D1247935

# CHIRAL MAD

## 5

EDITED BY MICHAEL BAILEY

# CHIRAL MAD

## 5

# FICTION

# FICTION

# POETRY

# THE BEGINNING IS THE END

## MICHAEL BAILEY

"This is my final anthology. I can't do this anymore."

I say that every damn time I begin working on a new collection of fiction and/or poetry. "After this one, the *last*, I'm done, ready to focus on my own writing." That's the plan, but then something bad happens. The magic is gone and suddenly there again as events terrible and triggering spark the need to collaborate with other creators: another mass shooting; the "righteous" instilling their beliefs upon others; an asshole driving a car into a crowded space; politicians poli-*tick*ing, sucking the life from those they serve; terrorists emerging from schools, from households, from *within*; one country fucking over another as the rest avoid conflict; child abductions; sex trafficking; rape; a rotten cop turning routine traffic stops into killings; basic rights wrongly stripped from the deserving; equality reverting to inequality; hate; humanity de-evolving. The list goes on as a colorful world reverts to black and white because of a four-letter word: *fear*.

All is quiet for a while, then not. As society crumbles, creators create. Empty pages must be filled and the need to anthologize that work emerges once again. "This is my final anthology. The *last*."

Books like these take work. Anthologists spend countless hours making it *just* right. Invitations are sent out while others invite themselves, eager to share their reaction to the chaos around them. When the collection begins to take shape, an open call invites the uninvited; yet there are only a handful of opportunities. Those who "make it" in the book love the editor while those who don't perhaps resent the editor, wondering why they weren't accepted. Sending thousands of rejections (non-acceptances) for a single book hurts.

"So, no, I can't do this anymore …."

# THE END IS THE BEGINNING

## INTRODUCTION

"No, this is not my final anthology. I have to keep doing this."

I say that every damn time I end the work on a new collection of fiction and/or poetry. "After *this* one, after redirecting attention on my own writing for a long while, maybe just *one* more." The magic is there and then suddenly gone as the world calms for a while, everyone focusing energy on the self. All the bad things keep happening, but everyone is so desensitized from the repetition of terrible things that it takes the next *really* bad thing, the unthinkable, to happen to cause the next big reaction. But until that moment, the seemingly black and white world reveals its beautiful, vibrant colors as fears are challenged and humanness progresses as it should.

And at some point, books like these are released into the wild. Full pages are there to be emptied into the minds of readers. Loved? Hated? That's for readers to decide as they move from the beginning to the end. "Will this be my final anthology. The *last?*"

One thing is for certain: this will be the final book in the *Chiral Mad* series. It's been a good run. Hopefully each volume has revealed an evolution of the editor, a personal effort to better represent the underrepresented. This is the most diverse of the five and features writers from Botswana, Bulgaria, Canada, China, Finland, Panama, Peru, Nigeria, Saudi Arabia, Singapore, Sweden, Sri Lanka, and the Divided States of America. As with the first in the series, all profit from *Chiral Mad 5* will forever be donated to a worthy cause. Have a problem (or don't believe there is one) with racial or sexual equality, with human rights, or with showing basic decency toward *all* people? Find another book. Voices need to be heard.

"So, yes, I have to keep doing this …."

# PERSISTENCE

## JONATHAN LEES

"We have become little more than pieces
of evidence in our own homes."
— The Archivist

*Hard white light obliterates the frame, a blur of dark flesh surfaces in and out
of visibility, some knocking about, until a man's weathered face fills the view, eyes
looking everywhere but at the screen, and he says:*

"Hello. Ok. Let's begin …"

*The camera swivels to reveal a hallway with floral flourishes, wood paneling,
and crammed hideaway bookshelves. An imposing grandfather clock crouches at
the end of the space, shrouded in enough shadows that its face is hidden.*

"Welcome, everyone. I am—"

*The audio cuts out.*

"I've never done a live video, so bear with me. We are inside the
home where my husband and I have spent the past six years of our
lives, and I thought it was time to share some of my personal work
for those of you still stuck in your homes and unable to get out to
a gallery in the indefinite future. So, I hope you are staying safe and
enjoy. The first piece is here, to the right of the front door."

*He points the phone's camera to a photograph in an antique frame.*

"This. The one I called Secaucus."

*He pauses, cocks his head slightly.*

"It's always at a slant because we strung up the wire incorrectly.
We'll get to fixing that soon, I think."

*The camera pulls back to show the entire picture. The lower half of the
photograph is filled with sun-bleached reeds, blue with the glow of swamp gas,
and above the gold of a promising sky. A centered bridge lies beyond, the old
defiant structure disappearing into a morning fog that erases the color of whatever
it touches. No entrance or exit, severed at both junction points.*

"I shot this back, obviously, when we were allowed to take the trains, when we were permitted to pass the wall. This is the one that started it all but not the one most people remember. Even now, a day doesn't go by where my camera isn't on me, although most of the pictures are of my husband and abandoned buildings."

*He smiles, lifts up a black metal Fuji digital camera, with an awkwardly long lens for the compactness of the body, and kisses it gently on the red capped shutter button.*

"Now, if you walk down this slim entryway, or the 'foy-yay' as Karl calls it, you'll notice the living room … and there he is."

*Theo nods toward a dark room. A man's face floats in the light from his laptop. The camera swings back and glides up the staircase. A succession of photographs disappears into the darkness above.*

"Let me get the light for you so we're not looking at nothing, right?"

*The hallway disappears and reappears as the camera adjusts to the burst from the hanging pendant lamp.*

"As you walk up, notice you are greeted by the same landscape, each varying slightly. A shift of light here, a heavier fog there. This entire series used to hang in gallery wall-sized frames at the International Center of Photography in Manhattan. I prefer the way it was shown in Berlin, which is the sizing you see here. It's not as quick to reveal its secrets, if you know what I mean. Rather pretty, but pedestrian works if you gaze from afar. As you look closer, I mean, *really* lean into it, in the second shot you'll just make out this dark figure …"

*He moves closer to the picture and centers his frame, the figure dwarfed by the steel bridge and nearly swallowed by its surroundings.*

"… and as the photographs progress, the figure blurs, loses its shape, and vanishes. Bloop. A stain removed. No one would have given a fuck about these pictures if it wasn't for that figure. Whoops, sorry about the language. Been home so long I forget myself. Now, if you look close in that second-to-last frame …"

*He moves upstairs to the third photograph.*

"… before the one where the man has disappeared. See? His shape has shifted, even though he is so distant as to be resolved in a blur, you can tell he has turned to look over his shoulder, as if he saw me shooting him. Impossible, since I took this series from a moving passenger train, my shutter speed high and my ISO even higher due to the weak light, which gives the whole series an increasingly noisy appearance. The larger you blow it up, the finest grain increases and breaks apart to become what appears to be a layer of static."

*He pauses and swivels the camera onto his face.*

"One critic called it 'a nightmare documented in panicked succession.' Another said 'it showcased the halt of societal progression and its representational lone figure lost in its crisis.'"

*He shifts focus to the photographs again.*

"This one's a bit of a strain, but it's basically the same as the first frame, although now the figure has vanished entirely, right? It's the context that makes it all the more haunting. Come with me …"

*The light falls, the image taking a moment to refocus as he steps up to the second-floor landing. The shadows turn blocky, muddy, mostly due to the compression.*

"Now that we are on the second floor, we won't bother looking into the bedroom—a mess, due to our terminal lack of closet space. Let's continue on into the study."

*The sun erases the frame and then the environment bleeds.*

"This is one of our biggest rooms, which used to have the best view of the city. We both have our desks up here. Karl's is the cherry-wood secretary and mine is the blonde workbench. They don't really go together but somehow it just worked. That's what some people have said about our relationship. Ha."

*Theo lowers the camera for what feels like forever in the world of online video where patience is not a virtue. The dark of his pant leg fills the screen. A faint sniff and a gasp, and then a giant inhale. He brings the camera back up toward himself and the movement halts. Theo's face fragments and falls apart or, rather, is not "resolved."*

The Archivist's hand cramps, and she drops her pen onto the pad. Her eyes are so raw and dry that the last tear squeezed out has the heat and weight of blood. Every time she looks at the words she's written, it's all so mad and illegible. Pacing the house and climbing into a pair of sweatpants makes her feel somewhat normal, as if she ever knew that feeling.

The drawn curtains allow enough sunlight in the room to function as an indicator of passing time. The coffee pot still chugs its second refill of the morning. The days are bleary, and sleep only comes whenever her eyes finally give up. There is nothing she wants to see out there. No, for her, right now, everything exists on those screens upstairs in her library. Ever since Theo and Karl went missing this widening rabbit hole has collapsed her sanctuary, and only the sounds of her nails dragging across the keyboard echo in the chasm as she plummets.

She became "The Archivist" when she surrendered her waking life going to work in that cavernous office, retaining status as a premier employee in a mandatory tech department that should have installed a revolving door instead of an espresso machine. Her little corner always dressed in minor comforts from home: a small cactus with one orange flower exploding from its tip, plush bears in various hues, photos of her and her sisters at the beach house before her grandmother died and family trips became a joyless force of habit, and little notes of affirmation that people are good and can all achieve great things. Yet, as she tucks in for the day's assault, she is cornered by screens that reveal another narrative, one of sickness, rot, and replicating imagery that would destroy the sanity of most citizens. With all the employees she's had to comfort over the years, she jokes that they should have called her "The Psychologist."

She sips her coffee and rewinds to a time when ugliness was committed under the cloak of night, in slit of shadow, or in abandoned areas. Now, everything happens anytime, everywhere. The birds scream, the sun rises, and someone else's history is snuffed out and recorded for prosperity. No minute, no hour sacred. She had taped over the clocks on all her monitors, no longer wanting to be reminded of the constant nightmare. She wants to believe these are isolated incidents, and not being shared, replicated, reproduced. The Archivist realizes that what she wants is often not realistic.

Every new hire boasted that they could manage whatever was

thrown at them, that they weren't bothered by the images they were being asked to locate and destroy. The "visuals," they called it, as if it were something to be entranced by, something to inspire; mostly a word to mask its insidious nature in their own minds. She'd seen muscular men with tattoos of more muscles go green in the face and have to be carted away, mumbling and in need of medication.

Employees sat at those monitors with their third shaky cup of coffee and some half-digested croissant rumbling in their stomach, all saying they wouldn't have nightmares. They barely cracked a crusty morning eye before assaulted by the purpling bruises of strangulations, the reddening flesh of the flagellated, the jaundiced eyes and foaming mouths of hate mongers. Words that would turn heads in the street strung together like some demented rhyme. Panicked, paranoid, poorly lit faces screamed into a machine that responded back tenfold with equally militant opinions and assured comments that aimed to rip up the skin of America. Shine a light in that particular patch of darkness, and there will be nothing but maggots squirming over each other, maximizing their mass and speed.

As she told her team before the day The Stain appeared, "Light takes energy to be created. Darkness just exists. So, you need a lot of fucking light to get rid of it."

The Archivist presses Play and Theo's face is back, speaking quieter this time.

"Alright, everyone, there is one more photograph. One that has never been seen in a gallery, a book, or online. It is the final in the series 'Secaucus' and there are reasons I haven't shared this with the world until now."

*The camera's eye trails around the study and refocuses on the back wall between two painful bursts of window light. Theo moves closer until the windows aren't in the frame and the camera readjusts to the dark wall where the picture hangs.*

"Might be tough to see, but here it is."

*It looks like the first in the series. The fog and the ominous glow of the swamp lights. The textural grain renders the photograph a sharper watercolor, the bridge sunken and disappearing on both sides. The figure nowhere to be seen.*

"The entire series, so far, trains your eyes to focus only on this location."

*He points to where the figure once stood under the ominous bridge looking toward the camera. That space now replaced by a smudge or a stain.*

"Let's back up. See now?"

*As he retreats, on the fringes of the frame, from different vantage points, Theo points to three figures approaching the spot where the man disappeared. Tucked in the shoulder on one is a rifle. Something happens to the video footage, blocks of breakup similar to any terribly compressed online video.*

"So, these three men are the reason this photograph has never been available to the public. It became a key piece of evidence after the discovery of a body in the same location. It was Karl who notified the authorities after seeing the repeating images on the news of the caution tape around the bridge. He recognized it from my photographs.

"The murdered man, later revealed to be activist William Rogers, was a brilliant figure whose retention of cultural knowledge was seemingly infinite and led our community, to dub him, jokingly, The Internet. He was an intellectual revolutionary with so-called "antagonistic methods," or, as more sensible people would see it, a truth seeker; a freedom fighter. They called him The Internet because he held histories accessible only if you asked the right questions. That is, before they were blown out of the back of his head and lost like so many other things in the putrid waters of The Meadowlands.

"He left behind a legacy of wise words against the systematic oppression of our people, but what he contested, what he *fought* against, still festered in the minds of millions like the grubs now rustling underneath his disappearing skin. Sorry, I am a bit dramatic when it comes to this subject. And there's reason for drama. When Karl reported it and showed the cops the image, nothing happened.

"I mean, they interviewed Karl and me separately about the day I shot the series and asked if I noticed anything else. They asked if I saw their faces after taking the pictures. I just laughed. New Jersey Transit is slow but not that bad. I told them I shot the pictures so rapidly I hadn't noticed them at all. Through the viewfinder, I hadn't even seen William. My eyes were on that bridge, the fog, that glow. I didn't see any of them until I developed the photos in my basement. And then that was it.

"They kept the print and the file we gave them. No follow-up. Unreturned calls. Even when the story hit the nightly news, there was never a breaking report where the photograph became the narrative. It might as well have never existed."

*Theo backs away from the camera, reacting to something outside the room.* "Karl?"

*Theo turns back with concern and his skull explodes. His forehead, his eyes, and his mouth gush color, blinding pinks and toxic greens and millions of degrading digital bits bursting out. This stain erases his features, drowning them and leaving nothing human behind.*

The Archivist stops the video and continues scratching out her thoughts into a small leather journal:

> *You have all dubbed it "The Stain" so we will progress with that title. Instead of wide eyes and an open mouth set in a human face, instead of a Theo, exists a flowering of every color imaginable, cascading over his skull as if melted in the most beautiful way. Beautiful at first, although, in its eventual persistence, it is more than unnerving.*

The Archivist stops writing and advances the video frame-by-frame. The colors pulse and cascade, covering yet retaining the shape of every human feature, and then, *there* … a slight skip in the chaos as she shuttles back and forth between the frames. Something new. A reflection in the glass frame behind what used to be Theo. The shape of a human. Karl? No, three figures.

It's this attention to detail—and observation she learned from her profession—where she got her nickname, why her videos are often archived and not scrubbed away from leering eyes. They become potential evidence. Images where you could almost smell the spoiled meat rot of a corpse after days of floating. A fetid hole not many can claim they've crawled back out of … a hole she lives in seven hours a day.

She drags the slider back to when Theo still has a face.

Backing out the door of the study where he would vanish, down the staircase, she pauses again to look at the Secaucus photographs, then shuttles back and freezes as Theo starts up the stairs. There is a slight peek of the living room. Barely lit by the electric blue of the computer and on the couch—

"… and there he is," Theo said.

By blowing up the video 300% and decreasing the resolution significantly, she is able to still make out Karl's face and the screen reflected in his glasses. The CNN logo and … something else. The colored blur covers a portion of the frame. And the text from the chyron below the reporter, barely legible, is the name William Rogers. The frame in the doorway, beyond the entrance to the living room, is a back entrance—a mud room, possibly. And in that entrance is a shadow, a very human shaped shadow.

The Archivist leans back in her chair and allows herself to close her eyes for only a moment because that's where most of the day's images replay, and there isn't a single one she would like to see again. She speaks into the camera.

"I started collecting the occurrences first reported, to the best of my knowledge, over six months ago …" She backs away from her desk, whispering into the live feed. "Here it is," she says and points at her laptop screen.

"The material you're looking for is buried in the Documents folder, in another folder called Inquiries, in yet another folder titled Transmissions. This is everything I have. Starting with the video rips, the news broadcasts, the screen grabs, and the correspondences I've collected since we first reported The Stain. Everything is encrypted, and everyone who knows me best knows how to access it. None of the correspondences are in my inbox."

The Archivist starts opening the videos hiding in the folders.

"I am showing you this now, not to scare you, but in case something happens. So you have your own record of it."

*The camera opens on a view of an unremarkable street and moves forward until it's hovering over a child's face on the pavement. There are voices too soft to be audible. Three shadows frame the boy's unmoving body. A lime green squirt gun in his hand. His head covered in The Stain. Every feature obliterated by a digital swarm of noise and bleeding color, yet an outline of the child's wide-open mouth. A shout cut short.*

She opens another video:

*A woman screams on a couch as her front door cracks open. She's shot fourteen times before her body erupts into colors and the screen goes dark.*

The next:

*A man swings from a tree, a bag covering his head, while the people who dance around his lifeless body remain in shadow. The Stain soon covers the entire frame.*

"These are three of the videos. There are countless more. They were archived and removed from the platform, yet somehow they still ... escaped us and were shared, replicated, used in news broadcasts, social media, memes. They were everywhere. In every instance, The Stain appeared. What you'll see in my folders are the raw videos I flagged initially."

She plays the unaffected video of the child and the squirt gun and visibly weeps as the camera floats over his lifeless body, his still sweating face frozen, his mouth wide open, his brown eyes staring at nothing. Three shadows loom over his tiny body.

"What scares me most is that the conversation has shifted to, and only to, The Stain. In every appearance, the commentary revolved around what The Stain was and where it came from. How it terrifies people, threatens their way of life, their beliefs, and affects their much-needed sleep. How they feared The Stain was a result of political sabotage, media trickery, made by foreign agitators looking to destroy America, and, yes, even aliens. The Stain alters the conversation, and the conversation has become The Stain."

She freezes, her eyes darting back and forth. She waits, the space behind her dark and the image swimming with noise.

"They want us to forget the suffering. They want us to forget these are people. Something wants us to stop looking. Someone wants to distract us."

A slam from a distance. The Archivist looks over her shoulder.

"They're here. You know what to do."

She takes out a gun and flicks off the safety.

"I'm calling upon you all to shine the biggest fucking light you can onto these maggots and burn every last one."

Her image is erased in a sickening display of color.

# COLORBLIND

## WRATH JAMES WHITE

I wish
I could be color blind
I wish I had that luxury
I wish
like a child
I could believe
that if my eyes are closed
I am invisible
I wish this black body
were not a target
That it could blend
into the mosaic tapestry
of this country
without casting a shadow
you find
so threatening
It must be choked
beaten
shot
silenced
I wish
It was as simple
as being polite
obeying the law
keeping both hands on the wheel

While also following commands
reaching for my license
both hands on the wheel
my insurance
hands visible at all times
my registration
both hands on the wheel
turning down the stereo
make no sudden moves
Stop resisting
the baton crushing my windpipe
stop resisting
the taser shocking me again and again
stop resisting
the fists, and boots, and batons
stop resisting
the knee upon my throat
I
Can't
Breathe!
Running for my life
Hands up. Don't shoot!
as bullets fly

toward
my back
I wish
that would make
the law
colorblind
This melanated skin
less threatening
My life
worth more
than property
I wish I could say
I love America
without feeling
like a whipped dog
that licks
the hand
that smacks it
I wish
I was never reminded
that you
and I
are different.

# ANCESTRIES

## SHEREE RENÉE THOMAS

In the beginning were the ancestors, gods of earth who breathed the air and walked in flesh. Their backs were straight and their temples tall. We carved the ancestors from the scented wood, before the fire and the poison water took them, too. We rubbed ebony-stained oil on their braided hair and placed them on the altars with the first harvest, the nuts and the fresh fruit. None would eat before the ancestors were fed, for it was through their blood and toil we emerged from the dark sea to be.

But that was then, and this is now, and we are another tale.

It begins as all stories must, with an ending. My story begins when my world ended, the day my sister shoved me into the ancestors' altar. That morning, one sun before Oma Day, my bare heels slipped in bright gold and orange paste. Sorcadia blossoms lay flattened, their juicy red centers already drying on the ground. The air in my lungs disappeared. Struggling to breathe, I pressed my palm over the spoiled flowers, as if I could hide the damage. Before Yera could cover her smile, the younger children came.

"Fele, Fele," they cried and backed away, "the ancient ones will claim you!" Their voices were filled with derision, but their eyes held something else, something close to fear.

"Claim her?" Yera threw her head back, the fishtail braid snaking down the hollow of her back, a dark slick eel. "She is not worthy," she said to the children, and turned her eyes on them. They scattered like chickens. Shrill laughter made the sorcadia plants dance. A dark witness, the fat purple vines and shoots twisted and undulated above me. I bowed my head. Even the plants took part in my shame.

"And I don't need you, shadow," Yera said, turning to me, her face a brighter, crooked reflection of my own. "You are just a spare." A spare. Only a few breaths older than me, Yera, my twin, has hated me since before birth.

Our oma says even in the womb, my sister fought me, that our mother's labors were so long because Yera held me fast, her tiny fingers clasped around my throat, as if to stop the breath I had yet to take. The origin of her disdain is a mystery, a blessing unrevealed. All I know is that when I was born, Yera gave me a kick before she was pushed out of our mother's womb, a kick so strong it left an impression, a mark, like a bright shining star in the middle of my chest.

This star, the symbol of my mother's love and my sister's hate, is another way my story ended.

I am told that I refused to follow, that I lay inside my mother, after her waters spilled, after my sister abandoned me, gasping like a small fish, gasping for breath. That in her delirium my mother sang to me, calling, begging me to make the journey on, that she made promises to the old gods, to the ancestors who once walked our land, to those of the deep, promises that a mother should never make.

"You were the bebe one, head so shiny, slick like a ripe green seed," our oma would say.

"Ripe," Yera echoed, her voice sweet for Oma, sweet as the sorcadia tree's fruit, but her mouth was crooked, slanting at me. Yera had as many faces as the ancestors that once walked our land, but none she hated more than me.

While I slept, Yera took the spines our oma collected from the popper fish and sharpened them, pushed the spines deep into the star in my chest. I'd wake to scream, but the paralysis would take hold, and I would lie in my pallet, seeing, knowing, feeling but unable to fight or defend.

When we were lardah, and I had done something to displease her—rise awake, breathe, talk, stand—Yera would dig her nails into my right shoulder and hiss in my ear. "Shadow, spare. Thief of life. You are the reason we have no mother." It was my sister's favorite way to steal my joy.

And then, when she saw my face cloud, as the sky before rain, she would take me into her arms and stroke me. "There, my sister, my second, my own broken one," she would coo. "When I descend, you can have mother's comb, and put it in your own hair. Remember me," she would whisper in my ear, her breath soft and warm as any lover. "Remember me," and then she would stick her tongue inside my ear and pinch me until I screamed.

Our oma tried to protect me, but her loyalty was like the suwa wind, inconstant, mercurial. Oma only saw what she wanted. Older age and even older love made her forget the rest.

"Come!" I could hear the drumbeat echo of her clapping hands.

"Yera, Fele," she sang, her tongue adding more syllables to our names, Yera, Fele, the words for one and two. The high pitch meant it was time to braid Oma's hair. The multiversal loops meant she wanted the complex spiral pattern. Three hours of labor, if my hands did not cramp first, maybe less if Yera was feeling industrious.

With our oma calling us back home, I wiped my palms on the inside of my thighs and ignored the stares. My sister did not reach back to help me. A crowd had gathered, pointing but silent. No words were needed here. The lines in their faces said it all. I trudged behind Yera's tall, straight back, my eyes focused on the fishtail's tip.

"They should have buried you with the afterbirth."


When we reached the courtyard, my basket empty, Yera's full as she intended, we found our oma resting in her battered rocker in the yard. She had untied the wrap from her head. Her edges spiked around her full moon forehead, black tendrils reaching for the sun. She smiled as Yera revealed the spices and herbs she collected. I pressed fresh moons into my palms and bit my lip. No words were needed here. As usual, our oma had eyes that did not see. She waved away my half empty basket, cast her eyes sadly away from the fresh bloody marks on my shoulder, and pointed to her scalp instead.

"Fele, I am feeling festive today, bold." She stared at a group of baji yellow-tailed birds pecking at the crushed roots and dried leaves scattered on the ground. They too would be burned and offered tomorrow night, at Yera's descension. And we would feast on the fruits of the land, as my sister descended into the sea.

"I need a style fitting for one who is an oma of a goddess. My beauty."

"A queen!" Yera cried, returning from our bafa. She flicked the fishtail and raised her palms to the sky. "An ancestress, joining the deep."

Yera had been joining the deep since we were small girls. She never let me forget it.

"Come, Fele," she said, "You take the left," as if I did not know. Year held the carved wooden comb of our mother like a machete, her gaze as sharp and deadly. Her eyes dared me to argue. She knew that I would not. Together we stood like sentinels, each flanking oma's side. The creamy gel from the fragrant sorcadian butter glistened on the backs of our hands. I placed a small bowl of the blue-shelled sea snails, an ointment said to grow hair thick and wild as the deepest weed of the sea. Yera gently parted our oma's scalp, careful not to dig the wooden teeth in. Before I learned to braid my own hair, Yera had tortured me as a child, digging the teeth into the tender flesh of my scalp. Now her fingers moved in a blur, making the part in one deft move. A dollop of gel dripped onto her wrists. She looked as if she wore blue-stained bracelets—or chains.

I gathered our oma's thick roots, streaked with white and the ashen gray she refused to dye, saying she had earned every strand of it.

"This is a special time, an auspicious occasion. It is not every year that Oma Day falls on the Night of Descension. The moon will fill the sky and light our world as bright as in the day of the gods."

I massaged scented oils into the fine roots of her scalp, brushed my fingertips along the nape of her neck. I loved to comb our oma's hair. The strands felt like silk from the spider tree, cotton from the prickly bushes.

Oma said in the time before, our ancestors used to have enough fire to light the sky, that it burned all morning, evening, and the night, from a power they once called electricity. I love how that name feels inside my head—e-lec-tri-city. It sounds like one of our oma's healing spells, the prayers she sends up with incense and flame.

Once when Yera and I were very small, we ran too far inside the ancestors' old walled temples. Before we were forbidden, we used to scavenge there. We climbed atop the dusty, rusted carcasses of metal beasts. We ducked under rebar, concrete giants jutting from the earth, skipped over faded signage. We scuttled through the scraps of the metal yard at the edge of green, where the land took back what the old gods had claimed. I claimed something, too, my reflection in the temple called Family Dollar, a toy that looked like me. Her hair was braided in my same simple box pattern, the eyes black and glossy. I tried to hide my find from Yera, but she could see contentment on my face. So, I ran. I ran to the broken, tumble down buildings with blown-out windows that looked like great gaping mouths. I ran into the mouth of darkness, clutching my doll, but when I closed my eyes, searching for the light, Yera was waiting on the other side.

That is when I knew I could never escape her. My sister is always with me.

Before the Descension, our people once lived in a land of great sweeping black and green fields, land filled with thick-limbed, tall trees and flowing rivers of cool waters, some sweet and clear, others dark as the rich, black soil. Our oma says when our ancestors could no longer live on the land, when the poisons had reached the bottom of every man, woman, and child's cup, they journeyed on foot and walked back into the sea, back to the place of the old gods, the deep ones.

But before they left, they lifted their hands and made a promise. That if the land could someday heal from its long scars, the wounds that people inflicted, that they would return again. In the meanwhile, one among us, one strong and true, must willingly descend into the depths to join the ancestors. This one, our people's first true harvest, will know from the signs and symbols, the transformations that only come from the blessing of the ancestors, when the stars in the sky above align themselves just so. Yera is that first harvest. She has wanted this honor her whole life. And from her birth, the signs were clear. Her lungs have grown strong, her limbs straight and tall, she does not bend and curve like the rest of us. My sister has the old gods' favor and when Oma Day ends and the Descension is complete, she will join the waters, and rule them as she once ruled the waters of our mother's womb, she will enter them and be reborn as an ancestress.

The ceremony has not yet begun, and I am already tired. I am tired, because I spend much of my time and energy devoted to breathing. For me, to live each day is a conscious act, an exercise of will, mind over my broken body's matter. I must imagine a future with every breath, consciously exhaling, expelling the poison because my brain thinks I need more air, and signals my body to produce light, even though my lungs are weak and filled with the ash of the old gods. Unable to filter the poison quickly, my body panics and it thinks I am dying. My knees lock, and I pull them up to my chest and hold myself, gasping for breath like our oma said I did, waiting in my mother's womb.

Oma gives me herbs. She grinds them up, mortar and pestle in her conch shell, and mixes them in my food. When I was smaller, she made me recite the ingredients daily, a song she hummed to lull me asleep. But as I grew, the herbs worked less and less, and my sister did things to them, things that made me finally give them up. I have given so much to her these years.

And I have created many different ways to breathe.

I breathe through my tongue, letting the pink buds taste the songs in the air. I breathe through the fine hairs on the ridge of my curved back and my arms, the misshapen ones she calls claws. I breathe through the dark pores of my skin. And when I am alone, and out of my oma's earshot, out of my wretched sister's reach, I breathe through my mouth, unfiltered and free. My fingers searching the most hidden, soft parts of myself and I am *light air star shine, light air star shine, light—*

In the suns before Oma Day, I spent a lot of time sleeping. My breathing tends to be easier if I sleep well, and so I slept. My lungs are filled with poison which means there's no space for the light, the good clean air. I have many different ways to expel the poison, and meanwhile my body goes into panic because my mind thinks I'm dying, so between controlling the exhalation, telling my mind that I am not dying, inhaling our oma's herbs through her conch shell, I am exhausted since I do this many times a day.

And then there is Yera. Always my sister, Yera. I must watch for her. I know my sister's movements more than I know myself.

This night, on the eve of Oma Day, which is to say, the eve of my sister's descension, I can feel Yera smile, even in the dark. It is that way with sisters. As a child, I did not fear the night. How could I? My sister's voice filled it. Outside, the baji birds gathered in the high tops of our oma's trees. Their wings sounded like the great wind whistling through what was left of the ancestors' stone wall towers. They chattered and squawked in waves as hypnotic as the ocean itself, their excitement mirroring our own. And I too was excited, my mind filled with questions and a few hopes I dared not even share with myself. Would I still exist without my sister? Can there be one without two?

As more stars add their light to the darkness, I turn in my bed, over and over again like the gold beetles burrowing in our oma's soil. I turned, my mind restless while Yera slept the sleep of the ages. For me, sleep never comes. So, I sit in the dark, braiding and unbraiding my hair and wait for the day to come, when my world would end again or perhaps when it might begin.

The past few days I've been aware that braiding makes me short of breath, and I realized that I am very, very tired. Last night I was going through my patterns, braiding and unbraiding them in my head, overhand and underhand, when I remembered what the elder once said to our oma. That she had done a lot in her life, that she, already an honored mother, had raised felanga on her own, and it was all right if she rested now. And I thought that maybe that was true for me, the resting part, which is perhaps why today I feel changed.

Δ

31

"Hurry, child. Hunger is on me."

Our oma calls but even she is too nervous to eat. Her hair is a wonder, a sculpture that rises from her head like two great entwined serpents holding our world together. My scalp is sore. My hands still ache in the center of my palms, and I am concentrating harder now to breathe. I rub the palm flesh of my left hand, massaging the pain in a slow ring of circles.

Yera has not joined us yet. She refused my offer to help braid her hair. "You think I want your broken hand in my head? You know your hands don't work," she said. I remember only once receiving praise from her for my handiwork. I had struggled long, my fingers cramped, my temple pulsing. I braided her hair into a series of intricate loops, twisting off her shining scalp like lush sorcadia blooms. Yera did not speak her praise. Vocal with anger, she was silent with approval. Impressed, Yera tapped her upper teeth with her thumb. Oma, big-spirited as she was big-legged, ran to me.

She lifted my aching hands high into the air as if the old gods could see them. Now dressed in nothing more than a wrap, her full breasts exposed, nipples like dark moons, her mouth is all teeth and venom. "You have always been jealous of me."

"Jealous?" I say and turn the word over in my mouth. It is sour and I don't like its taste. I spit it out like a rotten sorcadian seed.

She turns, her thick brows high on her shining forehead.

"Oh, so you speak now. Your tongue has found its roots on the day of my descension?"

Inside, my spirit folds on itself. It turns over and over again and gasps for air, but outside, I hold firm. "Why should I feel jealous? You are my sister, and I am yours. Your glory is my glory." I wait. Her eyes study me coolly, narrow into bright slits. The scabs on my shoulder feel tight and itchy. After a moment, she turns again, her hands a fine blur atop her head. She signals assent with a flick of her wrist. Braiding and braiding, overhand, underhand, the pattern is intricate.

I have never seen Yera so shiny.

I take a strip of brightly stained cloth and hand it to her. She weaves it expertly into the starfish pattern. Concentric circles dot the crown of her head. Each branch of her dark, thick hair is adorned with a sorcadian blossom. We have not even reached the water and she already looks like an ancestor.

"Supreme," I whisper. But no words are needed here. I pick up the bowl of sea snail ointment and dip my fingertips into the glistening blue gel.

My stained fingers trail the air lightly.

"Mother's comb," Yera says and bows her head. "You may have mother's comb. I won't be needing it anymore."

I smile, something close to pleasure, something close to pain. My fingertips feel soft and warm on her neck. They tingle and then they go numb.

Yera's mouth gapes open and closed, like a bebe, a flat shiny fish.

Her pink tongue blossoms, juicy as a sorcadian center. Red lines spiral out from her pupils, crimson starfish.

"Sister, spare me," I say. "Love is not a word that fits in your mouth."

The sorcadia tree is said to save souls. Its branches helped provide shelter and firewood. Its fruit, healing sustenance. Its juicy blossoms with their juicy centers help feed and please the old gods. To have a belly full and an eye full of sweet color is not the worst life. As I leave our Oma's house, the wind rustles and the sorcadia in Oma's yard groans as if it is a witness. I gaze at the sorcadia whose branches reach for me as if to pull me back into the house. Even the trees know my crimes.

Silver stretches over the surface of the sand. Water mingles with moonlight, and from a distance it looks like an incomplete rainbow. Our oma says this is a special moon, the color of blood, a sign from the ancestors. The moon is the ultimate symbol of transformation. She pulls on the waters, and she pulls on wombs. When we look at it, we are seeing all the sunrises and sunsets across our world, every beginning and every ending all at once. This idea comforts me as I spot our oma in the distance. I follow the silver light, my feet sinking in the sand as I join the solemn crowd waiting at the beach.

There are no words here, only sound. The rhythmic exhalations, inhalations of our people's singing fills the air, their overtones a great buzzing hum deep enough to rend the sky. Before I can stop myself, I am humming with them. The sound rises from a pit in my belly and vibrates from the back of my throat. It tumbles out of my dry mouth to join the others around me. Beneath my soles the earth rumbles. That night my people sang as if the whole earth would open up beneath us. We sang as if the future rested in our throats. The songs pull me out of myself. I am inside and out all at once. As my sister walks to stand at the edge of the waters, I feel as if I might fly away, as if every breath I had ever taken is lifting me up now.

A strong descension assures that straight-backed, strong limbed children will be born from our mothers' wombs, that green, grasping roots will rise from the dead husks of trees to seed a future. The others dance around this vision. When one descends, all are born. When one returns, all return. Each bloodline lives and with it, their memory, and we are received by our kin.

Music rises from the waves, echoes out across the sand, a keening. The elders raise their voices, the sound of their prayers join. I walk past them, my hair a tight interlocked monument to skill, to pain. The same children who laughed in my face and taunted me are silent now. Only the wind, the elders' voices, and the sound of the waters rise up ahead to greet me. The entire village watches.

Oma waits with her back to me, in the carved wooden chair they have carried out to face the waters. When I stand beside her, her fingertips brush the marks on my shoulder. Her touch stings. The wounds have not all scabbed over yet. She turns and clasps my hands, her eyes searching for answers hidden in my face.

"Fele, why, why do you such things?"

Our oma's unseeing eyes search but I can find no answer that would please her.

"Yera," I begin but her *tsk*, the sharp air sucking between her teeth, cuts me off.

"No," she says, shaking her head, "not Yera. You, Fele, it is you."

Δ

They think I don't hear them, here under the water, that I don't know what they are doing, from here in the sea. But I do.

I wanted Yera to fight back, to curse me, to make me forget even the sound of my own name. I am unaccustomed to this Yera. This silent, still one.

"Fele!" they call. "She has always been touched." "I told her oma, but she refused to listen." "One head here with the living, the other with the dead." "Should have never named her. To tell a child she killed her sister, her mother. What a terrible curse."

They whisper harsh words sharp enough to cut through bone. But no words are needed here. I have withstood assault all these years, since before birth. This last attack is borne away by the ocean's tears. They say my Yera does not exist. That she died when our mother bore us, that I should have died, too. But that was then, and this is now, and we are another tale.


It does not matter if she is on land or that I am in the sea.

We are sisters. We share the same sky.

Though some spells, when the moon is high and the tide is low, and my body flinches, panics because it thinks it is dying, I journey inland, to where the ancestors once walked in flesh, the ones we carved into wood. I journey inward and I can smell the scent of sorcadians in bloom, the pungent scent of overripe fruit, and feel my sister's fingers pressed around my throat, daring me to breathe.

Tiny bebe dart and nibble around my brow. They swim around the circles in my hair and sing me songs of new suns here in the blueblack waters. Now I am the straight and the curved, our past and our future. Here in the water, I dwell with the ancient ones, in the space where all our lives begin, and my story ends as all stories must, a new beginning.

# SPECTACULAR DEGENERATION

## ZOJE STAGE

The blind is lowered inch by inch;
the room darkens and becomes a fading photograph

She holds out her hands,
fingers reaching into the shadows
There is no comfort in the stumbling solidity
of matter,
Not when the darkness has stretched from the eyes
to the throat

She gasps for air as much as she squints to see

The world is gone, painted over with the non-descript
gray
haze
of mourning—
for all that has disappeared,
for the loss of stitching with thread,
reading a book,
glancing across the room for the pile of mail,
left until later

She didn't know *too late* would arrive,
and it is here

The blind has shuttered the remaining light;
the room is hostile terrain, the photograph a relic

There is only the unknown now,
the smothering newness of lost boundaries,
the terror of every step,
the certainty of loneliness,
and the creeping fear of something
approaching
in the dark

# THE TEARS THAT NEVER STAIN

JESSICA MAY LIN

They say that when you marry someone, you marry their family too.

You never believed this saying, and that's what I loved about you—the way you carved your path through life with pruning shears instead of myths, and how you weren't afraid to proclaim under starry nights that proverbs are stupid. We lived in a technological age, after all. We were young, so I guess I didn't know enough about scars and how they form. But it worked out, because I was ashamed of the secrets I bore, and I wanted to leave them behind too.

I never told you about the fires.

Maybe it was better that you didn't know about the time my sister pierced her ears without permission, and when my mother reached for her, my sister screamed and my mother's hands glowed orange. Or that on some evenings after dinner, for no apparent reason at all, my mother would explode in brilliant wreaths of white flame, and I would run away from her around our kitchen as the embers fell around me. I lied to you about the origin of the hardened, red skin on the tips of my fingers, when I grabbed her and tried to douse her in water once, because I could tell it was hurting her too.

Instead, you found out when I didn't mean for you to.

I stood in the backyard that Saturday evening while the sun burned, far away like my mother. My feet were bare in the grass, and I was talking to her on the phone about something silly. It always started that way. But it always ends with the fire. I could hear the crackle of her bones in the heat through the phone. I don't remember what I said, but I closed my eyes and listened to her burn.

When I came back in the house, you were looking at me like you didn't know me.

"Hey, when you were on the phone with your mother just now, I saw you through the window, and you were on fire. Did I imagine that?"

"Yes," I said. And I was filled with a deep shame—shame but also sadness, that her fiery blood ran in my veins too. If we fought, would I burn you? Someday, would there be a little girl in our kitchen too, running away from me, as I disintegrated into glowing blue cinders around her tiny body?

I told you it was just a trick of light in the glass. It's what I told myself too.

But I guess I was secretly relieved, later, when I learned that your family were freaks too.

Your father gave it away when we had dinner at your house, and you told him who you'd voted for in the last election. He slammed his fist into the table and the veins in his forearm bulged into creeping vines that bound his arm against the table so tight his skin turned blue. You ran to get the pruning shears.

After our fights, when you would disappear for days, was that why? Because you didn't want me to see you, slashing clumps of ivy and brush from your shoulders before they grew too thick to cut?

I asked you about it, and you told me you didn't believe in psychoanalyzing yourself.

It was at our wedding that our families met for the first time. And my sister, offended by a joke your brother told, threw herself across the table and ignited in a bright shower of sparks. Your brother responded by curling dense, thorny branches around her, and our families watched, mouths agape, as they disintegrated into ash over the white frosting of our uneaten wedding cake. That night, my mother burned, and your father choked, and we held them away from each other as the flesh of my hands singed and the bones of yours broke.

Later, we held hands in the dark.

"But I chose you," I told you. "I didn't choose them."

I tried to cry, but the tears that fell from my eyes transformed into light dusty flowers in the dirt. White asphodels that blossomed around our shoes and glistened in the moonlight.

You stood there and watched, until we were standing in a field of white petals, like ash. "You never told me you cried flowers."

"I didn't know," I murmured, as I brushed the white, spiny blooms from my eyes. "But I guess I got it from my grandpa. It started for him in his early twenties too. They're pyrophytes, they can bloom after the fires die."

After that night, I climbed the hill that overlooks the house I grew up in and watched my mother burn in the driveway. I marveled at the way her bones glowed pearly white through the dancing, translucent flames, the way her screams were muffled under the roar of fire. The flames wreathing her hair looked like a crown. Did I really think I could run from that? She and I wouldn't be us, if you took that beauty away.

But maybe that's just what I tell myself because I can't bear to face the truth.

I think back to a time, at the beginning of our love story, when we ordered kits from some genealogy company online. With a perverse delight, you and I lay on the bed and compared our results. No gene for baldness, no predisposition to breast cancer, although you were seven times more likely than me to develop pancreatic cancer if you took a drug I've never heard of. We giggled, amused at our luck.

How did they overlook the most important test?

These wounds were inflicted, I guess.

Sometimes, when I shiver alone in my bathroom late at night, because when I'm burning is when I feel the coldest, I wish I never met you at all. I would rather blister alone in the shadows, consumed by my private darkness.

But then the phone rings.

You're calling.

# AT THE DOWNTOWN UNIVERSITY

LUCY A. SNYDER

Our department director knows it's critical
to be on the right side of things. History
is happening just a few blocks away;
we can hear the chants while we work
and when the wind blows just so
we catch a whiff of pepper spray.

Each morning of the protests, she's sent
emails full of links to essays on black
history, social justice, racial sensitivity
which we are encouraged to read thoroughly
at our leisure at home or on our lunch break;
living history should not interrupt our work.

"We have a diverse student body," she reminds
us. "It's important to support them during this
incredibly stressful time." She offers no word
on whether students who are arrested or beaten
and miss class as a consequence can be excused.
Presumably, staff and faculty must burn leave,

assuming nobody's blinded by a rubber bullet
or suffers lasting brain damage under a boot
or a lung hemorrhage after a policeman
pulls down her mask to shoot tear gas
directly down her gasping throat.
No word on what happens then.

Our college campus is fully ADA compliant
but somehow, you never see a professor
in a wheelchair, nor a support staff member
with a service dog. Our department's faces
range from pale to golf-tanned. If a furious cop
sends the bravest of us to an unpaid retirement,

there's no word if we'll see a new black hire
or if he or she will find the support to last
longer than a white hire with attention deficit
disorder, or chronic depression or social anxiety,
all of which we're told are protected disabilities
but which somehow always end in an empty chair.

I'm sure that our director will hire a black instructor
just as soon as she finds one who can hold a mirror
that reflects back the qualities she most values in
herself: a PhD who's a photogenic morning
person, an outgoing able-bodied team player
who speaks and thinks just like everyone else.

# THE QUEEN OF TALEY'S CORNER

## GARY A. BRAUNBECK

"Here lies a most beautiful lady,
Light of step and heart was she ..."
– Walter de la Mare, "An Epitaph"

They can say whatever they want, but they weren't there, were they?

They weren't there on Talley's Corner on those Saturday nights when the East End of Cedar Hill was still the place to be, before the big fire in '69 reduced it to a place where those at the end of their ropes crawl into the shadow of poverty to fade away in slow, lonely, miserable degrees—but we're not talking about the way it is now, no; we're talking about the glory days, the grand days, the days of music and laughter and the lovely ladies whose ebony skin shone under the lights like fine onyx gemstones; we're talking about the days when Talley's Hideaway always had lines of people waiting to get in so they could listen to the entertainers play Ellington and Armstrong and Calloway and Ethel Waters just like it was the real honest-to-God Cotton Club, the Saturday nights when you could always find Mousey, Stringbean, and Jackpot harmonizing and scatting and snapping their fingers over an ashcan fire, waiting for a glimpse of Miss Hattie and her elusive, mysterious man, Mr. Granger, the music rising up from the open speakeasy windows and swirling with the street-dust dancing in the glow of the streetlamps that always shone brighter whenever Miss Hattie and her Mr. Granger would pull up in their elegant Minerva and she'd step out in the grandest of style.

See her then.

A stone marten fur around her shoulders, glistening from the smoke and the glow of the ashcan's flames, the golden silk tassel caught between the spring of its jaws, her coat of sable, a string of pearls around her neck that can't begin to outshine her smile or overshadow that laugh that Ashcan Boys waited all week to hear, back there in the glory days, the grand days, down at Talley's Corner where the crystal clink of glasses filled with gin echoed down to the street along with the music of the singers and the smoky piano and the big bands giving life to the jazz and the blues and the good old honky-tonk.

See Miss Hattie.

—*Sing for us, Miss Hattie, they would say.*

—*No, boys, I can't, not tonight. I got me some dancing and drinking and loving to do.*

Then she would glide up to her man, her Mr. Granger who looked like a king on these Saturday nights, and she'd slip a white-gloved hand through his fine strong arm, blow the Ashcan Boys a kiss, and the two of them would float up the stairs to Talley's Hideaway, leaving Mousey and Stringbean and Jackpot by their fire to shake their heads and wonder why they could never find a woman as fine as that to love them the way Miss Hattie did her Mr. Granger.

Sing to me now, boys; sing to me a song about Miss Hattie and those glory-day Saturday nights, waiting to hear her laugh. Sing to me and see her now.

See Miss Hattie now.


Emma looked up from the butcher's block when she heard the humming from the top of the stairs. Her sister, Rose, came into the kitchen, saw the look on Emma's face, and said: "Don't start."

"So long as you don't tell me Hattie's getting her dress out again."

Rose shrugged. "Okay. I maybe won't tell you, but that won't change anything."

Emma threw down the mound of fresh bread dough and untied her apron. "Not today, Rose. I can't take her craziness today. I like her just as much as you do, but every once in a while ...."

Rose walked over and took her by the arm. "You stop it, Emma. The woman's *old* and it's hardly her fault that she ain't … *all there* anymore. Just leave her be, she's not hurting anybody."

"I just wish the nursing home had told us about the way she gets before I told 'em it was okay for her to take our last room. I know she was a friend of Mom and Daddy, but she gives everybody the willies—ever notice how no one else comes down to eat with her except for you?"

"At least they thought to give us a call, instead of someplace like The Maples or one of them other places downtown."

"You mean in one of the *nicer* areas, don't you?"

"For pity's sake, Emma! Nobody lives in the East End unless they have to. And keep in mind that Hattie's money at the end of the month comes in real handy since Daddy died and left us this place."

"That's just it," said Emma. "We *know* that Daddy's gone, just as well as she knows her Granger is dead and has been for almost as long as you and me been alive. The difference is we don't make believe any different. Why do you insist on letting her go on pretending like she does? Putting on that dress and acting like Granger's coming by to take her out dancing and all that? I don't think—"

"How do I look?" came a voice from the doorway.

Rose and Emma turned toward Hattie.

*See her now, boys.*

*Her threadbare elegance and thinning, gray hair that now grows in patches. Sing to me a song of age, boys; snap those fingers and scat for Hattie, the Queen of Talley's corner, come 'round to grow old and frail, there in the shabby relic of her Saturday-night dress, smiling in the doorway to the kitchen of Emma and Rose Long's Rooming House.*

Hattie crossed to the table and seated herself almost daintily, taking care not to smudge or stain the silk white gloves that now bulged halfway up her sagging arms where once they glided elegantly nearly to her shoulders. The chair creaked when she sat, but no one said anything. No one ever said anything.

"Gonna be a grand Saturday night," said Hattie.

"You going out on the town again?" asked Rose, giving her sister a you'd-better-stay-quiet glance.

"That's what Saturday nights were made for, hon."

Rose smiled. "Got yourself a new beau we don't know about?"

Hattie laughed; despite the sandpaper rasp of too many years of too many cigarettes, something in it still chimed. "There is no man but my Granger, Rose—and you keep them young hands off him, hear me?" She winked.

"Oh, I don't know, Hattie. He's a looker, your Granger is."

"*Rose!*" snapped Emma.

For a moment the two sisters glared at one another, and then Emma turned away, donned her apron, and continued preparations for dinner, still three hours away.

Hattie reached for the cup of afternoon tea that Rose set in front of her. Her hands shook and the cup rattled against the saucer. She smiled to herself for a moment, took a small sip, then set it back on the table, releasing a soft, weary sigh. "Did I ever tell you that Granger used to read poems to me?"

Rose smiled. "No, you never have."

Hattie removed a small cloth-bound book from the tattered sequined purse that hung from her arm. "Granger, he said that a lot of the poems in this book made him think of me. Isn't that sweet? The poems, a lot of 'em are real pretty."

"Can I hear one?" asked Rose.

"You most certainly can … just give me a minute." She rummaged through the sparse contents of the purse until she found her bifocals. Putting them on, she gave Rose a smile, turned to a dog-eared page, and read:

> *If in the twilight of memory we should*
> *meet once more, we shall speak again together*
> *and you shall sing to me a deeper song.*
>
> *And if our hands should meet in another*
> *Dream, we shall build another tower in the sky.*

"That is one of the loveliest things I've ever heard," said Rose. "Wasn't that lovely, Emma?"

Emma grunted, pounding a fist into the bread dough.

"Who wrote that, Hattie?"

Hattie squinted at the faded name on the worn cover. "Can't rightly make it out. I think it says here the fellah's name was 'Carl' or something like that but spelled different."

Rose took the book from Hattie and looked for herself.

*But you know the name, don't you, Hattie? Remember the way you joked about it? You always insisted on saying it wrong because your eyes were never that good—or so you tried to convince Granger. Mostly it was because it always made him laugh, wasn't that it? You knew the name was Kahlil Gibran and that Granger always read him—it was the only book he owned. Saying his name wrong, calling him 'Carl Gibbons,' that was your grand joke, yours and Granger's, shared on soft, cool autumn nights as the two of you lay between warm sheets in one another's arms, inhaling the sweet aroma of the lovemaking still on your skin.*

*"If in the twilight of memory …." Remember how you said that was your favorite line, how it sounded like something from a dream?*

*But it's not a dream anymore, is it, Hattie? You're the only one who knows he still comes back for you on Saturday nights, that he can still take you back there to Talley's Corner when the music was hot and the gin was cold. Even now you hear his voice, don't you? And you love it so over there, because over there you're your old self, you're the Queen, the loveliest of all the lovely ladies in their fineries, not some used-up little bit of a thing who's traded the best of herself in for sadness and nursing homes and snickers behind your back as you pass by, never being able to tell anyone how scared you are, how lonely this place is, the way it is now; you can't tell them about his visits because they'd never believe you, they'd think you were just some crazy old lady, you've heard them call you that when they think you can hear them, and maybe part of you started to believe it, so you chose to play the part, didn't you? But now you sometimes wonder if maybe, just maybe, you aren't really crazy, after all, because how could your Granger love you enough to come back from the world of honky-tonks and speakeasies to take you dancing and drinking and loving while Mousey and Stringbean and Jackpot wait by their ashcan fire for just a glimpse of your smile? Slim and beautiful and the envy of all who see you on these Saturday nights, that's you. Listen: your ears fill with their compliments, your spirits soar with the looks in their eyes as they watch you, the evening vibrates with your laugh.*

Hattie reached over and took the book from Rose. "Some of the boys, they used to say they never saw a lady as light of heart and step as me."

"Oh, I've seen pictures of what you looked like back in the day," said Rose. "You were a heartbreaker. Put you next to Dorothy Dandridge and no man'd give her a second glance."

Hattie reached over and squeezed Rose's hand. "You are so sweet, hon. Thank you."

"I speak nothing but the truth. You were gorgeous. Still are."

"That's what Granger always said to me. But he was *never* the jealous type, nosiree, not him, not my man." She once again lifted her cup and drank her tea, this time with little shaking.

"That was delicious as always, Rose, and I thank you." She then excused herself and, humming some long-forgotten gospel hymn, made her way out the back door for her afternoon walk.

"*That* is one sad woman, you ask me," said Emma.

"Even if I didn't ask, you'd tell me anyway," said Rose. She watched Hattie walk down the path to the sidewalk before turning left and strolling away. Rose picked up the saucer and teacup. "Still, you've got to wonder why she can't … hey, can I ask you something?"

"Seein' as how I couldn't stop you if I wanted, you might as well."

"How did Granger die?"

Emma stopped pummeling the bread dough and stared at the wall. "Oh, my. It, uh …" She wiped her hands on her apron and sat down, gesturing for her sister to join her. "You sure you want to hear this?"

"Is it that bad?"

"Yes, it is. 'Bout as bad as it gets."

Rose sat down opposite Emma and gave a slight nod.

"Granger did bootlegging for old Bill Talley. Talley, he got most of his hooch from Kentucky, and Granger was always the one who drove down to make the payoffs and the pickups. Well, one night he ran into some Prohibition boys who didn't take too kindly to his 'uppity' attitude—that's what one of them called him, 'uppity.' That's all the excuse they needed to pull out their pistols and start firing. Some uppity colored boy in a Minerva full of booze gave them good target practice. But Granger, he was strong and he was big and he was fast. Made them Prohibition agents chase him all over hell's half acre before they shot out his tires and he had to take it on foot. You know what those bastards did? They shot him in the backs of both his knees and he dropped like a sack of wet cement. But that wasn't enough, not for them and not back then, oh, no. *Then* they turned their dogs loose on him. After that, they tied him to the back of their car and dragged him all the way to the downtown square where they strung what was left of him up by the neck so the birds could have a little snack. Papers back then, they said he was still alive when they hanged him. He stayed there for damn near two days before folks from Talley's come to cut him down. Daddy was one of the men who helped do it. Him and another fellow, they were the ones who went to fetch Hattie and take her down to identify Granger's body."

Rose exhaled and covered her mouth. "Dear God."

"You know how Hattie knew it was Granger? By feeling his hands. Daddy said she held his hands up against her cheek and knew it was him. Wasn't enough of his face left for her to—"

"Jesus, Emma, *stop*."

"You asked. Now, it's not that I don't have any sympathy for the woman, you understand that, right?"

Rose looked out the back door. "Poor Hattie."

"The whole damn world's got problems and heartaches, Rose. Everybody feels lonely and miserable because somebody they loved isn't here anymore and, yes, maybe some of them didn't die very nice, but so what can be done about it now? I know her Granger's gone and that she misses him something terrible, but so is Mom or Daddy, and you sure as hell don't see *me* going around setting two extra plates at the dinner table, do you?"

"Not anymore."

"Oh—why don't you go sweep off the porch or mop the bathrooms or something?"

Rose smiled to herself. "You raise your voice like you're ready to throw a skillet at my head, but you love me, Emma. Admit it."

51

Emma began kneading the dough once again. "Everybody needs a hobby. Some people put off doing the housework—me, I love my sister. Besides, I wouldn't damage a perfectly good skillet that way." She looked at Rose. "I'm sorry I've been so bitchy today, but Hattie kept me awake half the night pretending that she was talking to Granger. Half the time I swear she was talking back to herself in his voice. Gave me the shivers."

"It's a sad world some days, Emma."

"Isn't it, though?" She smiled. "But I'm glad I got you. You're real good company. So's Hattie, except when …."

Rose walked over and gave Emma a hug. "You're a good person with a good heart, Emma. You just hide it from us more than I wish you did."

Emma returned the embrace, and then said, "Are you still here?"

Hattie stands before the wall that is all which remains of Talley's Hideaway. When the Beaumont Casket factory burned to the ground in '69 it took over a dozen other buildings with it, including Talley's. The city decided that its money would be better spent making improvements elsewhere, and so Old Towne East—the East End—came to be known as "Coffin County." Hattie hates that nickname; it reminds her that too soon she's going to be under the ground in the cold, cold darkness.

Now the wall draws the ruined and the crazy to its shade. Today, it's a young man who's muttering about needing something cut from his face, but Hattie sees nothing wrong with the young man's face; it is, in fact, quite handsome. She smiles at him and gives him a dollar so maybe he'll go and get himself a cold drink of soda. The young man says something about this fish and staggers off, just another crazy who calls the shade of Talley's wall sanctuary.

She's thinking of Granger right now. For as much as she loves him, there are times when she wishes that he would just leave her be. At first, the Saturdays weren't every week, were they, Hattie? At first, they came only every few years, then once a year, then once a month, and now it's every week. You stand before the wall and worry that Granger's going to come and try to bring you all the way back, don't you? You worry because you like this here world you're living in, even if it means living without him. Somehow living without him makes your time here even more important; you want to honor his memory in the twilight of your days and turn your life into a tower in the sky.

But Granger, he doesn't like it over there without you, and you know that. But what's a soul to do?

It's up to Granger, Hattie knows this. Her Granger, her good, loyal, loving man. He's there behind everyone's smiles, in everyone's gaze, in the sounds of their voices as they pass by; near her always, somewhere just behind, or around the corner, gaining on her, calling for her to slow down, to give a body a chance to catch its breath.

You were so young, Hattie, barely twenty years old, and you'd never had a man treat you the way Granger did, never had a man buy you things, beautiful, sparkling, expensive things, things that cost more money than you'd ever dreamed of having, but those things, as splendid as they were, didn't mean half as much to you as the touch of his fingertips against your cheek in the middle of the night. Oh, and his *words*, his glorious words and stories whispered in your ear when sleep wouldn't come: stories of tailors and poets and bootleggers and thieves, of heroes and peddlers and songmen and train chasers; tales of healers and gamblers and summer nights on the run and they just made you *sing* inside, made you wish for a full and rich life by this adventurer's side so one day you could tell your friends and children and grandchildren about all the crazy, wild, dangerous, wonderful times you had in your youth.

Standing before the wall now, Hattie closes her eyes and holds out her hand.

*You comin' now, Granger? Look—I got on my best dress and my good gloves and those pearls you always said made you crazy for me. I think I want you to come, darlin,' but please do it quick before I change my mind and get all nervous and start to shake like I do. I can't stand it here without you, but it scares me something fierce to think about the place you want to take me. There, I'm the way I used to be, but it's always only for a while, and if you take me back there permanent, I might be the way I am now ... and I don't think you'd be too crazy over me now. I'm old and fat and tired and I got nothing in my life except these Saturday nights. But I still love you, I still try to make you proud to have a woman like me. You made me a queen, darlin,' you made me special, something I never was before and haven't been since. So, I'm holding out my hand, Granger, and I hope you take it and never let go. You comin' now, Granger? Please don't make me wait. Please don't leave me here. Please come before I change my mind.*

Hattie waits, holding her breath. She stands that way, a crazy old lady with her eyes closed, for almost half an hour before you think about giving up, but as she begins to lower her arm, to give up, to admit that it's all been in her head for all these years, she feels familiar fingers take hold of her own, and close tightly, and whisper to her of twilight memories and singing a deeper song as something in her chest pulls tight for only a moment, and then lets go ….


See her now, boys. See Miss Hattie, back with us at last.

Snap those fingers and raise those voices and harmonize those songs, Ashcan Boys; sing to the smoke and the lights and the scent of sweet gin from Talley's Hideaway; make room for night, boys, for those grand Saturday nights, and sing it proud.

The Queen of Talley's Corner done come home, and only we understand, don't we? Only us, and not the others she left behind. They never understood. They never would have.

But they weren't there, were they?

# ABSENCE

### SHANE DOUGLAS KEENE

Every time you call me it goes this way
I listen without speaking, mainlining loneliness
    through the earpiece; speechless with
    yearning, knowing the conversation has
    already ended
Every time you hang up, you end again
    So do I
I hit this terminal point every time, the shift from
    longing to mourning
The long night comes at me empty and cold, your
    silence, a thrumming wire in this echoing
    mausoleum where once we found home
When you betrayed me, sank into the abyss and left
    me here, I became a ghost in my own flesh
I began to haunt the creaking corners, the shadows
    my element, up and down halls, in and out
    of rooms, always ending at the top of the
    cellar stairs, hand rattling on the doorknob
If I twist it, drift down those stairs, what might
    begin at that ending, down in the formless
    darkness?
Will I look up?
Even lightless, will I see the marks in the beam, will
    I begin to see you again?
What end would that bring?
Dropping my hand from the knob, I turn, begin the
    midnight tour of your absence, trying to find
    a different way to turn
One more time around again

# A PLAGUE OF
# LOVING GRACE

## CODY GOODFELLOW

Excerpted from *Every Man and Woman Is a Star: An Oral History of the LamaVirus Plagues* by Les Moore.

[ CARMEN MALDONADO, TRUCK DRIVER, TAMPA BAY, FLORIDA ]

What infuriates me is how the world looks down on us now, you know? Our passports are toilet paper, we can't travel or emigrate, but what happened here was an apocalypse. God smote us for our arrogance. My parents came here on a raft, right? But I can't go back, even with a clean chromosome screening. But what can you do? Almost half of us have the same fingerprints, the same face, and the rest … No wonder Mexico built a fucking wall …

[ IRWIN NASH, AKA MC INTRON, ALLEGED RINGLEADER OF THE LAMA PROJECT BIO-HACKERS' COLLECTIVE, IS WANTED BY THE UNITED STATES, INTERPOL, AND CHINA. AT THE TIME OF THIS INTERVIEW, HE WAS IN PROTECTIVE CUSTODY IN A MAXIMUM SECURITY HOTEL IN TIRASPOL, TRANSNISTRIA. ]

It was more than a revolution. It was an evolutionary revolt. America enshrined into law that we were all equal and Hollywood promised to let us all be beautiful, but it was a lie, like everything else. The laws they used to prosecute us had yet to be written when they tried us in absentia. The Project wasn't a terrorist group, and it wasn't a plague, and it sure as fuck wasn't, what d'you call it, psychoplasmic hysteria.

The dream came true. We made everyone equally beautiful.

## CODY GOODFELLOW

[ ANDY NORSTROM, SAN DIEGO POLICE OFFICER ]

I don't know what they expected to happen … Maybe they listened to "Imagine" one too many times. If they thought this would bring peace, if they thought it was some kind of masterstroke to make the world more compassionate, I hope they're happy. In a lot of ways, they're just as bad as the guys who flew those planes into that tower. You know? Maybe worse …

[ DR. FABIAN MORALES WAS AN ED ORDERLY AT PROVIDENCE HOSPITAL IN SEATTLE ON DAY 12 OF THE PANDEMIC. ]

I was on duty when the first reported cases recovered. By then, there were negative pressure isolation tents out in the parking lot in front of the hospital, the ambulances couldn't even get in. We had refrigerated trailers in the employee lot, the morgues were overflowing. We were desperate for any good news.

We were two weeks in, and the infection rate was mushrooming, there was no test, no vaccine, nothing. Reusing N95 masks, bringing gloves from home, holding people's hands and just being easy when they're dying, and their loved ones can't come in the room. The numbers just kept getting worse … The hotels were all shut down and re-opening as quarantine wards, the schools as emergency aid distribution centers, and the restaurants and bars were all being looted or used to store corpses.

I remember people cheering in the ED when the initial reports came in from China and South Korea that the first confirmed recoveries were being evaluated. Then the other stories started coming up, first on people's phones from god knows where, so you didn't want to believe them. The ones about the Chinese summarily executing the ones who pulled through … Nobody knew what to think. People wanted to hold each other, but everybody was terrified. Back then, the mortality rate for smokers, anyone over sixty, was close to fifty fucking percent.

The head nurse, Leanne, was the first one to notice. Our first cases, we had a huge group brought in after the cops raided this tent village under an overpass on I-5. The whole camp was sick, they found three dead in their sleeping bags, and we had six more on jury-rigged ventilators in the tents outside because we couldn't spare the beds. These were advanced cases, and the first one whose fever was down, Leanne saw something was different right away.

I guess because she's a devout Buddhist … Did Peace Corps stuff or whatever over there for years. She dropped the tray and went to her knees, bowed her head and asked him in Chinese or whatever they speak over there, *What are you doing here?*

The guy was like barely conscious after his fever broke, he just said he was sick. He didn't speak Chinese, but we all thought …

Listen, I'm not racist, but you know things must be bad when you see Asians sleeping rough, you know? But this guy had an expired driver's license, said his name was Huggins. Looked nothing like him, but he swore up and down …

Leanne didn't say what she saw that set her off, but she was just staring at the guy as she walked away. I think she said to me, "Don't you know who that is?"

And then she saw the other ones, and she started screaming.


[ BREE PARK, FORMER KIRO NEWS REPORTER ]

How the fuck could we have predicted anything like that? We fully thought we were covering a good news story. The symptoms were comparable to influenza, but the facial inflammation—the recovery wards looked like the end of *Rocky IV*, everybody's eyes swelled shut—was a novelty. People were already freaking out about the outbreak, but when we found out those changes were permanent … when they led us into the room, I thought it was a joke, frankly. Can you really blame people for how they reacted? All I can say is, we probably shouldn't have had the news crew there …

Δ

# CODY GOODFELLOW

[ SCOTT PRUNTY IS A PRISONER AT WASHINGTON STATE PENI-
TENTIARY IN WALLA WALLA, SERVING A LIFE SENTENCE FOR 1ST
DEGREE MURDER; HE HAS BEEN INFECTED BY IRV STRAINS 1, 3, 14
AND 68. ]

I'm here for shooting Typhoid Mary and saving tens of thousands of people. I don't care, I like this place better than where I lived before. *You're* paying for it, how does *that* feel? These fucking questions, I swear …

My family got infected, and my wife had just died … the little ones were sharing a damned ventilator. I think I fought it off just long enough to see them through, when the symptoms started hitting me. These assholes came on the TV in the ward. All the staff were excited because the media was there to show the first recovery cases.

They didn't say anything about it. They just made happy talk about how we were gonna get a vaccine now, and nobody was talking about the elephant in the fucking room. Heads so far up their asses, their dumps must come out shaped like donuts.

I went out to my truck and got my rifle. I went down there, and I shot them. I got three of the six and winged a fourth. I would've got that bitch from the TV news too, but they dog-piled me.

I wasn't just angry. It wasn't just grief. I saw quite clearly what this virus was. It was an invasion.

They're destroying our way of life, they're destroying our economy, they dropped this bioweapon on us, and it was clear to me, if to no one else, that they were invading, taking our very bodies away from us … turning us into them. I'm just glad they stopped me, or I would've gone back up to the ward and killed both my daughters, then myself, before they could take us. That's what was running through my mind.

[ MR. PRUNTY'S DAUGHTERS, PEGGY, A T–3, AND RUTH, A T–4, LIVE
IN A GROUP HOME AT BEND QUARANTINE COLONY. THEY HAVE
HAD NO CONTACT WITH THEIR FATHER SINCE RECOVERING FROM
IRV-1 .]

[ DR. MEHITOBEL RHYS IS CREDITED WITH HAVING ISOLATED IRV-1, COMMONLY KNOWN AS THE LAMAVIRUS. ]

The laypeople who went for their guns weren't half as scared as those of us working in epidemiology. Think about it—there are only a handful of horizontally transmitted exogenous retroviruses known to infect humans, and none of them are airborne. Hairy-cell leukemia, HIV ... Further, there's no genetic basis for ethnicity ... there's no switch you can flip to turn white people Asian. So even before we isolated it, we got into some truly horrific speculation we didn't share outside our circles. Was this a whole cascade of reverse transcriptase insertions calculated to turn non-Asians into Asians? Ridiculous, but the obvious answer was even more frightening.

A whole suite of somatic changes went into effect in patients who survived because the invasive RNA was copied wholesale from a single cell donor. What we were looking at wasn't a plague turning people into ethnic Chinese, it was runaway gene therapy, turning them into clones, of a sort ... which raised still more frightening questions, because looking at this virus, it's not just doing something that nature would never do, if you look at the rate and geographical spread of infection, it's obviously man-made ... and someone was spreading it.

[ DR. YAEL RUBINSTEIN, BIOLOGIST CREDITED WITH THEORY THAT LED TO THE ISOLATION AND SEQUENCING OF IRV-1 ]

It's a question of not blasphemy—that's a Western concept foreign to Buddhism—but it is a poser of a question. Would a clone of Lhamo Dundop also be imbued with his holiness? Would their mind have the same supernatural inclination to compassion, at least? Did they seriously expect the infected to leap out of their beds to teach the Kalachakra tantra? I would speculate that the result would be similar to the genetic footprint of Genghis Khan, who introduced so much Mongol blood into Caucasian phenotypes. Some interesting trivia in those genes, but an atavistic streak of barbarian conqueror?

Not so much ...

The Lama Project was a hideous experiment. If they hoped to iron out inequality or racial differences, perhaps they're satisfied with what they did. If their aim was to put a gun to the world's head and force some new age of enlightenment, one has only to look at what happened with the cops in Chicago.

[ ANDRE RICE, CPD OFFICER ]

It was fucked up, man.

Right when we were needed the most, the bug was cutting us down. 15,000 positive cases in the city, and like half of them were cops. More than half the force out sick; a lot of us who had mild symptoms just kept coming in. I guess we spread it around, but if we weren't on the job, you would've seen some *shit*, believe me.

I was one of the first bad cases. In the hospital, on a ventilator and all that, but they said they had a handle on it. Give the bug what it wants, if you try to fight it, your shit just shuts down. I was back on my feet in two weeks, but ... I remember when I saw myself reflected in a steel tray—they hid all the mirrors, heh—and I remember thinking, *Who the fuck is that?*

They were trying not to show me, and I heard what to expect, but like ... damn. When you see your face, but it's not you, nobody can prepare you for that. They saw I was upset, I guess, and they drugged me. By the time I came out of it, I guess I got right with it, but I didn't have no like, epiphany about shit.

Hell no, it ain't changed me. I went right back to work. Protect and serve, motherfucker, but I ain't no bodhisattva of motherfucking compassion. My family, they didn't know what to make of me, and nobody around the neighborhood trusts me anymore, I never take the uniform off, not even to sleep. You know who you are, on the force. That's my skin, now.

They looked at me funny, sure, when I came back to the job, but I was ready to go, and they were short. They had us wear masks, they were worried we might still be shedding, but the real reason they made the mask permanent, it just scared the shit out of people, know what I'm saying? I mean, what would you do, if all the cops had the same dopey, smiling Chinese face?

They were just putting a mask over a mask.

[ DR. NADIA ALBAN, FORMER PROVIDENCE HOSPITAL EPIDEMIOL-OGY EXPERT, PORTLAND, OREGON ]

Once that [ the sequencing of IRV-1 recoveries ] happened, our whole treatment regimen changed, and we flattened the mortality curve. We realized the flu symptoms not associated with spreading the virus weren't the body resisting the infection; it was changing. The mortality rate in older patients was because they didn't have the resources to change.

What was really tragic was what happened in the prisons, the immigrant detention centers, even the mental hospitals, once martial law went into effect. Those people didn't have to die. And that's where the transformation was the most dramatic …

[ DELBERT WARGO, AKA LIL BARDO, IS A MONK AT THE OSSINING BUDDHIST MONASTERY, FORMERLY SING CORRECTIONAL FACILITY. ]

Our old name means "stone on stone."

We were murderers, thieves, and rapists. We deserved worse than what we got. When the pandemic overturned the old order, we were abandoned in our cells. Some of the trusties and a handful of the guards who were infected too took pity on us, or we all would have died in our cells. We watched the outside world until we could learn no more from it, then we turned inward. We began building a new library, we began meditating, gardening, caring for each other. We finally fulfilled the broken promise of this sorrowful place. We corrected ourselves.

How many of us are there? When IRV-1 came, the United States held 2.3 million in 110 federal and 1,800 state prisons, 1,772 juvenile facilities, and a couple hundred immigration and Indian detention centers. Not all of them have reformed as we have, but more than enough to create an archipelago of monasteries across this nation. Perhaps because we were the worst, with the least to lose, more of us awakened to the new voices in our blood.

We could be the leading force in a new age of enlightenment, but ... we still watch TV. We are consoled with the realization that we, of all people, may be the scattering of torches keeping the light of wisdom and civilization alive in the new dark age to come.

[ DR. SEPI RAHIMZADEH, FORMER CDC ASSISTANT DIRECTOR, ATLANTA, GEORGIA ]

It was for their own safety.

After Seattle, you couldn't tell anybody anything. We had it buttoned up in Washington, New York, L.A., and then it pops up all over the country, targeting first responders, and then this ugly backlash against the recovered. You couldn't convince people China wasn't waging all-out biological war on us. Even if we knew what was going on in China ... To paraphrase Ambrose Bierce, plagues occur to teach Americans biology.

These people were in danger. We weren't getting any direction from the White House, so we took it upon ourselves to round them up. Relocating them to Bend in the midst of everything else took a lot of doing. The Bend community had been almost totally wiped out by the lamavirus. A Buddhist commune there was the epicenter, they all voluntarily self-infected, and it spread to the town.

Some people cheered as they saw the train cars going by, maybe just because trains were running again, or maybe because they thought we thought we were carting them off to a concentration camp ... but we were trying to save them. We had to justify it by saying, Look, if there's a chance of making a vaccine, it's in their blood. They've beaten it.

We couldn't keep the trains up. Word got around, a couple of them were stopped and the militias burned them down on the tracks with flamethrowers. All we could do was announce the quarantine zone and encourage the recovered to find their way there …

[ FRANK GARGANO WAS AN FBI AGENT ASSIGNED TO THE LAMAVI-RUS TASK FORCE. HE NOW WORKS AS AN INDEPENDENT SECURITY CONSULTANT. ]

When an individual or group starts a fire or sets off a bomb, you can ascertain their capability by the materials used, and their motive by the target and timing of the attack. We thoroughly went over the spread of the virus and quickly ruled out theories pointing to China. They were hit first and while they went dark and we have only third-hand accounts of how they responded, their first priority was to crack down immediately on Tibet and their own dissidents at home and abroad. They were telling their people we did this. And they lie a lot, but in this case …

There were still only about a million infected worldwide at this point, and other countries got out in front of it, because they saw the bad example we set. But the distribution here made it clear that we were under attack, and the attack came from within our borders.

Their capabilities were massive. The last administration cut loose whole swathes of medical experts from NIH, USAMRIID and CDC, so you've got this huge pool of brilliant, bitter people. That's where they wanted us to look first, once we'd ruled out a foreign terrorist attack.

Of course, we soon found out this wasn't as unprecedented as one might suspect. The principal obstacles to the biggest break-throughs in biotech haven't been technological. They've been ethical.

So, there's a clinic in Singapore, another in Dubai, where gene therapy treatments have been applied to some of the wealthiest individuals in the world for many years. They infect patients with tailored retroviruses for medical and elective, cosmetic purposes. Of course, they don't do a complete makeover, but they'll splice in bits from unwitting donors to add height, muscle density, I don't know. They don't advertise it, for obvious reasons, but you can order traits off a menu with no prices on it.

But they won't guarantee success or even survival after age fifty. It works best in kids, adolescents, and the results aren't as unpredictable or hard to explain. These viruses are among the most precious commodities on Earth, they're implemented under strict confidentiality, and they take every precaution to prevent them from getting out. Modifying a virus to go airborne, it's not in my wheelhouse, but outside of a horror movie, that kind of thing doesn't happen.

We couldn't get anywhere with them if we tried. They greenmailed us, they bought out a Bureau legat who probed them and turned him against us. A few years ago, I wouldn't have said any of this ... but now, obviously ...

Anyway, we didn't have to go abroad, as it turned out. A lot of their best technicians, it's like a revolving door between Biotech Valley in California to the dark side, over there. If they were doing something off the clock in Singapore, they would've been beheaded, full stop, long before we knew about it. A whole cohort of Americans were in and out of there like it was a damned Starbucks. That gave us a triangle, and a much narrower field, but we ran out of time.

If we could've figured it out maybe a month earlier ... It haunts me, you know? Maybe we could've stopped a lot of what happened, if we could've prevented LamaCon.


[ IRWIN NASH ]

When the Black Plague was raging through Europe, nobody understood biology, but they understood quarantine. The rich retreated to their villas, but the people stuck in the cities, if they didn't die right away, they figured it out. They knew God had abandoned them. They knew they were going to die. They got together and partied. Orgies in cemeteries, fucking in church.

The Biohacking Conference was cancelled that year, obviously. The people emerging from quarantine were in even more danger from bigots. Ergo ... LamaCon.

We invited everyone who'd successfully beat the virus and

emerged in the new form. We set up a virtual hangout livestreaming the physical conference, which was in the Beverly Hilton. Rather than turn it over as a field hospital, they shut the place down, so we hacked it and threw a party.

Two thousand lamas in the ballroom. Another six million live viewers. It was beautiful, like a costume party where every single guest showed up wearing the same mask. Imagine a sea of that beatific smile, cracking so wide because they were finally freed from fear, finally exposed to the new world they were inheriting ... Why wouldn't they all start fucking each other?

Eighteen million infected just in the U.S. A million and seven hundred ninety thousand fatalities. Almost five million recovered with little or no permanent somatic damage (T-2). Roughly six million fully rescripted phenotypes (T-3), and maybe half of those permanently shedding the virus (T-4). Those are pretty acceptable numbers for a plague, but for a revolution ...

We accepted responsibility for what we'd done. We stepped out of the shadows and showed the world that the power to save humanity was in its hands.

[ PERI NOOTEN, PUBLIC HEALTH BLOGGER, UTICA, NEW YORK ]

Ever notice how nobody who says the Earth is dangerously over-populated ever just offs *themselves?*

[ PIERRE DIDEROT, A.K.A. DR. PESTIS, IS A PRISONER AWAITING TRIAL AT SERVICE CORRECTIONEL CANADA IN DONNACONA, QUEBEC. CURRENTLY FIGHTING EXTRADITION TO THE UNITED STATES AND THE UNITED NATIONS ]

We were reacting to their arrogance. Their sloppiness. Their myopia. If they would have chosen a less infectious, less aggressive virus, if they would've come forward sooner, so the treatment regimen could've been implemented, there would've been fewer deaths.

Sixty-three million infected worldwide. Almost five million dead, and these imbeciles standing on their corpses to take a bow. "We did this for you!"

Viruses don't want to kill you, they need you. Viruses are innately masculine, they make us all feminine. We are their whole world, their womb. What kind of organism would be so stupid as to destroy its own habitat? Viruses are not stupid, they are the sum total of all the hard lessons learned by the biome, but manmade viruses are only as intelligent as their creators, yes?

Nash and his crew were stupid gods. So, what happened at LamaCon was necessary. We had to call them out … We offered the world a chance to choose again. They opened Pandora's Box. We gave everyone their own box. (Laughs) Well, anyone with their own viral cloning lab facility, anyway.

We hacked their sequencing tools, their encoding protocols, their chat threads, and we made improvements. We democratized the plague. And we handed out the noisemakers … and the condoms.

Each was impregnated with a unique genome and a unique strain of retrovirus. We'd had to crowdsource and automate a lot of the process to get them out in time. Mistakes were made, I'll be the first to admit. The hardest part was getting viable DNA from reliable sources. We reached out to a lot of disgruntled personal assistants. We took it on faith in a lot of cases, and some might not have played out, but if you're looking for a test of viability, the Schwarzenegger genome acquitted itself handsomely. [ At present, eighty-one IRV-13 infectees are currently running for public office. None have emerged in the fields of acting or bodybuilding. ]

And how many fatalities from our bugs? Zero. Even the stupidest script kid following our protocols could make a more effective clone virus than IRV-1, without killing anybody.

[ BONNIE DURSTENFELD SITS IN A CRISIS COUNSELING CENTER IN DALLAS, TEXAS. THE WOMEN WORKING THE PHONES ARE ALL FIRST-WAVE IRV-1 INFECTED. ]

I took this call and the man on the line says he's Jesus Christ, freshly incarnated on planet Earth, and he wanted an ambulance to pick him up, take him to the hospital so he could begin healing the sick.

I laughed. What else could you do? We were under a lot of pressure then, and I follow Christ, used to attend church every Sunday; it was a huge blow to have that taken away. We didn't have the resources to send help, all we could do was lend an ear and try to talk them down, so I humored him. I asked which strain he thought he was infected with, and he said he was infected with the holy spirit, and the end times were at hand, and then he blessed me, and hung up.

Then the switchboards started to light up, and every caller was saying the same thing, like reading off a script. We had almost a hundred Christs that night. Three times as many the next … What a blessing!

[ DEWEY LATHROP, FORMER DALLAS EVANGELICAL MINISTER; IDENTIFIED AS PATIENT ZERO FOR IRV-27, HE PREFERS TO BE ADDRESSED AS LORD JESUS CHRIST, KING OF THE NEW ISRAELITES OF TRAVIS COUNTY. ]

In a holy war, no weapon is off-limits, not even the Devil's own instruments of darkness.

A plague of false prophets was abroad upon the land. You ask God and he doesn't answer, it's because He knows you know what's to be done.

Norm [ Pruitt, President and CEO of the Craft Castle retail chain ] brought us into it. He put together a team of god-fearing geneticists to sequence DNA from artifacts from the Holy Land in his private collection. He had it! The blood of the King of Kings. We were each of us entrusted with a vial to sow among our respective congregations on Easter Sunday.

We put out the word quietly, but you know the police and the centurions of the unlawful president tried to stop us gathering. 'Course, once they saw the sheer numbers of folks who came out, they stood back.

All the pews were full, the adjacent indoor waterslide park was in full swing, folks were camping out in the parking lot, folks hitched in and told stories of running from the police, all of 'em come in search of a miracle.

And we gave it to them. Poured it in through the heater ducts, oh, Lord, what a sweatbox. Folks were sneezing and coughing and having fits, but we had to turn 'em out to make room for a second show before the feds could shut us down.

Yes, we gave it up for God that day. I'm certain if more of us would've survived the incubation period and those travel restrictions didn't come down, we would have delivered all of this poor, godforsaken land come Judgement.

[ DR. MORTON TEITELBAUM, BEHAVIORAL PSYCHOLOGIST, CORNELL UNIVERSITY ]

Maybe that's the saddest part of all this.

In recovering from trauma, be it divorce, loss of a loved one or economic hardship, there's significant anxiety about loss of identity. Who am I? What do I do now? When the trauma itself atomizes one's previous identity, taking away their appearance, the problem is compounded.

So far as we could tell, the rescripting viruses had little or no effect on reconfiguring the brain, but we just don't know. Our neural networks are largely unformed at birth and configure themselves in the first years of life. Just because a virus overwrites your genetic makeup and changes your physical appearance, it doesn't make you into a whole other person. You're still going to be the same aggregate result of your nurturing, education and experiences, no matter what the mirror tells you.

But then you factor in the anxiety, the need to reconcile one's inner and outer selves. Even once the hysteria settles down and you're not a pariah, they'll treat you differently, and if everyone around you was rescripted by the same virus, how much more intense the pressure to adopt the identity foisted upon you? The plagues have left behind waves of previously very rare mental illness issues that become secondary epidemics. Prosopagnosia, the inability to distinguish faces; Cotard, or Walking Corpse Syndrome, have become the norm in whole communities recovering from successive waves of script plagues.

Those people were infected involuntarily. If a doctor prescribes medicine, you're going to take it in good faith and it might seem to work, even if it's a placebo. If your faith in your doctor is absolute, and the medicine is prescribed to you to rescript you into a reincarnation of Jesus Christ, you're probably going to come away thinking you can do miracles. When half the people who inhaled the sacrament at one of those megachurches or a Crafty Castle subsequently drop dead, it's far less stressful to question their faith than your own.

Speaking as a Jew, it's always been hard to take evangelical Christians' take on Jesus seriously. The sandy blond hair, the piercing blue eyes ... but these are the same people who blow a gasket when someone depicts Santa Claus as black. Now these mamzers are everywhere proclaiming they are clones of Jesus, and they make John Phillip Law look like Fivush Finkel.


[ RUPERT WANGROVE, AWARD-WINNING GOSPEL/COUNTRY RECORDING ARTIST, NASHVILLE, TENNESSEE ]

I don't see it.

People come up to me like you right now, saying it's my DNA they used in that there Rapture Flu, I say the Lord works in mysterious ways, fucker.

Wangrove out!


[ DOUG STRAHM, POLICE OFFICER, MOSS BEACH, CALIFORNIA ]

We had this beach community on lockdown before it was cool. Day One, folks came down from the City to seek refuge, we went door to door and put them in quarantine ... "I don't have anything, I pay your salary..." Within days, they're all showing symptoms and inside a week, boom ... They were all shook up ... (Laughs.) What? [ Strahm and the other fourteen officers on the force were subsequently infected with IRV-17, popularly known as Elvirus. ]

But seriously, it's been quiet out here, but we get some action. This one guy, lives out by the runway [ Half Moon Bay Airport ], calls 911 mad as hell, saying his neighbor infected him with something called the Beatlebug. Right off, this guy [ Daniel Ringquist, musician, entrepreneur, stay-at-home dad, infected with IRV-9 ] rubs me the wrong way. He works at home, never goes out since they closed the schools, he pays his taxes, all that, and he calls all the time to bitch about people eating out of his trashcans, people hoarding hand sanitizer. Now, his whole family's nearsighted, his wife broke up his band, he can't write songs for shit, and his neighbors are out to get him. I told him to get over it, we all got problems.

So, then we start getting calls about an outbreak cluster on his block. This fucking hippie infected his whole neighborhood, must've gone around licking doorknobs, or something. We were trying to get help from the City to come in and scoop them all out, but no dice. So, we lock 'em down. Return to sender, baby.

It was real foggy, that night, and we get this call. He's mad because the stores are out of toilet paper and lentils or some shit. The airport was closed to civil aviation, but the National Guard was airlifting into there, and I guess somebody smarter than me relocated the landing beacon onto the roof of the guy's house. A CH-54B helicopter dropped a cargo container full of toilet paper on the dirty damn hippie while he was haranguing us on the phone. How's that for instant karma? (Laughs.)

What? Hey, don't be cruel ...


[ ABBY FILNER, PRESIDENT OF BLUEGENES RETAIL RESCRIPTING CHAIN, PHOENIX, ARIZONA ]

You started to see these ads in your spam folder, the ones that used to be for black-market Viagra or Nigerian stock tips or whatever, but they're for celebrity viruses. Even when they got more reputable, you never know what you're sticking in your arm, it could just be tap water, it could be AIDS, it could be the genome of the scrub who took your money, but the odds of it being anywhere near what you're paying for are infinitesimal. Coming out of the plagues, people were still wary, but after months of seeing this fucking strange face in the mirror, they got desperate.

What we used to tell them was, look at the star's gross earnings. If they're still trending up, it's probably fake, but as these celebs top out, they look around and see their market share falling, the value of fame *itself* depreciating, and it's like any other bubble. They sell out and auction off their swabs, maybe even run the retail themselves. Being Brad Pitt only pays off for so long, it's like having a monopoly, but once you're too old, you cash in, and everybody gets to be Brad Pitt. At least until next flu season … (Laughs.)


[ CHAD ABOULAFIA, FORMER CELEBRITY GOSSIP COLUMNIST, NOW A BOUTIQUE VIRUS BROKER, WEST HOLLYWOOD, CALIFORNIA ]

You can't swab a barstool in the Marmont without getting Firecrotch [ IRV-52, commonly known as Lohanvirus ]. That bitch is everywhere, but nobody wants it.

Most of my offerings are pretty niche. We offer a free photo evaluation and personality test, and we send you a mystery virus from the genome we think you *need*.

Definitely, some are more infectious, more effective, than others. Once you experience them as a disease, you can see why some of these people are stars. It's just in their DNA … and now yours. The Lamavirus couldn't hold a candle to the Dalivirus. Idris Elba, Will Smith, Betty White, Mark Wahlberg—(Laughs) though you have to warn people about the superfluous third nipple issue.

I cultivate special relationships with celebs who don't go out in public, that are still in demand. I like to think my offerings bring more than just the phenotype, you know what I mean? You puke, you shit, you shiver for two weeks, and you look in the mirror and you're Julia Roberts, but you still have the same life, same clothes, same job, same car. Who cares? Quarantine spiked suicides because we were all told we were special, you know, participation trophies all around, but cooped up at home, you realize you're just another machine for turning food into shit, and you're hungering for annihilation, this came along at just the right time. It erases you and leaves a glamorous, beautiful, attractive person in your place.

But like, that's why stars with serious hereditary neurological imbalances are really hot right now. Your life sucks, but like, if you're Michael J. Fox, everybody will like and trust you, especially when the Parkinson's kicks in. You wanna be Werner Herzog, Shelly Duvall, or Mr. T? I guarantee you'll see life differently.

We don't guarantee it'll get you a leg up in the industry, but look at the pop charts, the rock charts, the country charts. The top three singles this week are by an Elvirus infectee, a Swiftee, and a Tupac/Jesus. Wangrove's last single topped out at #37. Don't try to tell me celebrity doesn't recapitulate virology.


[ REP. LENA DAHL, UNITED STATES CONGRESSWOMAN (D-MN-3) ]

We still don't have a vaccine, and because we've had to pick our battles, with new strains introduced every week, we're losing this fight. That's why I introduced legislation to write the Genetic Security Act, which would reclassify unlicensed synthesis of rescripting viruses as an act of domestic terrorism. And further, it empowers every citizen to contract for a one-time reinfection with a rescripting virus using their own archived DNA, and offers a one-time stimulus check to pay for it.

We don't expect it to pass. Religious conservatives have convinced themselves this is divine retribution, and the activist left has totally drunk the Kool-Aid the new applied biology lobby is pushing, that rewriting your whole phenotype is no big deal, like getting a haircut. But we think if we can get the opposition on record that they don't believe you should have the God-given right to be who you were at birth, we'll be eating their lunch at the polls come November.

[LUANNE O'LEARY WAS A NURSE AT THE SEATTLE HOSPITAL WHERE THE FIRST RECOVERED PATIENTS FROM IRV-1 WERE IDENTIFIED AND LATER ASSASSINATED. NOW A BUDDHIST MONK, SHE RUNS AN ORPHANAGE IN THE BEND QUARANTINE COLONY. AS SHE SPEAKS, SHE ADMINISTERS A TRADITIONAL TEST TO A FOUR-YEAR-OLD IRV-1 INFECTEE, SHOWING HER IMAGES OF OBJECTS WHICH MAY OR MAY NOT HAVE BELONGED TO THE FOURTEENTH DALAI LAMA TO DETERMINE IF SHE IS A REINCARNATION OF THE AVALOKITES-VARA. ]

I wish I could say the world is more enlightened now ... people are starting to accept the changes, but most are getting used to their bodies changing every year like fashions. It's made people more attached to the material world, not less. It's made it easier for them to forget about *us*, which, I guess, is a good thing. There are still a lot of people around here who're hostile to the colonies, even though they're all IRV positives, too. It's so scary when someone with your face wants you dead, to hear words of hate coming from his lips ...

There's a big evangelical Buddhist movement spreading now that preaches that the Dalai Lama himself shed his genome as a virus to raise consciousness, but I don't see any truth in it. I always said Buddhism wouldn't catch on in America until we found our own unique way to get it wrong.

But I do believe this happened for a reason. I know the Four-teenth was holding on as long as he could because of all this. But he couldn't wait any longer, and we have to believe he's come back, and maybe all this was to raise consciousness, to pave the way for him to reincarnate in the U.S.

I don't care why whoever did this to us did it ... whether they were trying to make a point in China, or whatever. I have to believe the universe was working through this person to bring us together, to reawaken something better in us, to take away a distraction from what really matters. We're the ones who messed it up, but the Universe always wins.

After what I've seen, I know I should just give up, but hey, we're up to our necks in shit, so there's gotta be a pony somewhere, right?

[ SHORTLY AFTER THIS INTERVIEW, A CAR-BOMB WAS DETONATED OUTSIDE THE ORPHANAGE, KILLING LUANNE O'LEARY AND THREE OTHERS, INCLUDING THE AUTHOR. ]


[ LES MOORE, FORMER CELEBRITY IMPERSONATOR, AMATEUR SOCIOLOGIST ]

I was one of *those* people. You see them on TV or in your news feed and you have a good laugh. Why would anyone get $150,000 of plastic surgery to look like Justin Bieber? Porcelain veneers, chin implants, drastic rhinoplasty, I even got the tattoos. People laugh, but you believe in yourself becoming someone else, even the scorn just makes you stronger in it. I was pulling down a couple hundred thousand a year doing public appearances, and I can't even sing with auto-tune going.

Then *this*.

It was worse than dying, I thought, watching my life's work, everything I'd made myself into, watching myself dissolve. I thought, fuck this, I'm checking out. I tried using sleeping pills, I slashed my wrists, I was determined. But every time, this voice spoke to me and said I was the author of my own suffering. I'd always been in Hell, trying to be someone else. If I wanted to end real suffering, I should look outside myself.

So, I did. I never realized how out of touch I was. How stuck up my own ass, trying to become someone else, trying to escape. When there were people all around me losing lives, they *wanted* to live. People losing their faces and then their minds. And worst of all, how quickly it all became normal. It was like my own sickness had metastasized and infected the world.

And I didn't want to forget how I felt, and I knew the world was going to forget because that's how we carry on, and I thought there's got to be a way to remind people that this wasn't always the way it was, so I started doing these interviews.

I don't know. Maybe I'll delete them later …

# THE INFINITE LIVES OF THE LITTLE MATCH GIRL

CHRISTINA SNG

The little match girl
Shivers in the cold,
Curled up in a doorway,
Freezes to death alone.

In a parallel universe:

The little match girl
Smashes the window,
Climbs inside to hide
And survives the night.

In another iteration:

The little match girl
Climbs unseen into
A passing carriage,
Survives in a safer world.

Yet this often happens:

The little match girl
Is rescued by a man
Who turns out to be
A violent serial killer.

Two things follow:

The little match girl
Is tortured, her face
Plastered in the papers,
Forever remembered.

Or:

The little match girl
Stabs him to death
With his own scissors,
Takes over his home.

More likely:

The little match girl
Saves a lost labrador.
Huddling together,
They survive the cold.

Or:

The little match girl
Is rescued by aliens,
Leads the invasion
Against the world.

And in another life:

The little match girl
In her fine carriage
Rescues a dying girl
Freezing in a doorway.

The one she chooses:

The little match girl
Sees all iterations,
Follows the cat and
Finds herself a home.

# FALLING DOWN
# THE WAYLE

## KEHKASHAN KHALID

After midnight, oblong shapes drift silently behind the frosted pane of my bedroom window. Abu used to say they were the tortured souls of our wrongfully murdered neighbors. Amma says it is my imagination. I've always wondered, if I dared to look directly at them, would I see my sister staring back?

She was trampled to death eight years ago, in the middle of an anti-Shia rally Amma had dragged us to. Amma said she must have flown straight to heaven, as martyrs did, standing up against disbelievers. She never said the same about Abu when he was bricked to death in the passenger seat of a white Toyota. She had taken one look at his face, a pierced mosaic of shattered glass and blood, and breathed, "I told him to be careful about the company he keeps."

Abu never turned anyone away from his corner store. Shias, Sunnis, Christians, Parsis, and Hindus alike could walk away freely with a bag of potato crisps. Clearly there were people in our neighborhood who didn't approve.

Losing him so soon after losing Farida broke me. I had never had any friends—even my birthdays were celebrated with Farida's friends—but now I began to make enemies. I was defined by a moment in fourth grade when a girl yanked my hijab, and I bit her finger until white knucklebone gleamed beneath a canyon of skin. People would veer away as I approached in my unironed, maniacally askew hijab. There was another time in fifth grade when a boy jabbed a mocking finger at my budding breasts—I caught him in a chokehold and stabbed his head with a ballpoint pen in a fit of rage till he fainted. But no one knew about that one.

People said we looked alike, Farida and me. Sometimes I can

see that, in the mirror across my bed, when I lift my chin and turn just so. But I don't think I can ever truly be like her. She was the prototype, and I am the crude copy. She was the obedient one who ascended to heaven, and I am the one struggling to follow in her footsteps.

After she died, the private school that had offered her a scholarship made the same offer to me, out of pity. I refrained from biting or stabbing anyone, but I could not rise to the same grade point average as her, and I still could not make friends. I know it was probably my personality that warded people off, but I am inclined to blame Amma. In a school full of waxed forearms and uniforms tailored to fit slim cylindrical bodies swaying like poles in their platform heels, she made me wear a teal polyester bag—unflattering on my pear-shaped sculpture—with short sleeves leaving bare an expanse of black stubble.

"It's the first day, so I've ironed the uniform for you, but from tomorrow you better get it done the night before," Amma said and stepped into the room. *Snick, snick, snick,* the plastic blinds rotated open, and the sun slid inside in long, elegant beams. She glanced at the book—facedown like a tent on my bedside table, its spine webbed with cracks like the veins in my bloodshot eyes—and pursed her lips. "Isra, you know what a blessing it is to be able to go to this school. The least you can do is get to bed on time!"

I lifted burning eyes to her face.

"I don't feel well."

"Well, that's to be expected if you refuse to sleep," she said grunted, shoving my patchwork *ralli* off my legs. "Go take a shower. The geyser isn't working, and the cold water ought to wake you up."

Amma skimmed the *malai* off the top of the canister of milk and drizzled honey onto it. She handed me a hunk of bread and sat to watch me eat. I struggled to eat bite after bite of soaked bread. The desire to lose weight always hit me, like an anvil dropped on an unsuspecting cartoon, the day summer holidays ended. If I could lose enough weight, maybe the elegant shape of my bones would be visible even beneath my baggy clothes. When Amma's appetite had been satisfied, I left the table and made my way to the backyard.

There was a room under our backyard stairs. A triangular hovel where Sanu Masi lived. I guess she had been living in this dilapidated manor long before Abu acquired it, and Amma, who believed the prayers of elders would bring us *barakah*—abundance—must have allowed her to continue living there. This neighborhood was unsafe and real estate was cheap. Why pay with money when you must pay with lives? Amma kept the manor going by renting out our first floor to a madrassa. It wasn't just the rent she was counting on. There were rumors our house was haunted—rumors that, according to her, were nonsense and only made my imagination run wild—and the saintly boys in the *madrassa*, swaying and chanting *quranic* verses, would keep the demons at bay.

Amma was simultaneously obsessed with the existence of demonic djinns who could cause us harm and dismissive of the shapes that my imagination constructed in my bedroom window every midnight. Djinnat were not ghosts of the dead, lingering in the world due to unfinished business. Djinnat were beings of fire and freewill, banished by the existence of humans. The virtuous ones made their homes far out to sea. And the malevolent ones lived under our feet, in an infernal, septenary abode, the Wayle. These ones arose from the Wayle, clinging to pipes in dank bathrooms or ensconcing themselves in the necks of humanoid dolls, and waited, with infinite and unwavering patience, for humans to make a single misstep so they could swoop down and claim them.

Farida and I had known Sanu Masi since we were five years old. We had been scared of her at first. She fit a five-year-old's idea of a *churail*, a witch, with her thin braid hanging by white threads on a balding scalp, her disproportionately skinny body as if her skeleton had fallen apart and pieced itself blindly back together, and eyes that never stopped following us around the backyard.

She never strayed from her doorstep. She stood there, watching us with an ambiguous smile. Then, a few days after Farida's death, while retrieving a tennis ball that had rolled into the yawning cavity of her doorway, I stumbled into her arthritic fingers. And, instead of a witch or a curse, I found someone who could bear to listen to me.

"You're unhappy," Sanu Masi observed. She was standing, once more, at the doorway of her room under the stairs.

"I wish Amma and Abu hadn't enrolled me in a private school," I said and shrugged. "I prefer friends to a good education."

"You have me." Sanu Masi wrapped her arms around me. She was bony but her arms oddly fleshy.

"I wish I could just …" I said and glanced at Sanu Masi reluctantly, but her face was impassive and nonjudgmental, "rip their heads from their bodies. Break pencils in half, till my palms are grazed with blood, and stab them into their eyes."

My fists shook with imagined rage.

"I know," Sanu Masi said and sighed. "I'm proud of you for holding back, Isra." Her knuckles bumped over the ridges of my spine as she stroked my back "You just wait. One day you'll get back at them."

"Since it is your first lesson of the year, we're going to do a little ice-breaking exercise." The whites in the teacher's hair gleamed under the tube lights as she paced at the front of the classroom. "If you saw my email, you should have bought in a little token of anything that represents your holiday."

My hand, inside my bag, closed over a fist-sized fabric doll. I had hunted for it this morning as the school van blared the horn outside our gate. A dainty little bride in a red dress with gold trimmings, kohl-rimmed eyes, and woolen black hair. It wasn't that I lacked Barbies—we had a few relatives who had been to America and brought back blonde leggy dolls in clothes Amma disapproved of—but the Barbies were too realistic and Amma, afraid they would draw the demons, had drawn crosses with permanent markers over their eyes, like knocked-out smiley faces. Besides, Abu had bought this doll for me from our one and only vacation to the hilly city of Murree. That would be an interesting anecdote to share.

I settled in to listen to the other students but the boy in the seat in front of mine turned around. "Hey, do you want to fuck me?"

I recoiled from his sneering. My eyes slid from him to his friends, watching me with their elbows on the backs of their chairs.

"Um …" My throat emitted a bovine sound, and my ears burned, rattled by this diversion. My heart plummeted as the words I had been rehearsing in my head blurred.

"I don't think she understands what that means, Asad," one of his friends said and snickered.

"Is that true?" Asad's eyes lit up maliciously. "Do you not know what 'fuck' means?"

My knee trembled, jerked up and down of its own accord. I clamped my hands down on it, but it wouldn't stop.

"I think she's a virgin," the friend on the other side chimed in.

"A horny virgin."

"Is that true? Are you horny?" Asad's eyes, hard as nails, were trained on my face.

"I don't think she knows what 'horny' means."

The teacher called out my name just then. I stumbled to the front of the classroom, realized I had left the fabric doll on my desk, mumbled something illegible and returned to my seat amongst laughter from my classmates and disapproving noises from my teacher.

My heart drummed with anger long after the class was over. If only he had dared to approach me alone, without his cronies there to egg him on, I would have shown him who he was messing with.

"Look at that, she's staring at you."

"She's fucking creepy, man. She looks demented!"

Asad's friends jostled his shoulder.

I pretended to ignore them and headed toward the stairs. I had to go across the building to make it to my next class. They whispered behind me.

"*Just push her.*"

Before I could react, two palms planted themselves on my back and gave me a violent push as I descended the staircase. My bag fell first, arcing through the air, scattering books like I would scatter blood, and then I followed its trajectory. My elbow hit the stone banister, my lip burst on the bottom step, and my glasses cracked a couple feet away.

"*What* is going on here?" A teacher pushed her way through the burgeoning crowd.

Asad called from the top of the stairs, "She slipped. We tried to catch her, but," he said and shrugged, and the classmates surrounding him nodded like marionettes.

"Come on, let's get you up." The teacher clamped a hand around my arm and pulled me to a standing position.

I lifted the hem of my shirt to wipe the blood from my lip and found that my nose had been running mucus down my moustached upper lip. It left streaks of glutinous green and red on my hem. I turned and began to collect the things that had scattered all over the hall, shoving them back into my bag. My fabric doll was nowhere to be found.

"I think you should go to the nurse," the teacher said. "I can write you a note for your next class."

My breaths came in short gasps; tears flecked the corner of my eyes. Where was the doll? Had I forgotten it in class?

I pushed past the teacher and raced up the stairs. As I approached the dimly lit door of the classroom, voices sniggered inside.

"What the hell is *this?* Did she think this is an elementary school show and tell?"

I pushed the door open just in time to see my classmates tear the head off the fabric doll. The ripping noise seared my ears, and I clapped my hands to them with a sob. Asad pulled an arm off, and little fluffs of cotton filling drifted to the floor. And then they noticed me blubbering in the doorway. They exchanged awkward looks, pushed past me, and left me alone in the classroom with the shreds of my only vacation in fifteen years.


"What are you doing?" Amma was looking over my shoulder as I trailed my finger down the page of the dictionary. *F* ... *Fuck*. She had seen the word I was searching for. I had been too busy wondering what sexual intercourse could entail to hear her footsteps. I slammed the book shut, my finger still between it, and cried out. She whirled me around; the book slipped from my fingers, flying across the room.

"*What* do you think you're doing?"

"Nothing. I'm looking at a dictionary, for crying out loud!"

"I'm disappointed, Isra." Her lips were tight. "How did you even hear that word? What have you been doing?"

"Nothing! People use that word, and I sit there like an idiot not knowing what it means!"

"Who uses it? Is it kids at school? Should I be speaking to the school management about this?"

"Yeah, that's just what I need. My mom going to the principal to ask about *fucking*."

Her slap came faster than I could anticipate. It rocked me back on my heels. I crouched on the floor, the strands of my black bob barely covering the burning redness that crept across my cheek. Tears, like angry dewdrops, grew on the edges of my eyes.

"Isra, the path to hell is a slippery slope. All it takes are a few wrong footsteps, and then you can't stop the fall."

"I already am in hell."

I pulled myself to my feet, pushed past her, and ran out of the room.


"I can't take it anymore, Sanu Masi," I sobbed against her flat chest.

"I know, sweetness, I know." The nails of her ropy fingers dug into the flesh behind my ears. "I don't think we should let them get away with this anymore."

"What should I do?" I sniffled.

"Remember what I told you about *Chathan Seva*? Binding a demon to your service?"

"Come on, Sanu Masi, Chathan Seva is as real as Amma's version of hell."

"Tut, tut, who says your Amma's version of hell isn't real? I think the Wayle exists, deep underground. And *Chathan* Seva is how you call those who live there." Sanu Masi pulled my head back and scanned my face.

"But, if she's right, then those demons just want to claim our bodies."

Sanu Masi shrugged, like her head dipped between her shoulder blades for a moment. "There's always a price to pay, Isra," she said, "The question is, how badly do you want revenge?"


It was a little after midnight. The clock in my room ticked like the clucking of a disapproving tongue. *Chathan Seva … binding a demon to your service.* Sweat beaded my brow. It was a compelling idea. I glanced at the shapes in the lounge, drifting mournfully past the window. They seemed disinterested. I climbed out of bed and crawled over to the mirror to look at my sunken, sallow face, peppered with sunspots. My hairline had the unfortunate quality of immediately acquiring copious amounts of grease, even after a shower.

Sanu Masi had laughed at my expectations of blood and incense. She said calling a demon was as easy as calling someone's name, and mirrors were proximate doorways to other dimensions. I repeated the name Sanu Masi had told me, loud and clear in the emptiness of my room, until the words lost meaning through repetition.

A light appeared in the center of the glass, like a lantern carried in a fog. I blinked and rubbed my eyes, but it wasn't sparks dancing behind my eyelids; it was real, and coming closer. The light began to grow—a blooming blue lotus, caught between gentle fingers, spinning round and round. But as the image touched the surface of the mirror, I recoiled. The arms surrounding the light were not periwinkle petals. They were fleshy, translucent tentacles, riddled with suckers. They burped their way through the mirror, dragging a burning golden core. A fiery organism curled like a fetus amidst that writhing mass.

"This world burns," it lamented. The voice seemed to emit from the tentacles, the fetus at the center silent. The tentacles slapped the floor of my room in agony. "What do you want?"

"Revenge, against those who deserve it."

The tentacles swayed in the air, assessing me.

"And what do you deserve?"

It started slowly. The creature from the mirror snaked its tentacles along my arms and climbed onto my back. The proboscis I assumed was its mouth tickled my neck. It spilled black ink onto

Asad's bag, turning pages full of assignments illegible. It snapped pencil nibs every time certain classmates attempted quizzes. I was forced to sleep on my stomach but at least I was sleeping, soundly. And then the strange dreams began.

I was falling down an interminable well and the first time my skin touched the edge of the wall it sizzled and popped like the fresh liver Amma tossed on the cast iron tawa. The heat peeled my dermis like starving hands on fruit and the fat leaked out, fueling putrid flames. When I stopped falling, I was walking on iron-hot ground, my skin melting and repairing itself around heat-contracted muscles that moved of their own accord. Hundreds of forms, alight with translucent fires, stumbled beside me. I tried to stop but movement was necessary to stave off the pain.

There was a thunder-clap above us. Pieces of metal with glowing, molten cores tumbled toward us like streaking meteors. The people around me weren't looking up. They were looking at me, the teeth in their melting faces bared. They brandished steaming iron pokers and twisted their bubbling feet toward me. Pain had enraged them, and they would direct that rage at me.

The next day, I had to sneak into Amma's room, mix foundation with her moisturizer, and lather it across my arms to hide the burns that looked as though cigarettes had been extinguished on my skin. I assumed my arms were sore from the suction of those tentacles.

"Do you think you should go now?" I asked the golden body of the djinn.

It seethed with warmth like an oven door left ajar.

"What will you do if they start again?"

I nodded in agreement. I went to see if Sanu Masi was there so I could show her my new companion, but she was gone. She did that from time to time, to visit relatives who still cared.

That was the day things began to pivot out of control. My slightest distress enraged the demon. The Pepsi bottles Asad bought for all the classmates, except me, burst apart, scattering fizzy black liquid and glass in every direction. Everyone stood stunned as he screamed at his outstretched arms, pockmarked with shards, until the nurse took him away.

"You really need to go." I shivered in the girls' toilet. The demon perched on my back in the mirror, leeching off my neck, strangling my arms.

"Your anger sustains me," it said and made a rippling sound of pleasure.

"But I'm not angry anymore, you've made it all better."

It made no response, but I could see it thrumming like a baby suckling its mother. I wished I had asked Sanu Masi how to reverse the Chathan Seva.

I was falling again. A burst of frigid air sliced past my cheek as if I was falling into the embrace of stalagmites. I relished it for a second—an escape from the fiery above—before I realized ice burned as much as fire. I crashed onto unforgiving ground that shattered the feeling in my frozen legs. I couldn't get up. I tried to move forward with my arms, but they were wrapped like a straitjacket around my naked blue body in futile protection against the cold. So, I sat there, a twisted ice sculpture of limbs, numb except for the parts of my body that screamed as they touched the ice. *At-at-at.* The sound of the friction of my bones ricocheted around my skull. I swung my eyes right and left. There were hundreds of me. Pale, lifeless, deformed, huddled inexorably onto the cold ground. And the painful orchestra of our shivering filled the air with a remorseless buzz. *At-at-at-at—*

Three days with the demon and I was afraid to sleep again. The sensation of falling in my dreams was too real. I sat on my bed, knees pressed to my chest, afraid to see my reflection in the mirror. What if it drank my very soul through my veins? Tears trembled across my face, but I swept them away with aching fingers. It was ravenous for emotions, and I didn't want to feed it.

I knocked on the classroom door and edged it open, late because I had fallen asleep during lunch break out of sheer exhaustion.

"Excuse me, Miss, could I come in?"

"You're late, by fifteen minutes!" The teacher continued to write numbers furiously on the blackboard.

"I'm sorry, I had a project deadline today, and I was working on it during lunch …"

"I don't want your excuses. Come inside and stand with your face toward the wall."

"I said I'm sorry …"

"Do you want to go to the principal, Isra?"

I dropped my bag near the door and turned to face the peeling paint on the wall. The classroom heaved with silent laughter behind me. Seconds later, I felt a nick on my calf. Somebody had thrown a compass from their geometry set at me, and it was stuck in my shalwar, the pointy edge digging into my leg. I bent to remove it.

"Can you stop fidgeting in that corner?" the teacher barked from the front of the classroom. "You're already late and now you're messing around?"

I stood up straight again, the compass still pricking my leg.

The teacher turned back to face the board. The missiles picked up pace. Erasers, wads of crumpled paper, stubs of overused pencils. My eyes clogging with tears, the djinn on my back quivering in ecstasy. There was a knock on the door.

"Oh hi, miss!" A boy waltzed into the room. "You look absolutely gorgeous today, if you'll forgive my saying so." His eyes, wide with feigned infatuation, bore into the teacher.

"Oh, stop it!" She blushed and batted her hand at him. "Get in here and take a seat."

The class giggled as the boy dumped his bag near the closest desk, winked triumphantly at the girl next to him, and took a seat.

I struggled to curb the rage that festered inside me, the djinn thrumming like a tuning fork—its excitement swayed me from side to side. I needed to get out of here.

"Miss," I said and raised my hand and turned, my mouth sour, "I don't feel well."

She ignored me and continued to tap the chalk gratingly on the board in the shape of numbers. I burped and clapped a hand to my mouth as the class burst into laughter. Their hilarity seemed to expand and echo across the blurring room.

The djinn whispered succulently, "Let me, Isra, let me ..." There was something unbearably familiar about it.

It slithered off my back and onto the floor, dragging its golden body across the tiled surface. Every object its molten core touched burst into fuelless flames. Through hazy eyes, my classmates flickered in their seats like shadows on a wall, their faces melting from laughter into screams stifled by the demon's translucent, shapeless limbs wrapped across their mouths. Within minutes, the classroom had become a burnt-out shell in the middle of a pristine building, populated by the charred remains of my former classmates. I ran before the demon could climb back onto my shoulders.

I leapt over the school boundary wall and took the first rickshaw home. I couldn't be around when they discovered the remains. Maybe they would think my ashes were amongst that desecrated classroom. Anything that would keep me from being the culprit. I ran through the house, ignoring Amma's shrieks to leave my shoes at the door, and made for the backyard.

"Sanu Masi!" I ripped open the door to her hovel. "This is all your fault. You come out right now and help me!"

"Isra!" Amma and her rolling pin stood akimbo behind me. I turned a weeping face toward her. She bolted forward, grabbed me by the shoulders, and then wrinkled her nose.

"Isra, what is that charred smell? And why are you yelling into this empty cottage?"

"Empty cottage?" I echoed.

"Yes, this room has been empty for years." Amma touched my forehead. "Isra, you're burning up."

I squirmed out of Amma's arms and ran back up the stairs.

My room was dark when I opened the door, but I could make out the faint outline of a thin white braid hanging onto a balding head, like an ivory dagger.

"Sanu Masi?"

When she turned around, she illuminated the room with her phosphorescence. Her tentacles swayed above her head, and she smiled as if two index fingers were hooked into the corners of her lips, pulling her mouth upward.

"Sanu Masi ..." I whimpered, "I don't understand."

She shuffled toward me, sometimes backward, sometimes forward, a spinning body below a stationary head. A bell rang below in the depths of the house, and I heard Amma answer it, "Is Isra in some kind of trouble?"

I turned to the door, but Sanu Masi drew it toward herself again.

"Oh, Isra, they're never going to appreciate you. Trust me, I've been through this. Stabbed to death in my own home. Just because I believed differently. But I got my revenge and look at me now. I'm resplendent."

"What am I going to do?"

Sanu Masi's tentacles nudged me toward the mirror on my wall, pitch-black and oval—a cavernous mouth—and her puckered lips whispering frantically in my ear, "Fall with me. Come to a place where you are unafraid to be yourself."

I looked down the gaping hole that was the mirror.

"What are you going to do to me down there?"

"Nothing you haven't already experienced."

She gave me a sidelong look and I knew she meant the dreams had been real. I had been falling for days.

"Is this hell? Am I going to hell?" I trembled, sobs I had held in for days cascading down my cheeks. Farida might have gone to a heaven I could never ascend to, but I was quite sure I would never find Abu either, down where I was headed.

"This is no longer hell for me but, in the beginning, it might be for you."

"What about all those people who were hurting me? Why aren't they here?"

"But my sweet girl, you already dealt with them. They've paid their price. Now you only have to pay yours."

She pushed me, and I tumbled headfirst down the well.

Δ

The Great Lotus was a burning land with fringes of ice. The fire and the ice whipped our amorphous essence into shape. Without it, we were nothing. Occasionally, in my dreams, I would drift to lands I had once known. I would float across strange landscapes of objects and cloths, and I would sense the sleeping presence of nearby beings that were both like and unlike me. But no matter how long I waited, watching them sleep from beyond the frosted panes of their windows, I could never approach them. Not until I was called.

It was years before I was summoned. A large, inflexible fist whisked me toward a shimmering surface. I was inside a mirror and a young boy was watching me with mingled hope and fear. My body cried out against the blistering air of his world as I emerged through the glass.

"It burns," I whispered. "What do you want from me?"

"Power. To fight someone who deserves it."

My tentacles swayed in the air, assessing him.

"And what do you deserve?"

# EVERY DAY CAN'T
# BE APRIL

## NNADI SAMUEL

A little'un guns his two fingers at me,
startling me to a killed posture.
he styles his wrist
& flashes a teaser to make his mania prank real.
this lad, with face like mine disremembering to be kin.
he tucks a finger to leave one poking at me,
shredding my skin,
a bizarre smile swelling on his lips.
he had a toy car with a siren gulping my first cry for breeze,
& softened his grip only when he knew I was limp.
his cheek sells the lies how he takes a near-death for leisure,
how he turns this to April Fools',
now, when his shrugs would scare the hell out of me.
I grope my wrist and find my watch stuck in March
    —a docile March.
a little white snails on his skin to jeer the thing he outdid
    —this negro priding as his kin.
I wouldn't kneel on him to drown my message home,
no, his breath would go.
I'd make a prayer like this,
bringing back to my lips the news of the recent death,
restraining the urge to kill the little white on his skin,
& repeating this phrase:
"No one kills a boy with a stomach for mood swings."

# FEELING LIKE A BIG KID AT THE BEGINNING OF THE END

## PAUL MICHAEL ANDERSON

Addie couldn't find a light blue bead anywhere in the bowl, and the little girl next to her hugged the other bowl to her chest, picking through it. The girl's pigtails were uneven.

"Dad?" Addie asked, turning to the other table.

Dad's eyes looked up from his book. "You need something, lovebug?"

Addie held up the plastic bowl. Beads fell against the side, like the rain stick Ms. Mitchell brought into class last year. "I can't find light blue."

Thunder rumbled outside, close enough to rattle the craft store's tall front windows. The kids at her table jumped, as well as most of the parents at the other table, looking up from their phones.

Dad glanced through the glass, frowning; the sky was clouding over with a gray wool blanket. "Sure, kiddo."

He took an empty chair at her table. He was the only dad here, surrounded by moms; even the clerk had stared at him when he'd signed Addie onto the attendance clipboard. A year ago, Addie would've announced her dad—Daddy back then, not so often now, unless she was upset—had summers off because he was a teacher, and he would quickly guide her wherever they needed to go. Dad sometimes felt embarrassed about being the only man around—

Mom worked all year, at an office nearby—and it was only recently Addie had noticed. At nine, she had an idea about embarrassment; it was why she called her dad *Dad* instead of *Daddy*.

"Okay," he said. He looked at her bead template, a circle shape the size of small plate, the only one left because they'd come late, and the littler kids had taken the person, animal, and house templates. "What're you making?"

"Planet Earf." She frowned. "*Earth.*"

"Good pronunciation, bug," he said, smiling. He stuck his tongue between his teeth, softly made the *Th*-sound. Addie grinned and mimicked, and thunder rumbled harder. A little kid across the table cried out.

Dad frowned again. "Gonna get soaked when we leave." He leaned toward her template. She'd gotten most of the continents, the tubular beads rising from the yellow plastic pegs, saving on green by using brown for the Sahara desert and white for Antarctica. "This is pretty good."

She beamed. "We did hemispheres last year."

"You're gonna need a lot of blue." He slid the bowl to her. "Dig through this." The other girl had let go of her container and slid it closer. "I'll go through this one."

*Scrabble, scrabble, scrabble.* Addie liked the sound of the beads clicking as they searched. She checked the other kids scattered along the table, watched over by the clerk guarding the clothing iron used to finish the projects. Addie thought all the kids looked younger, and she almost felt embarrassed, but she was out of beads at home, and Dad said they could pick up some more. One little boy slow-walked his plane template to the clerk, holding it with both hands as if carrying a bowl of water. Another boy bumped his template, spilling some of the beads off their pegs, and his mom was right beside him, already giving calming *shooshes* as the boy's face reddened and eyes got teary.

Outside, an emergency siren burst into life. It made Addie's shoulder's tense, the way the sound *jumped* into her awareness. It was as startling as the thunder.

"Gotta couple," Dad murmured, setting them in the pile on top of his book. He had the cover down. Most of the covers of his books scared her, even though she said they didn't, to show she was a big girl, and turning them over was a habit, she thought. It gave her a warm feeling. Dad wasn't gooshy—he routinely hugged and kissed the top of her head but wasn't the kind of parent to give calming *shooshes*—but things like that showed he cared. Thinking like that made her feel like a big girl.

"Gonna need more," Dad said. Mom made fun of how often he talked to himself. Addie had once heard him say, "I'm a great conversationalist, so of course I talk to myself." She'd asked Ms. Wadas—this was when Addie had been in second grade—what the word 'conversationalist' meant, and Ms. Wadas had said she was proud of Addie knowing a big word. That'd also given Addie a warm feeling. She was getting older and actively looking for that sensation. Being nine, she realized, was trying to always feel like a big girl until she actually *was* a big girl.

The mom of the little boy who'd slow-walked his template got up from the parent's table. The other moms stayed with their phones. Outside, another siren came to life, the sound skittering along her nerves. She scooched her chair closer to Dad.

"Accident on the Interstate, probably," Dad said. He set the bowl back. "I think that's all I can find, kiddo. See what you can do."

Someone's phone beeped with a message, like Mom's did, and someone gasped. It seemed very loud in the store, and Addie realized the store didn't have speaker-music, what Dad called Muz-*ak*, playing. She couldn't remember ever being in a store where there wasn't *some* music overhead.

Addie set her bowl with her Dad's—both snatched up by the girl next to her, one uneven pigtail beginning to unravel—and got to work, plugging in the blue between the continents. It took a lot of concentration; the pegs were small, the beads close together so that when heat was applied, they'd soften and merge, and you had to be careful not to knock other beads over when putting new ones down.

She fell into the rhythm of building the world. Dad starting reading again. Around her, the crying boy finished his template, ironed it, and left. The girl next to Addie kept adding greens, reds, and blues to the bottom of her house template, then removing them—she was trying to make a garden, Addie thought.

"Oof, it's gonna be a big storm," Dad muttered, and Addie looked up. He stared through the tall storefront windows. The sky was a weird mix of ropy gray-black clouds with patches of red bleeding through. The clouds seemed to be rolling against one another, like the hot dog machine at 7-Eleven. The sight bothered Addie in the same way the emergency sirens did.

She looked down at her template and tried setting a blue bead down, only to knock out part of the United States. "*Darn* it."

"What's your daughter making?" a woman asked, startling both Addie and Dad. The woman stood at the head of the table. She hadn't been with the other parents. Addie had never seen her before. She looked older than the other parents, too. Not *old* old, like Gram-Gram or Nini, but older than Dad. Little wrinkles beside her eyes kept flexing, lines around her mouth—*parentheses*, Addie heard Ms. Mitchell say when they'd learned punctuation—tensing and relaxing. Her eyes were bright, but hard, reminding Addie of plastic gems.

"Um," Dad said. "She's making the Earth."

"Like the lord," the woman replied. The parenthesis around her mouth tensed and relaxed, tensed and relaxed.

Dad looked at Addie, and Addie didn't like his expression. His eyes were wide, but hard, the way he got when he was annoyed, or about to say her first *and* middle name. He put an arm around the back of Addie's chair. "Do you have enough blue, hon?"

The northern hemisphere was almost done, South America, Africa, and Antarctica still dying of thirst. "I think so," she replied, her throat dry.

"Let's finish up," Dad said. "Try to beat the storm."

She nodded and picked up some blue beads. The woman behind them hadn't moved on. Addie snuck a glance, and the woman was watching the windows. Now the rolling clouds were black, the patches of red the color of a crayon. The sight of it made her hands curl into fists, the beads pressing against her palms. Another siren filled the air, then another. Her shoulders hunched.

"Hurry up, bug," Dad said, softly, meant only for her. The sound of his voice goosed her. The little girl next to her shoved the bead bowls away with a triumphant squawk.

"Sorry," the woman said behind them. "The storm distracted me."

Addie started to raise her head, but Dad's hand moved to her shoulder. Redirection, and she recognized it, the way a big girl would.

"S'okay," he said. Thunder banged over the store. "It's gonna rain hard."

"It looks like it might do more than that."

*What does that mean?* Addie thought.

"I didn't mean to bother you," the woman said. "It's just ... I come into the store, and they always have these little summer activities for the kids, but you never see fathers around—"

"I'm a teacher," Dad said, and Addie, knowing all of Dad's voices, could hear the strain in it.

"Well, isn't *that* nice!" the woman said. The words sounded sarcastic, but the woman seemed genuinely pleased. "You get to spend some quality time with your daughter." Her voice reminded Addie of warm honey, the kind Mom would add to her tea. Addie had tried it once; it'd tasted awful, sweet like a candy, but hot like dinner. "And I bet she doesn't lose any learning when not in class."

"Probably not," Dad said. "Listen, I—"

A rumble filled the room, followed by a hollow *whoosh*. Addie saw something out of the corner of her eye and at first couldn't understand what was going on outside.

"Holy shit," Dad breathed. "Lookit all that rain."

Once he'd said it, it clicked in Addie's eye—god's big shower-head, turned to full blast, obscuring even the parking lot just beyond the overhang of the store's marquee, leaving only vague shapes and a lot of gray-blue. Like a thick shower curtain obscuring the world, imperfectly erasing it. It put a flutter in her chest, right where the warm feeling of being a *big girl* went, but it wasn't a good feeling.

Everyone in the store froze, watching. It never changed from its constant intensity, as if god was trying to get rid of all the water in the world, at once. Her parents weren't religious, but she'd heard the story of Noah's Ark, of course. Her dad hated boats.

"Well, your mom won't have to water the plants," he said and grinned. It was a shaky affair, and he was putting effort into it, but seeing it—seeing him *doing* it—calmed the weird flutter in her chest. "If she has any plants left, that is." He nodded toward her template. "Let's get it done, love."

Addie got back to work, the sound of the torrent eventually becoming almost calming. Ms. Mitchell's rain stick hadn't sounded like *this*. She surrounded South America in blue, then south toward Antarctica. "Almost done, Dad."

"Wonderful."

"Does your wife teach, too?" the woman asked, and Addie's calm shattered like ice. She'd forgotten about the weirdo.

Dad sighed. "No, she does not." He turned in his chair and Addie, very distantly, thought she heard more sirens. "Look, can I help you with something?"

"Maybe," the woman said, and she said it in a way that reminded Addie of snakes. Her fingers fumbled, willing them to move faster but more carefully. She'd been proud of her Earth art, but now she just wanted it to be done. A part of her—a big girl part of her—mourned the idea that she may never look at this piece without thinking of the weird woman; the rest of her, though, just wanted to be done so Dad—*Daddy*—could take her home.

There was a pause long enough for Dad to say in his irritated voice, "And?"

One of the other parents pulled her phone away from her ear. "Lost the call while it was still ringing," she said, as another mother held up her own phone and said, "My internet just went out."

Addie dropped beads and dropped beads. *Plunk, plunk.* The oceans rose around Antarctica, India, and the little half circle meant to represent Australia. The planet Earth filling with water.

"I came in here," the woman said, still in that snake-like voice, "for art supplies. I have my own Etsy store."

"Uh-huh," Dad replied, not hiding his exasperation. The mom who'd lost a call squinted at her phone screen and said, "Won't even *let* me make calls now. *Dammit.* I was trying to call Kyle's work—"

"And I got a message," she said. "A message about—*that.*"

"You got a message about a storm?"

"A message about a *disaster*. A disaster that's coming, when I'm not home, away from my children."

Dad grunted, and Addie knew that sound. She'd heard it the last time she'd forgotten about the bouncing ball rule in the house, and she'd knocked over the lamp. "Look, miss—"

Addie elbowed him. "I'm all done."

Dad startled.

She pointed to her completed Earth.

"Good," he said. "Go get it ironed so we can go." He pointed at the other end of the table. "Go around that way."

At first, she was confused—the clerk with the iron was directly across from her and they were both at this end of the table—but then she realized that she'd pass right by the weird woman that way. Dad didn't want her going anywhere near that person.

She slid out of the chair, taking her template and passing the mothers whose phones had stopped working. She carried the planet with both hands, like the little boy earlier. She looked out the store-front windows and that fluttery feeling came back. The world was, for all intents and purposes (one of Mom's favorite sayings), gone beyond that thick curtain of rain. One bonus, though, was that she couldn't see those black clouds or that red sky.

Addie approached the clerk. "All set?" the clerk asked, trying to smile, but it looked as forced as Dad's. The clerk had a walkie-talkie clipped to the pocket of her jeans—to talk to other clerks, Addie guessed—turned low and people were babbling on it.

Addie nodded and handed her the planet. She turned toward her dad and the woman was leaning forward, focusing all her energy, and Dad was leaning away.

"I can't get to my kids," the woman was saying. "You can't get to your wife. She's going to be gone. My kids are going to be gone. That's the point, sir. That's the *point*. You hear those sirens? That's the *end*."

Addie glanced at the clerk, putting a sheet of wax paper over Addie's template and running the iron on top of it.

*Why doesn't anyone do something about this woman?*

Dad got up. He towered over the woman—she was shorter than Mom—but that didn't make her less intense.

"Miss," Dad said, trying a different tone, the kind Addie heard when he ran into the parents of students. "Your kids are fine. My wife is fine. The storm—"

The woman pulled out her phone. "No, they are *not*. This message I got—"

"Your phone is broken."

The woman gaped and he pointed. It was far away, but Addie could see the way the store lights hit the cracks in the phone screen.

Dad was looking around, over the woman's head, as if searching for someone. "Excuse me—"

The woman's face twisted, getting red, and she slammed her phone into Dad's chest. "My phone is *not* broken. I *did* get a message!" Her voice was rising. "A message of *the end!*" The biggest rumble of thunder hit, overriding the thrum of the storm, shaking items on the shelves. Someone yelled, as if in pain.

Dad staggered and the clerk heating Addie's art rushed over. "Ma'am—"

The woman wheeled around, slamming the phone into the side of the clerk's head, sweeping the clerk off her feet. "I'm not *crazy!* I *know* what's happening, and we have to *prepare!*"

Addie grabbed her art off the counter, burning the tips of her fingers, and rushed to her dad, who was rubbing his chest. He straightened when she came to him, taking her free hand and pulling her close, partially behind him.

More clerks, all young girls like the one assisting the art project, came out as the injured clerk pulled herself away, hand on her cheek. Blood between her fingers.

"*This is a time of judgement!*" the woman yelled. "*Do you GET that? Do you? We have to prepare for that! We're going to have to rebuild! And HE—*" She whirled and pointed at Addie's father. The woman's eyes were wide, banishing the lines beside them even as the lines bracketing her mouth seemed deeper than ever. "*—he can help us do that!*"

"Jesus Christ," Dad breathed, backing away—toward the doors, Addie realized. "All this for a storm."

One of the clerks pulled out a phone. "I'm calling the cops, Miss. We all know what you look like, now just calm—"

The woman interrupted the clerk by laughing, throwing her head back like a bad guy in a cartoon. *"There are no cops—"*

A final rumble of thunder hit them, but it was almost an earthquake, a burst of sound that crushed their ears and shook the floor beneath their feet. Everyone staggered, crying out. Addie pressed herself close to Dad's back, the vibrations traveling up her legs. Glassware around the store tumbled and shattered.

Everyone froze, even the weird woman. Addie realized the sound of the rain had stopped. Sirens again, distant, but there were a lot of them. Her heart beat hard, high up in her chest.

"Addie—" Dad started to say. The digital chime of the store front doors sliding open—*bing bong*—interrupted him.

*"Help!"* a woman cried, and everyone spun to see a young lady, soaked to the skin with rain and blood.

The woman's face hid beneath the black-and-red streaks, one eye bulged, too big and too shiny. Dad pressed Addie behind her, and Addie complied, cringing into her daddy, everything in her chest locking up, the sight of the woman freezing in the center of Addie's mind.

*"Help me!"* the young lady yelled, staggering and falling to her knees. She blew blood bubbles as she spoke. *"I was—"* She collapsed, flat on her face.

"Jesus," Dad said and grabbed Addie by the arm.

Everyone was frozen, the kids, even the crazy woman, though she had a look of someone who was extremely happy to win a game.

*"Let's go—"* Dad said through his teeth, and yanked Addie along, away from the collapsed woman, keeping himself a barrier between Addie and everyone else. They circled around her, heading out the doors—*bing bong*—backward, Dad keeping her from seeing. "Can't help her. Can't—"

The heat hit them first, then the smell. The heat was a thick washcloth run under a hot tap and then shoved against their faces. The smell, though, punched their noses—the high, sweet stink of garbage, like Mom's compost bins in the backyard but with something metallic beneath. Sirens punctured the air, too many, and screams from all directions. Cars jammed on the roads beyond the plaza, some half in their lane and half out. Addie couldn't see any people, though some of the cars had open doors. In the direction of Mom's work was a wall of black smoke, and above all this a sky the color of the blood on the collapsed woman, glaring through holes in clouds of purest black. The woman with the one eyeball was the scariest thing Addie had ever seen, scarier than any book cover, until Addie saw what was outside.

"Daddy," Addie said, squeezing his hand. He squeezed right back, his hand shaking. That fluttery feeling filled her entire body.

"It's the end," the weird woman said, coming outside. She sounded like a witch, like in old Disney movies. "It's the end, and we need you. *I* need you."

Daddy's hand gripped Addie's again. Addie looked down at it, then at her partially completed planet Earth. The clerk hadn't finished ironing it and some of the light blue pegs had fallen off.

"We have to go," Daddy said, his voice struggling not to shake like his hand. "We have to find your mother." He led her off the curb and into the parking lot.

Addie couldn't see whatever had harmed the bleeding lady, but she kept looking at the blood-red sky, the same color as the bleeding lady's face. She didn't feel like a big girl right now, although she knew she was because the sky was like the cover of Daddy's books, but it couldn't be flipped over and hidden, and she was staring right at it and not looking away.

# SING MY CARNAGE IN A HAYFIELD

### SARA TANTLINGER

The butterflies are coming
hidden survivors, strong-willed.

I am not.

The butterflies are coming
and they all hold tiny axes.

I am laying
in the middle of a green field
full of wildflowers, the sun shines
on my body. I am wearing a black
dress because this is a funeral
in a hayfield.

butterflies are here
with their sharp little axes
and when they chop into my body,
god it takes months before
they've severed me properly,
split me up,

but when they're done they peel away my flesh
and shape it into wings molded from my own blood
and veins, this body is so red, black dress covered
in crimson, but the death of me was lovely
and the rebirth was one worthy of constellations.

I fly away with them,
the leftovers from my carnage.
We're even now,
and we have found peace together.

That's the whole point
of a self-inflicted
massacre.

# WE ARE VIGNETTES

## TLOTLO TSAMAASE

### HIM

Early morning, a baby cries and a dog howls.

Laraso wakes up, face spitting sweat. He's not superstitious, but sometimes the world tries to tell him something.

He enters a five-storied building. Brick-charred building. Dark windows. No sun, no sky. Tight corridors lean up into dank stairs into dark corners, no straight walls. The ceilings are low, forcing him down a concrete path. He's looking for someone. *Her.*

He finds a tiny room with large equipment, desktops of the late 90s, a vinyl record spinning splayed fingers. He chokes back. Hurries out of the room. Shadows and dark objects smear into the corners of his eyes, obscuring his sight. A sickness swells inside his body but he can't purge it. His feet grow slow and panic builds in his chest. This dream, fuck this dream: sometimes a premonition, sometimes a manifestation of the anxiety and work stress he's undergoing. He can't tell which for now, but it must be that fucking exhibition. He checks each room. She's a creative director, where's her office?

All the rooms are empty but they're so full of spirits, spirits he can't see but his spirit can sense. It's like when someone stands behind you or watches you too long, you get that sense that you aren't alone. Scopaesthesia, it's called. He tried to illustrate it once in his work, the enlightenment of senses. And in these rooms of this five-storied building, the rooms are empty, but they are heavy with spirits, just watching him bound from one room to another. Who are these spirits or whose demons do they belong to?

*They can't touch me, which means something protects me. God, my ancestors, my grandparents' prayers, I don't know.*

The corridors narrow as he finds his way up to the alfresco rooftop space. His heart screeches. Holds his breath. Large snakes lie by their patrons, like dogs, but without leashes, held back by warnings. He tries to see these patrons, but his eyes become sick, his sight blurs and it hurts too much to stare. He can't make out their faces.

Witchcraft.

Someone's trying to bewitch him. It always happens. Maybe he should've weaned off his antidepressants rather than pulling off cold-turkey; the dreams now are too psychedelic, too vivid, the night sweats drowning him in his bed. He should've weaned off the antidepressants, but he couldn't smoke a joint with them because the after-effects jettisoned his thoughts, bombarding the landscape of his mind. It felt like he was eternally falling, a permanent prison of vertigo. He needed the weed for his art, it melds reality with his fantasy well. So, he had to stop taking them.

Now the snakes see him.

He can't let them bite him, that's how they'll poison him through his dreams. He wonders which fuckers these are. His stepmother? His ex-girlfriend? A jealous neighbor? Someone wants to see him suffer, that's why they're attacking him through his dreams. Spiritual attacks, his mentor used to say. Just pray. Just pray and you'll be fine. Instead, he flees when the snakes strike forward. He wakes up just as they bite his leg. Sheets and pajamas drenched with sweat. Wonders, were they successful in bewitching him?

THEM

"Don't bother screaming. The room's sound-insulated."

The voice splits my eyes open. A den of darkness. Four bullet holes of splintered sunlight. Melting black liquid drips like rain. Blues and jazz drum the wall. A man screams, or sings, I can't tell. There's smoke and a polyrhythmic sound; our heartbeats render the percussive beat. Our? I'm blind by sight, but I can see through my other senses that I'm not alone. I can smell people near me. People or animals? Breaths stench the air. Fears cuddle every corner.

"Hello?" I say.

"Don't be afraid," a bass voice says. "This is your first waking."

"My first waking?" I touch my head and it's full of fluffiness I can't explain. I feel weak, tired.

"We all woke up in this prison of dark. We don't know what it is or where we are. Strange things happen here."

"Prison of dark?" I ask, fingers trying to read the eclipsing wall.

"The room runs six meters by six meters. Three meters high. The acoustics are good, so I'm guessing it's sound insulated. Don't bother screaming." His voice seems to point to another entity in the room. "She's been screaming all hours, all day. The only sign of existence outside this wall is the people who've been collecting her voice through those holes." I stare at the tiny round holes, like they are simple architectural décor.

"Don't bother screaming if you don't want your voice taken," Bass Voice repeats.

"She heard you the first time," a soft voice says from the entity's direction. "And *you* should be afraid." I feel the "you" directed at me.

"I was trying not to scare her," Bass Voice says in Setswana.

"It won't last. She needs to mentally prepare herself to be scared," Soft Voice says. I detect vague hints of a Zambian accent, buried under the heavy cloak of a Saffer accent.

"Scared of what?" I ask. "I'm sorry, can I come closer? It feels weird speaking to just a voice."

Bass Voice towers higher as if he's grown past the ceiling. "Stay back. If you get any closer, you could curse me with your death."

Soft Voice trembles. "Best we don't move. The other two, they were too close. They died together and were born into death as twins, I guess. So, stay back. The rules are that fast to learn."

"I don't understand …" I say. "What am I doing here?"

"'What am I doing here?' Who took us? Why us? Why me? Those questions after 139 wakings still torture us," she says.

"You've lived 139 wakes? I've only seen through 23," Bass Voice remarks.

"What does *wakings* or *wakes* mean?" I ask.

"All of us wake up in this cell with no recollection of our past. That is a waking. 139 people have woken up in here and … faded into sleep."

"139 wakes and 139 sleeps. Jesus. You saw all that? Why didn't you say anything?"

"No one asked."

"Why the fuck are you still here?" Bass Voice asks suspiciously.

"I don't know," she cries. "I don't know. Tell them to kill me already."

139. "That means 139 people ... slept here?" I say.

"Died." Soft Voice starts crying. "Can't you smell it? The air is rigor mortis."

"The way you talk is strange," I say. " A rigor mortis air—I don't understand."

"You will soon. This is your new reality now. There's about eight of us, soon there won't be."

If we're eight, then why are the remaining five quiet?

HIM

Exhibition is in six weeks. Six weeks. *A five-room event show of paintings and various multimedia installations of the prolific digital / mixed-media artist, Lasaro Bogosi, who hails from Serowe village and is Botswana-based in the opulent folds of the Phakalane suburbs ...*

"I am fucked," he says to himself in his open-kitchen plan over a cup of espresso, peering down at his cellphone, reading the morning headlines. He has nothing to show except empty canvasses in his studio, no sculptures and only lies launched virtually to the terrains of his agent overseas. He drank and smoked his way through his advance with friends and socialites at a cigar lounge not far from home. And now they're at work, safe with their jobs and salaries. They don't understand the pressures.

DMs slide into his phone. Bribes, threats, and slurs.

"I am truly fucked," he repeats.

He told his agent he was halfway through with his work, blamed network issues and technical failures each time he tried sending pictures or through video calls. He's sure they've caught on. Next on his tour will be Cape Town, London, New York—

"Fuck, I am fucked."

Anxiety is claustrophobic now. Artists' block is different this time round. He bought this home as a retreat overlooking a spacious plot, but over the last few days it's been hell, disturbing.

"My first work, it was easier," he says on a call to his girlfriend, Naya, who's a creative director for an advertising agency in Kgale Mews. "No one knew me. Knew what to expect from me. I was free to create as I wanted. Now with the pressure of the success from the first project and the harsh criticism, how can I create something as valuable as the first without being too repetitive?"

"Shut out the world," Naya says. "And stop scrolling through social media; it's like letting in this crowd of bad people peer over you as you paint. Cut the world out and focus on your project."

"You don't understand," he says. "I can't breathe, I can't think. I'm paralyzed with panic each time I try to paint. I haven't been in my studio for three days—I'm utterly scared. What if I fail?"

"So what if you fail? Las, you fucking debuted with incredible pieces of art that no one in this lifetime can do. All those oldies are so fucking frustrated because even with the wisdom and experienced piled on them, they can't do what you do."

"I can't ride on my old work to carry me forward. I'm starting from scratch here."

"Listen, take a hiatus from social media and cut all contact from everyone. Lock yourself in your studio, bring out all your research books, your old work, listen to your jams—I know the fusion of Fela, Hugh Masekela, Miriam Makeba gets you started, smoke a joint and just let loose, get loose."

Let loose, get loose. That's exactly what he did.

But his work was amateurish, the themes redundant. There was no narrative, no concept he could explore.

His friend, Tefo, came over that night, some IT personal who landed a decent job that offered benefits in this day and age. Most of Lasaro's friends could hardly make rent, buy a car, maintain transportation fees, struggled with maintaining their medical aids—so he set up a trust from which they received a monthly donation. He understands their struggle. For one, he'd rather be heartbroken in a mansion than weeping, broke and sad in a combi. Now word got out, and everyone's been trying to be his friend.

They sat outside by the boma, watching the fire fold in and out of the night. Tefo, an old laaitie from primary school, sat cross-legged, lean and neat, drinking whisky.

"Remember, DJ Steez and that stint of unemployment he went through? His mother was a chemistry teacher at school."

"Ja, ja, I do." He leaned forward, sipping on a cider.

"I heard this from a guy who heard it from someone within DJ Steez's social circle. Apparently, guy went to a traditional doctor, and that's how he got to where he is."

"A traditional doctor or witchdoctor?" he asks. "There's a difference between the two. There's a reason the latter is called a witchdoctor—they don't procure blessings through holy means. It's evil work. And now traditional doctors are often lumped into that category when they do natural, healing and holy work. My great-great grandfather was one and he was burned by that stereotype."

Tefo stares at him thoughtfully, smiling. "No one cares about the difference when they're desperate for something. No one fucking cares about that fine line when the landlord has kicked you and your mother out. No one cares about morality and ethics when starvation has welded their flesh to their bones."

"So, what, Steez saw one and miraculously became a successful EDM DJ?"

"Well, I don't know the fine details, but that's about how it goes." Tefo took a long sip, agonizing him with a stare. "How's it going for you not crossing that fine line?"

THEM

Are they going to feed us? Whoever *they* are?

They put us in here, I don't know why. Experiments, or the voyeuristic nature to watch creatures burn in the flame of death. Torture can be fun if you like that kind of thing.

Pockets of light slam through our walls. No bullets, no shells.

Just adorned shadow licked in light. A woman, a scamper of a thing, rockets to the far corner, eyes yielding fear more than anything. Our cell is an inferno of urine, shit, fear, and blatant cowardice. Sweat frolics from one end to another. We tell the days by the number of deaths.

*Where did they take you from?* he asks.

*My bed. I was passed out.*

*You?*

*The basement parking. In my car.*

*You?*

*The office toilets.*

*You.*

*The walk home.*

*You.*

*The bus stop.*

*You?*

*I was whistling at night—*

*That's bad luck you know—*

*And a snake took me—*

A burst of laughter. *A snake?*

*A terribly huge one. Wrapped itself around me, dragged me out, sealed my screams inside itself.*

*Jesus, are you serious?*

*What the fuck is this place?*

*At least we're not alone, that'd be worse.*

No physical traits connect us. One tall. One short. One pudgy. One thick hair. One loose fingers.


HIM


Early Wednesday morning, the controversy stuns him. He can still turn it around, his situation, that is. Monomaniac, he is; his art a hybrid of human and celestial atrocities—the well of creativity is dry. He stares at the far redbrick wall of his house, prizes and framed pictures of events with legends and celebrities, the limelight affixed above his head like a halo. A god, he is. *Eclectic Afro-surrealist artist, Lasaro Bogosi, 25, dazzles audience with his smile and charm*, the description reads. His sophomore work lies in the mortuary before it's even born.

Puts the world and his phone on airplane mode. Then, a cup of espresso, yoga. Before he became famous, he'd shoot videos in the morning, spend hours editing them on VDSC and Adobe Premier Pro, splitting, trimming and speeding clips to ascertain that quiet cinematic appeal and loading the right type of royalty-free songs from either SoundCloud or Epidemic Sound at the opportune time—which, once done, he'd upload to his YouTube channel. Then there was the newsletter he had to update fortnightly. And the Instagram scheduled posts he planned weeks before. And sneak-peaks and gifts he prepared for his Patreon. Packaging orders. *That* was his day job. That and his illustrations and sculptures, which required intense and obsessive studying of artists' works, analyzing tomes of human anatomy and outer space and the animal kingdom of which he married in his works, stringing them with artistic flair. Both paid well once they picked up.

And now he has all this free time, in no need to do all that admin. He's beyond rich. He could retire and not need to work a day in his life. But he is an artist before he is a person, brand, or business.

He stands in his studio, forlorn and perturbed. His whole life contained in an assortment of drawing ink, gouache, compasses, magnifying glasses (for detailed drawings), scissors, masking tapes, tracing paper, flat-bed scanner, lightbox, acrylics, reclining glass table. Canvasses of varying sizes, sketchbooks piled on the desk. Books on cyberspace, celestial bodies, myths and folklore, human anatomy, spirituality, astrology and the likes. He takes a shot of his espresso. Tries studying the greats: Frida, Izquierdo, Barragan, Marquez, Head—fusing whatever form of art and translating it from ecopoetics onto the canvass, from Mexican architecture onto the canvass, from surrealist paintings onto the canvass. But he needs a body. A muse. And quick. His deadline is not that elastic. He's postponed about four times now. They're losing his trust in him. Millions are riding on his back. Jobs, thousands of them, are resting on his shoulders, nesting in his chest. His agent is patient with him, but he sees the weariness. He needs to prove himself with his sophomore work. People say he was lucky with his first work, as if he didn't put in the work. He needs at least eight pieces of abstract surrealism. Of horror. Anything to tack onto, a string of narrative, of morbidity. A backstory most importantly infused with the societal issues.

That fine line. That fine line. That *fucking* fine line.

He's never considered such, but then desperate measures et al.

Like saving grace, his girlfriend's caller ID fills up the screen. He's smoked two joints, drank through a bottle of Vodka, and he hasn't bathed for eight days since Tefo was over. He's AWOL. He can't let Naya see him this way. Hear him this way. She doesn't know this side of him, naked and fragile and dark. She only knows the protégé who has come to sudden riches. That's the façade every-one loves: invincible, talented, intelligent, charismatic— "What's the worst that could happen?" his girlfriend, always the optimistic, would say, trying to comfort him. "You fail, but you live on to create more work."

So, he ignores her call yet again. Her message slips in: *Sending me an "I am OK" text or "busy talk l8r" and then ignoring my calls and other messages is not on. You've been ignoring me for eight days. Eight days. Las, WTF?*

Fuck. Now he's put her on read.

He doesn't have the same craving he used to have. To study and create. For his next work, he wants to do something different, chal-lenging, thought-provoking, and new. If he could, he would splice that narrative from someone's memory banks. Memory banks were saturated with histories upon histories absorbed in our DNA from the past lives of our ancestors. Someone else's memories encoded in us. Things we forgot but remained in us and took up brain-space. Whole narratives, archived in the genes. That he wouldn't need to skim with his eyes or study.

And that was the problem.

By the time the words or art got inside him, its identity, its essence, was already diluted. Before it reached him, it started with the author researching to collate information, translating it into a book print through their bias. Then his eyes would translate that before it got to the core of him. The essence of such narratives getting translated myriad times loses their significance. Whereas if it originated within him, it would pour as is. There's a deep and intimate aesthesis to obtaining first-hand data before it's sullied by modes of translation. This is no hit on translators, which are an entirely different respectable art. He wonders, *Who will tell our stories? Who will know our history when all these stories are clammed up inside these people? Someone. Someone had to disinter them. Graft them into art pieces that will show the world who we are and what we are.*

It would be in him and in no need of having to bypass several mediums. It had to originate from him and pour out of him. One must respect their art. Every new piece always called for something from him. Now he knows why his new work wasn't speaking to him because it seeks deep devotion that may see him crossing boundaries. He stares at his past days objectively, the signs, the dreams—his friend's suggestion. All signs, a calling. If he answers this calling, he gains the wisdom to create another set of magnificent work that will supersede his debut work. He must answer this calling.

Someone must release all these stories tied up within bodies, useless to imagine their power into beauty.

He reaches for his cellphone, texts Tefo to connect him to the witchdoctor.

THEM

"You have a beautiful voice, by the way," Soft Voice says.

"Thank you," I say.

"Maybe you're a singer. Try a note."

Bass Voice: "Jesus, a psychopath has us locked in here and all you care about is songs. What's next? Painting your nails?"

"I'm trying to take my mind off things."

"Don't sing," Bass Voice says. "I think we're getting picked based on our talents or something. Last guy was a historian. Then a professor, herbalist, dancer, spoken-word artist, doctor—"

"I remember the doctor," Soft Voice says. "He mumbled some medical terms when, dear God, that poor man's brain was leaking from his head. And when he touched him … he died."

I gasp. "What the hell is this place? Why can't we remember anything?"

"Whether you sing or not, you're chosen," Soft Voice says.

"I sing," I whisper, "but not professionally." A sharp pain to my head. "I'm remembering something, but it hurts to remember. "I … lead a team … of creatives. Something to do with concepts and projects and clients."

Bass Voice backs away. "Shit, it's happening again."

Something soft crosses my leg and I jump. "Can you hear that?"

This room is feeling tiny again, a processing of some sort.

"Someone has to know we're missing. They should be looking for us soon," Soft Voice says.

"How do we know that? What if we don't have family?" Bass Voice asks.

She shrugs. "Why the fuck are the other five quiet? I think they're already dead. I can't even see them and won't bother looking around this hell-hole cell."

"We only have each other," I whisper, pain growing inside me.

HIM

The odor began to burn into his nostrils, militating against his senses, a few days after he visited the witchdoctor. It smelled of shoes, filled to the ankles with rain, except there was no foot to stop the breath of this smell. A car-boot smell. A dead donkey smell. It probed his mind like the angry fist of a migraine. He wished to take a knife, cut cleanly through his skull, to transplant the pain out and into someone else for there is nowhere else pain can rest except in the human body. Let it lie too long outside the body and it'll castrate nations into political rife things, into corrupt poison, into the climaxed inferno of climate change.

He stood still in the hallway of his home. A luxurious build from the proceeds of his art. Sustained on the aesthetic cultural infusion of his native Tswana traditional architecture with motifs echoed on the façade in patterns he used to watch his grandmother paint by hand on the walls of their rondavels back when his grandmother was still alive. His heart burns coldly in pain when he remembers her. Died too early. His grandmother: the museum of their past. Things you couldn't find in books or the internet or this new generation came from her lips. Her eyes burned blue by cataracts, she'd roam the hallways in a white gown, like she was a ghost. Sometimes he does still see, her scent carried strong by the dust of the graveyards.

But he knows where this pain comes from: the dreams, the nightmares—the spiritual attacks.

Someone is entering his mind from his dreams. The dreams are the doorway to his consciousness. *They're in now. Who the hell are they? How the fuck can I get them out?* Spiritual warfare. If he believed in such a thing, he bestowed its birth faith, its longevity faith, its power faith. This witchcraft blossomed in his brain, trickled into his frontal and temporal lobe, the control center of empathy and control, and trembled his fingers with the arthritic condition of a geriatric. What would they find? A tumor? An aneurysm terrorizing him in the steely morning of a noon-day sung high by a cockerel. Fuck, he can't go this way. It's done and did.

Naya calls again. She wouldn't understand. Lets it ring.

Later: The intercom buzzes. A delivery guy. "Delivery from Ms. Naya Isang."

Homecooked food. Thank god. He knows she's working on an intense project, but she prides herself in cooking food at home, healthy at most, which she packs in Tupperware to last her several days. When he opens the package, it's stewed goat meat, couscous and sweetcorn with a dash of butter and parsley. He's never had a woman who was both intelligent, wealthy, beautiful, and an excellent cook. *She* actually takes care of him. He wonders if he should call her to thank her, but that would turn into questions of worry and a long conversation. If he texts her, she'd call and he'd have to let it ring, but he doesn't want to miss another one of her calls for fear of getting into more trouble. So, he foregoes communicating with her and sits in the garden, finally eating a full meal since his last one five days ago. He daydreams about her. Having her is like having a home. She's a good singer. He told her to go pro, but she's passionate about her job. Endless days he'd listen to her sing, and he'd paint inspired by her voice. Her voice, if he could have it pour through him.

Now satiated, he treks backs, checks his schedule.

He contacted a witchdoctor just to assist. Some village up north.

"I could be the machine that draws the art, the narrative," he said as the witchdoctor stared at him in his hut. "I just need subjects and their life stories that would make it easier to download onto the canvass, me as the medium, my hands the machine parts bleeding these stories into what will be my sophomore work."

"Are you sure? To be able to extract such detail of a story, well, the subjects would die. It would be murder."

He gasped. "No other way?"

"No."

He swallowed. "I mean, important stories can be found in useless people. People who don't bring meaning to society. A homeless guy, for example. A cleaner. A thief. A thug. The low of the low. Then that would make it okay, right? I mean, they have all this history tucked away in their genes and it's all going to waste. I'm helping our country by documenting it."

"If you see it that way. I'm here to assist in every way possible."

"It won't get back to me, right?"

"No."

"Then, I'm sure."

The witchdoctor gave him some stuff wrapped in soft plastic, a flimsy thing. Looked like an assortment of dried herbs and elsethings. He didn't need to know the subjects. Better that they are strangers. He was watching a documentary once about serial killers. Apparently, they have patterns consistent in their choice of victims, weapons, and ways of disposing the body. As long as his patterns were inconsistent, it wouldn't get back to him. But even inconsistency is a pattern. He is an artist, after all.

The avant-garde serial killer.

No, that's crass, beneath him. He can't think like that. Their death on his canvass is a posthumous honor they'd never receive if they were alive. The dried herbs and elsethings to spike drinks of strangers. It'll take effect in eight hours, remove them from their environment and transport them to an unknown place.

He'd done it before he left the village, at a bar, to a man who was spitting tales of his late uncle. Then at the library at Main Mall's civic hall. Every day he was spiking about thirty people in restaurants, public toilets, the post office, the bookstore, the gym, parking lots, the bank, clubs ... as his girlfriend called and called seriously worried about him until she saw an Instagram post of him chilling with friends.

Now he sat with a joint, sending a slither of smoke into the wood-ribbed ceiling of his studio. He sat, waiting for the stories to somehow enter his mind from wherever they were. A dainty teacup set of his grandmother patterned in azure sat on his coffee table. Inside floated dark debris unlike tea leaves that the witchdoctor prescribed for the connection to his muses, his subjects, who will be part of a critical moment of history, and they don't know it. No one tried archiving and reiterating history this way. Controversial as usual, he is. He drank it. Stood across his canvass, across his tools of wires and chisels and—

Thirteen hours every day, he didn't stop for seven days:

*The blood of time fills the streets.*

*Burn your breath.*

*The drowning of wo-men in their tears.*

*The phallic cross in their crotch, its blade licked wet by all elders.*

He stands back, watching his work, wondering from which subject, which victim, this story was downloaded. What kind of person was this that they held such a dark story of religious allegory, pain and domestication and a withering section of veld inside them? He exhales, utters: "People, *Jesus*, people can't realize the power within them. How useless they are to let it go to waste. Now I am powerful. I hold history. I am the museum of untold stories. Now the world will know."

This shit here is better than weed.

THEM

"What are these things floating in here?" I ask, pointing at what looks like dust particles gilded by sunlight as they float about.

"We don't know. We found them here," Bass Voice says.

"Why's your voice muffled," I ask.

"I don't want to inhale them."

Soft Voice adds, "He took one of the other Waker's hair and wrapped it around his nose and mouth, to act as a filter, I suppose. I doubt it works. These particles are too fine."

"Well, I haven't died, have I?" Bass Voice says.

"Neither have I," Soft Voice says, "yet I haven't masked my face with a deceased person's hair."

"I had to. It was infecting us, making us feel unwell. I think that's how the others died." I feel his eyes on me now. "You should be dead. When you remember, you die."

"What is that on the floor?" Soft Voice asks.

"It looks like a cross," Bass Voice says. "Shit, it's happening. Someone's about to die."

"Quickly, hurry! Tell us more. What do you remember?" Soft Voice says. "It could help us."

"I was having tea ... someone gave me tea."


HIM

Naya is over. Handbag on the barstool. Braids tied into a top knot. A flurry of floral perfume. He stares at the clock in the kitchen; he should be in his studio, working, but she came suddenly, and he couldn't kick her out or she'd explode.

"I'm sorry," he says, hoping this will appease her quickly and she'll leave or something.

She leans against the island as he fills a glass with water for her. "You keep doing this," she says, arms folded. "If this is how it'll always be, I'm sorry but I can't stay. I'd rather you let me in instead of locking me out. Then what's the point of us?"

He sighs. So, an argument it is. Appease, appease, appease and it'll be over soon. "I know," he says. "I'm sorry."

"There are other women who prefer this type of arrangement, I'm sure. Not me."

"I know."

"I work long hours too. I work weekends. Work is stressful and hectic, but I'm always trying to make time for you, which you reject. I believe we have the same predicament, but you choose to close me out."

"Ja, but you don't have the whole world watching you, waiting for you to fail, or desperately pressurizing you to release your next work, telling you that you'll do better than your last, or your last was crappy and this one will be too." Damn it, now he's opened the door to further argument. He should shut up, apologize some more, kiss her and she'll be on her way. It always works. Today, he's tired.

She narrows her eyes. "So, I have it easier?"

He raises his shoulders, steers his eyes elsewhere, lowers his shoulders. "Honestly, ja."

She laughs and it's that type of laugh a woman makes that unnaturally forebodes the end of your world. "Three years we've been together. Three."

"You're not like the other girls," he adds in frustration. "The other girls I've dated."

She places the glass down. Raises her eyebrow. "You used to say that as a compliment, now what's changed?"

"I'd send them and their friends on trips to wherever they want in the world. I'd buy them high-end clothes, cars, jewelry, phones, everything they wanted. They wouldn't … bother me. They'd leave me to my art. To focus. Because they knew how important my work was to me. That I couldn't always be available."

She smiles. "It was a good deal, huh?" He keeps silent. To answer is a dangerous thing. She continues, "You funded their life-styles, and when you needed their bodies, they'd avail themselves. A very good deal."

She steps closer, and it's almost menacing if it weren't for the fact that she was a woman and a head shorter than him, but something about it curdles his testicles. She's known to be feral in clinching huge deals for her firm with such a cool bravado and ease that people are oft-weary of her calmness. With that poker face, you wouldn't know if she was blowing up the world, panicked, or saving people.

"You'll come to learn later in life," she whispers, eyes fringed with naturally thick lashes, "when you're an older man, the things you could afford were in fact putting you in debt. Debt of true living, the things that bring meaning to your spirit. The only things that age in beauty is a true-meaning spirit, not a body, or a car, or jewelry."

It's funny she's saying this, being that she's four years younger than him. He hated such lectures. But he knows why she speaks this way, because her mother died a lonely and regretful life which she confided in him. Through disciplinary acts, she avoided the same thing happening to her too.

She raises her hands, gesturing to his mansion: "You've got all this money and fame—you can't afford my spirit. My spirit is not a transaction." She picks her handbag and coat. Heads to the front door. "I can afford my lifestyle without you."

Just then something boils in his spirit, speaks louder than his mind and he knows he must stop her, but he doesn't know why he must stop her. Like he's realizing he's entering a bad deal if she leaves, like the one a company almost hooked him into of which his agent advised him against.

"Naya, please," he begs, pulling her gently by the arm. "One last chance. Let's talk. Please. Listen, I'll get the tea running."

She reconsiders his pleading eyes. Changes tack. Follows him back into the kitchen.

From his cupboard, he pockets the flimsy plastic with the herbs and elsethings.

THEM

Sonic landscape. A pastiche of smoke and sound. Gluey voices. Mélange of marimba and fires. It's all familiar. Too familiar.

"My name … is Naya." It's all coming back to me. A rush. Work. Going over to his place, frustrated.

"What do you remember? What are their names? Who gave you tea?" they ask.

"My … my boyfriend," I whisper. "I remember. I was dating him. No, no, no—it can't be him. It can't!"

"Stand back," they shout. "She's about to go."

"Who is he?" Bass Voice asks. "Give us his name."

"What's the point of knowing who put us in here if we're going to die now?" Soft Voice says.

Bass Voice: "If I die, I will know who to haunt."

"Lasaro Bogosi," I whisper.

"The famous artist?" they ask in panic.

I stare all around, horror drowning me. Motelike things floating, from ground upward, in slow dizziness. Too small and detailed for the eye to see. I run my hand through them, inhale them. Images. Images. Images. Of us. I stutter, "T-t-these are someone's thoughts. This is not a building. This is a mind. It's someone's mind. We're trapped in someone's mind."

A substance of his thoughts, floating like small particles of rain in reverse.

"What?" they all say. "You can't be serious."

"Who would hear our screams from inside someone's head?"

"It's a sound-insulated room. Basement at best," Bass Voice says.

The realm of the mind, an invisible transcendent thing.

I stare at the walls. Grip at hope, mercy. "But why? I loved you. I. Loved. You." A sharp pain. I double over, regurgitate my thoughts onto the floor, slick creatures slippery-clawed on the floors. They yield back, afraid. My sickness. My back crimps. Hold my head. "My brain—" a little explosion emanates inside my skull, the brittle shell of cranium, and I drop before my soul gives. I soul-stand back, watching the disease bomb of myself on the floor.

Soft Voice screams. "What the fuck is going on? Fucking kill me now. I can't take it anymore. Kill me."

The tea, something in it is controlling me. I can't stop. The cross takes solid form on the floor. I take it. Stab myself on the pier of religion. The brain concocts what the faith relies upon. Weeping shadows. My face, skin shaved thin, peeled into a macabre mask of ebony gold—

### HIM

He stares at his next piece. Her face, skin shaved thin, peeled into a macabre mask of ebony gold, circa-*now*, though not circa-*later* when millions adorn her mask in the museums. Her death potent in the air. Behind her, the curio cabinet of dark skin-wood stands.

Outside, the crickets' tempo increases, hottest it has ever been. Mirages everywhere. He blames the pain. It's the pain that's the serial killer, not him.

*I've killed them in every unimaginable way except by hand.*

A disfigured body lies on his floor. No housekeepers, his number one rule. Turpentine mixes with the decaying scent of flesh—how can he translate that onto his canvass? How do you portray scent with the texture of a paintbrush?

He bends low, gently moves aside the wet matt of fried hair. "Shh, don't move."

His smile, dazzling. A chipper. He had to. The creativity well ran dry, arid like his country.

The skull. The den. Them, inside. Inside him. His head. He hears them, whispering, screaming, detonating. They won't stop. A woman. She screams. Something lifts her voice from her larynx cleanly, splices it through the night. And now she is without voice. The canvass, he sculpts the abstract images: *Time is not a corrupt fabric, not the man who burns the white off the bone into the toddler's skin; bone, crush it real good, sniff it. One puff, two puff. We smoking each other now. Flashing neon skins blind him. A spirit trapped in the façade, motifs on the wall, appropriated.* He goes on and on.

Time evolves things. He's never had his thoughts living beside him like this, like insects, cockroaches flicking in and out. But the maddening heat of the night silently crawls on his skin. By the easel, his thoughts eat at him, tearing bits of his sagging skin. He can't watch. He must look away. Just a little sip, a tiny glass, a whole bottle will drown everything away. "Crack open my skin and I know what you'd find," he whispers.

He surveys his installation art: the estuarial souls clammed up, like a myriad of jelly fish, bobbing in and out of the framing, puddling in and around the frame. The gnarly voices twist around the stem. Tributaries of their blood. Seven pieces of work for the exhibition. He looks aside. He is number eight.

The creator becomes consumed by his creations, his work. Now he is his artwork, his voice a moonlight across a monsoon.

The smells are gone. His oeuvres remain alive, curators of the strangers he fed. Him. Them. They are vignettes. Outside, sensing this heinous killing, a baby cries and a dog howls; but their souls are gone, taxidermized on sepia tones, a photogravure.

# PARABLE OF THE BLUE MAN

## JAMAL HODGE

A Blue Man placed a pointed ear to one of the forty-one holes he'd made in the skin of God's favorite black clothes.

"All I hear is havoc," he said, voice unsteady.

"*Listen deeper, past the rage.*"

"I hear his days, given little chance; but he's accountable for his behavior and cannot claim happenstance," the Blue Man cursed, defiant.

God remained silent.

"I hear his tears born of his fears. But all men weep …. What of my fears? These people aren't gentle sheep. He is the one who chose to live violent! God, why are you so silent?!"

From within, God's voice rose, but it could've been his conscience, the Blue Man supposed.

"*Is he the one to unmake you? Shatter you down to chains, scar the pride from your back, entomb you in lack? Did he fill your neighborhood with crack? Redline your hope for a better dream. Enlist savagery as a theme for his image across your screen. Does he own the factories manufacturing the guns, killing his sons? Yet you fear him in monstrous ways, shouldn't it be him who's terrified these days? Should he not refuse friendship every time you seek? Should he not doubt every word you speak?*"

"Those are not my ways. I wasn't born in those days. Everyone struggles. We all face adversity. Some make it and some fade away. You made this order. Isn't this your way?"

"*Should the fading fade quietly? Or should they shout and roar? Shouldn't they take from your mouth, and rage at your door?*"

"Let them come. I'm ready. I put forty-one shots in this one already. Injustices happen. The past can't be changed, but I'll protect mine and what remains. The heritage of mine is not all spent, defined by the story your black clothes lent. There is love and glory and victories true; there is goodness in the story we've written in the name of you."

"*When much is taken, much is spent. The quality of the seed is the nature of the crop lent. Your ways are not my ways. Good does not wash away the bad. Gaze into the holes of your favors. See the future of your labors.*"

The Blue Man investigated one of the forty-one holes he'd made, weary. Knowing the truth is always scary. Visions of an empire's fading glory on a foundation of red. Its legacy unsteady, in the storms of time. Cain and Able replayed with both brothers slain. Blood on each other's hands. "Am I my brother's keeper?" replayed again and again, on the lips of unaccountable men. Sins dealt for sins wagered. Injustice accepted in the name of dominant skin.

Every shade of God's clothes, full of holes, leaking a rainbow of tragic colors.

The Blue Man convulsed in repulsion, eyes wet with history's tears. Looking higher than his justifications ever allowed, he searched for God's true face behind the mask he'd sculpted to suit his own reflection. And then, for the first time in his life, he asked her sincerely,

"Lord, how do I fix this?"

And things began to change.

# THE UNBURDENING
# OF LAVENDER

## GENE O'NEILL

PROLOGUE

*Millions died during The Collapse.*
*The Rule of Law disappeared.*
*The strong prevailed.*
*It was the Time of Cal Wild.*

Cal Wild had grown increasingly dry, hot, and polluted. This afternoon, a rare fog had crept in from the nearby Pacific Ocean, falling
like a wounded cloud over most of the greater San D Ruins. It eventually blanketed the remnants of the village of Solana Beach, thirty
miles north of the San D Shield. The mist gradually dispelled the
heat. But as darkness fell, the fog began to dissipate, leaving behind
an air turning chill.

A young woman squatted, hunkered down among a cluster of
oaks, madrones, and bushes on the northern border of the village,
screened from view of an old Quonset hut that was isolated from the
ruins proper. As the moon finally broke through the dissipating mist,
she stood and shivered, moving about and rubbing the goosebumps
along her bare arms. The moonlight illuminated the skin color she
wore from head to foot—one of the lighter shades of blue, a faded
lavender. She was tall and slimly built, her graceful movements and
faded denim eye color complimenting the unusual shade of her skin,
adding to an almost regal bearing—a lavender lady.

She'd paused in the oak grove in late afternoon, intently watching the hut and the immediate surroundings. The young woman

wasn't overly concerned with a passing Freemen surprising and confronting her. The permanent inhabitants of the Cal Wild wasteland could sometimes be abusive and combative bullies, but usually they ignored those of her kind, as if they were invisible. Only occasionally were they dangerous. But as a female she was specifically concerned with the possibility that a dyed male would enter the hostel. Mostly, her kind sought refuge from the hot, dry wasteland in one of the Dyed Person Hostels by late afternoon. In her nine months of wandering Cal Wild after being dyed, programmed, and banished from San Fran Shield, she'd encountered other DPs only on rare occasions. Almost always a male. And twice she'd had bad experiences after entering one of the shelters to find a male already established inside ahead of her. Once an emerald man had stolen everything of value from her backpack when he arose early and left the shelter the next morning.

About a month ago, a more terrifying incident occurred when she'd encountered a midnight blue man already eating and drinking tea when she entered the hostel. The man's darker shade of color indicated he'd been dyed for one of the more serious blue offenses, sexual assault. And this immediate recognition of a violent sexual offender would have normally caused her to make a hasty retreat, forsaking the minimal comforts offered by the shelter. Except, there had been a rare third person already in the hostel, a lemon-colored woman. The yellows indicated different *political crimes* against the Company's conservative authoritarian rule, lemon a much lower offense than amber for treason. So, the lavender lady believed herself safe enough with a third person in the hut.

The women ignored the blue man, ate, and had a brief conversation. The lemon woman shared that she'd been wandering with her burden of yellow for over three years, after being rendered a judgment of color for protesting equal rights for shield women.

The lavender lady had gone to bed early in one of the sleeping cubicles at the end of the cinderblock building, falling asleep quickly.

But she'd been startled awake by a huge hand pressing tightly around her mouth, and another strong hand clutching her neck in a strangle hold. A hoarse whisper: "Be very quiet, not a peep, or I will snap your neck like a twig." It was the blue man. His heavy body positioned between her spread legs. He was naked, pressing against her. Terrified, her heart beat wildly and her pulse raced.

"Do you understand?" he whispered in her ear, tightening the grip on her throat. "We don't need to wake up your friend the mustard girl, while we have a little fun." The offensive smell of his breath and unwashed, sweaty body was overwhelming, but she was paralyzed by her fear, and couldn't draw away from his foul odor. The lavender lady managed a slight nod, even though she remained frozen stiff with terror.

"I'm going to slip off your underwear now," he whispered, the hand on her mouth. She closed her eyes, held her breath, as he touched her bared cleft, thinking: *Oh, please, no—*

There was a sharp metallic *click*, accompanied by another voice, leaning in close behind the blue man, a loud and clear order: "Remove your hand, and let her up, *now*."

The man's body eased off the lavender lady, and she scrambled to her feet.

The lemon woman had the tip of a long switch-blade knife against the right side of the man's throat, pressed so firmly that a drop of blood rolled down his neck. "Now, you pick up your clothes and pack, then move your smelly ass to the door and get yourself outside to dress … but carefully. Do you understand *me?*"

Barely audible, he said: "Yes."

Still holding the tip of the knife pressing firmly up against his throat, the lemon woman marched the blue man on his tiptoes to the door, with belongings in his arms; and then, with a foot in his back, she gave him a firm shove outside and pushed the door shut. After being forced from the hut, the blue man would not be able to re-enter this hostel for at least four days. And the nearest shelter was at least a distant six- to eight-hour hike from the present hut.

"You need to carry one of these for protection," the lemon woman said, clicking her switchblade closed. "Save some of your Smoke to barter for one at a trade-off."

She referred to the drug capsule DPs were allotted with their nightly meals. Most cracked the capsule and eagerly inhaled the drug immediately after eating, never saving any. Smoke was addictive. Their drug dependency motivated DPs to find a new hostel at least every other night, making it easy for the Company to record and track their current locations. But the lavender lady had been advised early on in her travels by an older DP to *not* immediately use all her Smoke allotment—she tried to save one capsule each week. The lavender lady had traded three capsules early in her travels for a carved walking stick with the polished knob resembling the head of a mountain lion—a creature extinct in Cal Wild. The walking stick doubled as a weapon to ward off attacks by wild dog packs. A danger she'd fortunately rarely experienced.

"We can leave the hut together tomorrow and separate later," the lemon woman added. "I'm meeting my sister from San D Shield at a secret location outside the dome. She will be bringing me shield credits. I'm heading south to check out a rumor of an escape route for DPs, a safe crossing of the border with the Latin Confederation. It may be costly, if it even exists …"

The lavender lady thanked her savior, then added: "Yes, I'd like to leave at the same time as you in the morning."

As the lavender lady continued watching the Quonset hut, nighttime fell—an unusually chilly night for the wasteland. She shuddered, took several deep breaths, clearing her thoughts of the rape attempt. Again, she rubbed the goosebumps along her arms and then cautiously approached the DP hostel. She glanced about, then placed her hand on the palm sensor right of the heavy door and pushed, her location registering automatically in the Company's computers. As the door swung fully inward, she squinted, peering inside. With the illumination provided by moonlight at her back, she surveyed the dimness. Nobody at the table or either of the three sleeping cubicles or the toilet at the rear of the hut. The hostel was unoccupied. The lavender lady let out a big sigh of relief. It was unlikely by this late in the evening another DP would enter this shelter.

Feeling relatively safe, she lit the thick candle on the table. She dropped her walking stick and backpack in the closest sleeping cubicle after removing her mug and bowl. She crossed the narrow room to the Company vending machine and placed her bowl and cup in the proper slots. She palmed a sensor, the bowl filling with a vegetable stew, her mug with tea. While at the machine, she palmed another sensor for her allotted capsule of Smoke. Neither of these specific sensors would work for her again for at least four days.

She secured the drug in her backpack with five other capsules she'd managed to save during the last six weeks or so. Then, she slowly ate the stew and drank the tea. She went to bed staying fully dressed, exhausted by her day's hike in the oppressive heat and her nervous two-hour surveillance of the hostel. Her sleep was restless, plagued by a recurring nightmare of being attacked by a faceless phantom.

In the morning, the lavender lady rose early, left the hut, and wandered south, planning to visit a large trade-off on the northern fringe of the greater San D Ruins. She usually avoided all trade-offs because these were spots where her kind *could* run into confrontations, the gatherings packed with Freemen buyers and sellers.

The undyed inhabitants of the polluted wasteland were distinctive, especially in the fierce heat because of their bundled-up garb—head coverings, facemasks, and long coats, usually a duster covering them from neck to ankle. The coats were often decorated with amulets, charms, pendants, feathers, and other items—many believing the charms had supernatural significance.

After the Collapse, the Freemen had bundled up against the heavily polluted environment, including the several areas of radiation and the pervasive threat of UV poisoning. This bundling-up started long before the mysterious Company finished constructing the Shields. The five domed cities spaced along the Cal Wild coast, from San D Shield in the South to Couver Shield in the North, offered residence, but only to the more affluent wasteland survivors and emigrants. As time went by, the Freemen attire took on a mystical significance, many believing the various charms protected them, and some believing they prevented them from bearing deformed children, the wasteland sprinkled with defectives. The bundled-up, masked, and weirdly-decorated appearance gave the Freemen a disheveled, fierce, and threatening appearance, which occasionally erupted into a violent encounter for a hapless DP.

In the early evening, the lavender lady stood beyond the fringe of dancing shadows cast by the flames from 55-gallon drums spaced around the perimeter of the trade-off. She was mesmerized by the size and hustle and bustle of the crowd, mostly bundled-up Freemen buyers and sellers—some obviously drunk or twisted on drugs. But a small group of shield residents stood out, wearing their distinctive neon-colored, one-piece modtrend, venturing out of the San D Shield for an evening's exotic recreation, which might include using the drugs Soar or Rush, watching the bloody whip fights, or sampling the wares of painted women—unauthorized activities usually overlooked by the Company.

The lavender lady's gaze was momentarily drawn to four pitiful defectives in the nearby crowd, all dressed in rags and begging. But her senses and attention were constantly bombarded and distracted by the clashing senses and excitement suspended in the air.

**Sounds:**

Sellers hawking goods from nearby tables, blanket spreads, and stands offering a wide variety of wares for shield script or barter:

*"Hooks, lines, sinkers, poles, fresh fish."*

*"Clean shirts, pants, dusters, hats, caps, and other apparel."*

*"Soar, Rush."*

*"Your pick, fresh cuts of meat."*

**Smells:**

*Mouthwatering cooked food.*

*Barbecue.*

*Steamy stews.*

*Assorted items flavored with the aromas of sweet, bitter spices*—all hot and ready to eat from bowls, plates, or on sticks.

**Sights:**
*The painted ladies.*
*Roulette.*
*A boxing match.*

**Touch:**
*Tingling electricity palpable in the air, like before a thunderstorm.*

The lavender lady sucked in a deep breath, focused, steeled herself, let out the breath, and cautiously made her way into the crowd to an area offering a selection of cutlery. She couldn't find a switchblade knife for sale, and finally decided to trade four capsules of Smoke for a long hunting knife with a leather scabbard. She attached the weapon to the side of her belt, then departed the potentially dangerous trade-off.

Consulting the programmed mental map for Cal Wild hostel locations, she headed easterly from the San D Shield, a shelter a good five hours' hike to the southeast.

She arrived sometime around midnight, feeling safe enough at the late hour to enter the cinderblock hostel without surveilling. Planning to wash up before eating, the lavender lady stared into the rare fragment of a mirror left over the wash basin.

A stranger looked back at her from the mirror. The woman had deeply etched wrinkles across her forehead and at the corners of her mouth, crows' feet extending from the corners of her eyes. But it was the dull, worn-out blue eyes that not only shocked but saddened her. Of course, the lavender skin was familiar. She sucked in a deep breath acknowledging the recognition. She'd been twenty-six years old when dyed and banished to Cal Wild. In nine months of wandering the wasteland, she was transforming into a middle-aged woman. The polluted environment, including the UV rays, were partially responsible. After a few moments' reflection, the lavender lady knew the primary cause was the constant state of stress and anxiety. She finished washing her face without looking back in the mirror.

Early the next morning, the lavender lady wandered along in the shade of oaks along a shallow creek, looking for a place deep enough to bathe.

*Splashing, laughter, joyful sounds.*

She moved cautiously, locating the source. She stood atop a slight knoll overlooking a bank and a shallow pool. Two female children—perhaps five and six years old—were naked and cavorting in the water. Their bundled-up but unmasked father watched from the bank, smiling. It seemed an eternity since the lavender lady had been able to enjoy watching children at play. Actually, it had been less than a year—one of the busiest playgrounds was near her conapt inside San Fran Shield.

*Growling* interrupted her revelry.

Three huge mixed-breed dogs, led by a pit bull, had crept up and circled the father, baring their teeth ferociously. Vicious and hungry. The girls shivered in the water, obviously frightened.

The pit bull darted at the bundled-up Freemen, leapt, clamped down on a shoulder, knocking the man to the ground.

Before the other two beasts could attack the downed Freemen, the lavender lady shouted, gaining their attention, and bounded down the knoll. She held her walking stick at the foot end like a bat, swinging the carved knob solidly into the side of the head of the nearest dog. The beast collapsed, quivering, legs making slow climbing motions as if running uphill. Shifting the stick, the lavender lady moved closer to the downed man, jamming the smaller end of her bat-like a sword into the chest of the pit bull, drawing blood, giving the Freemen time to struggle to his feet. The giant man delivered a forceful kick to the crotch of the dog, knocking the wind from the beast, who grunted and gave ground.

Simultaneously, the largest dog attacked, a mastiff, leaping at the lavender lady's throat. She protected her face from the beast's slobbering mouth and bared fangs. The dog clamped down on her arm near her elbow, the force driving her flat onto her back. The huge beast shook its head violently. Instinctively, the lavender lady rolled to the side, pulling her knife from the scabbard, and drove the blade up to the hilt below the dog's front shoulder. She twisted the blade with all her strength before withdrawing it. The dog released her arm and made a puppy-like *yip*. Bleeding, it backed away as the lavender lady got to her feet.

The mastiff limped away and joined the pit bull. The two wounded dogs retreated into the woods. The first dog she had batted in the head was dead, blood leaking from its ear and mouth.

Her arm bled and hurt, but she made her way to the two frightened and shivering girls still knee-deep in the water. She held out her hands.

"You're safe now, girls. Let me help you out of the water—"

"Don't you dare touch my girls," the Freeman father shouted. "You, you, you … filthy degenerate!" He brushed past her, scooped up the girls in his arms, and scrambled up the bank. Then he turned back and shouted before disappearing into the woods, "You disgusting queer!"

She'd heard versions of these words shouted at her during her wandering. A scarlet man had once called her *a fucking lesbian* when she didn't respond to his sexual advances, but none of those words had been used at her judgment of color.

*You are assigned lavender for sexual congress between adults of the same gender.*

She'd never been intimate with the wife of the Companyman, as accused. They'd only casually hugged publicly. Yet the black-clad security chief for the Company had made a formal complaint against her, and his word was all the evidence needed.

Now, the lavender lady wasn't sure of her sexual orientation, if any, usually leery of the sight of any DP or Freemen—male or female. She was more than a bit surprised by the Freemen's obvious recognition of her rare shade of blue, which indicated her *supposed* sexual crime. She was bitterly disappointed by his lack of gratitude and the expressed fear.

Despite her father's attitude, the youngest girl made a little hand wave as they turned away and disappeared into the forest. This gesture, and the ache in her arm, reminded the lavender lady that she'd saved all three Freemen from the dog pack at great personal risk. She knelt, dug out her first aid supplies from her backpack, and dressed her bite wound, thankful no bones were broken. She wandered southerly.

It was early evening, dusk settling, as the lavender lady spotted a fire north of her DP shelter. Curious, she cautiously moved in closer.

A small group of Freemen gathered around a bonfire, their shadows dancing against a backdrop of trees. An unmasked Freemen turned away from the oak behind him with a wide grin on his face—

The lavender lady stared at the tree in disbelief.

A naked man, dyed scarlet, hung from a limb, a noose around his neck, head lolling to the side … and a bloody gash from his forehead running back—

*The scarlet man has been hanged and scalped!*

She looked again at the apparent Freemen leader. Instead of charms on his duster, he wore a wide belt with three scalps dangling from it, including a fresh bloody one from the scarlet man. The Freemen leader signaled in the direction of the DP hostel, giving an order: "Bring me the yellow woman. It's her turn to swing."

*Yellow woman?*

The lavender lady turned and quickly made her way down to the shelter, moments ahead of the two Freemen. She found her friend tied to a tree near the hostel and cut her loose. The lemon woman gasped a thanks, taking the knife in hand as the two Freemen appeared.

The lavender lady struck the closest Freemen, her walking stick making a crunch against his knee. The lemon woman attacked the other, stabbing him twice in the chest. Both men were down, groaning. Then the lemon woman turned to her rescuer.

"We better flee. Others will be here soon to investigate."

Δ

Several miles south, they both stopped to rest. The lemon woman explained: "Those Freemen belong to a group called the White Lightning Boys. Their stated goal is to 'cleanse the wasteland of all people of color.' I'd heard rumors of them, but I thought they were just an insignificant cult centered in the mountains to the east, a threat, but only to the few far eastern shelters. Never expected to encounter them so close to the coast."

"And they are hanging and scalping DPs?"

"Yes. They believe the scalps give them supernatural strength and protect them from enemies and pollution."

The lavender lady nodded. She sat, resting, still catching her breath, then said, "We need to place some distance from them, but where do we go now?"

"Well, first we have to find a young woman named Amara at a fortune teller's tent in the ruins near a trade-off not far from here." With an excited expression, she added, "She apparently can introduce us to someone who can guide us safely across the dangerous Latin Confederation border and point us toward a Baja escape route from Cal Wild.

The lavender lady took a moment to digest the revelation. She shook her head, looking a bit discouraged. "The price may be too high. I only have two capsules of Smoke to barter. I'm guessing they won't be nearly enough."

The lemon woman smiled. "Don't worry for now. My sister gave me a hundred and seventy units of shield script that the White Lightning Boys never thought to search for in a pouch in the back of my shorts. It may be enough for both of us."

The tent was located on the fringe of another large trade-off, where a sign read:

MADAME SHELLEY
SOOTHSAYER, CLAIRVOYANT, DREAM GUIDE

At the entrance, the lemon woman said, "Hello, we're looking for Amara."

A tall young woman, her blonde hair secured in a ponytail, appeared in the doorway, smiling. Only her oddly-clouded blue eyes marred her exceptional beauty.

"I'm Amara, how can I help you?" It was clear from clouded eyes and the angle she held her face when talking that she was blind.

"We're interested in crossing the border with the Latin Confederation," the lemon woman said. "Can you help us?"

Amara moved closer. She gently touched each of their foreheads with the palm of her hand, thought a moment, and nodded. "Ah, I can tell you're both dyed—lemon and lavender ... But you are good women. You'll want to go much farther than the border. Down Baja, then across the Sea of Cortez. A skin clinic in Mazatlán will be able to dissolve your color. My friend, Karch, will get you safely across the border and introduce you to some other reliable guides, who will lead you the rest of the way—Surf 'n' Volley cultists."

The lavender lady's pulse raced with excitement.

They followed the blind but psychically-gifted young woman. She told them they were crossing a parking lot for the once world-famous Balboa Park Zoo, abandoned after the Collapse. Acres of asphalt were a faded gray and broken up in many places, brown grass poking up through the cracks. She led them into a grove of eucalyptus trees on the southwest side of the lot.

Amara stopped in front of the entry to an old stone hut that had once served as zoo restrooms but were now living quarters. She knocked on the door.

"Lute, I have visitors to see Karch."

A smiling stooped-shouldered older man came out. "Hi, Amara. Karch should be back from servicing his rabbit traps soon. Have a seat. I'll get tea." He covered his mouth and coughed, then indicated an old picnic table with benches.

Before they finished their tea, an amber blur bounded into the area, stopping at Lute's side, frightening the dyed women. "Hello, Lion, old boy," Lute said, ruffling the fur on the huge mastiff's head. "Lion is Karch's guard dog. He should be along any minute."

Sure enough, the boy appeared in the clearing near the old restrooms, his physical appearance surprising the two visitors.

Karch was missing both arms. He walked up to the table, balanced on one leg, and with the other foot unstrung two jack rabbits tied to a wide leather belt with metal hooks all around.

"Only a pair to clean, Lute." He turned to the blind girl and said, "Hi, Amara. You have friends who want to cross the border?"

"I do."

They all sat at the table, the huge amber dog resting at Karch's feet. They discussed details, Karch explaining that it was best to cross around noon. Less chance of being spotted by a Latin Confederation hummer patrolling the border. They had infra-red capability to aid their surveillance. He described their guides on the other side of the border, the Surf 'n' Volley cultists. "They have good relations with the LC."

The lavender lady nodded, then said, "We have concerns about cost."

"Clinic is expensive—seventy to eighty credits apiece, depending on shade of color. I appreciate whatever donation you can afford, even something to barter. I use it for Lute's cough medicine from the Shield. The Surf 'n' Volley people are coastal refugees from Cal Wild, very anti-Company. They charge nothing for their services."

Karch was delighted with the five caps of Smoke the women donated, and they were delighted the lemon woman's script would be enough at the for the clinic for both of them.

After dinner, Karch filled their canteens with water. He pointed with his feet to a pair of tanned blanket rolls. "These will keep you warm at night. But tomorrow, if we hear a hummer, you flap them out and hide, like this." He demonstrated, snapping one of the blankets with his toes, out and up in the air, then ducking and lying flat underneath. "The blanket matches the desert-like ground. The hummers won't notice us. But lie still, till I give the all-clear. Okay?"

Both women nodded their understanding, again more than a

bit impressed by Karch's physical ability with his feet and armless body—agile and flexible as a cat.

At noon the next day, Karch and Lion brought them to the border, pausing at a sign.

DANGER

AREA MINED WITH EXPLOSIVES

NO TRES—

"Follow me carefully, stepping in my footprints, just like Lion," Karch instructed. He led them slowly along an invisible trail, winding through a sandy area covered with dried scrub oak. At one point, he pointed with his right foot at a stand of Torrey pines in a nearby draw to the west. "One of my best rabbit runs." They continued single-file through the mined field, until he announced: "We're safe now."

"There's the road," Karch said, indicating an old asphalt highway that stretched south through sand dunes, the tired gray broken up with brown patches of dead growth—burnt field grass and chaparral. "Welcome to Baja," the boy said.

They walked for about an hour, the hills growing steeper; and the coastline becoming more irregular, steep cliffs dropping down into beaches—

Lion suddenly froze, facing the ocean.

Two women in halters and shorts appeared, accompanied by two bare-chested men, all heavily tanned. One of the women held out her hand and Lion bounded to her side.

Karch introduced the dyed women to the Surf 'n' Volley folks. Minutes later, he declared, "I need to get back to Lute, but leave you now in capable hands. Good luck."

"C'mon, Lion." Then the armless boy and his dog headed north.

The women stayed overnight at the Surf 'n' Volley encampment, and the next day began their safe journey south.

EPILOGUE

The two women eventually reached the Mazatlán clinic and were cleansed of their color. In time, Karch became a legend among DPs, known as The Armless Conductor. Both undyed women dedicated themselves as conductors, successfully guiding DPs along the section of the underground railroad from San Barboo Shield to the San D Shield. Neither woman's life would ever be filled with riches or fame, but in the wastelands of Cal Wild, any life lived in freedom, adventure, and peace was one worth celebrating. And they did, together, for many years.

# MAGMATIC

## LH MOORE

The first time
I fell through
It was with an inferno blazing
In my eyes
And hands
Poised, ready
To strike.
The next time
I fell through
I was a whirlwind
A storm raging
With no end
To my fury.
The last time
I fell through
There could be no doubt
Of the voice as
All the masses heard
My roar.
Then …
I got up.

# WHAT IS LOST
# IN THE SMOKE

## LAURA BLACKWELL

Like all smoke-eaters, Allumbra resides in the troposphere and lives off the remains of things that burn. Some of their kindred swirl around the uglier sources of smoke: arsons, incinerators, atrocities. One of the gentler ones of their kind, Allumbra has always preferred offerings. A lean year for a smoke-eater is a good one for humanity, and Allumbra, who feels an affection for the imaginative little creatures, begrudges nothing.

Allumbra is in California when the wildfire starts. At first, this scent of pine and cedar smoke is pleasant, but it quickly becomes overwhelming, stifling even in the sky. It smells of trees meant to remain tall and alive on the hillsides for decades to come. This fire is no offering. No one wanted it to happen.

Allumbra floats through a smoke so thick with fear and pain and loss, it's choking even to a smoke-eater. But although there is more than enough here to eat, they have a purpose: A smoke-eater bears witness. Allumbra has watched some of these humans and animals for many years—and has come to love many of them—but one in particular is the reason they came to live above the stands of pine and cedar.

A tiny house is nestled in the hills, isolated by acres of trees and a gravel drive with several switchbacks. Allumbra has followed its owners for over half their lifetimes, since Tom was fighting for the Allies in the European theater in 1943. Allumbra fled Hamburg's firestorms in July, and then the October fires in Kassel, determined to starve rather than live on the smoke from burning cities. It was cowardly—smoke-eaters are meant to be witnesses to all that burns, however horrific—but every being has its limits. Allumbra knew that if they stayed to witness, they would die of the horror. As he marched, Tom burned his letters from his fiancée, Sally, determined that if he were captured, no one would be able to harass her from afar. Ever the romantic, Allumbra latched onto those small bits of hope and joy.

Sally's neat penstrokes detailed her attempts at a Victory garden, sketches of a shorter nightgown (so patriotic, saving the cloth for the war effort), brave lies that everything was going well and vulnerable truths about how glad she would be to see Tom on his return. Salt from dried tears—hers and his both—seasoned some of those letters. Admiring Sally's resourcefulness and their mutual devotion, Allumbra followed Tom home at the end of the war and settled in to sup at the barbecue pits and wood-fire chimneys in these sleepy California hills. They have stayed for over half a century, settling over the hills and valleys and all those who live there.

Slipping through the crack between door and door frame, Allumbra coalesces into a shape, swirling the various grays and the firelit pinks—the only colors a smoke-eater has—until they somewhat resemble a human being in a filmy robe. They find Sally and Tom in the bedroom, door closed and air purifier doing its grim best.

Tom's eyes widen above the oxygen mask he uses to help with his emphysema. He croaks the words, "Is this it, then? The angel of death?" and Sally's head swivels in alarm. Her eyes, red with smoke irritation and ill-hidden tears, stare at Allumbra over her filter mask. The mask is only N95, not strong enough for easy breathing, but perhaps it helps a little.

Allumbra bends the stripe of pink on their newly made face into something meant to pass for a smile. "I've been watching you a long time. You need to leave your home."

Tom looks to Sally with the frustrated bewilderment of one who has recently begun relying on a translator. Sally adjusts Tom's mask with trembling hands and says in a clear, loud voice, "Just a visitor, honey. We'll talk in the hall." She rises with some difficulty and leads Allumbra out of the room, coughing at the smoke that tinges the rest of the indoors. Drawing herself up as straight as she can, she tells Allumbra, "I'm not sure who you are, but if you've been watching, you know we got rid of the car after I lost my license last year. The nearest neighbors are miles away. If our caregiver had shown up for her shift, we'd have left with her ..." Sally's voice wobbles inside her mask, "... but she didn't. The phone lines are down. We don't know if we can get out." She locks eyes with Allumbra. "Do you know if we can?"

Allumbra has no alternatives to offer. They have all the weight and strength of smoke and can carry nothing heavier than a message. And as much as they appreciate humans' ideas, they have few of their own. "I will wait for your rescue," they say with the deepest gravity they have. "If it does not come, I will bring you peace myself." Better than letting the oxygen tank explode in the fire.

Sally inclines her head in a shaky nod. Although Sally may not know exactly what Allumbra is, Tom's question about angels was not completely wrong: Allumbra lives in the sky and survives on superheated longing. When Allumbra does not walk out the front door, but flattens and slips through the crack, Sally does not appear surprised.

Next Allumbra visits Odiseo, an artist who sometimes burns his unsuccessful sketches in his charcoal grill. They've known him since he was a small child who blew out each birthday candle separately, making a different tiny wish each time. Allumbra longed to grant these wishes for a pencil with lead the color of a toyon berry, a dragonfly to alight long enough for him to draw it, the ability to translate the smell of his mother's pork tamales to something the eye could see.

Perhaps it is because smoke-eaters cannot create that Allumbra loves artists. Allumbra loves Odiseo especially because they took their current name from him: All umbra from his umber paint and his use of shadow; *alumbra*, "light," from a letter he wrote to an ex before losing his nerve and burning it.

Odiseo is sleeping, and Allumbra's voice is too soft to rouse him. The smoke detector's battery is dead, so Allumbra tickles his nose with smoke, but Odiseo only coughs and shifts. Allumbra has no power to wake him.

Allumbra leaves him to visit the Chung home. The Chungs have always burned paper money for their ancestors. About ten years ago, the older daughter thought it would be fun to start a New Year tradition of smearing sticky *nian gao* on a drawing of the Kitchen God, telling the deity happy stories about the family, and then burning the image. For the past five years, many of the stories have featured a shy kitten—then a skittish cat—named Boots. The younger daughter's delight in the cat was sweeter than the sticky rice cake.

The human Chungs got out of the house before the roads closed, but Boots remains squeezed between a piece of furniture and the living room wall. Though left behind, she is not an offering willingly given; she was hiding behind the entertainment center, and the family had to break off their search to flee. Allumbra tries to help, but they have no hands to free her, no hands to comfort her. Boots responds to soft shooing by cringing deeper into the crevice—not that it matters. The doors and windows are closed.

There are others, too, human and house-pet and wildlife. Allumbra can't save anyone but dares not make the same offer they made to Tom and Sally. To accept what Allumbra can give, one must have a reasoning mind and eyes wide open.

When it's obvious that the fire has made the roads impassable, Allumbra visits Sally and Tom one last time. When Tom and Sally see Allumbra, they look at one another with eyes already filling with tears. "No rescue," she says. It is not a question. "You promised to make it peaceful."

"I will keep that promise," Allumbra assures them. Sally curls up in Tom's arms as Allumbra dissipates into thicker smoke, fills their lungs as gently as possible, and waits with them until their end. It seems to Allumbra that it doesn't take long. Allumbra has a good sense of these things; they have always been a being of endings.

The fire spreads, and the smoke that climbs from it is foul with polymers never meant to melt, with the bitter tang of metal from wiring and furniture and rebar. Allumbra has more books than they can read—schools and libraries full—and they want none of them. Even the meat excites no appetite, for this meat was tucked into refrigerators for a cozy meal or burned off the bones of animals and humans who were not yet meant to die.

This time, Allumbra tries to do their duty. They do not flee. Spread over the California landscape, Allumbra grows immense with smoke they would rather not ingest. They are black, white, grays all between, and sunset-pink from the light of extinguished memories and dreams. *Alumbra* and all umbra at once.

There is only so much a being can witness. Allumbra cannot stand the loss, cannot withstand it, cannot contain all these particles of homes and life's work and lives. Allumbra cannot live on death. Full beyond bearing, Allumbra bursts like a thunderhead and rains ash for miles.

Counties away, humans cover their faces with masks and bring their animals indoors. Schools close. Offices close. Everything shuts down, trying to shut the ash out.

Allumbra was never able to imagine a different ending for themself. Unlike the humans, they had little imagination. They were only ever a being of endings.

# MY PEOPLE

LANGSTON HUGHES

Dream-singers,
Story-tellers,
Dancers,
Loud laughers in the hands of Fate—
    My People.
Dish-washers,
Elevator-boys,
Ladies' maids,
Crap-shooters,
Cooks,
Waiters,
Jazzers,
Nurses of babies,
Loaders of ships,
Porters,

Hairdressers,
Comedians in vaudeville
And band-men in circuses—
Dream-singers all,
Story-tellers all.
Dancers—
God! What dancers!
Singers—
God! What singers!
Singers and dancers,
Dancers and laughers.
Laughers?
Yes, laughers … laughers … laughers—
Loud-mouthed laughers in the hands of Fate

# I'M NOT SAM

## JACK KETCHUM & LUCKY McKEE

I wake up in the morning to Zoey's crying.

I've heard it before, many times. It's familiar. It's not the usual sounds cats make, it's miles from a *meow*. It's more of a muted wail. As though she's hurting. Though I know she's not.

It sounds as though her heart is breaking.

I know what it is.

She's got that toy again.

Zoey's a tuxedo and so is her old stuffed toy. I don't recall who gave it to her, some friend of ours who likes cats, I guess, but that was long, long ago—and though there's a tiny patch of stuffing leaking out over the back of its left ear, it's miraculously still intact, after years between my nineteen-year-old cat's not-always-so-tender jaws.

She protects that toy. She gentles it.

And there's that yowl again.

I glance over at Sam beside me and she's awake too. She yawns.

"Again?" she says and smiles.

Zoey pre-dates Sam in my life by nearly nine years but she loves this cat as much as I do.

"Again," I tell her.

I get up and shuffle across the chilly hardwood floor and there's Zoey out in the hall looking at me with those big golden eyes, her toy face-up lying at her feet.

I lean down to stroke her, and she raises her head to meet my hand. I use this opportunity, this distraction, to steal the toy with my free hand and tuck it back into the waistband of my pajamas.

I pet her head, her long bony back. She's arthritic as hell so I'm very gentle with her. I know exactly how to touch her, the exact weight and pressure of my hands on her body that she likes. I've always been able to do this. With animals and with people. I've always known how to touch.

And here comes the purr. Soft these days. When she was young you could hear it from rooms away.

"Hi, girl. Good morning, good girl. Hungry? Want some foodie?"

Yes, *foodie*.

Cats respond to *i-e* sounds. Damned if I know why, they just do.

She trots ahead of me into the kitchen, a little wobbly on her feet but always game for breakfast.

I pull her toy out of my waistband and give it a good toss into the living room. She'll find it sooner or later but for now there are other things on her mind.

*That toy. That tuxedo with roughly her own markings.* There's a mystery to that little stuffed animal. One I know I'll never penetrate.

It's the only toy she ever cries over. All the rest are passing fancies. She bats them around awhile and then loses interest. I find them gathering dust beneath the sofa, in a corner under my desk in the study, and once on the grate in the fireplace. How it got beyond the screen only Zoey knows.

Zoey came scratching at my door one cold March Saturday evening. She wanted in. I was drawing in the study when I heard her. I opened the door and there was this scrawny cat, probably six months old at the time, the vet said, with mites in both ears, a sweet disposition, and obviously starving.

I always wondered where she came from.

We're pretty much out in the middle of nowhere here.

She came to me spayed. So, she had people somewhere. Somebody had cared for her.

Were there others out there? I wondered. Her mother, maybe? Was she part of a litter?

And at some point, I started to ask myself, could there be a connection between toy and cat? Could this small inanimate object possibly remind her of something? Family? Was that why this ordinary, no-catnip stuffed tuxedo kitten seemed to resonate for her, to stir something long and deep inside? It seemed possible. It still does.

If you heard the *yearning* in this sound she makes, you'd understand why.

It was years ago I got to considering that. I remember feeling at the time that I'd stepped into mystery, into the realm of the inexplicable. Into enigma.

I've never shaken it. It gets me to this day, every time.

In the kitchen I pick up her water and food bowls and put them in the sink and while she sits waiting patiently I open up a can of Friskies tuna and egg and flake it into another, fresh bowl, pour her fresh water and put them on the floor and watch her set-to.

I hear water running in the bathroom. Sam's up. I hope she gets out of there fast. I've got to pee. By the time I've got the coffee brewing she's standing behind me with her hand on my shoulder and we're both of us staring out the window over the sink out onto the river.

It's a lovely spring morning. Hardly a breath of wind in the trees. There's a bald eagle gliding thermals over the water. He hits its surface and veers away toward the pastureland beyond the far bank and he's made a catch. We can see the gold glint of fish scales in the sun.

Hardly a day goes by when you don't see some sort of wildlife out here. We've got foxes, coyotes, wild pigs. Zoey stays inside. She'd never have made it to twenty if she didn't.

I turn around, give Sam a peck on the cheek and head for the bathroom. She smells like sleep and fresh soap.

On Sam, not bad at all.

I'm not much for breakfast—just a coffee and cigarette kind of guy. I figure food can wait on my break from the drafting table. But Sam is. The coffee's ready and she's already poured herself a cup with cream and sugar and I can smell the raisin bread in the toaster.

I pour a cup for myself and sit down at the big oak table. I like my table. Found it at an estate auction in Joplin. Hell, I like my entire house. We're surrounded by five dense acres of woods and a river, like a surprise waiting to happen.

The living room is all stained wood with high oak hand-carved beams maybe a hundred years old. There's an ancient stone fireplace.

The room opens to the kitchen so I'm looking out at all this space in front of me.

It occurs to me—watching my wife of eight years slather her toast with butter and strawberry jam—that we've made love in practically every square inch of the place. All over that hardwood floor. Couch and overstuffed chair. Scorched her lovely ass one night on the fireplace. The memory of which makes me smile.

"What?" she says and swallows her toast.

"I was just thinking."

She squints at me. "You've got that look, Patrick."

"Do I?"

"You do. And what I've got to do is finish my breakfast and pee, shower, and drive forty-five minutes to Tulsa so I can autopsy Stephen Bachmann and decide whether it was pills, scotch, plain old Dutch stupidity, or any combination of the three that put him in our drawer. I don't have time for you."

"Aww ..."

"Don't, 'Aww ...' me, mister."

"Aww ..."

"How's Samantha coming?"

"She's about to blow her brains out with a shotgun at the behest of her tormenters. By tomorrow I should have her resurrected. Tomorrow or Saturday."

She takes a long, man-sized swig of coffee, gulps it down, and smiles.

"I'm still not sure whether to be flattered or distrustful of the fact that she's named after me. You splatter her brains all over the wall for godsakes."

"Yes, but then she comes back. And I would never splatter you."

I love it when she arches her right eyebrow that way. She gets up and steps over, leans over and kisses me. It lingers.

After all these years, it lingers.

She breaks it off.

"I know, I know," I tell her. "Shower, pee, brush your teeth and off to your Dutchman. You want company? In the shower, I mean. Not the Dutchman."

"I don't think so. Maybe tonight, after work. I'll reek as usual. What are we doing for dinner?"

"Leftover teriyaki-beef bourguignon. From night before last. You liked it."

"It was yummy," she says and disappears around the corner into the bedroom.

I hear her Honda Accord pull out of the driveway a half hour later and think how lucky I am. I'm doing what I want to do, drawing my graphic novels—and making a pretty decent living at it. I've got a home I love, a well-loved old cat, and this forensic pathologist person who's crazy enough to love me.

I'd say I go to work but that would be a lie. I go play.

Play goes well.

When I hear the Honda pull back in again, the blood splatter pattern on the wall behind Samantha's head is complete. I'll have Sam check it for accuracy, but I've learned a lot from her already and I think I've got it right.

Splash page indeed.

It's nearly seven o'clock, getting on to dusk, her normal arrival time. I've fed the cat and the bourguignon is simmering on low. The garlic bread's buttered and seasoned and awaiting the caress of the broiler. All I've got to do is boil the broad-noodles, pour the wine, and dinner's ready.

I cover the work, get up and stretch and pad barefoot into the living room just as she's coming through the front door. I realize I haven't put on a pair of shoes all day. One of the perks of the game.

I walk over and hug her and plant one on her cheek. She really doesn't reek. She's already showered at work. She always does. But sometimes, with the really bad ones, it's a three- or four-shower evening. Tonight, just a little tang of something in her hair. Just enough to let me wrinkle my nose at her.

"I know," she says. "It wasn't the Dutchman."

"No? What did the guy in?"

"Booze, a Pontiac, and an obstinate oak tree. He had a nice dinner before he died, though. Sauerbraten, red cabbage, potato pancakes, and about a pint of vanilla raspberry-twirl ice cream. But the scent you detect belongs to somebody else."

"Who?"

"Gentleman named Jennings. Turkey-farmer."

"Ah, that lovely ammonia smell."

"Right. He had all this turkey shit piled up next to his barn. Looks like he was about to spread it out over his field when he had a heart attack instead. Fell right into the stuff. He was covered with it. We figure he was breathing in it for a good half hour before he died too. The inside of him almost smelled worse than the outside. Did you say something about a shower this morning?"

"I did."

"If you wash my hair, you're on."

"I love to wash your hair."

"You hungry yet?"

"Not really."

"Turn off the stove."

She turns the shower on, letting it warm up, and I watch her undress. As always, she's businesslike about it, but to me she's a Vegas stripper. At thirty-eight she looks twenty-eight, everything tight, the bones delicate. We've both felt sad from time to time that she's infertile, that we won't be having any children. Me a bit more than her, I think—I've got a brother for what he's worth and a father and mother while she's an only and both her parents are dead. So maybe I'm more used to family. But I shudder to think how far south her body might have gone were that not the case. It's shallow of me, I guess, but as she is right now, she's a joy to behold.

She throws the curtain and steps into the spray of water and I'm right behind her, watching her nipples pucker, watching her glisten. She turns toward me and shuts her eyes. Her long hair's plastered to her head. I reach for the Aussie Mega and lather her up.

She smiles and makes these little *mmmmm* sounds as my fingers dig in for a good, firm, gentle massage. Little lava-eddies of shampoo roll over her collarbone, over her breasts, and down to her navel.

"I think I could go to sleep like this," she says.

"Standing up?"

"Cows do it."

"You are no cow."

She smiles and tilts her head back to rinse, straightens up, and wipes the water from her eyes. Then looks down at me.

"Oh," she says. "Oh, really? Already?"

"I guess so. Turn around, I'll do your back."

She does. I wash her back, her ass, her breasts, her stomach. She raises her arms and I wash her armpits, her arms, then her back and ass again, into the crack of her ass, into her cunt. She soaps her own hand and reaches down to me.

She's got my cock in her hand stroking the shaft and rolling around the glans and my fingers are moving inside her, my other hand clutching her breast and we're both of us making sounds now. She's gone baritone.

I know exactly how to touch her. I know exactly what she likes.

And god knows she knows me. What she doesn't know is that my legs are giving out and I'm coming all over her ass.

"Okay, enough!" I tell her. She gives me this look over her shoulder. "For me, I mean."

"Thank *god*," she says. And she comes too, for the first time that night.

The second time she comes we've already closed my own deal and I've got three fingers inside her. There's debate about whether the g-spot really exists but she's living proof there's *something* there. She likes this hard, not smooth and easy like in the shower, so that's what I'm giving her. She's starting to buck and groan and I'm grinning down at her like I'm listening to my favorite rock 'n' roll song of all time.

Then she says those magic words.

*I'mmmm commming!*

I could cry or laugh out loud, this is such fun. I stay with her, ratcheting up the pace, the pad of my thumb buffing her clit, fingers pressing hard, sliding along the warm wet wall of her insides.

*Oh!* she says and *ohhhh!* and holds the moment suspended inside her so I hold too while she trembles all around me and then lets go. I work her a little more, smooth and gentle now and she jerks and spasms. Internal electricity. I know the feeling.

She laughs. The bawdy laugh. The one reserved just for me.

"Bastard!"

"You love it. You know you do."

"I know I do."

She kisses me the way you kiss your lover when he's made your day. I kiss her back. She's made mine.


While I'm heating up the bourguignon, preheating the broiler for the garlic bread and boiling water for the noodles, I ask her to go into the study and have a look at Samantha, see if I've got the spatter right. She comes back in a little while.

"You've been doing your homework," she says. "Studying the photos. Good."

We've got morgue photos and crime-scene photos pretty much all over the place. In my study, in the bedroom, on the bookshelf in the living room. We have to hide them from the guests.

I'd made the mistake a few years back, before her mother died, of leaving a series of full-color shots of a Mexican drug dealer lying by the roadside—his severed arms and legs piled on top of his chest and his head split open by a machete—left it on my drafting table when her mom flew in from Boston. One look and her face went white.

Try explaining to a sixty-five-year-old woman that this was research for what she'd consider a comic book.

"It's pretty much perfect," Sam says, "in a larger-than-life kind of way."

That makes me feel good. She's got it exactly.

"Right. That's what we're after. Realistic and over-the-top."

"I can't wait to see how you're going to put her back together."

"Neither can I."

Dinner's fine. I don't burn the garlic bread and the noodles are *al dente*. We're lingering over our second glasses of Merlot when I get this *look*.

"What?" I ask her.

She smiles.

"I was just thinking," she says.


Unusual for me to go twice in one night but not unheard of and we've had that excellent dinner and the wine. There's a familiar moment of unease when I glance over her shoulder at the glassed-in hutch and her eight thirty-year-old Barbie dolls are staring at me, not to mention Teddy Davis, her very first teddy bear, threadbare and crunch-nosed, with these strange, droopy, deeply-cleft buttons for eyes—buttons that actually *resemble* slanted squinty eyes—and this down-turned pouty mouth, so that he looks sort of like Bette Davis on heroin. It's unnerving.

But that passes. She sees to that.

And this time, for me at least, it's even better.

I go a lot longer and she's right there with me all the time. We're a two-person band. She's on rhythm and I'm on lead. She's figure and I'm ground. We don't exactly come together but it's so damn close that I'm still hard inside her when she does.

We always make love with the light on. We figure the dark is for sissies. So that when I roll away, I'm able to see the sheen of sweat down her body from her collarbone to her thighs. Sweat that's part her and part me.

And I think, *Don't ever let this stop. Don't ever let us get so old or tired or used to one another that we don't want this.*

The thought comes to me just as I'm about to nod off to sleep.

Be careful, brother, what you wish for.

Δ

I wake to a sound I've never heard before.

It's the middle of the night, it's pitch black but I'm awake so fast and so completely it's as though somebody's slapped me. It's a high thin keening sound and it's sure not Zoey with her toy. I reach over to Sam's side of the bed. It's empty.

I pull the chain on the bedside lamp and the bedroom suddenly glares at me. That keening sound rises higher and more urgently, as though the light were painful.

I see her. There she is. On the floor in the corner wedged between the wall and the hutch, facing the wall, her naked back to me, her arms clutching her knees tight to her chest. It's not cold but she's trembling. She glances at me fast over her shoulder and then away again, but I see that she's crying.

That sound is Sam, crying.

But I've heard Sam crying when her mom died, and it doesn't sound anything like that. This doesn't sound like her at all.

I'm up and out of bed, going to her, to take her in my arms and—

"*Nooooooo!*" she wails. "*Noooooooo!*"

It stops me dead, but I think, that's not her. *That's not her voice.* All the time knowing that's impossible.

"Jesus, Sam ..."

"Don't!"

And now her left hand is darting through the air over her head like she's shooing away a sudden flock of birds.

I reach for her. She sees me out of the corner or her eye.

"*Don't ... touch!*"

The voice an octave higher than it should be.

What the *fuck?*

"Don't touch," she says, a little calmer this time. Through sniffles. And that's when it hits me.

It's a little-girl voice. Coming from my Sam.

Under other circumstances I could almost smile at the sound. *Sam playing the middle gurl.* But these are not other circumstances. The look in her eyes when she glances at me is not funny.

Okay, she won't let me touch her, but I need to do something to comfort her. Plus, she's naked. For some weird reason that bothers me. I get up and pull the blanket off the bed. Kill two birds with one stone.

I go down on my knees behind her and hold the blanket.

"Sam, here. Let me—"

She bats at me with both hands, hard and fast, and now she's crying again.

"Don't touch me ... you *hurt* me!"

"Hurt you? Sam, I'd never—"

"*Not Sam!*"

"What?

"*I'm not Sam!*"

And now I'm way beyond confusion. Now I'm scared. I've slid down the rabbit-hole and what's down there is dark and serious. This is not play-acting or some waking bad dream she's having. She's changed, somehow overnight. I don't know how I know this, but I sense it as surely as I sense my own skin. This is not Sam, my Sam, wholly sane and firmly balanced. Capable of tying off an artery as neatly as you'd thread a belt through the loops of your jeans. And now I'm shivering too.

In some fundamental way, she's changed.

But damned if I'm simply going to accept it. I put on my best comfort voice. Comfort and reason.

"Of course you are. You're Sam. You're my wife, honey."

"Wife?"

She stares at me a moment, sniffles, wipes some snot from her upper lip, then laughs.

Actually, she giggles.

"Not your wife. How can I be your wife? That's silly."

I wrap the blanket over her shoulders. She lets me. Clutches it close around her.

"I'm Lily," she says.


There are silences that seem to peel away layer upon layer of brain matter, leaving you as stupid as a gallon-a-day drunk.

"Lily," I say finally. Or at least I think that's me.

She nods.

I get up off my knees and sit on the bed. Our familiar bed.

She's stopped crying. She sniffles but that's all. I'm still getting these distrustful looks, though. I notice Zoey sitting in the doorway, glancing first at me, then at Sam, and then back at me again, like she's trying to puzzle out the situation as much as I am.

"Why do you say that? That your name is Lily?"

"Because it is."

I point to Zoey. "Who's that?"

"Zoey," she says.

"And me?"

"You're …" Tears well up in her eyes again. "You're … I don't *know* who you are!"

Then she's sobbing. Her whole body heaving.

I can't bear to see this. I don't know what to do but I've got to do something so I get off the bed and go down to her again and before she can stop me I wrap my arms around her. She tries to wriggle free of me at first but I'm nothing if not tenacious, so I hold on and her body's betraying her anyway—the sobbing's got hold of her bad.

It takes a while but at last she subsides. Her muscles drift slowly from high-wire tense to slack. I'm stroking her head exactly like you would a little girl's.

She seems exhausted.

"Come on. Let's get you to bed."

I lift her carefully to her feet and point her toward the four-poster.

"No," she says.

"No?"

"No. Not there."

I want to ask her *why not there* but I don't.

Maybe I figure it doesn't matter. Maybe I'm afraid to know the answer.

"Okay, the couch? That all right?"

She nods. She turns and stares into the hutch, frowning.

"What? What's the matter?"

"You locked up Teddy. I want him. I want my Teddy."

Good grief. She wants the goddamn bear.

"No problem."

I throw the latch and open the glass doors, pluck him out from amidst his Barbies and hand him over. She hugs him to her breasts. And I'm about to tell her hang on, I'll just get some sheets and a blanket and pillow, when she's already stepping out past the cat and down the hall into the living room. She seems to know exactly where she's going. Zoey follows along behind her.

I gather up the bedclothes and a pair of light pajamas I know she likes and when I get into the living room she's already lying down, holding on to Teddy. Zoey's curled up at her feet.

"I brought your pajamas. Can I get you anything? Water?"

She shakes her head. Lets the blanket fall away and stands and steps first into the pajama bottoms and then slips into the shirt and buttons it up, top to bottom. She's not shy about it. I'm watching her. It's a woman's nude body I'm watching her clothe but the move-ments are wrong somehow, they're quick and jerky, full of restless energy, without Sam's smooth flow and glide.

*Where are you, Sam?*

She sits down on the couch. Looks at me. Like she's studying me, trying to figure me.

"I could have the water now," she says.

"Sure."

In the kitchen letting the water run to cold I'm aware of her standing behind me in the doorway. I pour the water, turn off the tap, and when I turn around I could almost laugh. She's standing there straight-legged, with her hands on her hips and head cocked to one side. A kid's cross-examination pose.

"Who are you, really?" she says. Then pauses, thinking. "Are you my daddy?"

Her voice is so very small.

"I'm ... no, Lily. I'm not. I'm not your daddy."

There. I've said it. I've addressed her by the name she wants me to use. Lily.

"Who then?"

"Patrick. I'm Patrick."

I hand her the water and watch her gulp it down. She hands me back the glass.

"I'm sleepy, Patrick."

"I know. Come on."

I fix the bedclothes and fluff the pillow. There's something I've got to know. I tuck my wife in. My wife who thinks she might be my child. I'm sitting beside her on the couch. She's watching me. Holding Teddy. It takes me a while and she must be wondering what I'm thinking but I finally get up the nerve to ask her.

"Back in the bedroom. You said I hurt you. How did I hurt you?"

She shrugs.

"Come on, Lily. Tell me. How? So I don't do it again, y'know? How did I hurt you?"

She shakes her head.

"Where?"

She gazes down and slowly pulls away the blanket and sheet over her thighs, and points.

Points there.


The first scotch doesn't help nor the second. No way I can go back to bed. No way I can sleep. So, I sit in the dark in our overstuffed chair and watch her, fetal on the couch, her face as innocent as a baby's.

I'm wondering what the morning will bring. Is it possible she'll sleep this off and I'll have my Sam back again? And where in hell did this come from in the first place? The phrase *multiple personality disorder* keeps banging around in my head like a soup spoon on a frying pan.

What's next? A teenage boy who likes to burn things?

I know her history. Her childhood was apparently just fine. Nobody abused her. Not as far as I know. There were no traumatic car accidents. When her father died, she was twenty. Nobody in her family got murdered. There were the usual middle-class adulteries in the family but nothing that would scar her.

So where does this come from?

The hour of the wolf arrives and with it that peaceful eerie silence it has, when the night-creatures go to ground just moments before the birds greet the day. The sky out the window slowly brightens. She turns in her sleep. I finish my third scotch. Its magic has eluded me.

I've worked a few things out over the course of the night, though. So that whichever way this goes I know what I've got to do. At least initially. I get up and rinse out my glass in the kitchen and get the coffee going. I sit down at the table and at some point realize that I've been staring at my hands.

Are these guilty hands?

*Don't touch! You hurt me!*

This stings. This aches.

And then I think, no. That was a woman I was touching. My wife. And she was touching me back. I won't have the fucking guilt. I won't permit it. I didn't hurt her. I knew exactly how to touch her. She came, for godsakes. Three times.

The coffee's down. The buzzer buzzes, telling me so.

I stand at the table and there she is in the doorway, yawning, arms stretched out above her.

This is the moment. Either she'll want the coffee or she won't. I can smell it rich and sweet and so can she.

"Is there juice?" she says.

There's a lump in my throat like something won't go down. These hands are sweating now. But the thing is to maintain control.

"'Morning, Lily."

"'Morning." She thinks for a second. "'Morning, Patrick."

She shuffles over to the refrigerator, opens it, pulls out the grapefruit juice and then hesitates, puts it back on the shelf and takes out a carton of Newman's Own All Natural Virgin Lemonade instead. She turns to me.

"This okay?"

"Sure," I tell her.

Δ

Breakfast is coffee for me and raisin bran with milk and a glass of lemonade for her.

"I've got to make a few phone calls," I tell her. "Why don't you go play with Teddy for a while, okay?"

"Okay. Can I have the dolls too?"

"The Barbies?"

The Barbies are collectors' items by now. I hesitate. She pouts. Hell, they're hers, not mine.

"Why not."

I pull all eight of them off the shelf and arrange them sitting along the edge of the living room table for her. When I leave the room, she's smiling.

Back in the kitchen, I use the wall phone. I dial her office first. It's early so I get the machine.

"Miriam? Hi, it's Patrick Burke. Listen, Sam won't be in today. Something fluish. I'm calling Doc Richardson. She probably just needs a shot and some antibiotics and she'll be fine. But you'll have to cover for her, okay? Sorry. Thanks, Miriam. Talk to you soon. 'Bye."

Next the good doctor. Who we've known for years.

"Hi, Doc, it's Patrick Burke. I know it's early, but if you could call me back as soon as you get this, I'd really appreciate it. Something's up with Sam and I'd like you to see her right away if it's at all possible. I'm kind of … I'm really kind of at my wits' end, Doc. Thanks, Doc. I'd really appreciate it. We're at 918-131-4489."

I repeat the number slowly and hang up. My cheeks are hot and my heart's pounding. It isn't shame or guilt or even anxiety. It's fear. I feel like Doc's my one and only lifeline. What if he has no idea what to do? What then?

I pour myself another cup of coffee. When my hand seems steady enough, I take it with me into the living room. Two of the Barbies are undressed—the 20's flapper and the one in the 18th century handmade gown, both of which she designed and created herself—and Sam's busy swapping clothing.

She looks happy.

I sit and watch her for a while. She pretty much ignores me. She's humming something but damned if I know what it is. Sam's not much of a singer but Lily seems to have perfect pitch.

Goddamn.

A half hour later, the phone rings.

Doc Richardson says he'll see us right away. I've made up the guest room for her—since something tells me she's not going to be wanting to sleep in our bed while she's still this Lily person—so I lay out a pair of jeans, an Elton John tee shirt, and a pair of panties on the bed. No need for a bra. She never wears one except for work. But it occurs to me to wonder if, as she is now, she'd even know how to put one of the damn things on.

I tell her to go brush her teeth and get herself dressed. But first she's got to arrange the Barbies and her Teddy *just so* on the bureau across from her bed. I watch in the bathroom while she brushes. It seems to take her forever and she's awkward about it. As though the toothbrush were too big for her. It's very weird.

We're going on a little trip, I tell her. She wants to know where. To visit an old friend, Doc Richardson, I tell her. *Oh*, she says.

"You remember him?"

She shakes her head. Very definite about it. *No.*

She wants to take Teddy along. Fine.

In the car I have to remind her to buckle up and need to help her with the strap. As we're driving, she's dancing Teddy around on her lap singing "Frosty the Snowman" in that high clear voice that's suddenly hers even though Christmas is still seven months away.

The doc's office is on the corner of Main and Steuben Street, flanked by Bosch's Hardware and the Sugar Bowl, our local soda shop, on either side. There's a parking spot three cars down from Bosch's so I pull in. She flings open the door, forgets she's buckled in, lurches against the seatbelt.

"Easy," I tell her and press the release. She smiles in a way like *silly me* and flings open the door.

174

"Uh, leave Teddy, okay?"

She frowns for a moment, but then shrugs and seats him neatly in the passenger side and slams the door. I come around and take her hand.

We look pretty normal, I think. Husband and wife out for a stroll. And Sam, at least, looks happy.

Which is probably why, when Milt Shoemaker exits the hardware store, a bag in each hand, there's a big grin on his face as he walks toward us.

I try to match it.

"Milt."

"Patrick. Miz Burke. Fine day, ain't it?"

"Sure is, Milt."

He's a big man carrying too much weight on him. He's sweating and snorting like a bull.

"Listen, Patrick. I need to apologize to you. I ain't forgotten about those widow-makers you got up there. It's just that with those storms last month I been busy as a two-dollar whore in a mining camp. Pardon, Miz Burke."

I glance at Sam. She's still smiling. Maybe a bit too much.

I want to get us gone.

Milt runs Shoemaker's Tree and Stump. It's six months now since he promised to come out to our place with his crane truck and shear some high dead limbs off our old oak tree—struck by lightning last year—about twenty yards from the house. Dead limbs are brittle and dangerous and prone to falling at very inconvenient times. A tourist in New York's Central Park was killed by a widow-maker last year.

I'd wanted his chainsaws out there as soon as possible. But I think, not now.

"No problem, Milt. Tree's held up so far."

"You should call the office and make an appointment, Patrick. That way I'd be sure to get to it pronto."

"Well, I may just do that."

"You should. Out of sight, out of mine, y'know?"

*Mine?*

"I will, Milt. I will call. You take care, now. Best to Elsie. You have a good day."

He's looking at Sam strangely. A puzzled look.

So, I glance at her too.

Good grief. She's picking her nose.

I can't fucking believe it.

"Have a good day …" he mutters as we pass him and walk away.

A doctor's office should have music, I think, to lighten things up a bit. Doc's doesn't. Walking into Doc's is like walking into a sepulcher. The second we close the door behind us I can feel Sam stiffen. I can tell she doesn't like it. There are two old stringy ladies seated whispering in a corner, clutching their handbags as though fearful of a city-style mugging. There's a bald man in suspenders reading a newspaper. When he turns the page it's the loudest thing in the room.

Thankfully, we know none of them.

We walk past them to the counter. Millie, Doc's receptionist, is typing at her desk. She gets up smiling as we cross the floor.

"Hi, Patrick. Hi, Sam."

"Not—"

I cut her off. "How've you been, Millie?"

"Not half bad, Patrick, for a little old lady. You two have a seat. The doctor will be with you in a minute."

I'd outlined what the hell was happening on the phone as best I could, and Doc assured me he'd see us right away. I hope he keeps his word. The ladies are eyeing us as we sit. And Sam starts fidgeting immediately.

There are magazines on a low table beside us. I'm tempted but I don't want my own page-turning to add to the din.

Sam's staring straight ahead at the counter. I wonder what's so interesting, so I follow her gaze. There's a big three-quart glass jar on the counter and it's filled to the brim with wrapped hard candy—what appear to be cinnamon and grape and peppermints, lemon drops and lifesavers and root beer barrels.

"Patrick?"

And that little-girl voice coming from this big-girl person gets everyone's attention.

"When we leave, okay?"

She sighs. "Oh, okay."

Millie opens the door. "Mrs. Burke?"

I get up but Sam doesn't recognize her name, of course, so I lift her gently by the arm and walk her to the door and I see she's confused so I whisper to her that it's all right, she shouldn't worry, and we follow Millie's ample figure to the Doc's office. We enter and she closes the door.

Doc rises, all six feet, five inches of him. I clear my throat.

"Doc, this is Lily."

He extends a meaty hand. "Lily," he says, smiling.

Doc's about the warmest, friendliest person I know and if he weren't a giant and had a little more of that snow-white hair on his head and a matching beard he could pass for Santa with the best of them. She takes his hand and shakes it.

"Sit down, Lily. Make yourself at home. Patrick? Can I talk with Lily alone for a little while? Would you mind? Get to know one another a bit?"

There's a small dish of the same hard candy as on the counter in the waiting room sitting on his desk. He pushes it toward her, selects a root beer barrel for himself and proceeds to unwrap it.

"Help yourself, Lily," he says. He pops it into his mouth.

"Call you in a bit, Patrick," he says around it.

I'm dismissed.


Back in the waiting room, the ladies are eyeing me with suspicion. I've jumped ahead of them in line, after all. With this strange woman. A story across the clotheslines.

I pick up a copy of *Time* magazine. Astronomers have found a new planet that orbits three stars. There are articles on last year's continental freeze in Europe, on what it means to be a Conservative in America. Britain is banning photoshopped ads in which the models look *too* perfect.

I can't concentrate.

*People* magazine? *Scientific American*? *Cosmo*'s out of the question with those ladies present.

I solve the problem by doing nothing at all.

And I'm only a bit surprised when I wake up to a hand on my shoulder. Millie's.

Sam's standing beside her. She doesn't look disturbed at all or the least bit unhappy, which is good.

"Ben would like to see you now," she says. "Lily? Here's a magazine."

*Sesame Street.*

"We won't be long," she says.

Sam settles in with the magazine and I follow Millie inside.

Doc's sitting behind his desk making notes in a folder I can only presume to be Sam's. I sit across from him, and he puts down his pen. He shakes his head.

"Patrick, it's the damnedest thing I've ever seen. Physically she's just fine, same old Sam as always. The only physical changes I can see are those she's apparently made by choice, for lack of a better word. The vocal change is all tongue-placement. The jerky movements to the limbs and shoulders, you and I could imitate them pretty easily if we concentrated on it hard enough. So, the question is not what she's doing but why she's doing it."

"You mean you think she's faking?"

"Not at all. Quite the opposite. Talking to her just now, there's this strange kind of disconnect. It's as though she remembers selectively. She knows who Lady Gaga is but not her mother's or her father's name."

"She knew Zoey. Our cat."

"Did she now. That's interesting. The only time she got the least bit nervous or upset was when I asked her who you were, who Patrick was. That seemed to confuse her. I didn't push it. But she can identify everything around her perfectly well. I'd point to a chair or a window or a bookshelf and she'd rattle the word for it right off. I knew when she got bored with it too. You could tell. Her vocabulary, by the way, is at about a five-year-old level. She could identify flowers but not the vase, for instance. Called it a jar. She can add and subtract but not multiply or divide.

"This … transformation. What strikes me most is that it's uncannily consistent. Sure, you and I could imitate each of these child-aspects of hers if we tried. But I doubt very much if we could imitate them all at once, choreograph them all together—and do it for hours at a time, as you say she's been doing. That would take one hell of an actor."

He pulls out a prescription pad, picks up the pen and writes.

"Here's what we need to do. First, eliminate anything physical."

"You mean, like a tumor?"

"I've never heard of a tumor causing these kinds of symptoms, but yes, a brain scan's definitely in order. I want you to phone this number at Baptist Regional and arrange for it right away. I'll call ahead and grease the skids for you as soon as you're out of here, tell them to slip you in ASAP, tomorrow if possible."

He tears off the paper and hands it to me.

"Go home and make the call. Then try to get some sleep. You look like hell, Patrick."

I head for the door. He's right. I'm suddenly exhausted. But one other thing's bothering me bigtime.

"Doc, what if this isn't physical?"

"Yeah, I know. Multiple personality disorder. You see any other 'personalities?'"

"No."

"Keep a good sharp eye out. If there are any, one should surface soon. My understanding is that these things tend to cluster. She under any particular kind of stress lately?"

"Not that I know of."

"Work, maybe?"

I want to say hell, *she loves cutting up people for a living,* but I resist that.

"Sam loves puzzles. She sees her work as puzzle-solving. I think she'd want to do it even if they didn't pay her for it."

"Marriage okay?"

I want to say *it was until last night,* but I stifle that one too.

"We're fine, Doc. I just don't understand this."

"Well, fact is, me neither," he says. "Not yet, at least. Listen, try this. Try getting her to remember things. Jog her memory. Maybe, if we're lucky, you'll find something to jog her right back again."

I tell him I will, thank him, and walk out the door.

Doc's as good as his word. I phone and give them my name at the hospital and a moment later I'm speaking with a receptionist in radiology who gives us an MRI appointment for noon tomorrow.

For lunch Lily wants peanut butter and jelly.

We've got strawberry and peach preserves. Not jelly but close enough.

I make myself a fried egg sandwich and we eat in front of the television. I don't know anything about kid's programming, but I figure PBS must have something and they do. It's called *Clifford the Big Red Dog* and it's about ... a big red dog. Also, a purple poodle named Cleo, a blue hound named Mac, and a yellow bulldog named T-Bone.

She giggles occasionally.

There's a commercial for something called *Dinosaur Train* which is coming up next. Friendly dinosaurs. Why not? Consider Casper.

But I'm really bone-tired now.

"You be all right out here for a little while? I'm gonna go have a short nap. Or maybe you want a nap too?"

"Nah. I'll stay here, Patrick."

I no sooner hit the bed than I'm asleep.

But I wasn't kidding. It is a short nap. Half an hour max.

It's Zoey again. Her toy. That yowl. Rising up from the floor at the foot of the bed.

And Sam's heard it too because here she comes, her brow knit with concern, tucking Teddy under her arm and stooping down to pet her. Zoey flinches slightly, hunkering her shoulders beneath Sam's touch. This is an old cat with arthritic bones. She's stroking too hard.

"Easy," I tell her. "Go softer."

She slows her stroke and lightens her touch. Concentrating. Serious. Much better.

For her reward she gets a purr going.

Against all expectations, that short nap's been quite restorative. I feel much better. Maybe I can get a little drawing done.

"How's your TV?"

"Good. Can I watch some more?"

Exactly what I want to hear.

"Sure you can. If you want me, I'll be in the study."

"Study?"

"The room with the big table. You know."

"Oh," she says, but it's clear she doesn't, not really. It's also clear she doesn't much care. She's into those cartoons.

I get to work.

Samantha, I find, is resisting me today. A cynic might say, well, what do you expect? You've got half of her head blown the hell off. But I've dealt with more difficult problems before. Maybe it's that I've introduced a new character, Doctor Gypsum, a Strangelovian sort of guy in dark glasses and aviator cap whose task at the moment—as it will be in the future—is to put Humpty back together again.

It's weird, though. I have the sense that I'm drawing both characters just fine. He's all angles and she, as usual, is all soft lush contours masking the tensile strength within. But somehow I seem not to be getting the distances right between them on the panels. The balance is off composition-wise. Maybe it's a problem of perspective. They're either too close together—even when he's bending over her apparently dead body he seems too close, almost as though he's inside her in the frame—or they're too far apart. You get the feeling they're so far away he might be shouting.

This isn't like me. I know my shit.

I try it a few different ways and finally I get a page layout I like which seems to accommodate the panels as well as open up or close these distances as the case may be.

Time to go on to the next page.

That one comes easier. I'm into the rhythm of it now.

So into it, in fact, that when the phone rings it barely registers. Work's like that for me—everything in the real world goes away. I get into this zone where it's just me, line, story, and characters. Which is why I need total silence when I work. I need to hear it sing.

But the phone *does* ring and it's only when I hear Lily's voice— not Sam's—politely saying *no, sorry, there's no Sam here, guess you got the wrong number, sorry, that's okay* that I panic, realizing I've momentarily forgotten just exactly who's out there to answer and I race out of the room and into the kitchen just in time to see her cradle the receiver.

"Wrong number," she says.

The phone rings again. She reaches for it but I'm faster.

"Hello?"

"Patrick? Hi."

It's Miriam, Sam's boss. Nice lady.

"I just wanted to check in on Sam," she says. "How's she doing?"

How's she doing? She's fucking *missing* is what I want to say. And thinking that brings me close to tears or hysterical laughter or both, I'm not sure which. I feel like some mad doctor in an old black-and-white horror movie.

*She's gone! It's alive!*

What I do say is, "Just as we thought, it's flu. She's going to have to rest up for a few days, bring down the fever. In fact, she's dead asleep now."

"Well, tell her we've got everything covered here. Tell her not to worry. It's been a slow week for axe murders and floaters. Chloe and Bill say hi. You take good care of her, now."

"I will."

"Give her our best."

"I will. 'Bye, Miriam."

I let out a big sigh of relief. We lucked out. She really did figure the first call was a wrong number and not that I'm holding some little girl hostage here out in the boonies.

"Patrick? Whatchu doin' in there anyway? You're quiet."

"Drawing. Want to see?"

*Jog the memory.*

"Okay."

She follows me into the study. Stands off to one side of the drawing board. But her attention's drawn immediately to the shelves. We keep a lot of books in here, mostly art books and Sam's medical texts. But I've been collecting comic-book and horror action figures for years. I've got Superman, Batman and Robin, Green Hornet, the Mummy, the Wolf Man, Frankenstein, Godzilla, Rodan—there's probably two dozen or more. Hell, I've even got a plastic Jesus.

"You have toys!" she says.

Wide-eyed, like she's never seen them before. So much for memory-jogging in this room.

"Yeah. I guess I do."

"Can I play with them?"

"They're not really for play. More just to look at."

"Oh."

I can tell she's disappointed. Like it or not, right now she's just a kid. And all she's got are some Barbies and Teddy to play with. I point to the drawing board.

"Here, check this out."

I lay out the Samantha pages one by one on the board.

"This is what I do in here."

These are pretty good, I think. Some of the best work I've done. Moody, and with lots of action.

"You do this?"

"Yes. You like it?"

"Yeah. There's no color, though."

"Color comes later."

I keep turning the pages and I can see she's interested.

"If would be better if they moved," she says, "like on TV."

And then she's looking back at the shelves again. Distracted. I'm only halfway through the pages.

I can't help it, I feel a flash of irritation, maybe even anger. And yeah, it's anger, all right. Anger at *Sam. Not at Lily but at Sam.* Sam for doing this. Sam for leaving me. And then anger at myself for feeling that way. It's not her fault. Is it?

I put the pages down and cover them over.

"Let's go see about dinner. What do you say?"

Δ

Dinner is hot dogs and french fries. Her choice. What did I expect? I zap some beans and sauerkraut in the microwave too, but she doesn't touch either one, just slathers her dog and fries with ketchup. I've never seen her use ketchup on a hot dog before. Hitherto she's always been a Gulden's mustard girl.

Around a mouthful of fries she says, "it's not fair."

"What's not fair?"

"You've got toys."

"They're not really toys. They're just for show."

She's pouting. "They're toys," she says. "And all I've got is Teddy and some stupid dolls."

"I thought you liked those dolls."

"They're okay, I guess …"

*But.* I'm not stupid. I get it.

"You want some other stuff, right? Some of the stuff you saw on TV, maybe?"

She brightens right away.

"Yeah!"

"Okay. After we eat, we'll go on the net and see what we can find. How's that?"

"The net?"

No memory of the net either. Sam has sites and files saved by the dozens.

"You'll see."


She's fascinated by the computer. I remember reading somewhere that all kids are. At least at first.

We hit the merchandise sites. She's standing behind me pointing out what she likes while I'm punching in the site addresses and click-ing on the items. During the next half hour, we purchase an Abby Cadabby Bendable Plush Doll, a *Once Upon a Monster* video game, a knot-a-quilt package, a Teeny Medley bead set, a Stablemate Deluxe Animal Hospital—complete with quarter horse, foal, donkey, goat, resident cat and border collie, operating table and bandage box—and a pair of Curious George pajamas. The pajamas come in kids' and moms' sizes, so I've bought the latter. By the time we get to the Easy Bake Oven and Super Pack, she's leaning on my shoulders.

She smells of fresh soap and traces of hot dog.

The Oven and Super Pack alone set me back a hundred dollars but who's counting. The plush Clifford the Big Red Dog another forty-five. I buy them all and arrange for overnight express delivery.

She yawns. She's having fun of course but for her, maybe, it's getting near bedtime.

She's tired. So, she walks around and proceeds to sit on my lap.

"Uh, not a good idea, Lily."

"Why not?" She points at the screen. "I want that," she says.

And I'm not sure I like either of these developments.

What she's pointing to is a Baby Alive doll. At forty bucks a Baby Alive doll speaks thirty phrases and comes complete with a dress, a bib, a bowl, a spoon, a bottle, diapers, doll-food products—whatever the hell they might be—and instructions.

I imagine the instructions are useful.

The doll says, "I love you, Mommy," and "kiss me, Mommy," among other things. Eats, drinks, and wets its diaper.

I'm not sure I like that. I'm also not sure it's wise to have her on my lap. I might have been better off when she distrusted me. Because right now this warm woman's body, my wife's body, is in serious danger of giving me a hard-on.

And this body *thinks* it's about five or six years old.

"You're too heavy," I tell her.

"Am not."

"Are so."

"Am not."

To prove it, she *wriggles* on me. Bumps gently up and down.

"Off," I tell her. "You want me to buy this or not?"

"Oh, okay."

I'm a grouch. A spoil-sport.

She gets up.

I buy the fucking doll.

Δ

I'm sitting in the chair in our guestroom watching her sleep. The moon is nearly full and through the window behind me it bathes her face in slants of milky white. The night's unseasonably warm so she's pulled the covers down to just below her waist and I can see her belly between her pajama top and bottom, her navel like a tiny pale button pressing up and down against the mattress cover.

My wife's an outie.

I'm thinking about how we met, eight and half years ago. I'd just landed my first job in the publishing business, as a colorist for Arriveste Ventures—garish, primary-color-only work on their *Blazeman* line. Nights I was brushing up on my anatomy at the adult ed department at Tulsa Community College and Sam, who already had four years under her belt in the coroner's office, was guest lecturer. Her subject that night, the integumentary system. Skin.

A lot was familiar to me. That skin was the largest organ in the body. That skin was waterproofing, insulation, protection, temperature control, guard against pathogens, all rolled up into one. That skin was the organ of sensation. But there was something she said that I'd never considered before, at least not in the way she put it.

She said that skin *permits* us access to the outside world.

"All the orifices in our bodies," she said, "our eyes, noses, ear canals, mouths, anuses, penises, vaginas, nipples—they're all there and function as they do because skin, by not covering them, allows them free communication with the world which is *not* us. Even our pores exist where they do and where they don't, solely by permission of our skin. Pretty smart stuff, skin is."

That got a laugh. But this Samantha Martin person was pretty smart stuff too. And I was already thinking about her own skin.

It had been a year and a half since Linda had e-mailed me from New York saying—apologetically but baldly—that she'd fallen out of love with me. She didn't know why.

Was there another man? No. Something I did or said? No. It just happened. She'd been meaning to tell me for a while now but hadn't gotten up the courage. I was twenty-four years old, and we'd been lovers for four of those years. I was still completely crazy over her. Those seven stages of grief they talk about? I went through all seven at once, I think, rattling from one to the other like a game of bumper-pool gone berserk. At the end of it, I more or less vowed that love and even sex could wait. Until I was thirty, maybe.

But then here was Sam's skin. The complexion of her face, her bare arms in the sleeveless blouse, her long graceful neck.

It's always been one of her loveliest features. Arguably her best. Winter-pale or summer-tan, it's always seemed to smolder with some warm inner glow, an even interior lighting. There are tiny dances of freckles across her shoulders, hands and forearms. And one beautiful dark mole just to the left of the small of her back.

I didn't get to see the mole that day. But from my desk in the second row of our classroom the rest was pretty clear to me. That she was smart, and she was lovely. Neither fact was lost on anybody in the classroom. Especially the guys.

So, while I listened carefully to what she had to say about *parting* epidermis, dermis and hypodermis, about scalpels, about where and how to cut in order to get at all that good stuff inside, I was doing some fantasizing too. About what it would be like to touch her.

I hadn't done that in a long time. Touch a woman.

And when her lecture and the Q&A were over I did.

It's always amazed me to hear beautiful women—actresses or models—say that they hardly ever get asked out, that most men are intimidated by them, tongue-tied by their beauty. Me, I just don't get it. That's never been my problem. Maybe it's this artist's eye of mine that just can't help being drawn to beauty, to want to be in its presence as much as humanly possible. Maybe it's because I grew up in a pretty secure family.

Maybe I just don't know any better. Fools do rush in.

But as the class filed out Sam was talking with our teacher, Mrs. Senner. She stood with her back to me, and that gave me all the excuse I needed. I touched her lightly just beneath the shoulder and said *excuse me?* and the smooth warm softness of her skin and firmness within hurtled straight to my brain like a flaming trail of gasoline.

She turned and smiled.

"Sorry to interrupt," I said. "But I've got a couple of questions. Could I maybe buy you two ladies a cup of coffee?"

I was being disingenuous in the extreme. I knew perfectly well that Mrs. Senner always raced home after class to fix supper for her husband, who was just getting off his shift at Tartan Industries. We all did.

She introduced us, said I was one of her better students, and then gracefully declined.

But Sam accepted.

I don't remember much of what we talked about over coffee first and then two glasses of wine each, and the walk back to our respective cars, except that she seemed as interested in the business of making graphic novels as I was in what went on in the autopsy room. More importantly, the current was there. The connection loud and clear.

Later, after our third date and first night in bed, she would tell me that my hand below her shoulder that evening had startled her, gone through her like a shot. She called herself a workaholic and said that after an affair gone south with an older married man it had been a very long time between drinks for her too and that my touch felt to her like a wake-up call from a long dry dreamless sleep.

It was and still is the loveliest thing anyone has ever said to me.

And now I watch her sleep.


I won't cry. Not yet.


I wake up like somebody's hit me with a cattle prod.

I wake up horrified.

Zoey's climbed through an open window which should have a screen in it but doesn't and she's out on the ledge of a tenth-floor apartment, looking fascinated by what she sees below and then frightened and finally bewildered and as I'm crossing the room to get to her, carefully, afraid to startle her, she tries to turn on the narrow ledge when she should just be backing up the way she came and falls out of sight into space.

I'm instantly awake, stunned, my arms outstretched in front of me, reaching hopelessly for my cat. Inside the dream and right here in my bedroom I've been shouting, both worlds melded into one. Now they break apart. Zoey stares at me from the foot of the bed.

She gets up and meanders over. I scratch her neck and chin and she tilts her head back and closes her eyes, content. When I stop, she steps onto my lap and nuzzles my chin. Breakfast time.

"In a minute, baby. Got to piss." I step into my jeans. Tuck in my tee shirt. Habit. It slightly amazes me that I still have habits.

On the way to the bathroom, I can hear the TV. Cartoon voices. Lily's already awake.

The guy I see in the mirror disturbs me, so I don't dwell on him. I just finish my business and get out of there.

In the living room Lily's kneeling in front of the TV set, watching a commercial for Sid the Science Kid.

She's also naked to the waist.

There's that mole.

She hears me behind her and turns and smiles.

"'Morning, Patrick."

Even after all these years it is wholly impossible not to take in her breasts.

Sam's breasts are small. You can cup one in each hand and not get much overflow. They're quite pale. So pale that in a few places you can see the dim blue traces of vein beneath the flesh, traces of vulnerability, I always thought. Her areolae are a very light brown, almost perfectly round and about an inch wide. Her nipples are pink and a quarter-inch long at all times, permanently erect.

And her nipples have a direct phone line to her cunt. I've made her come dozens of times without ever going below her waist.

If she notices me looking at them she doesn't show it.

"Something wrong?" she says.

"Where's your pajama top, Lily?"

"On the bed. It got hot."

"Why don't you go get it for me, okay?"

"I'm *still* hot!"

"Girls are not supposed to run around with their tops off, Lily."

"Who says?"

"I say. Trust me."

She sighs again. I'm getting used to that sigh. But she gets off her knees and stomps past me toward the bedroom and as she goes by, she brushes my bare left arm with her right breast.

I could practically swear she's done this on purpose.

Like she's flouting her body, flirting with me.

But that's impossible. How can she know how this makes me feel? If this were Sam, she'd damn well know of course. Sam's very self-aware. But Lily?

The answer is, she can't. She hasn't got a clue. Kneeling there in front of the TV she was the picture of innocence. Brushing against me's just the sullen, pouty thing any kid might do who isn't getting her way.

Forget about it, I tell myself.

Sure.


I've showered and shaved and dressed and as I'm cleaning up the dishes she appears in the kitchen doorway.

"What are we doing today, Patrick? Can we go on the 'puter some more?"

"Actually, I need you to get in the shower for me and then get dressed, okay?"

"Ugh! I *hate* the shower!"

No she doesn't.

"Water gets all in my eyes. Can't I do a bath instead?"

It's all the same to me. "Okay. You want to run the water, or should I?"

"You do it."

I finish the dishes and run her a tub, bend over and test the water with my hand.

"Ready," I tell her.

I stand and turn and there she is in front of me, naked, naturally, clueless again, her pajamas in a heap on the floor. *Jesus wept.* I avert my eyes. I pick up her pajamas and get the hell out of there.

Sam is a neat-freak, but Lily obviously isn't. Her clothes from the day before lie on the floor of her bedroom where she dropped them in a more-or-less straight line from the door to the bed. Shoes, tee shirt, jeans, panties, socks.

I make her bed and fold her pajamas and put them in a drawer. But for them, the drawer's empty. If this goes on much longer, if Sam's going to be Lily for a while, I should probably move more of her stuff from our room to this one but I'm damned if I'm going to do that right now. We've got this MRI coming up at noon. Nothing changes any more than it has to until I get the results on that.

I pick up her clothes. I lay her jeans out on the bed, the Avia running shoes beneath the bed. The socks and panties go in the laundry basket but that's in the bathroom and I can hear her splashing around in there. I'm not going in. I carry them into our room and select a fresh pair of each, go back to her room and lay them out beside her jeans.

I realize I'm not thinking quite straight. I'm carrying her used socks and panties around instead of just tossing them on my bed until she gets out of there. So that's what I do. Go back to our room and drop them on my unmade bed.

Something catches my eye.

The panties.

Sam says she has little time to shop and she's not like most women anyhow, she doesn't really like shopping. So, the panties arrived via UPS from Victoria's Secret along with a half dozen other pairs a few weeks ago. They're ivory. And ivory shows up stains.

There are skid-marks on Sam's panties. Or should I say Lily's.

She hasn't wiped sufficiently.

So now I've got a problem. Do I call her on this or no? If I do it'll likely embarrass her. I don't want to embarrass her. I figure maybe it's a one-shot. I figure I'll spray the damn things with some of our eco-friendly stain remover and leave it at that.

Δ

In my red Sierra 4x4 the radio's tuned to our classic rock station—The Band doing "The Weight"—and wonder of wonders, Lily's singing along.

"You remember that song?"

"'Course I do."

"You remember any others?"

"I dunno. I guess."

"Which ones?"

"I dunno."

"Name me one."

She shifts uncomfortably in the seat. "Why are we going to the hospital, Patrick?"

"We're going to test something."

"Like in a quiz?"

"Nope. There's a machine that does the testing. All you do is lie down and watch a bunch of pretty lights."

"You too?"

"No, just you this time. I already had my test, a long time ago."

Concussion. I slipped on the ice six or seven years back.

"Did you pass?"

"Yep. And so will you."

I'm trying to sound nonchalant but secretly I'm worried about how this is all going to go down. For an MRI to work you've got to lie perfectly still—not an easy thing to get a kid to do. The machine is noisy as hell and if you're at all given to claustrophobia this will definitely bring it out in you. An MRI can be a scary creature.

I'm worried about how Lily's going to take it. All sorts of scenarios flit through my head. Lily screaming, crying, banging on the tubing, refusing to lie down, scrambling off the table, hiding. Lily in tantrum.

I know how bad this can get. My first clear childhood memory is of me doing pretty much all these things when faced with my first hypodermic needle. The doctor was not pleased. I doubt a radiographer will be either.

Ignorance being bliss though, she doesn't seem at all concerned. She's gazing out the window at the cows and horses out to pasture, the corn stalks, the fields of soy and wheat. We pass a produce store, a used-car lot selling car-ports, the RoundUp Grocery and the River Winds Casino.

Yep, gambling and wheat fields, that's us. There are any number of Indian-owned casinos out here, with names like Buffalo Run and Stables. They're wildly outnumbered by the churches, of course. But attendance-wise the smart money's always on the Indians.

When we pull into the parking lot of Baptist Regional Health she's singing along to the Kinks' "Missing Persons."

She can remember these songs. But she can't remember me.


We find our way to radiology and the room is packed. Almost entirely older people. I'm wondering if there's an Early Bird Special on MRIs and CAT-scans these days.

A young woman in Admitting hands me a clipboard and a pen and we find a seat. While I'm filling out the papers Sam's fidgeting, openly staring at all the people around her like she's never seen this kind of crowd before. Fascinated, just short of rude. Across from us a skeletal white-haired woman smiles at her, a little flustered by being stared at you can tell, and Sam smiles back like this woman is her very best friend in the world. The woman hides inside her magazine.

"What's that?"

She's pointing to a guy about my age seated by the wall to our left, wearing overalls and work boots and cradling his right arm up into his chest. Luckily, he's talking to the woman beside him—presumably his wife—so he doesn't notice.

"A sling. The man hurt his arm. But it's not nice to point, Lily."

"It's pretty."

She's right. The sling's a deep burgundy, some sort of paisley print.

"You've got one a lot like it. Only yours is blue."

"I have a sling?"

"It's a scarf. You make a sling out of a scarf. Normally you wear it around your neck. Or over your head."

"Can you show me when we get home?"

"Sure."

I finish the paperwork and bring it to the desk. Sam's sort of baby-stepping along behind me. The woman in admitting smiles. "You can go right in," she says.

"Excuse me?"

"They're expecting you. Right through this door."

I knew that Doc had clout, but this is amazing.

I open the door for Sam, and we're greeted by the radiographer, a short slim guy in hospital scrubs who introduces himself as Curtis. First or last name, I don't know.

"Mr. Burke. Lily. Right this way, please."

*Lily?*

*Samantha* was what I wrote on the chart. Talk about greasing the skids. The Doctor has outdone himself this time. He leads us down a corridor and opens a door to our right.

Sam steps inside ahead of me and her eyes go wide.

"It's all white!" she says.

Which it is. The whole room looks like it's made of porcelain. Walls, scanner, scanner bed, chairs, stretcher, linens. Everything except a long wide window directly ahead of us—Curtis' monitoring station.

"Are you wearing any jewelry, Lily?" he asks.

"No."

"What about the ring?"

"Oh, that."

She tugs off her wedding ring and hands it to him.

"Good. Then all you have to do is lie down on your back here and relax."

"She doesn't have to change? No scrubs?"

"Nope. She's good to go as-is."

She hops up on the scanner bed. Curtis plumps her pillow. She lies down.

"It's going to be a little noisy," he says. "Want to listen to some music?"

She nods, smiles. He produces a pair of headphones.

White.

I hear faint Muzak coming from them as she puts them on. Sam would have died.

"Would you like to stay, Mr. Burke?"

"I think I'd better, yes."

I'm still apprehensive as to how she's going to take this.

"Then I'll need your watch and your ring. Anything else metal? Any change in your pockets?"

"No."

I hand him the ring and the watch and he turns to Sam again.

"I'm going into that room now, Lily. I'll be able to see you and talk to you and you can talk to me if you need to and I'll hear you—but only if you really, really need to, okay? Otherwise try be real quiet. Like pretend you're sleeping. Try not to move at all, you know? Make believe you're asleep."

She nods again and smiles. This guy is pretty good.

He exits the room. I sit in a chair. A few moments later Sam begins to move. Headfirst into the belly of the beast.

She's a fucking trooper.

Not a wiggle out of her. A half hour later we're back in the car headed home. And our timing's perfect because as we turn onto the driveway, the long clay road that cuts through our forest, there's a UPS truck just ahead of us.

Or maybe it's not perfect. The driver's going to meet Lily.

Anyway, our toys are here.

The driver's a woman of about forty who I've never seen before, not our usual driver, very pretty even in her baseball cap and over-sized drab brown uniform. 'Mornin', she says as she gets out of the truck and we both say 'mornin'. She hauls open the back.

"I've got nine for you today, Mr. Burke, Miz Burke."

"I'm Lily."

"Glad to meet you, Lily."

"What're these?"

"We ordered them, remember? On the computer."

"Toys!" she says.

The driver says nothing, but it can't possibly be lost on her that this is not the voice of your normal thirty-something woman. We help her unload. The silence is pretty thick except for Sam, who's humming "It's Not Easy Being Green." And I can't help it, I'm embarrassed for her. Or maybe for me, I'm not sure. Either way it sucks.

When we've got them all inside and I've signed for them the driver gives me a smile as she climbs back into the truck but she won't meet my eyes.

"You have a good afternoon," she says.

And I can almost hear her thinking *She's so pretty, too bad she's retarded. And too bad for him too.*

She pulls away. I almost want to throw something. But I don't.


Lily wants to open everything right away but it's way past lunchtime, so I make us some tuna sandwiches and a pitcher of lemonade and we take them outside to the old stone barbecue and eat at the wooden table there. The sun is glinting on the river. There's the scent of earth and trees and grass growing. It's a relaxing, Saturday-or-Sunday kind of thing to do and Sam and I have done it many times. But Lily just wolfs it down. She really wants at those packages.

"You remember this?" I ask her.

"Remember? 'Member what?"

"This. Doing this. Us being here together."

She shakes her head. "I never did."


It seems to take forever but by the time I've got the animal hospital ready for surgery in the living room, the Easy Bake Oven alive and bake-ready in the kitchen, she's already got the *Once Upon a Monster* video game running and Teddy and Abby Cadabby are having tea under the watchful eye of her new Baby Alive doll.

That goddamn doll is spooky.

I figure I've got to log in some drawing time.

I work for maybe an hour, hour and a half, but something's wrong again. Now it's Samantha herself who somehow seems to be eluding me on the page. She doesn't look right. I've been drawing this woman for weeks now and know exactly who she is. Hell, I've even put her face and head back together after a shotgun blast.

So, what's my problem?

I go back through the first few pages and study her, then flip to today, go to the middle and flip again, back to the first few and flip to yesterday, back and forth until finally I've got it. She's consistent until yesterday, when I had that difficulty with perspective. And today's an extension of what I did yesterday. I'd have seen it then if I hadn't been occupied with composition. It's subtle but apparent now.

Sam would have caught it in a minute. I try not to think how much I miss that.

Samantha's gotten slightly slimmer. A little less heft to the breasts, a bit narrower in the hips and thighs. A little more like the real Sam.

More like Lily.

And I'm thinking, well, what the hell, fuck it, I can fix that—it's ridiculous and annoying to have to do over the last three pages but it's no big deal and god knows I've been preoccupied with the real Sam so that it's no huge surprise that she'd have crept a bit into my work—I'm thinking this when I hear a crash from the kitchen.

In the kitchen the scene would be funny if it weren't so pathetic. There's Sam at the counter, hands raised in what looks like surrender, her eyes wide and mouth agape like she's just seen a ghost scutter across the floor. Only what's down there is a sodden paper napkin beside some buttery toweling, each of which is soaking up a mixture of what turns out to be flour, baking powder, vanilla, vegetable oil, and round red sugar crystals. *Barbie's Pretty Pink Cake.* Which is also all over the tail and haunches of my cat. She's skulking toward the door.

I grab her before she can make her getaway and now it's all over me too for chrissake.

I rush her to the sink.

"Jesus, Sam! What the hell …?"

"My elbow I hit it and it fell and she was there and *I'm not Sam!*"

"Okay you're not Sam, goddammit, but gimme a goddamn hand here. Turn on the tap, will you? Warm, please. Not hot."

I can't keep the edge out of my voice, and I don't try. What the hell was she thinking, doing this without me being here? My cat hates water unless she's drinking it.

"Here. Hold her here. Around the shoulders."

She does as I say and miraculously Zoey's behaving, so I tip a bit of dish detergent into my hands and rub it into a lather, rinse and do it again.

Then I go to work on my cat.


Zoey keeps giving me these disgusted looks until at last I've got her toweled dry and we set her free. Sam hasn't said another word to me through the whole thing.

"Look, I'm sorry I snapped at you," I tell her.

"I'm not Sam. You keep calling me Sam. Why?"

I have no good answer to that. At least none she'd understand.

"You remind me of somebody."

"Who?"

"Somebody I know."

"Is she nice?"

"Yes. Very nice."

This is killing me.

"Let's clean up this mess on the floor, okay?"

"Okay."


At around eight that night I turn the sound off on a show about elephants on Nature and pull out the photo album. We stopped taking photos a few years back for some reason, but there we are in the old days just after we met, Sam thirty and me twenty-eight in front of the Science Museum, taking in the fireworks at Carousel Park, down by the Falls, Sam on a bench in City Park, waving at me.

"She does look a lot like me," she says.

I say nothing.

There are three pages of photos I took at the St. Augustine Alligator Farm back in our 2008 vacation and these seem to fascinate her. The crocks and turtles, the albino alligators, the wild bird rookery, the Komodo dragon. She's forgotten Sam entirely.

I turn to some of the older family photos. My mother and father, my brother Dan, her parents on her father's birthday. She doesn't seem interested in these at all.

"They're nice," she says. "Can we watch the elephants?"

I'm awakened by Lily's voice.

"Patrick? I'm scared."

She's turned on the light in the hall behind her and she's standing in the doorway in her Curious George pajamas, hands and cheek pressed to the doorjamb like she's hugging it. I'm still woozy from sleep but through the open window I can hear what's bothering her.

Above the chirping of crickets, the wind's whipping the howling and yipping of a pack of coyotes across the river. They'll try to take cows down now and then over there and they tend to like to celebrate when they do. There seem to be a lot of them tonight, and the mix is eerie, from the long sonorous wolf-like wail of the adults to the staccato *yip yip yip* of the young. Which sounds for all the world like demented evil laughter.

Even the crickets sawing away in the darkness sound vaguely sinister tonight.

No wonder she's scared. Even to my ears it's spooky.

She looks so vulnerable standing there. Shoulders hunched, legs pulled tight together, her thumbnail pressed against her upper front teeth. More like a kid in some ways than I've yet seen her. So much less of Sam, so much more of Lily.

Almost like the daughter we'll never have.

"It's okay. It's just a bunch of coyotes. They can't hurt you. They're way out there over across the river."

"Patrick?"

"Yeah?"

"I'm scared."

"I know you're scared but you don't have to be. To them it's a kind of music, like singing, only because we're not them, it sounds weird, a little scary. That's all."

"Singing?"

"Uh-huh."

"I don't like it."

"Try to go back to sleep, Lily. They really can't hurt you. Honest."

"Can I … could I stay with you, Patrick?"

*I want her to. I don't want her to.*

Contradictions slam together.

"You'll be fine over there, Lily."

"No I won't."

"Sure you will."

"No I won't. I'll be good, I promise. I won't wriggle around or anything. I promise."

I can hear the tremble in her voice. Almost like a desperation there. She really is scared.

"Okay," I tell her. I scoot over to the far side of the bed by the window. She scampers to the bed as though the floor's on fire and hops in. Throws the light summer bedcovers over her shoulders and snuggles up next to me. She's shaking.

It's automatic. I put my arm around her and then her head is resting on my shoulder.

I haven't done anything like this for days.

It makes me almost light-headed.

It's as though this is Sam again, as always. As though nothing's changed. But one thing reminds me that everything's changed.

Her hair.

When Sam comes to bed and we hold one another close like this I'm always aware of the faint traces of shampoo in her hair, Herbal Essence or Aussie Mega. It's a clean smell, as familiar to me as the scent of her breath or the feel of her skin beneath my hand.

Lily hasn't shampooed today.

It's not a bad smell, just flat and slightly musky. But it's not Sam's smell, not at all.

I'll have to remind her in the morning. Shampoo your hair.

Meantime, if I close my eyes, the rest of her is Sam. My hand on her arm, her cheek on my shoulder, her leg against mine.

Lily keeps her promise. She doesn't wriggle.

But it's a long time before I'm able to sleep. And it isn't the coyotes.


In my dream I'm telling somebody or other at somebody's dinner table how extraordinary I think it is that I'll die someday, just disappear tonight or tomorrow or whenever, and I'm wondering out loud just what will disappear along with me when I do. I awake with a raging hard-on tenting up the covers and a sense of puzzlement that one should somehow coincide with the other.

Mercifully, Lily's already up.

It makes no real sense and actually the thought's briefly annoying but I'd rather she not see this. So, I peer out into the hallway to make sure the coast is clear before I head for the bathroom. Then standing there peeing I wonder if she's *already* seen it. It's possible.

The call from Doc Richardson comes at nine-thirty.

"She tested out just fine, Patrick. Is she still …?"

"Yeah. She's still Lily."

I don't know whether to be relieved or not. If it were a brain-thing it might be treatable. But then again …

He sighs. "Well, there's nothing physically wrong with her. Everything looks perfectly normal. Have any other personalities appeared?"

"No."

"And no sign of Sam at all, I assume."

"None."

"Then I think you need to have her see a therapist. I'm out of my league here. But I know a good one. Have you got a pen?"

I write down the woman's name, address, and phone number. I do it mostly for the doc's sake. I'm pretty sure I'm not going to use the information. Call it pride or stubbornness—I want to see this through on my own if I can. I'll keep it by the phone as a last resort.

"Thanks for what you did at the hospital, Doc."

"My pleasure. Hey, they owe me. Good luck with the therapist. And keep me posted, all right? You know I'm very fond of Sam."

"I know. I will." I thank him and hang up.

I'm thinking that with or without a therapist, this could take a while.

Lily's on the couch, nibbling from a box of raisin bran. Her left arm's poking out of a paisley scarf. Her sling. Herman the Human Cannonball is about to be launched by the gang over at Sesame Street.

"Lily, as soon as the show's over, I want you to run a tub for your bath, okay? And be sure to wash your hair. You forgot yesterday."

"Okay."

She doesn't seem the least distressed so I'm guessing she missed the woody.

I go back to the phone and speed-dial the coroner's office.

"Miriam, hi. It's Patrick Burke. Listen, I wasn't being completely truthful when we spoke. In fact, I wasn't telling you the truth at all—I don't know why. There's no flu. Never was. Physically, Sam's fine. This is … something else …."

"You mean like a breakdown?"

"I guess that's what you'd call it, yes."

"God, I'm so sorry, Patrick. Are you all right? I mean—"

"The two of us are fine, Miriam. Well, we'll be fine once she gets through all this. But I'm afraid I'm going to have to ask you to give her a leave of absence for a while."

"Absolutely. You take all the time you need. Your wife works like a soldier. She deserves it. Can I speak with her? Would that be okay, do you think?"

"I don't think so. She's pretty fragile at the moment. Maybe in a week or so."

"Is she seeing somebody, getting therapy?"

"Yes."

Two lies inside of twenty minutes. Not bad, Patrick. I give her the therapist's name just to seal the deal.

"Good. Well, give Sam my best, will you? From all of us. And if there's anything I can do …."

"I will."

And that lie makes three.

Δ

I'm at the drafting table working on Samantha duking it out with The Torque, trying to keep her from going all svelte on me again, when I'm aware that the television's gone off and there's water running in the tub. A little while after that I can hear her splashing around in there. She's left the door open.

"Lily?"

"Yeah."

"Close the door. And don't forget to wash your hair!"

"You do it."

"What?"

"You do it. I get soap in my eyes."

"No you don't."

"I do too. You do it, Patrick."

She'll be naked in there.

I tell myself that I'm being silly. That's my wife in there and I've seen her naked thousands of times. *Get a grip, Patrick.*

"All right. I'm coming."

I finish crosshatching Torque's ugly mug, get up and walk to the bathroom.

She's sitting in soapy water up to her breasts, small peaked islands in the waves. Beneath the water I can see her pubic hair. She hasn't depilated in a while, so it drifts like tiny dark strands of seaweed. Her left thigh is under water but her right leg's bent so she can get at the toes, which she's soaping vigorously. It tickles. She giggles. Her thigh gleams.

There's a small line of soap like soul patch on her chin so I wipe it off with my finger.

"You ready?"

"Uh-huh."

"Duck under."

She tilts her head back into the water and comes up sputtering, wiping her eyes. Meanwhile I've got the shampoo off the shelf. I pour some into my palm and smooth it into both hands, kneel beside the tub and work it into her smooth fine hair. She smiles at me.

"Don't get it in my eyes, Patrick."

"I won't."

And I'm careful not to. But I can't help thinking of our last real night together, starting with our shower, starting with me shampooing her hair just as I'm doing now.

Then telling her *turn around, I'll do your back.*

*She does. I wash her back, her ass, her breasts, her stomach. She raises her arms and I wash her armpits, her arms, then her back and ass again, into the crack of her ass, into her cunt. She soaps her own hand and reaches down to me.*

This is not a good place to go.

She's looking up at me with those very innocent eyes.

I turn on the water behind her. Fiddle with the hot and cold until it's luke.

"Okay, rinse. Close your eyes." I'm trying to keep the thickness out of my voice.

I cup my hands, collect the fresh tap water and pour. Collect and pour. Over and over again until her hair is clean and shiny. She stands up, raises her arms, and smoothes her hair back off her forehead. The gesture is so *Sam* it floors me for a moment but only for a moment because with her arms raised I can see the dark stubble in her armpits. Three days' growth now. Sam shaves every day.

I wonder if Lily's noticed.


While she's toweling off, I go into her room and retrieve yesterday's tee shirt, socks, and panties.

The panties are stained again, worse than before.

I'll have to talk to her.


"Dad?"

"Pat? Hey, how are you?

My father is Daniel Patrick Burke and he and my mother are the only people in the world allowed to call me Pat.

I don't phone him nearly enough. But he's good about it. I think he understands.

"I'm okay. How about you?"

"Not bad. Got a little golf in this morning. I'll never be any good at the damn game, but it gets me off my butt now and then. My partner was Bill Crosby. He asked about you, sends his best."

Bill always does. Like my father, he's a retired schoolteacher. Only my father taught math in Tulsa while Bill taught history in the Bronx. Bill's a little rougher around the edges.

"Tell him I said hi."

"I will."

There's a pause on the other end and I hear the flick of a lighter. My father's Zippo. My dad's got emphysema. He shouldn't be smoking at all, but he figures half a pack a day will buy him a little more time than two packs would. He's content to leave it at that for now.

"How's the weather been?"

"You know, sunny Sarasota. Weather's fine. I just wish the snowbirds would hurry up and go home. You can't get a parking space anywhere in this damn town. I went to visit your mother yesterday and then decided to grab a bite to eat. I had to walk five blocks to the Bonefish Grille and then waited half an hour for a table. Sometimes I think everybody down here's from Minnesota."

So here comes the inevitable. The dreaded question. The reason I don't call too often. But I have to ask.

"How's Mom?"

I hear him pull hard on his Winston.

"She asked me who I was, Pat."

He lets it lie there a moment. On this end, I'm frozen.

"Sometimes she knows me and sometimes she doesn't. I wanted to take her out for some ice cream. You know she loves ice cream. They tell me that's typical. That with Alzheimer's the sweet tooth goes last. But she gets so confused, you know? She wanted to get a sweater even though I told her she didn't need one. She couldn't find her own clothes closet. She went looking in the bathroom."

My father knew he needed to put his wife of forty-two years in a managed care facility when she decided to make a frozen pizza for a snack one night and put the pizza in the oven, box and all.

"Anyhow, I got her out of there and we went for a drive and I got her a chocolate sundae. She seemed to enjoy herself, to have a good time. She even reached over and smiled and had some of my banana split, just like a little kid. She was sweet. But, you know, she never once asked about you or your brother. And I'm not sure she knew who I was, even when I kissed her goodbye. Even then she looked puzzled."

He sighs, coughs. After two years this is still always rough for him. He changes the subject.

"You hear anything from your brother?"

"No."

And now the pause is on my end. My brother Ed is two years older than me—he became a D.C. cop after the Marine Corps. He thinks what I do for a living is ridiculous. I think what he does is probably just short of criminal.

Besides, I'm thinking about Sam.

"Something wrong, son?"

"No, Dad. Everything's fine. I'm just a bit tired, that's all."

"How's Sam?"

"Sam's fine. She's glued to the television."

Which is true. I just don't tell him what show it is.

"Give her my love, will you?"

"Sure, Dad. Of course I will."

Another pause from me. I'm picturing my mother and her chocolate sundae, her reaching across the table.

"You sure you're okay, Pat?

And I almost tell him then. I almost blurt out the entire thing, because I love my father and maybe he can comfort me, maybe he can tell me it's going to be all right and make me believe him the way I always believed him when I was young and he was the dad, the schoolteacher you could always go to, who always knew that you treated kids the same as you treated adults, with respect and an open heart.

I want to tell him that I miss her—that I miss us. Because we've always been one hellova pair, Sam and I, not just lovers but the best friends either of us has ever had, who tell one another when we're hurting or need help and love to crack one another up with some silly goddamn joke. We love the same cat. Respect the same books. Smile to the same Tom Waits CDs in the car. Share a grave distrust of politics, lawyers, and Wall Street.

I want to tell him that I feel abandoned. Like part of me's living alone.

But my mother's burden enough for him.

"I'm fine, Dad. Honest."

I can't tell if he buys it or not. Finally, he breaks another silence.

"Okay. The two of you come visit your old dad one day soon, all right? It's been too long."

"Sure, Dad. We will. I promise. Love you."

"Love you too, son. Love to Sam. 'Bye."

Over the next two weeks I slash away at Samantha. I'll tame that lovely bitch, keep her juicy ass big if it takes everything I've got. My deadline's not until the end of next month but when I'm not with Lily I'm obsessive about this. The pages don't exactly fly—I keep having to correct them—but I'll have it done way before then.

We've fallen into a kind of pattern, Lily and me. She fixes her own cereal in the morning, and I make lunch and dinner. I work while she plays. I make sure she has a bath every day and—over her protests, at first—that she washes her own damn hair. Once was quite enough for me. I order out for groceries. I do the laundry, skid marks and all. Can't seem to bring myself to talk to her about that.

But Lily's meanwhile become more demanding. Can't blame her. She's bored. Television and beads can only go so far. Same for Barbie's two-story Glam Vacation House, Glam Convertible, and Glam Pool and Slide. For a few days she's into her Easy Bake Oven. She masters Barbie's Pretty Pink Cake and goes on to Snow Mounds, Raisin Chocolate Chip Cookies, S'Mores, and Easy Bake Brownies.

All a bit sweet for me. But I pretend to like them fine.

Her Baby Alive doll likewise exerts its pull. Temporarily. She feeds it, bottles it, listens to its inane prattle and changes its diapers. Teddy seems to be acting as surrogate daddy for a while, but I sense his ultimate discouragement. Baby Alive is so screamingly *dull*.

The weather's been fine. She wants to go outside, meet other kids. She wants to go out and play. But other kids are out of the question. When she asks me why, I tell her that you have to go to school to meet other kids and she's not going to school right now. Which puzzles her. But for a while at least she lets it lie.

Zoey wants to go outside too from time to time, I think. Always has. I'll see her gazing out the window, chattering at the birds, or else she'll be peering around my legs at the door. But there are critters out there who'd be all too happy to tear her limb from limb. There are critters of the two-legged variety who'd do the same for Sam.

*Re-tard.*

There's an old rusty swing set and slide left here by the previous owner over by the side of the house. We never use it. But now I set it in order for her. I sand down the rust on the slide, steps, chains, wooden seats, and test the chains. I oil the hangers. I have to solder one of the hangers and two links on the chains but other than that it's in remarkably good shape.

I buff the slide with S.O.S. pads, hose it down to a shine and test it out myself. I land hard on my ass, which makes Lily laugh. *I'll have to get some sand.* She lands gracefully, of course, on both feet and giggling, on a run.

Never mind the sand.

She's happy to be out. Happy with the swing set in particular. Some days she wants me to push her, so I do and it's a curious feeling. It's like I'm playing two roles here at the same time, parent or playmate to the kid who shouts *higher, higher*—but then in our quieter moments it's almost romantic, like we're a new pair of lovers again, doing the kinds of silly kid-things that lovers do.

I think of Sam and me at the amusement park in Kansas City years ago, before we were married, the way she kissed me from a bobbing horse when I managed to grab that brass ring.


Then there's the river.

She wants to know if it's okay to go swim in the river.

There are water moccasins and snapping turtles in there. Snappers are shy usually, but water moccasins can be aggressive as hell. They'll swim right at you. Sam knows enough to look out for them but would Lily? Lily would not. I figure I can be her eyes, though. She wants to swim. It's hot. We've got a dock. Might as well use it.

I still haven't gotten around to transferring Sam's clothes to Lily's room, so I go into her drawer and pick out Sam's favorite two-piece. Cobalt blue. When last seen wearing it she was making guys stumble into their wives at the bar at the Pelican Grove Palms.

While she's putting it on in her bedroom, I pack a cooler with a couple of cold Pepsis for her and three Coronas for me and slap together two bologna and cheese sandwiches. I'm not sure I'm all that hungry but I can always feed the crappie with mine when she's finished swimming.

"Patrick?"

I'm wrapping sandwiches. "Uh-huh?"

"Could you do this?"

She's standing with her back to me. She's got her sandals and bottoms on but the halter's hanging loose from her shoulders.

There's that mole again.

Did I mention that her back comes complete with the Dimples of Venus? Two deep indents on either side of her backbone down low at her hips. I snap together her halter.

"There. You ready? Got the towels?"

"Yup."

We make a stop at the tool shed. Against the possibility of water moccasins, I select a rake with steel tines. You never know.

She's all nervous excited energy. Practically jumping up and down. She runs ahead of me out to the dock and before I've even gotten there she's cannonballed into the silty water. She surfaces smiling and wipes her face and sputters.

"How's the water?"

"It's *freezing!*" Maybe it is, but not enough to stop her.

The water on the river moves with a slow steady current here but she swims easily back to the dock, turns and swims out a bit further and then back again and holds onto the dock kicking her feet behind her and I realize that it's Sam's crawl I've been watching. She remembers perfectly how to swim.

I almost say something, but I don't. Every time I've spoken Sam's name the reaction hasn't been good.

So, I shut up and watch my wife swim.


We do this nearly every day when the weather's good. I'm not about to let her swim in a storm. I have to explain to her about lightening. I don't go in myself; I just sit on the dock with my rake and my cooler and watch her and watch for snakes. I was raised around chlorine swimming pools, and natural water—lakes, rivers, oceans—just don't seem right to me.

I do like to fish, though. And crappie are great eating.

I dig out the fishing rods and the tackle box. Besides crappie, my favorite, you can pull bass and perch from the river. Catfish, of course, if you're bottom fishing. And gar, which look like fucking prehistoric monsters and are vicious on the line. Their bodies are heavily armored and their jaws are filled with long sharp teeth. You catch a gar, you don't touch the damn thing, you cut away the hook, leave it to him as a souvenir. I've seen gar with three or four of them hanging from their jaws like some kind of Goth mouth-jewelry.

You can use practically anything as bait—chicken liver, frozen shad, dough balls—but I prefer nightcrawlers myself. There's a ravine about a half mile from the house and at night after a heavy rain there are hundreds of pale fat bodies wriggling through the grass trying to keep from drowning. All you need is a flashlight and a jar with a perforated lid and some dirt inside and you'll have your bait in no time.

So that's what we do.

Sam never liked this part. I mostly did it alone. But Lily's delighted at discovering this strange living world writhing under our flashlights at her feet. Even more so at finding some of them stuck together. I'm not going to try to explain to her about hermaphroditism.

She has no problem at all picking one up, examining up-close and then dropping in the jar. The problem comes the following day when we start to fish.

She *hates* worming the hook. Won't have any part of it. Hates to watch me doing it too.

She's feeling the worm's pain.

I always wondered exactly how much pain is really involved in this. It's not as though a worm has much in the way of a nervous system. But it's important to push the hook through the flesh of the worm several times so it doesn't slip off in the water. Usually, three will do. But after the first invasion of that flesh the writhing can get pretty intense. As though the worm were angry, indignant at this unwarranted piercing. You can look at the worm and imagine you're seeing torture up close and personal.

Lily really can't stand to watch. So, our fishing expedition is a short one. We go home with a perch and two crappies.

I guess that'll do.


When Doc calls, I'm unprepared for it.

It's past 10:00 A.M. I've just gotten up. I've slept late again. I'm on my first cup of coffee. Yesterday was our grocery delivery and some of the Frosted Flakes Lily requested are scattered across the kitchen table. Bowl's in the sink, though, so I suppose that's something.

"I just spoke with Trish Cacek," he says.

*Doctor* Cacek. The shrink.

"She says you haven't brought her in."

"No. I haven't."

"Why's that?"

"I want to wait, Doc. See if she comes back on her own."

"I'd advise against that, Patrick. She needs to be in therapy. You seeing *any* improvement at all?"

"Sometimes a look, a gesture. She was yelling in her sleep a few nights ago and I could swear the voice was Sam's. But you know, we don't sleep in the same room anymore, in our room, and by the time I got there she was asleep again."

He sighs. "Take her to Dr. Cacek, Patrick. You can't do this alone. You're too close to it. How are *you* holding up, anyway?"

"I'm fine."

I'm staring at the Frosted Flakes.

"I'm really just fine. We're doing stuff together. Things we used to do. We watched *Sleepless in Seattle* night before last. One of her favorite movies."

"And?"

"Well, she paid attention. Smiled at the end."

"I'll say this once again. You're too close to this. It's not good for either of you. Get her into therapy."

"I'll think about it, Doc. Honestly, I will. I want to try, though, just a little while longer. Thanks for calling. Appreciate it."

We hang up. I wipe down the table. Sit and drink my coffee.

I'm unprepared for the second call too. It's not a half hour later. I'm just finishing the dishes.

"Hello?"

"Hi, Patrick."

"Oh. Hi, Miriam."

"How are you? How's she doing?"

"Better. A little better, maybe."

"Good. That's great. Can I say hi? Just a quick hello? And I promise not to talk shop."

"I don't think so, Miriam."

I'm tempted to put Lily on the line. Miriam's a good lady but she's being nosy. I can hear it in her voice. Two minutes with Lily would give her plenty to talk about down at the office.

And now Zoey's standing in the kitchen doorway, yowling, her toy—her little stuffed tuxedo-cat—sprawled at her feet. Thought I'd hid the damn thing.

"Good god, what's that?"

"Our cat, Zoey. She does this sometimes."

"Sounds like somebody's murdering her. So, can I talk to Sam?"

Insistent. Zoey's insistent too.

"Not a good time, Miriam."

"Will you have her call me, then? We're concerned about her."

"I know. Wait. What do you mean?"

"We're ... concerned. That's all."

"I'm taking care of her, Miriam. I'm not holding her prisoner or anything."

"I didn't mean … of course you're not. Just … have her call me when she's up to it, okay?"

"Yes. Fine. I will. 'Bye."

I reach down and grab up the toy. Zoey gives one last long yowl as it disappears behind my back and into the pocket of my jeans.

I don't know whether it's Miriam's call or Doc's call or Zoey's whining or all three of them together but right now I'm boiling.

I take a few deep breaths and sit back down at the kitchen table. Zoey ambles over.

It's not her. It's never her. I stroke her fur.

I just touch her.


Lily's outside playing with her Barbies in the sandbox I built for her, pretending it's a beach and the girls are out sunbathing drinking piña coladas or whatever Barbies drink these days while I'm at the drafting table trying to figure out what the hell is wrong here. *Everything* looks wrong to me now, not just Samantha's look and Doctor Gypsum's and the various loathsome members of the Abominations' League but perspective again, the framing of the panels strikes me as flat, dull, something I could have done better twenty years ago. I'm well into the third act and it's just not working for me.

I keep thinking of that conversation with Miriam. *I'm not holding her prisoner or anything.* Where the fuck did that come from? Why did I have to say that?

Screw this. This isn't going anywhere.

I lean out the window.

"Hey, Lily! Want to go for a swim?"

She looks up, seems unsure at first. Maybe I was a little loud.

"Okay, Patrick."

"Suit up."

Skippy peanut butter and Smucker's Concord Grape this time. I've got them wrapped and packed away in the cooler along with the beer and Pepsi but still no Lily.

She's not in her room. She's not in the bathroom. I peer into mine. Found her.

"What's up, Lily?"

She's been in the bedroom drawers. Sam's drawers. She holds an orange and yellow two-piece out to me.

"Could I wear this one instead of the blue?"

"Whatever one you want."

"This one's pretty."

"Well. You should wear it, then."

She opens the closet door. Sam's closet. Fingers a strapless blue and white silk dress. Sam bought it in New York City.

"All this stuff," she says. "It's really, really pretty. Do you think I could play dress-up later, maybe?"

There's a buzzing in my head. A disconnect. I think she says something else to me. I'm not sure.

"What?"

"Later maybe, Patrick? After the swim?"

"I … I guess so. Yeah, if you want. All right. Go put on your suit."

She hurries out of the room and I'm left standing there looking at Sam's clothes hanging neatly in the closet and disheveled where Lily's been pawing through the open drawers.

I'll straighten them out. Only not just now.


I'm halfway through my first beer when I see the snake.

The beer hits the deck and I'm up on my feet with the rake in my hands and it's coming toward her, its body a black undulating streak in the water behind a raised head as it rises over a drifting branch and she doesn't see it, doesn't even know it's there and I'm yelling *Sam! Lily! Get out of the water! Get out of the water NOW!* and she hears the panic in my voice and looks confused but starts swimming anyway, Sam's powerful stroke, yet the damn thing's gaining on her, no more than ten feet away.

*Faster, Lily!* I yell and bless her she really pours it on so that she hits the side of the dock and starts to hoist herself up just as it raises its fucking head to strike but I lash it with the steel tines of the rake. It writhes furiously in the roiling water and tries to bite, the snow-white mouth hitting the wooden handle just above the tines and Lily's out of the water now watching wide-eyed as I flip the rake around and bring it down again and again on its back, on its goddamn head, until at last the snake's had enough and turns and glides away.

I drop the rake as though it's poisonous.

I'm shaking so hard it's hard to stand so I don't even try. I drop down beside her on the dock, our feet dangling over the muddy water. Lily pulls hers in as though that thing still might be out there somewhere.

The look on her face is pure shock. She reaches out for me and I reach out for her and then I'm hugging her wet body tight to mine and we're both of us trembling in a sudden cold wind of our own devise.


"Anything I want?"

"Uh-huh."

It's about two hours later and Lily's at the bedroom closet. Seems she's forgotten all about the snake. I sure haven't.

Sam's got a half dozen conservative suits for work front and center in the closet, but she pushes those aside to get at the more interesting stuff in back. She turns to the drawers and opens and closes them one at a time, inspecting them.

"You go 'way now," she says. "I'll come when I'm ready."

I grab a beer from the fridge and plant myself on the couch in front of the TV and watch a rerun of *Bones* and I think how Sam used to enjoy that show, even though it was utter hokum—the day a medical examiner partnered up with a detective in the field was the day Wall Street worried about ethics. But that was part of the fun. That and snappy dialogue and the charisma and chemistry of the two leads. I think about us early on, Sam and me, when we first started dating. How people used to say that when we walked in, we lit up the room.

My understanding is that mismatched clothing is all the rage with the kids these days but when she comes out grinning with a flourish and a *ta-da!* I can't help it, I have to laugh. She's got on woolen knee-socks, one green with yellow polka dots, one blue and red with alternating wide stripes. She's teetering on a pair of black brushed leather three-inch heels. The dress is shiny red satin, sleeveless, with a scoop neck, cut to just above the knee. Ralph Lauren. I was with her in Tulsa when she bought it.

She's wearing Sam's three-strand, nickel and black agate necklace, her turquoise necklace, her red coral necklace and her fossil bead necklace, a brown and yellow camouflage-pattern silk scarf, and a pair of long white gloves with pretty much every ring in Sam's drawer slipped over them. And to top it all off, Sam's wide-brimmed floppy straw sunhat.

"Well?" she says.

"You look … stunning," I manage.

"You like my shoes? You like my dress? You like my hat?"

"I like all of it."

And I do. Just not necessarily all at the same time.

She turns around and back again a couple of times just like they do on the TV fashion shows, I guess. A kind of awkward pirouette.

"Wait! I'm gonna do it again."

She half-rushes, half-staggers back to our bedroom.

I think about her put-together, about what she's selected. At first it makes me smile and then I realize something. Together they're all wrong. Together they're the *Clash of the Titans*.

*But each piece individually is one of Sam's favorites. Every one.*

I picture her standing with the bedroom door closed gazing into the full-length mirror on the door, choosing her selections. I asked her once, a week or more ago, what she sees when she looks into a mirror. Wondering, did she see a little girl? "*Me, silly*," she said and shrugged and wouldn't say anything further.

But what's she seeing now? Bits of Sam? Bits of Sam's history, her likes and dislikes, her memory?

It gives me an idea. I go hunting around in our collection of DVDs until I find it. A couple of years ago we converted a box full of VCR tapes, early home movies, to DVD. Since the photo album was such a flop, I'd never bothered to play them for her. But what if it were all a matter of timing? What if she simply wasn't ready then? What if she is now?

It's exciting. Definitely worth a shot.

I key up the DVD player and wait.

When she comes out, I'm floored. But this time I'm not laughing.

Her wedding dress. It was in a box on the top shelf in the closet. She's standing in front of me in her wedding dress.

All the jewelry's gone except our wedding ring which she's been wearing all the time throughout all this and seems to think nothing of, like it's part of her. But she's looking strangely shy. As though the dress has power, as though the dress has tamed her somehow.

It's floor-length, lace, with delicate spaghetti straps and a modest train. It's supposed to hug her body from breasts to hips, but it doesn't quite do that because Lily's not managed the buttons up top. She's holding the veil out to me.

"What's this for, Patrick?" she says.

It's a moment before I can speak. I go to her and take the veil.

"It goes in your hair. Like this."

I arrange the comb in her hair and spread the veil down first over her face which makes her smile and wrinkle her nose and then back over her back and shoulders. I step away.

"You look ... beautiful."

"I do?" She's delighted.

"Yes, you do. And you don't know that, do you."

"Know what?"

"That you're beautiful."

"You think?"

"I think."

Her expression is serious all of a sudden. Then, "You're silly, Patrick," she says, and turns to head back to the bedroom.

"Wait. Come here. Sit down a minute. I want to show you something."

I pick up the remote to turn on the DVD player while she sits down next to Zoey curled up on the couch. The dress slides up a bit. I see that she's barefoot.

Zoey seems to regard her lap and the dress as a possible nesting place but apparently decides she's comfortable where she is.

"You need anything? A Pepsi or anything?"

"Nope."

"I'm gonna go grab a beer. Wait right here, okay?"

"Okay."

I do and she does.

I've orchestrated our home videos with old rock and country songs and the occasional show tune. I know exactly where I want to go with this because there she is beside me on the couch, sitting there *in her goddamn wedding dress* so I fast-forward through our first trip to the Big Apple with Gene Kelly and Frank Sinatra and Jules Munshin squeaking their way through *New York, New York, it's a wonderful town* and there's the Empire State Building and the Chrysler Building and Sam eating a huge pastrami sandwich at the Carnegie Deli and gazing out over the city from the second of the doomed Twin Towers and then we hit the fireworks here in Tulsa, our first fourth of July together, and she says *wait, stop.*

I hit PLAY. Fireworks bore me to tears now though not as much back then. But Lily's interested. The music is the Beatles' "For the Benefit of Mr. Kite" which is something, at least. Still, I want to get on with it. I let her watch for a while and then fast-forward again. And there we are at Yellowstone, "where hell bubbles up," and Tom Petty's singing "Saving Grace" sounding like Alvin's Chipmunks while we're viewing geysers and waterfalls, pools of emerald water and turquoise water, incredible sunsets—and from a distance, a herd of grazing bison. There's Sam in her cutoffs in the foreground, smiling and pointing out at them.

Next, we're in Kansas City at Worlds of Fun Amusement Park. There she is opposite me on the Ferris wheel, on her bobbing yellow horse on that merry-go-round where I snagged the ring, screaming bloody murder on the roller coaster and *wait wait wait go back!* Lily says so I rewind to the roller coaster again, my aim with the video camera jiggly as hell, Willie Nelson doing "On the Road Again" while Sam screams silent screams and Lily giggles beside me.

The giggling unnerves me. I want her to wake up, snap out of it. That's what this is for. Instead, she's giggling.

The bumper cars are next. *Ooooo* she says, and claps her hands, fascinated, so I know there's no point in fast-forwarding. She'll only want to go back again.

She's pulled the veil down over her face and she's chewing on it absentmindedly.

On the screen Sam's getting battered from all sides. She's getting creamed. I remember this. Sam was talking to another woman, a parent, about something or other while we were standing in line waiting to ride. There were a bunch of kids behind me, maybe ten of them, all ages, and I turned and got their attention, waving my arms and then pointing to Sam and mouthing *get her!* which made them laugh.

And which they did.

When the segment's over Sam and I are at Broken Bow Lake and it's beautiful and Sam's in her cobalt blue two-piece but I want to get through this so I fast-forward through Roy Orbison's "Blue Bayou" and finally we're there.

At the wedding.

And I'm wondering, does this have a chance in hell of beating out the bumper cars?

But it's uncanny, it's as though I knew back then when I was putting this video thing together that this was going to be important someday. Because I've emphasized it. I've left it utterly, completely silent. No scoring. Just us.

It's a professional behind the camera so the shots are tight, focused, not jittery like my own. So there we are on this nice sunny July day in front of St. John's Episcopal, my own limo pulling up first and me getting out in my tux with my best man McPheeters, both of us grinning, the three Johnny Walkers doing their work on us, and even my brother is smiling for a change, saying something that my groomsmen Joe Manotta and Harry Grazier seem to find actually funny.

It cuts to my mom and Sam's mom being seated by the ushers and I look to her for some sign of recognition but there isn't any, none at all. Next thing I'm standing at the altar with McPheeters watching my brother, Joe and Harry escort Miriam and Sam's two pretty college roommates down the aisle, trailed by our cute little flower girl—I forget her name—very serious about the business of tossing her rose petals *just so*.

Then the moment I'm waiting for. Sam, arriving in front of the church and stepping out of her limo and then beaming on her father's arm, *in the dress*, moving slowly down the aisle.

It's hard to look away but I do. I need to watch Lily.

And I'm rewarded.

She leans forward, intent. She's hardly blinking. She lifts the veil.

I remember this part from the tape. The photographer actually irritated her father slightly by focusing almost entirely on his daughter's face. Almost nothing of him or the priest or the actual ceremony. Even I got short shrift. But I never could blame the guy. It was no wonder he was captivated. Sam was standing bathed that day in a single streak of gentle flame-red light, glowing through a stained-glass window.

This is what Lily's seeing.

I glance at the screen. I know what's next. The ring. The kiss.

I don't watch the kiss, but Lily does. She looks puzzled. Her eyes go to me and then back to the screen and her lips seem almost to be forming words or the beginnings of words, her eyes flicker.

They go to the gown and back to the screen again.

*Come on*, I'm thinking, *come on*.

And then the silence breaks apart into a million pieces and Kris Kristofferson and Willie are singing "Loving You Was Easier," our song back then, and I know we're on the dance floor at the reception, our first dance together as husband and wife, and Lily leans back on the couch more relaxed now while Kris is singing about coming close together with a feeling he's never known before in his time, and I turn to the screen in time to see that second kiss which is just as public as the first one, with everyone watching us tinkling their knives against their wine glasses but this one's real, I remember this one all right, I can almost feel it, this one's just for us, just between us two people so much in love and there's nobody in the room at all but Sam and me.

I begin to sob into my hands. Can't stop it. Can't stop shaking. It's like every moment of the past two weeks is flooding through me all at once, pouring out of me, all these moments away from her and it isn't fair, it isn't right.

"Patrick? Patrick, what's wrong?"

*And the voice is Sam's voice.*

I feel like a jolt of electricity. It's almost the same as when I saw that snake. I've done it! I can't fucking believe it!

"Sam! Jesus, Sam! Sam!"

I reach for her but she's up and off the couch so fast I don't even come close.

"*I! Am! Not! SAM!*" she screams, her face a twisted mask of frustration and anger and goddammit it's suddenly Lily again, Lily in full-bore tantrum mode as she bats my beer bottle off the table, tears away the fireplace screen and flings it across the room, sweeps my John D. MacDonald books off the mantle and as I'm standing trying to grab hold of her and talk to her saying god knows what to try to calm her down as she throws the standing lamp so hard against the wall that the light bulb explodes sending Zoey into a panic so that she leaps off the couch landing hard on her arthritic legs, skitters across the floor and races out of the room.

Lily's screeching loud and high as she tears my framed Jack Kirby print of *Hulk Comics #1* that I've had since I was seventeen off the wall and smashes it to the floor and she's barefoot and glass is everywhere—I never want to hear that screech again as long as I live, it's like an animal in pain—and then I hear another crash coming from the study.

"Stay there," I tell her. I'm thinking about the glass. "Don't move."

I know what I've got to do. My being here's no good. My being here's making it worse. She's looking at me like she'd like to strangle me, tear my head from my shoulders so I back off and head for the study. At least I can see if my cat's all right. So that's what I do.

I hear the coffee table go over behind me.

In the study, the first thing I see is my LightPad smashed beside the drafting table and my pages scattered all across the floor. There's Zoey huddled in the far corner of the room beneath the window. She must have made a leap for the high ground and failed. Glass crunches underfoot as I go to her, reach down. She cringes. But I persist.

"Hey, girl. It's all right. It's okay. It's all right."

It's not all right at all but in a moment or two she relents and lets me touch her, stroke her back, scratch her head. Her eyes soften.

I'm hearing nothing from the living room so I'm hoping the worst is over. I figure I'll give it a little more time just to be sure.

I crouch beside the drafting table to gather up my pages and the world suddenly tilts on me, nearly sends me down to all fours.

I'm staring at the pages.

I'm looking at Doctor Gypsum and Samantha.

Only I'm *not* looking at Doctor Gypsum and Samantha.

I'm looking at myself. Myself and Lily.

In every frame. I've drawn us exactly. Our faces, our bodies. Lily's and mine.

Battling the Abominations League. Stepping out of the rubble of an old building, wounded, taking shelter, healing. More battles, more wounds. Whirling through space. Diving deep into the safety of the sea.

I've been doing this every day for weeks now.

I stare at the pages and feel a weariness I've never known.

I gather them up and place them carefully on the table.

Then turn and leave the room.

Lily's standing where I left her. The table overturned beside her. The living room is a shambles. There's an acrid electric smell in the air.

She's naked. The wedding dress lies torn and crumbled at her feet. And she's cut herself. On the hem of her dress are three drops and one long bright smear of blood.

She's crying softly. Her shoulders trembling.

"Lily."

"I'm not Sam," she says.

Only gently this time. Almost, I think, with regret.

"I know," I tell her. "I know."

And then a moment later, "Don't move. I'll come to you."

I cross the room and sweep her carefully up into my arms. Her face is still wet with tears against my cheek as I carry her into our bedroom. I lay her down on the bed and have a look at the cut on her foot. It's not too bad. I go to the bathroom for sterile pads and peroxide, bandages and bacitracin. I tend to the wound.

The night's warm. She makes no move for the covers.

I lie down beside her and look into her eyes and she looks into mine. I don't know what she sees there but she holds my gaze and doesn't turn away. I'm not sure what I see in her eyes either. I think of Sam and I think of Lily. But in a little while I reach over.

It's perhaps a blessing, this thing I have, and perhaps a curse. I've always thought blessing but now I'm not so sure.

I know exactly how to touch her.

I know how to touch.

# MY PEOPLE

## LULU L. WONG

My people sew in sweatshops, getting paid by the piece,
who were once OB/GYN surgeons, architects, engineers
in the old country.

My people hid in jungles, ate rats, to escape the Killing Fields.

My people arrived on Angel Island as paper sons,
with $2 in their pockets, and worked three jobs
washing dishes, laundering clothes, sweeping the floors at Google.

My people wrote stories about Women Warriors and slayers of demons.

My people founded Yahoo, Zoom, Alibaba, created Google Maps.

(Some of) My people have worked hard to achieve white privilege,
like the daughter of the peasant with no shoes
who graduates from Yale, magna cum laude.

And yet, the daughter who dreams of being the next Maxine Hong Kingston
is told by the peasant father,
there ain't no trust fund to pay you rent, baby girl.

My people are diverse, ambitious, resilient.

My people—model minority or salvo to divide people of color?

# THERE ARE NO BASEMENTS IN THE BIBLE

## JOSH MALERMAN

The overburdened mother dragged the son across the street by his wrist, unaware she was delivering him to a place with far darker potentialities than the loneliness she feared he'd experience if left home alone.

She dragged him to the new neighbor's house to play.

"Oh, for God's sake, Maxie." She knelt in the middle of the street, licked her thumb and flattened a cowlick in his black hair. "They're gonna think we don't bathe. You look dirty. Come on. Don't make me be this kind of mom."

"I'm not doing anything."

"But you are." The hair popped back up. She flattened it again. "*Think* for a second. Think for me. I need you to make friends. I need you to make *one* friend. That's all I'm asking for here. We don't have money for a babysitter. And I can't work from home. Capiche?"

"Yeah."

"One friend, Max. And this feels like a winner."

They reached the curb and stopped to look at the house. The big blue cross on the front door wasn't the only element that spoke of lives lived differently than Max and Golda Stein. The bright white shutters, the spotless welcome mat, the pruned bushes and manicured lawn. The cutout of an Easter egg hanging in the front bay window.

His mother frowned.

"What's his name again?" she asked.

"Christian. Christian Dove."

"I mean ... are you kidding?"

"I'm not."

"Jesus, Max."

"Mom."

"Okay. One friend."

She didn't need to drag him now as he walked beside her, from the street up onto the grass, then the sidewalk, and the weedless concrete path to the swept front steps.

"I don't think we've ever looked as Jewish as we do right now," she said. Then, "But you know what they say: opposites attract."

Up the steps to the door.

She eyed the bell.

"If your father still lived with us, we wouldn't have this problem." She fixed her own hair in the reflection in the smudgeless storm door. "But you know … fuck him."

The inner door opened before she rang it.

His Mother smiled. Her words still ringing, it seemed, even as the blonde woman behind the glass smiled in return. The woman eyed Max momentarily before returning to her. She didn't open the door when she asked:

"Can I help you?"

"Hi!" his mother said. Full-cheer now. "We're new in town. Just moved in across the street." She thumbed over her shoulder. Behind her, boxes covered the front porch of hers and Max's new home. The doors to the Escort still open in the drive.

"Oh," the woman said. She placed a hand over her chest. *Silly me*, she seemed to say. But Max thought he saw a little more there. Something like, *How did these two end up affording the same street as us?*

She opened the storm door.

"Welcome."

"Max tells me you have a son?"

"A son?" The woman eyed Max as if he were the IRS. "Why, yes. We do. And I'm Peggy. Peggy Dove."

Max could almost hear what these names were doing to his mom. People who believed in Jesus was one thing: *Christian* and *Peggy Dove* was another.

"I was hoping Max and Christian might get along," she said. "We're new, he needs friends. I'm sure Christian does, too. Anybody does, right? Ha. So why not just skip to the chase."

Peggy fingered the gold cross flat to her white blouse.

"Who's there?" a man called from farther in the house.

Max looked past Peggy as the man stepped down from a chair flush to an empty wall. His white shirt matched his wife's blouse.

"Michael," Peggy said. "New neighbors. They have a son."

Michael Dove looked to Max. Looked to his mother. Said, "Oh," and stepped out of view.

"I'll just get right to it. I could use a place to put Max today. I've gotta get to work and we don't have a nanny, or day care, we don't really know anyone yet. I'm not sure what else to do and I was hoping you guys might help. I seriously don't mean to sound like a mooch, the first time we meet. I at least like to hide that until the second."

A beat of silence. Then Peggy smiled.

"Oh," she said. "Oh, you're funny."

His mother half-bowed.

"Is Christian home?" Max interrupted.

"Good question, Max," his mother said. "Yes. Is he? And if so … would he wanna play with Max?"

Down the hall beyond Peggy, a door opened. A young face appeared, blond hair, a white shirt like Mom and Dad's, his buttoned to the neck.

He waved, stoic-faced, to Max. Max waved back.

"Christian?" Peggy asked. "Would you …" She eyed them again, as if deciding upon something. "Would you like to play with the new neighbor boy?"

Christian only stared at Max.

"How long will you be gone?" Peggy asked.

"Well, ha, I don't expect you to host him all day. Just like … a few hours?"

Peggy touched the cross at her chest. Turned to Christian again.

Michael Dove peered around the corner at the end of the hall. "Christian?"

Golda held her breath. Max could practically hear her hoping.

"Okay," Christian said.

"Okay! Great. Talk about good neighbors. I'm not sure how to thank you other than to say … thank you."

"It's our pleasure," Peggy said.

Golda knelt beside Max.

"So, why don't you be the gentleman you are and say thank you and promise me you'll behave the whole time you're here?"

Max looked to Peggy. To Christian at the open basement door. To where Michael had been peering around the far corner but was no longer.

"Thank you," he said.

Golda got up. She patted Max on his back, and he understood it meant he should go meet Christian in the hall.

He passed Peggy on the way, smelled the soap of her. And something else, too. Something like matches extinguished.

"Hi," Max said, extending a hand to the blond boy. "I'm Max Stein. That's my mom, Golda."

"I'm Christian Dove."

"I know."

"How did you know my name?"

"When my mom brought me to the school, to show me around, someone in the office saw our address. Said we lived right across from the Doves and that they had a boy my age. Christian. You."

Christian smiled and it was the first genuine smile Max had seen all day. His mother's was made of worry. And Peggy's … he didn't know yet.

"Are you any good at video games?" Christian asked.

"Yes. Very. What games do you have?"

"Tons."

"Wanna go to your room?"

"The basement," Peggy called. "Play in the basement only, Christian. Absolutely nowhere else."

Michael rounded the corner, his white shirtsleeves rolled to his elbows. A flashlight in one hand.

Max looked to the chair facing the empty wall.

"Come on," Christian said, taking Max by the hand. "Let's see how good you really are."

He led Max down the basement steps, but not before Max got one more look at his mother talking to Peggy again, slipping him a little wave and a relieved shrug, as if to say, *So it all worked out. Good. Good for us that it all worked out.*

One last look before the basement door closed behind him.


Shelves.

That's all Max could see: the rows of shelves that lead from the finished part of the Dove basement to the unfinished (and unlit) beyond. From where he sat, on the brown couch on the brown carpet (this like an island in the concrete basement; silver steel support beams and poles), he saw tools on the shelves. Metals objects he and his mom didn't have much of yet. The extra items a family accumulates while living in one place for a long time. Back home, at their new home, they had a single toolbox, still unpacked. And if something were to break? Well, it might stay that way for a while.

"Dad is handy," Christian said. He held two controllers in his hand, the cords flowed from the carpeted square to the base of the TV, to the game system there.

Max eyed the far side of the shelves, the dark perspective pointing where the aisles they made ended.

It was unsettling if you let it be.

But the sudden blue light from the TV brought him back to the couch, and to Christian.

"My dad couldn't change a tire," Max said.

"Really?"

"Yeah. One time we got stuck up north forever because Dad couldn't figure it out. Mom was pretty upset about it."

"Why didn't she just do it?"

"She's no better at that kind of thing." Then, "But if I had to put money on who would survive in the wilderness on their own, I'd take her over him."

"I see. You ready?"

Max looked to the screen. A title card with bright yellow letters: *Siren Light.*

"Holy shit!" Max said. "You have *Siren Light!*"

"I do," Christian said. He looked to the exposed pipes and beams in the ceiling. "But let's not swear like that."

Max reddened a bit.

"Really?"

Christian smiled kindly. "I'm not sure how it is in your religion," he said, "but it's a no-no for us."

"Okay."

"You got it?" Christian asked.

"Got it."

"Cool. Fucker."

Max turned to him, eyes wide.

And the boys laughed.

And they started their game.

Above, the ceiling creaked. Someone stood there.

"It's actually a tough one," Christian said, flipping through potential avatars.

"Good," Max said. "The easy ones are boring."

Above, a thud. Michael's voice, raised.

Max looked up.

"I agree," Christian said. "But within reason. Right?"

Peggy's voice, responding. Raised.

Max stared at the beams.

The Doves, he understood, were arguing.

"I mean, I love games," Christian said, "but I don't wanna spend my entire summer trying to win one."

Max opened his mouth to respond but the voices above got louder, and the ceiling creaked, and Max heard the word ghost.

When he looked to Christian, Christian was looking at him, too.

"Are you paying attention?" Christian asked.

"What? Yes. Yeah. I agree. I don't wanna play one game all summer, either."

Christian looked past him then, to the shelves.

"We *do* have board games," Christian said. "If you'd rather."

"Me? No way. I've been wanting to play *Siren Light* forever."

"Why didn't you just get it then?"

Max didn't hesitate: "Because it's expensive."

"Yeah, but if we live on the same street, we must have the same money. Or thereabouts. Right?"

Max considered this.

Had he heard the word right? Did Michael Dove say *ghost?*

"I guess so," he said. "But my mom, she's a single mother now."

"Ah. Can I ask you something?"

"Of course."

"Are you Jewish?"

"I am."

"I thought so. And aren't Jewish people really good with money?"

Max laughed. "Mom? Good with money? Oh boy."

Christian didn't smile though, and Max let himself get more serious about it.

"Naw, not all Jewish people."

"And the house?"

"Mom's mom and dad helped."

"Ah."

Upstairs, quiet now.

"Well," Christian said. "Let's see if we can't kick *Siren Light*'s ass together."

They settled deeper into the couch. But as Christian set up the avatars, and told Max what he knew of the game, Max glanced once more to the shelves.

And he wondered if he and his mom would ever have so much stuff that they needed aisles of shelves, such long aisles that they bridged the distance between light and darkness.


He told his mom about the Doves' argument over dinner. They sat at the kitchen table; a small one they'd been gifted by a friend of hers at her last job. The living room harbored their unopened boxes and what furniture they had, some of it still on its side. She wore her work pin, her name in green on a yellow plastic card.

She'd had the fork halfway to her mouth when Max told her what he'd heard.

"Hey," she said. "Don't turn this into a thing."

"I'm not."

"I know you, Maxie. Next, you're gonna say you don't wanna go over there because they argue. Well, too bad."

"I didn't say that. I had fun. I guess. With Christian."

"Damn straight you did. Look at the option."

They both looked to the boxes.

"Whatever," Max said. "They just … argued, is all."

"So?"

"I don't know. Worse than when you and Dad argued."

"Really? How so?"

"I don't know." But he did. "Well, for starters, they were trying to be quiet about it. You and Dad never did that."

"No, we sure didn't."

"And I guess I like it better that way. Like, you're not hiding anything when you yell about it."

"Don't you think they were being quiet because they had company?"

"I don't know if they had company."

She finally forked the food into her mouth and smiled. But it wasn't easy to laugh and chew at the same time.

"*You*," she said. "*You* were the company, Maxie!"

"Oh. Right."

Max reddened. But not so much. It was funny. Yet, it also made sense. He hadn't felt much like company while he was at the Doves'. He felt more like a spectator, listening to the family from a room away. As if he was outside the theater doors and had to wait until intermission to be allowed back into the movie.

"What were they arguing about?" she asked.

"I don't know. We were in the basement."

"The whole time?"

"Yeah."

"Literally?"

"Yeah."

"Didn't you guys have any snacks or anything? Not that I'm being picky. Believe me."

"Yeah. Peggy came downstairs with pretzels and dip."

"What kind of dip?"

"Ranch."

She rolled her eyes.

"Well, that's something."

"I heard the word *ghost*," Max said. The way he said it, like he'd been wanting to say it, wanting to hear how it sounded out of his mouth, out of his head.

Bur his mother didn't seem to think anything of it.

"That's it? *Ghost?* That could be anything. Literally."

"I know."

They ate. His mother looked to the living room, eyeing the box with the stereo stored in bubble wrap.

"I gotta work tomorrow again," she said. She leaned back in her chair. "You think it's too much to go over there again?"

Max shrugged.

"I could stay here. Empty the boxes. We gotta do it eventually."

She smiled.

"You're a good kid, Maxie. A really good kid." She reached over and patted his hand. "But still, you're *just* on the other side of too young to be trusted alone in an empty house with valuables boxed up and nails and screws lying around."

"I won't get hurt."

"Probably not. But … maybe one more day with the Doves? Then we can unpack together tomorrow night. Do it right."

"Okay."

He thought of *Siren Light*. How they'd made it pretty far. It didn't sound like the worst idea, going for it, trying to win it tomorrow.

She got up and carried their take-out boxes to the kitchen sink. Max got up, too, crossed the living room, stood at the window, eyed the Doves' across the street.

"Hey, they're up," he said to himself.

Inside, a single flashlight roamed the otherwise dark space. Max thought of Michael Dove holding that light.

Was their power out?

Max went to the living room wall and turned on the light to test it. Then, he turned it off quick, irrationally fearful that the Doves might see into their home.

Through the window he saw the flashlight go off. And the Dove house went dark. It felt not unlike the two houses had winked at one another from across the street, both saying, *Goodnight.*

But winks, Max knew, often implied a deeper knowledge. Like, wink-wink. Like, uh huh, okay. Like, sure.

*Goodnight.*

*Sure.*

*Okay.*

*Goodnight.*


"Wanna have a staring contest?" Christian asked. They'd been playing *Siren Light* for less than an hour but it was clear neither were as into it as they were the day before. And while Peggy Dove had seemed relieved to see Max at the door (she vocalized how much it meant to her for Christian to be "occupied" today), she'd also seemed distracted. Max heard someone else knock not long after he'd come downstairs.

*Company*, Max thought then.

"Sure," Max said. "What are the rules?"

Christian got up off the couch.

"Come," he said.

Max followed him to the edge of the brown carpet, where Christian sat, cross-legged.

"Come," Christian said again, and Max sat facing him. Facing the shelves and the far side of the basement, too.

"No blinking," Christian said. "And obviously no looking away."

"That's it?"

"Yes, but …" Christian's eyes glittered the way people's eyes do when they're excited to reveal the catch. "How much experience do you have with staring contests?"

"Well, not much."

"Okay. Have you ever stared into the mirror long enough that your face changes, that you look like someone else?"

A muffled voice from above. The person they let in, no doubt. A man? Max thought so.

He smelled something familiar, too. Something like a mix of a cigarette and thanksgiving.

"No," Max said. "I guess I'm not obsessed with my own face enough for that?"

"Ha," Christian said. "Funny. But it's true. It happens. If you stare at something long enough without blinking, that thing will look like something else. Something entirely new. Something that shouldn't be in the room with you."

Max looked over Christian's head to the aisles of shelves. Above, the visitor sounded like he was giving instructions.

"Who's here?" Max asked.

Christian looked up. Shrugged.

"You don't know?"

"You ready?"

"Um, yes."

But was he? Had Christian been warning him of something? No. But still, that's how it felt.

"Okay," Christian said. "No matter how my face changes, you can't look away. Even if you totally believe it's not me sitting here anymore facing you. Okay?"

"Okay."

"Okay." Christian intentionally blinked many times and wiped his eyes. Max did the same. Then Christian said, "On three. One … two …"

A heavy thud from above. The man's voice. And had Christian said the number three? He must have, the way he was staring into Max's eyes.

Max stared back, without blinking.

He discovered, immediately, a groove in this game. He didn't feel the need to blink at all. Not yet. Maybe it was because of that smell, here again. Thanksgiving stuffing. No, mint. No … a variation of the weird cigarettes Dad used to smoke when he got home from work. Yes. Something candle about it, too. Max focused on that. And the movement above. Sounded like they were slowly sliding furniture across the room. It was hard not to nervously smile, it being so still down below despite the low hum of the furnace coming from the dark path made by the shelves; tools, papers, and boxes, yes, boxes and boxes of who knows what. Max could just make out those boxes (not unlike the boxes still taped shut in the living room of his own home across the street), could just determine that's what they were in his peripheral vision as he remained focused, and unblinking, on Christian. He could hear Christian breathing, too. And the sound mingled with the scent from above as if Christian's breath were this burning weed, this aroma both calming and unsettling at once. Did the shelves end there? In the dark? Where he thought they should? How much space between the end of the shelves and the far basement wall? Hard to say. Harder to see. Especially without looking. Yet, that's just what Max was doing: *looking* into the corner of his vision while keeping his eyes on Christian.

It looked like Christian was holding in a smile, too, as the corners of his lips rose, the smallest bit, so that, to Max, it almost looked like he was made of rubber now.

But Max didn't look away.

Not even when he heard distinct footfalls in the hall at the top of the basement steps. Not even when he heard the conversation from above, nor when the smell got stronger and the image of Christian breathing that smoke got stronger, too.

"Sage," a voice said. Man? Woman? So hard to tell, a dual tone, the door between the speaker and Max, the distance, too, down the steps, across the basement, all the way to the carpeted island where the boys sat facing each other, their features, yes, taken for granted, now changing, as neither relinquished with a blink.

"What are they doing up there?" Max asked.

Because he had to.

And: "What's 'sage'?"

"I'm not falling for any chit chat," Christian said. His face was waxy white now. "That's exactly how you get someone to blink."

"I wasn't …"

Something moved in Max's peripheral vision.

In the far corner of his eye.

"Christian …"

Down an aisle of shelves.

"Christian …"

"I'm no fool."

Someone stood back there. Max could make out a complete silhouette where one had not been.

"Do you have a sister?" Max asked.

He meant it.

"Not doing it," Christian said.

The wax of Christian's face drooping now. His face longer. Just those two eyes holding their place.

"Sage," someone said again, above.

Max tried to define the silhouette without looking directly at it.

"Is there a coat rack back there?' Max asked.

His eyes started burning.

But he didn't want this game to end.

He didn't want permission to look.

"Why?" Christian asked. A smile in his voice. "You see some-one?"

No. Couldn't be. No one there. Only Christian's face moving now. Shallow ripples that burned Max's eyes.

"I can do this all day," Christian said.

And Max believed it.

"Okay," he said. Admitting defeat without yet giving up. Christian would fall for that.

But beyond the stranger's face, the silhouette lifted an arm.

And waved at Max.

Max didn't mean to blink, didn't mean to stand, didn't mean to run from where Christian remained, cross-legged on the edge of the brown carpet square.

But that's what he did.

"Ha!" Christian cried triumphantly.

Max stood by the stairs, one hand on the railing. He looked to the shelves.

"I saw …"

But maybe not. Nobody there.

The basement door opened. That smell rode a wave of curling smoke down the steps.

"Not the basement," Peggy said.

And the door closed again.

"Are you being a sore loser?" Christian said.

Max looked past him, to the shelves.

No silhouette.

Then: "I gotta go."

"But your mom isn't here yet."

"I know. I just …"

"You *are* a sensitive pussy, aren't you?"

Max stared back at him, Christian still cross-legged with the basement expanding into eternity behind him.

"Yes," he said. Because he just wanted to get out. To go home. Mom or no mom. "Yeah, I am."

And he took the stairs up and out of the basement.


"The hell are you doing here alone?"

His mother looked more stunned than angry.

"I opened up the box of books."

"Wait, what? You came home to *read* of all things?"

Max nodded. He picked up the encyclopedia and walked it to her. It was open at: SAGE.

"They were burning this upstairs in the house. While Christian and I played in the basement."

She eyed the book, then Max. She set her bag down.

"Max. I can't have you doing this."

"I've only been here an hour."

"I understand." Then, "She let you come back alone?"

"Peggy?"

"Yeah."

"I don't think she saw me leave. She was somewhere else in the house."

His mother took the book.

"It's for warding off evil spirits," Max said.

"I know what burning sage is for."

"Well, I didn't. And I was there. Why'd they do it?"

"Slow down, kid. Have you eaten?"

"Kinda."

"What does that mean? A cheese sandwich?"

"Yeah. I had a cheese sandwich."

"Maxie. You're making this harder on me than it already is. This whole situation is nuts. Work, single, you, the house."

Max pointed to the color picture of the burning sage. To the black and white rendering of a pilgrim using it to "clean" her home.

She eyed the illustrations, too.

"Christian people," she said. "They do stuff like this. Religious, is all. You don't have to act so scared. They'd think the world had turned upside down if they were in a house of hardcore Jews."

"I don't wanna go back there."

"Then don't."

Settled then.

"You said we'd unpack the boxes tonight," Max said. "I can stay home and put things away tomorrow."

"Ah shit, Maxie. I'm exhausted."

"When will you not be?"

"Hey, kid. You win some, you lose some, even in the course of a single conversation, you got it?"

He did. But he didn't like it.

"Where would I go tomorrow?"

She exhaled heavy. She looked to the living room, toward the windows, beyond them, too, to the Dove's home across the street.

"You're sure it was sage?"

"Positive."

She entered the living room, stood at the glass.

"I don't know. People have their rituals. Everything's a ritual."

"But I heard them say the word *ghost*, Mom."

"Yeah, I thought of that, too." Then, "You were in the basement the whole time again?"

"Yeah."

"Okay."

"Okay, what?"

"I don't know. Sounds like a classic case of weirdos, is all. You know any other kids in the area?"

"No. Do you?"

"No. And I can't take off work tomorrow. Way too soon for me to start acting like I eventually will."

They eyed the Dove house. The sun lowered on the street, but they saw Peggy fingering the cross at her chest

"What's she doing?" his mother  asked.

"She looks scared."

"You know what?" She pulled the drapes closed. "No. None of this."

"Why'd you do that, Mom?"

"Because people make total sense if you have all the information, and nobody knows everything about anybody else and so we think everyone's crazy but us."

Max went to open the drapes again, but she stopped him.

"I mean it, Max. And you can stay here tomorrow."

"Alone?"

"Alone. But we're gonna need to unpack some of the stuff first. Like the knives and toaster."

"Aren't they safer where they are?"

"Hey, you win some you lose some, even in the same conversation. Now do as I say."

"Okay." Then, "Thanks, Mom. I'll be good. Promise."

"Alright. I'm starved. Make me a cheese sandwich? They're so good."

"So good," Max said. Then he was off, to the kitchen, a little more pep in his step for not having to go to the Doves' tomorrow.

As he went, and as he called across the house about the staring contest and video games, Golda peeled the drapes aside and glanced across the street. Not long. Just enough to see Peggy and Michael in that bay window, staring across the room to a place Golda couldn't see, crossing themselves as they did.

Δ

The next afternoon, Max stood alone in the same living room. He and his mother had emptied more boxes than they planned the night before; turned out to be the sort of thing that fueled itself; you opened one, you opened many. They set up the bed in Max's bedroom, too. No more of the mattress on the floor; his room was beginning to look like a real one. His books were on a shelf, his figurines on the nightstand. They'd set up his desk another time.

Now, restless, Max opened the remaining boxes, deciding with almost every one of them not to do anything with the contents. Putting silverware away might be easy on its face, but what if Mom wanted it done differently? What if she wanted forks on the right, spoons on the left? Wasn't worth the work, it seemed.

He looked out the window regularly, to the Dove house. He watched it close. It was a regular Tudor, brick and half-timber framing, white wood here, a black gutter there, a small, sloped roof. And the Doves inside. But Max felt uneasy, even this far away.

"Something's going on over there," he said, even as the front door opened, and Michael came outside. His glasses made it so Max couldn't see his eyes and his hair was messy enough for Max to think his mind was on other things. Michael lumbered as he moved, without looking up or down the sidewalk, straight to the garage, where he punched in a code and waited as the door slid open. At the front door, Peggy. She called out to her husband. Michael looked frustrated but returned to the front door and held out his hand.

Peggy handed him something that was clear as day to Max, here across the street, behind glass that needed cleaning.

A small, empty vial.

Michael went back to the garage, got in the car, pulled out the drive, and drove away.

Peggy watched him go before turning to face the house, collecting herself and entering again.

Max eyed the windows. No sign of Christian.

Was he in the basement? Playing games? Was he winning *Siren Light* this very minute? Or was he sitting, cross-legged, still smiling for having won the staring contest, or worse: still staring?

Max left the window. Suddenly his own house felt big. Empty.

Cold. Quiet. And like at any moment he might hear the thudding of people rearranging furniture, muffled voices arguing, visitors walking the halls, burning sage in all corners.

But not the basement. No. And why not?

Max crossed the living room, entered the kitchen. He'd make himself a sandwich. Hungry or not, he needed to do something. But the kitchen felt confining, too, and so he exited through the back glass door, onto the little deck, and took in the same cloudy day the Dove house took in across the street.

No chairs out here, not yet. So, he stood, and looked back through the house through the back glass door, a little afraid of seeing movement inside, something out of the corner of his eye.

He heard a car, no, two, and walked the length of the house where he had a clear view of Michael Dove returning. He was not alone. As Michael pulled into the drive, another man pulled an old yellow car to the curb. And as Michael got out, so did the second. He was much older than Michael, had white hair, and dressed entirely in black. In his hand, a vial.

Max knew without being close enough that the vial was now full.

A black book, too, under the arm.

Max wanted to know who this visitor was. He got closer to the corner of the house, slowly along the side so he might hear what they said if they spoke.

He heard his name instead.

"Max!"

He started at the sight of Peggy Dove on his own front porch.

"You're home," she said. "Thank God." She smiled and Max saw adult fear there. Across the street, Michael walked the man in black to the Dove's front door.

"Hello, Mrs. Dove," Max said.

Peggy gripped the cross against her chest.

"Is your mother home, too?"

"No, she's at work."

Peggy nodded.

"Do you think you could come over and play with Christian today, please, in the basement? His father and I have work to do."

She didn't sound like herself. Or Max heard in her something he'd only ever heard in his mother: desperation.

"I don't know," Max said. But he did know. He could easily cross the street and play games with Christian.

But why?

The man in all black entered the Dove home and the front door closed behind him. Max looked to the windows, expecting Christian.

Waving.

"Max?" Peggy asked. She sounded hysterical then. A pitch he'd not heard in his own mother's voice.

"Um ... yeah. I can come over."

"Oh, thank God."

She smiled and sorta sunk and Max was worried she was going to fall to her knees on the porch. He stepped toward her. But she just placed her hands on the porch railing and was sweating.

Then, before he had to time to assess his decision, he was crossing the street with her, and the overcast day felt even more so. He thought of the man he'd just seen walk up the Doves' front steps, thought of the man's black hat and the items he carried with him. Next to Michael Dove's white shirt (Max now suspected Christian's father hadn't changed his shirt since the day Max met him), the visitor's clothes were black as ink.

"Christian is already in the basement," Peggy said, halfway across the street. "He's no longer allowed in his bedroom. No."

Max had to ask, "Why not?"

Peggy looked to him and her face and blonde hair was framed by that gray sky and Max understood she hadn't meant to say that last bit aloud, perhaps she'd forgotten she'd come to fetch him at all. He thought of something his mother once said, how people would be able to tell that she and Max's father had been through "some shit" because people can sense that about each other, are "attracted to that" in each other, and can't help but stare.

*Stare.*

Max imagined all their faces changing: Peggy, Michael, Mom, Christian, and now the older man with the vial in his hand. When they reached the curb, Peggy almost tripped.

"Downstairs," Peggy said. "Immediately. Okay?"

Fervor in her voice. Sweat at her temples. Max even spotted sweat at the chest of her blouse, but he quickly looked away.

"Downstairs. Good little boys. Play your games. Downstairs."

She opened the front door and Max peered down the hall, half-expecting Michael Dove and the man in all black upon chairs, shining flashlights on the empty wall.

But he heard them moving upstairs instead.

"Downstairs," Peggy echoed, and she took his wrist the way his mother had when she first dragged him to the Dove house.

The house no longer smelled of sage.

It smelled of something much worse.

"Do you have a dog?" Max asked. Why did he ask it? He knew the answer.

Peggy looked to him like he was mad. She opened the basement door. *"Christian!"* That note of hysteria again. *"Christian! MAX IS HERE!"*

Max looked down the steps. Thought of the things he'd seen or not seen the day before. Saw first Christian's shoes, then his khaki slacks, his white shirt, and finally, his face.

A scar on one cheek. No, two scars there.

"What happened?" Max asked.

Christian looked to Peggy and Peggy shoved Max inside.

She shut the door behind him.

"Hey," Max said.

"Hey," Christian said.

"What happened to your face?"

"Shut up, okay?"

"Well, what happened?"

Christian looked up. A lot of noise up there. Quick footsteps and a knock at the front door and Peggy's voice and then a man's voice and then Michael's voice and then another man's voice, too.

Max took the stairs down.

He had researched more than *sage* in the encyclopedia, as the word had led him to other words, as the encyclopedia tends to do. He read about ghosts. Rituals. A home possessed.

"—off-stage," Christian said.

Max only caught the end of it.

"I said I got hurt by a character off-stage."

"What does that mean?"

Max looked to the far side of the basement. Wished he hadn't. The aisle created by the shelves seduced, even as it chilled.

"I was asleep, Max. Are you listening to me?"

"Yes."

"I was dreaming of myself sleeping. Same bed. Same room. All of it."

"Really?"

"Yeah. And I was looking up to the ceiling in my dream and then something slashed my face."

"Jesus."

"Don't say that." He ran a finger across the scars.

"Who?"

"That's what I'm saying. A character off-stage. That's how Mom described it. She said sometimes a character can do that to you in a dream. Dad said I probably did it. But …"

He raised his hand to show his nails were clipped and clean.

Upstairs, many voices. The two men, the two visitors, were speaking at the same time. But it didn't sound like an argument. It sounded like they were saying the same thing. Like when people chanted the same words at a baseball game.

"Okay," Max said, his voice shaking. "Who do you *think* scratched your face?"

"Come," Christian said. He stepped toward the carpet. "I don't want them hearing us."

Max didn't think the adults would hear anything they said down here. Not the way things were going up there. The voices, louder now. In unison. Peggy had joined in on the chant.

"Listen," Christian said. "Mom and Dad, they argue about this a lot."

"Your mom thinks there's a ghost in the house," Max said.

Christian looked surprised. A little bit. It was the first time Max had seen him this way.

"Yes."

"And your dad doesn't?"

Christian looked up.

"Dad isn't sure. He once told Mom we have to be careful, people like us, people with faith. Careful what we put our faith in."

"He thinks your mom is overreacting?"

Christian shook his head.

"He *did* think that. But now … well, a lot has happened."

Upstairs, hard footsteps. Chanting.

*Off-stage*, Max thought.

"Mom says a little woman hides in the chimney," Christian said. He said it so suddenly that Max started laughing and the laugh became a nervous lump in his throat. Christian went on: "She'd smelled something bad one day and she followed the smell to the chimney, and she looked up in there and a little woman looked back. That's what Mom said. Dad got mad about it. But then Mom got mad because she said …" Christian was whispering now. "She said Dad *fucked* her."

"What?"

"Yeah. Mom said Dad and the woman in the fireplace did that while Dad was asleep. And then I saw something upstairs, and Dad said Mom was poisoning my mind but then we had ghost hunters come over and they were supposed to spend the night, but they left before the morning came and that's the morning *you* came."

Max looked to the ceiling beams.

"What's going on up there right now, Christian?"

But he knew.

Ridding the house of a ghost. Off-stage.

He thought of his mother. At work. The overcast sky. The man in all black and the second visitor.

"Mom has seen her all over the house," Christian said. "I think maybe she's attached to her. To Mom."

"I'm gonna leave," Max said.

"Don't be a pussy," Christian said.

"Where did you learn words like that?"

"She's not a woman, I don't think. She's something else."

"I'm gonna go."

But something crashed upstairs, and the voices rose, and the two visitors were shouting now together. Peggy yelled too, and Max thought he heard Michael barrel up the hall.

Max shrank further from the stairs.

"Here," Christian said. "Help me."

Christian stood at one end of the couch. Like he wanted help moving it.

The two boys slid the couch beneath the bulk of the noise upstairs. Christian got up on the back of the couch and gripped the beams above.

"Come on," he said.

Max joined him.

The voices were clearer now, but not by much.

"They're using Jesus to get rid of her," Christian said.

"You said it's not a woman."

"It's not."

Max looked to the far side of the basement.

"I don't know if Jesus can help with this," Christian said.

Above: did someone fall? The ceiling warped toward them.

Then, a voice unlike the others up there.

Christian and Max got down from the couch fast. Neither spoke as those last muffled syllables played over in their heads.

"Why are we in the basement?" Max asked. He didn't want to be here. Had to leave.

"Because Mom thinks it's safe."

"*Why?*"

"Because there are no basements in the Bible."

"What? Oh, Christian … what are you talking about? We need to get out of here."

"You're not wrong. And Mom actually was. There is an instance. There is one basement in the Bible." Then, he cited it: "*I saw also that the house had a raised basement round about: the foundations of the side-chambers were a full reed of six great cubits. So.*"

"Christian, I saw her yesterday."

"You probably did."

The boys looked to the aisle of shelves.

"I've seen her down here many times," Christian said.

Max moved fast to the stairs. He was five high when he heard the voice again: not Peggy. Not Michael. Not the men.

*A little woman hides in the chimney.*

Max stopped, his eyes on the door at the top.

"There's nothing to be done about it," Christian said. He'd come to the foot of the stairs. "If someone like Mom could overlook something as simple as a basement, how can we trust her interpretation of anything else?"

But Max wanted to go. Had to go. He climbed another step.

Someone was at the other side of the door.

"Max," Christian said. "Jesus won't work. Nothing works."

"I'm not thinking about Jesus," Max said.

"It's beyond religion, this thing."

Up top, the knob turned.

"It was attached to a Muslim before it was attached to us."

Max climbed another two steps.

"It's bigger than our ideas of God, the son of God, the Virgin."

Another two steps.

"Did Mom go fetch you?" Christian asked.

Max looked to the foot of the stairs. Christian, alone down there.

"What do you mean?" Max asked.

But up top, the door opened.

Max gripped the rail, prepared to run back down. If the silhouette was there. If it was anybody but Michael or—

"Peggy," he said.

Yes, Peggy Dove at the top of the stairs.

Tears in her eyes.

Max had seen this expression before. His mother had it when she broke the news of the divorce to him. A sense of being forced to say something she didn't want to say.

"Max," Peggy said. "Could you come upstairs for a minute, please?"

Max looked to Christian.

"Don't do it," Christian said.

"Christian, what's *wrong* with you?" Peggy said. But it was forced. She didn't want to be saying this. "Max, I just need … I think it'd be good to …"

Max watched her search for the words. He thought of the aisles of shelves below.

No. He didn't want to go back down there. Not for the world.

"Don't do it," Christian said.

"Would you please, Max?" Peggy said.

Max thought of the staring contest. The corner of his eye.

"Sure," he said. "I'm coming up."

He climbed the remaining steps. Peggy couldn't look him in the eye and Christian stepped away, silent now, from the bottom of the steps.

By the time Max was in the hall, facing the man dressed in all black and a second man in similar clothes, facing Michael and Peggy Dove, too, the lot of them in the thin hall, each of them sweating, all of them eyeing him like they needed him, like he was their last hope, Christian had already turned on *Siren Light*.

The blue and yellow glow from the screen was the last thing Max saw before Peggy shut the door.

"Thank you," the old man in black said.

But his words were interrupted by wood moved in a fireplace. The unmistakable sound of logs against the grate of a chimney.

# ASPHYXIA

## MAXWELL I. GOLD

Shadows danced against particulates of my breath, falling into the soft bleakness of night. Slowly, deliberately, without changes in rhythm or tempo, every exhalation dripped apprehensively from my lips, crumbling into molecular oblivion at my feet. Trembling and cold, I could hear those ancient ululations thrash within my consciousness, an unbridled metaphysical trauma of generations unborn, unable to breathe, unable to speak, strangulated by the historic instruments of pragmatic complacency, mired and muffled by the songs of silence.

Ethereal fingers slammed against tissue and terror as my lungs contracted under the weight of what felt like a billion terrible stars, a billion eyes gazing into the atomic blackness without any real consequence as every last pitiful ion was crushed. The rhythm picked up, fingers tapping over the fleshy surface of the sky, where inhalations felt more like tiresome infinities arpeggiated in some twisted symphonic beat.

Colors began to blend, everything merged into some wild spectral hue of what-ifs and someday-soons, it was beautiful, like I had taken one last breath; until the horizon bled with fissures, preparing to burst under the pizzicato of ghostly fingers plucking away on strings of some unholy tool.

And there was no more color, no more beauty, a world drenched in grotesqueries and grayspaces. Slowly, deliberately, without changes in rhythm or tempo, every exhalation dripped apprehensively from my lips, crumbling into molecular oblivion at my feet. Shadows danced against particulates of my breath, falling into the soft bleakness of night.

# LIFETIMES

KOJI A. DAE

The parenting clinic jutted up from the concrete like a golem protecting the city from haphazard pregnancies. Alex, with his crooked, half-grin, strolled into its shadow without pausing.

"Aren't you worried at all?" I rushed to grab his warm but not sweaty hand and slow him to my pace.

"Worried?" He stopped and kissed my cheek, his eyes twinkling. "We're going to be great parents."

I would have skipped the test if it wasn't a legal requirement, but the only way we could free our gametes was to jump through the Future First Organization's hoops. I'd promised Alex I would try.

We reached the reception desk as the clock ticked to 14:00. A woman with a high bun and glasses that slid down her nose waved us into a room.

"These rooms block out external signals, so there'll be no interference during the examination. Please turn on your implants."

Alex always kept his on, but I reached behind my ear and held the soft nub toward my skull until my neural system started up. The familiar fizz behind my eyes let me know it was working, but the interface failed to pop up. Probably part of the block the consultant was talking about. She read our serial numbers from a computer—a string that should be too long to memorize—and we confirmed them as ours. "I'll just step outside and dim the lights. Try to relax. The simulation is full immersion, so you won't have to interact on a conscious level. I'll monitor you, in case there are any problems."

Alex reached across the table and squeezed my hands. "You'll do fine, Shauna."

Alex called our first son Pete, but he was always Peter to me. The neural labor coach made the birth experience pure ecstasy. Peter shot through me in waves of color and fizzing pops of excitement until I was floating on a cloud of endorphins. I looked at the squished baby with dark, wet hair and my insecurities melted. We could raise this tiny being. I would do anything for him. I didn't expect him to ask for everything.

As Peter grew, Alex took him on adventures in the park and taught him to be a man. I envied their carefree excursions as I wiped his butt, scolded him when he was naughty, and tried to teach him to be a good person.

Pruning a person toward goodness takes more time and energy than turning him into a man. My body withered, shrunk like a raisin, and Alex didn't want to touch me. Or maybe I didn't want to be touched. I blamed it on the baby that split me apart and wormed his way between me and Alex. My friends said it's common with the first kid. The anger will pass. Just hold it in, don't show too much of it or it can spoil everything.

I swallowed as much resentment as I could, but when I died at sixty-two, my last coherent thought was that it wasn't fair. I gave Peter my whole life, and he would keep living after I died.

Next, we had a pair: Tiffany, and two years later, Tony. A set was supposed to be easier than a single child. They leaned on each other, taking some of the weight off me. This helped stave off the bitterness that had consumed me with Peter. I tried to put Peter out of my mind. Tiffany and Tony were a fresh start, and they deserved a fresh mother.

The first years were not that golden bliss parents go on and on about. Two kids are more expensive than one. Alex spent more and more time at his computer station, writing code for coins. He didn't have time to go to the father-daughter dance with Tiffany or fishing with Tony.

"What if I went back to work?" I suggested when Tony was six months old. "Even part-time. It could free up some money and you could spend more time with the kids."

Alex gave me a quick kiss on the temple and ignored my request.

In the years I'd been out of the workforce, my status had crumbled. One of us needed to keep professional momentum.

That left me to do all the parenting. After spending years steeped in pampers and puree, my vocabulary mirrored the mush our kids ate.

When Tiffany was ten, I tried to get my mind back. I signed up for an experiencing sharing course. My teacher was a young man with a handsome smile who taught the basics of curating and editing experience. But all I had were the everyday stories of two average children. Nothing worth sharing.

"I feel like a shell," I admitted to Alex when Tiffany was fifteen.

"Don't talk like that." He looked around as if someone was listening, even though we were alone.

After they went off to university, things got better. But I never felt as full of life as I had before I gave birth. I was surrounded by loved ones on my deathbed. It wasn't bitterness or anger that filled me, just a will to be taken into the nothingness where I belonged.


Cherry was the most difficult. She came out wailing pink and with a hole in her heart.

"She won't live past her first birthday," the doctors told us.

Part of me was relieved. Children were exhausting. I could do my duty for a year and be free. But the nights I spent cuddling her frail body changed my mind. I wanted her to fight—to live.

Alex spent long nights at the office. Went on trips far away. He didn't want to get attached, and no one blamed him. But no one kept me from filling with love for Cherry.

When her second birthday came and went, I assumed we were in the clear. My little Cherry was stronger than the doctors understood.

But by her third birthday, just when she was growing a spunky attitude, she was gone. Part of me left with her.

"It'll be okay," Alex comforted me. When had he come home? It felt like he had been gone for years.

I tumbled into a depression so deep I might as well have joined her.

Δ

The lights came up and Alex withdrew his hands from mine. A shadow of concern flickered over his bright green eyes before the door opened and our consultant came in.

She reached over and hit a few strokes on the keyboard. My mind cleared and my shoulders relaxed. "I have your results here. Do you want them as a couple or as individuals?"

"A couple," Alex said. He had to have known I failed, but maybe his score could level us out and we'd still get approved.

"No. Give him his score as an individual," I said. Maybe he could adopt without me or find a surrogate mother with which to parent.

"Alex, you scored a forty-five out of fifty. You're fit to be a parent."

My heart caught in my throat. Nearly perfect. How could he be a nearly perfect parent when he barely parented the kids? When he left me alone for hours and days and even weeks? A piece of skin flaked off my lip and the metallic taste of blood swirled into my saliva.

"And Shauna?" Alex asked, not looking at me.

The woman shook her head. "With classes, maybe."

I lowered my gaze. Going to the VR center twice a week, living out the lives and deaths of twenty-four children each month? I couldn't do that. Alex couldn't possibly ask that of me.

"It isn't fair," Alex said. "You only gave her difficult situations."

*And you never helped me*, I wanted to add. But my mouth continued sucking on my lip like a baby sucking on a morbid tit.

"The system creates realistic situations based on your personal profiles. It is quite an accurate example of possible futures." The consultant paused by the door. "Some people just aren't cut out to be parents."


By the time Alex abandoned me, he had become a tight-jawed, sullen stranger.

"You promised me forever," I cried.

"You won't even take the classes! Won't even try."

It was the same argument, first every month, then every week, and finally every day. I had no more answers, and he had no more patience.

"You're the one who wanted kids in the first place."

I sulked. He left.


"You don't want kids, do you?" Alex, the laughing, careless one I was set to marry in a few days, snatched his hands back from me.

"Maybe I don't," I said.

He stood, the betrayal of lifetimes creasing around his eyes and lips. "I guess it's better to know now than ten years from now."

I held my arm out to stop him. "We still have two scenarios. One could be better. One without kids? Or maybe if you stay at home instead of me ..."

He snorted. "I know what I want, and I've been clear from the beginning. I don't need two more lifetimes to know you're not the woman I thought you were." He walked out of the VR center and out of my life.

It took me months before I started dating again. When I set my profile to available, the first line read: *Wanted, equal partner to share a child-free life.*

# SEASONAL MEAT

## JAMAL HODGE

The law of the jungle
Is the law of the land.
Transcend the kind illusion,
Blood on your hands.
Red on those who hunt,
Those who watch,
Those who cry.
Observe how readily we dance,
The familiar dance.

The moves rehearsed as if from birth.
The questions,
the opposition,
those regurgitated platitudes,
usher in the same false cleansing.

Blood on so many hands,
Satisfied by a "Maybe this time,"
Complacency celebrated as faith,
To soothe the cotton-picking truth,
Of your proud national status,
As seasonal meat.

Justice doesn't cradle the weak.
No ownership?
Look at these sheep.
Hands up, pleading for mercy
In a land apparently without sin.
It's just tradition,
Christened when the black boy bleeds,
Blue light,
Red light,
Blue eyes, stern.
Red wounds, earned.
By breathing too loudly,
Too proudly,
Too black.

On a jog through the butcher's town,
Where innocence is a feeling,
And facts can be explained,
In upside down riddles,
Of the many wrongs you were about to do.
Violent fantasies,
Warrant violent acts,
In the pale predator,
Who fancies himself the prey,
But not today,
Never today.

But then, when?

# OBSERVER DEPENDENT UNIVERSE

## CHRISTA WOJCIECHOWSKI

The rain streaking down the window makes me crave a home I never had, an epigenetic memory threaded into my DNA. No matter that this precipitation will sear canyons into my flesh if I ever step outside to stretch my arms and soak it in, bash the glass and tumble into the gray-amber sunset to melt under drops of sulfuric acid.

This is comforting on two levels. One, I get a cozy feeling that we must have felt on the planet we were made from, where nature made it so that the sound of rain tempered our restlessness with melatonin. We don't ask for it, yet the sleeping potion is released, cued by dark skies, allowing our minds to dissipate like the fog that lifts from the lake of poison next to our current base. The second consolation is that death is waiting just outside this door, if only I could meet it halfway.

"Your sustenance is ready," the voice from the ceiling says. It's a strangely tender voice, like an aunt you never talk to but have always loved because you were her favorite.

I scramble to the unit where my meal awaits behind a clear door. It opens as soon as my hand comes within range. I am hungry and I do not complain about this pile. Food is food. And salivary glands flood my mouth on cue. I eat. Like a primordial creature wriggling in the ooze, pressing my lips to the plate and sucking it through my parted mouth without a slurp. I ingest. Parted mouth that was pressed to you. To your shoulder. To the head of the organ between your legs. I swallow, my stomach hungry for the paste, loud and roiling.

If my limbic system fails in its graceful and undulating peristalsis, pushing the molecules through my inner tubing, I starve. If it malfunctions, the follicles will not absorb the nutrients within the sludge. But it works, in mindless efficiency. I feel the sustenance break down, the glucose already entering my cells, each one in the warm afterglow of renewed energy. They are happy. I am not.

I talk to the body. Will it to stop. It's running on a program without my consent, billions of years old that began with the first prokaryotes. Funny how the cells, all separate little worlds, cooperate in this alliance of which I am blocked from participating. I ask it: How can you disobey me? How can you make me hungry when I don't want to be? How can you force me to take my next breath when all I want to do is stop breathing?

I didn't give you permission.

Not for this breath either.

And I know that even if I could crash through the dome and lay supine under the drizzle, the pain would trigger a reflex that would have me leap to the closest shelter before I had a chance to make a deliberate choice to stay under the shower of acid, to let the flesh separate from my bones and seep into the alien ground. But part of me has prevented myself from doing anything drastic. Part of me, purely out of morbid curiosity, is simply wondering if you'll come back.

I fall asleep listening to the pulse behind my ear. Relentless.

This body isn't mine. It never was. Yours isn't either.

*Seelho, Seelho. Come the rain and cleanse the system.*


At dawn, when the slide moon cusps the mountain range, this is our time to rise. We are startled awake by the kind voice in the ceiling, the voice of someone who, no doubt, died decades ago. All that remains of her is a nameless disembodied vibration. We go to our posts beneath the sky pavilion, a wide convex structure that distorts the inhospitable bile-green skies and the slick and jagged land outside, making it seem more wondrous and monstrous than it probably is. The dome, a god's magnifying glass and we are an experiment. It is possibility that is poisonous.

Dressed in threadbare sleeveless shirts and underwear, our slick, rubbery skin prickles in the damp. Again, this physiological reaction I did not mandate, did not want to show that I felt anything. I vowed to be beyond sensation and yet my skin reacts to the world outside. The organism continues to disobey. The cells conspire.

"Get into formation!" the general shouts. Spittle flies from her mouth, her eyes yellowed like they've been stained by the jaundiced light that radiates from the skies beyond the glass. Her oily hair is tacked under a saturated cap. She shines like obsidian, tarnished as if from a black sun. Dirty, yet clean like polished steel. "Twelve and twelve!"

We do our exercises. Twelve of each: push-ups, burpees, squat jacks, planks, dips, lunges, sit-ups, fly jacks, mountain climbers, high knees, skips, scissor jacks. We do only twelve reps because it is enough to retain our fitness for flight without requiring excessive oxygen, water, and calories. It's moments like these when I'm standing in muster or straining myself to the point of exhaustion that I replay our conversations, talking into cameras with imitation wine-stained teeth. If we thought about the lightyears between us, we would choke with panic. Mercifully, the human brain was fitted for our small world. We can't think big enough. Impossible to consider that maybe we never mattered at all.

The tranquility the sound of this noxious rain brings is deceptive, tapping on the glass as I pump my knees up to my chest. Our lungs heave in an accompanying rhythm that remind us we are running out of air supply with every breath. And I dream of you, with a constant, obsessive, subtle perseverance.

You are with me, waking and sleeping, and I force myself to recall the days our bodies were together, operating on that ancient program beyond our control. No matter how much you valued your duty to Masha, or I to Samir, the organism doesn't understand language. It has its own rules that we are powerless to disobey. Propagation, a dirty trick that feels like love. That is what Samir told me when he found out about you. What we call love is a tool of evolution to inspire us to procreate and successfully raise offspring. There is no such thing as love, and I should be easily able to let you go. But I could not. And even if it was an illusion created by hormones and pheromones, it is an illusion to which I gladly surrendered.

We've long since proved that love doesn't need a body. Sex does, but love does not. Did it matter we were electronic signals skidding over the com net? Your green eyes muted and pixelated, voice stuttered and tinny, and that was enough. And all I have now to arouse me are memories of your words distorted by time and space into frequencies that bend, with only a hint of what your voice might have been if I remembered accurately, my body calling and now I have to answer its requests with reluctant fingers.

Of one mind. Of one evolution. *There is no Seelho. We are Seelho.*

After our morning exercise, we meet in the debriefing room. Rows of barely clad women, eel-like and lubricated, are ready to slide through any discomfort. General wears that strange, misty look as she outlines today's plan. She believes in this mission.

But I have a mission of my own.

"Today we are exploring the west quadrant." She taps the corner of the screen at a crinkled ridge of mountains. "You will be aimed at this range. We think there could be liquid water there."

There is a collective sigh from the women's segment that says, *if only*. We are lean, gleaming, fit, efficient. And we are filthy. Our science division has not found a way to distill any molecules of $H_2O$ from the air or the rain yet, and so we are all chronically unbathed, our bodies encased in their own residue. At night, we rub down with thick, frothy oil and scrape our skin off with the backside of a comb. The dead skin cells curl up behind the bulldozer to form a milky dander paste we fling into communal cans. These drums of oil were something they brought in droves when they created the outpost centuries ago, only to discover much better ways to fuel our nomadic society. But they had spent so much to send the payloads of obsolete sludge that we are ordered to use it. Nothing goes to waste. The oil is full of antiseptic properties, we are told. Reduces inflammation. These dead bodies of ancient creatures and plants have fermented to perfection over millions of years. How they've given themselves to protect us eons into the future, wrapping us in a filmy embrace light years away from the home where they became extinct. The degraded blood from the dead Earth.

*Seelho. Seelho. There is no Seelho. We are Seelho.*

Our acrid body odor mixes with the thick, metallic smell of the oil. Like worms that slithered up from tannic soils, if we ever found life, no living thing would want to be near us. I simmer over this. We worms. The general's eyes bulging in her grimy face, and I realize that I am just as vile. We are stained—the grinding, interlocking parts of an old combustion engine. As we get warm, the sweat beads up through the oil, it bleeds, runs down our arms and legs in streaks, this golden, black blood.

I try to leave my body, send an energetic feeler to all corners of the universe. Find you floating in some metal can through space with hundreds of other beating hearts. Are you at another outpost, musing at an alien sky just as I am? Or are you dead? Particulate matter drifting like motes in the starlight. I call you.

Your smiling eyes and easy jokes made the fear foolish. We were both assigned partners, I with Samir and you with Masha, to make the most of our genetic diversity. We interlocked. Gave birth. Let go of our children in the name of Seelho. Humans can be made with virtually nothing. Saliva and breath and zygotes. *But we can't feed you, children. May you find a home and be fruitful.* Blast them to the next coordinates where we increase our chances of finding the perfect planet. Even if we found it, or they found it, we spread so far apart that the race could not rejoin at any place one of our teams found. Ninety-nine percent of us will end up nowhere and eventually wither and die.

"Let's just be happy," I said to you. "Why this constant search for an adequate place that does not exist? We could live out our lifetime here, now, together and then go out as we choose."

"We need to go as far as we can. It is a test. Your instinct is there for a reason. You can't deny it."

"What if I can?"

You laughed at me. "Have you ever tried? Hold your head underwater, your body will fight. That is Seelho. Even if you try to go against him, your body obeys him first."

And that's when I really noticed Seelho. Felt it. More tricks. Keeping a secret from me inside my own body. I always thought it was mine. But why would I ever think that when I was not the one who created it? I strain to remember before I was born, but I can't.

That is why I loved you hard, meanly, with bites and slaps and gritted teeth. To leave marks on you because we knew that being together was impossible, and we would be ripped apart for this worthless quest. Do not let us perish. Do not let us fade into the murky records of history like the terrible lizards and the entire tree of life that resulted in us. We cannot let them have died in vain. They are our parents, and we must go forth. Why? Because Seelho says so. It has programmed us to always try. Life never stops fighting.

So, we crawl through the Milky Way looking for a place to settle, somewhere we can rummage for materials, or best outcome, to stop and grow. Sometimes it's a few decades, or a hundred years, but no place has had enough resources to sustain us. It takes so much effort. We are in the negative, expending more than we are gaining. The chances of finding a suitable planet are so remote that it strains the mind. But we can't stop. Not until the last tiny life goes out.

I pull on my flight suit. The rough material scratches my oily skin in a way that makes me tingle. *Alive. You are alive. The pain means you exist.* The body tells me. It is responding to this message, and it makes me angry. You know, my love, I'm always angry first, stoic second. And I did not sign up for this shit.

"Officers, mount up!" says General. Each of us female flight agents line up at our cannons. We slide into the hatch on the side of the gleaming gun metal tube, slip into the capsule and check the instruments. These craft are hundreds of years old by now, built on Earth for the first explorations. Now they are battered workhorses. We make use of what we have. No working propulsion system, we are simply chucked as far as possible, shot out like cannon balls to land and scout around for anything we can possibly use. The interiors are near to falling apart, the cockpits musty with oil and sweat and decomposing synthetic materials. The vinyl seats are cracked and pinching. New navigation panels are glued over old like technological barnacles, the windows foggy and pitted. *As I am Seelho's vehicle, so this is my vehicle,* I think wryly.

This craft will listen to me, but I can't will my heart to stop beating. I have tried—just to see if Seelho would show itself and make its presence known.

"You don't have to see Seelho," you said. "You cannot."

"Why?" I asked.

"Because you are Seelho. The wordless processes of the body prove its existence."

Oh, but you are, or were, so wise. You said to stop asking why. Trust. That was all I had to do to be at peace. But I can't stop asking, for my mother and father, for our daughter, for you. All of us.

Father died before I learned how to remember. I try to extract his face from some repressed part of my brain. He must be locked somewhere in there, the same place you're fading into. There is only a smudge and a murmur of his that may be something I concocted to soothe me. I like to think that he was a great man, that I am special and destined for great things, but the older I get, I realize he wasn't. I am not either. And Mom was a stone woman who loved in a way that felt like oppression, resistance no matter which way I went. But that was so I would be capable of surviving. She loved me so much that she made herself into an enemy. A good mother. When they came to claim me for the service, I was ready.

"What happens if there is no one to remember us?" I asked my Mom once. She stared blankly at the wall. "Does a tree fall in the woods?" she said. I asked her where that saying came from. She didn't know. But I know what it means.

I excelled during training, lead scout for the female regiment. You were the lead of the men's. I liked that we were the two top scouts. Recklessness has its merits. Until we were cleaved, spread far and wide like spores, but your ship tumbled away by some force we cannot yet explain. Out of range. Never to be heard from again. There are many ships we cannot reach and many outposts that may have successfully found a place to stop and rest, or live, and continued. It has been fifteen years and we may never know. We always knew this could happen but never thought it could happen to us. It's too painful to think of all the horrible ways you could've died. With the way things are going, hope is childish. I am forced to operate according to the colony's delusions anyway. I have no choice. But it isn't really hope, I told you. It is fear of never having existed.

A junior trainee comes to yank on our belts to make sure they hold. She is the same age as I when I came—just after their first menses, another ancient cycle that operates independently of our wishes. "What's it like?" she asks me. "Going out there?" She is smiling, white teeth against all the black buttered skin.

What do I tell her? That it's terrifying. Claustrophobic. That my instinct was to stop this futile pursuit. That it feels like I will be yanked from your skin. The body, the only home that I have. One that Seelho will lose use of if I let it die. I want out.

"It's freedom," I said, trying to smile, my lips stretched beyond their limits.

She finishes the preflight check on my tube. "Remember Seelho," she says before sealing me in. I see her small face in the window, the precious smile of someone who can't comprehend how doomed we are. Such a sweet creature. Maybe our daughter is out there smiling at a stranger like this.

Thirty field agents are scheduled today to cast a wide net and see what we can bring in. Impossible to use rovers on this land, which is crisscrossed with scars of rock and shaped by geological violence, like this place was in a cycle of destroying itself, failing to do so, and healing, only to try again. Repeatedly bleeding and ripping off the scab.

I hear the same sweet voice that announces my breakfast: "3, 2, 1."

With a great sucking noise, my capsule is launched by some local propellant that smells like sulfuric rot. Even in the airtight capsule, I smell it. Either that, or my mind is sensing beyond my body. Maybe I am hallucinating. Some of us go mad.

I force my eyes open. I want to see it all. G-forces push into me. It feels like the weight of your body when you used to yank me into a hallway and press me against the wall. The rain is still with me, making trails that tremble psychotically as they streak across the windows, catching and glowing with green and pink and yellow light. The momentum in low gravity allows me to cruise unimpeded by friction above the cragged impossible land, gorges so deep our instruments cannot detect the bottoms. Cruelly teasing us with the possibility of water that we will never reach. The atmosphere is an opaque whorl of tarnished colors until I pierce the clouds, and I am vaulted, suspended at the apex for a moment, like the space between inhalation and exhalation. I hold my breath as my insides rise inside me.

It is silent, except for the soulless rush of wind. I yank my belts and think back on the girl who made sure I was safe. I arrive at the other side of weightlessness. Like coming back to life. Relieved and disappointed, everything rattles wildly as I descend. If I don't release my parachutes, my capsule will fall into one of those bottomless abysses. I'll be dashed against the cold rock, where the acid rain can penetrate and rinse me from my bones. My instincts won't be able to do anything about it. I'll be pulverized before I have a chance to react. If my signal disappears, the retrieval craft will not waste resources to find me.

Will Seelho somehow intervene? Will it finally speak to me in a language I can understand so I can know if we really did have to keep searching, keep fighting so hard? I feel the exhaustion of generations. I do not want to obey anymore. We need to accept the reality. It is time to fade out.

*No.*

I hear it clearly, inside my head and out, a thundering negation that permeates everything. Was it the powerful launch forcing the blood from my brain, gas leaking into my capsule, oxygen leaking out, the madness? But I *feel* you, as surely as if you were in the cockpit next to me, as surely as if I *am* you.

And I'm paralyzed by a sequence of thoughts, listening to them rather than thinking them. A digital transmission or the spark between neurons—they are almost one and the same. When we talked in real life, or when our ships were still close enough to chat on com net, or now when I talk to you in my head—they are all equally valuable moments. We are not merely juicy, thrumming bodies executing some program beyond our control. We are Seelho's mind as well. Our thoughts are its thoughts, and your voice is the voice of everything. I can never tell where you end and I begin.

Because there is no end or beginning.

This is Seelho thinking.

I'm suddenly aware of It. A jarring moment of pervasive clarity explodes out in all directions and dimensions. The journey of every atom burning in every star. The muck of creatures that seal my skin, scaled ancestors who turned their primitive eyes to the stars without ever questioning Seelho. And I feel those Earthling humans, so long ago, who toiled out of fear and courage to invent such things that would get us to a new world. The first launched into deep space with no guarantee of anything except a slow and lonely starvation. My mother and father, the junior who smiled at me with a knowingness of a much older person, like she knew I was in for a surprise, and you. Your face. Your voice. You exist in me. Your face is my face. Your voice is my voice.

I drop below the murky clouds. The rain is heavy, angrily batter-ing my window. The ever-constant protest of a world that does not want to become ours. But we won't listen. Obstinate and enduring. And I know I will not let you die, even if you've been reduced to a faint spark between the synapses in one lonely woman's head. One spark started the whole Universe, didn't it? One spark started life itself. Every thought is valid. Even if existence is a dream. Even if love is a dream. It is real to us. We make it so.

I initiate the parachutes. The capsule's velocity is violently halted. I'm yanked against my harness and heave against it as it bruises my chest. The craft hits ground with a deafening thud and the sound of wrenched metal. A great hoarse sob scrapes up from my lungs, and I let go, a grief held for fifteen years. I know you are dead because I feel you permeating everything around me, absolute joy I never experienced. Tears and oil run into my mouth. Crying out precious brine, I lick it up and swallow. I laugh. It feels right letting my smile take up space. Even if your heart is no longer beating, your heart is my heart is Seelho's heart. A secret my cells know, my DNA knows, the body knows. I must trust it. I must try.

I raise a trembling hand to the touchscreen and initiate com net. "*Scout 22* to *Retrieval*. We have touched down."

"*Scout 22*. Copy that."

"Preparing to complete area survey."

"Stay safe out there. Remember Seelho."

I release my belts and grab my helmet. Our reflection smiles from the golden polarized shield. "I have a feeling we might get lucky today."

# CHASING
# THE SERPENT

MARGE SIMON

The player hums
the disc begins …

Starting soft,
squential chords
moving upward to crescendo –
at the peak, a vast ocean vista,
the sky, a sheet of slate,
wind rising,
waves parting –

con calore
con fuoco
con moto

*It is a big one, a dragon breathing notes aflame, the power of its impact
pulls me into that churning wave of melody, chasing the serpent with
its scaly and slippery skin … I grab its whipping tail, but it coils
around my wrists as no bondage I've ever known,*

hurting
weeping
intense

*I become the music, sucking froth from the shining dragon's lips, the unchangeable joy as its fiery breath caresses my neck; then with an allegro of shimmering scales, I am released as my dragon rises to meet the sun.*

I fall to earth,
holding ecstasy
not unlike a prayer ...

then trembling, I press
*Replay*

# SABLE'S BESTIARY FOR THOSE WHO REMAIN

### HAILEY PIPER

The tattered yellow notebook you hold represents a promise I made to myself. I spent my old life learning to navigate a world that hated me for who I am and who I love. I promised myself that I can survive a world that hates everyone else, too. Each week, I'll compile my notes into another creature entry. You'll survive our new neighbors by learning how I survive them. Let's begin with an easy one.

ENTRY 1: THE UNDER-SWARM

I hate to chronicle them as a separate species, but two years after the Flare, I have to accept that the under-mothers aren't entirely human anymore. Keep away from their eggs and they won't hurt you. When I first joined the walled compound that Dante and Brian founded, their group had planned an egg raid. Dante said they're tasty and the super-rich protein keeps you fed for a week. I convinced him it wasn't worth it.

If the under-swarm drones catch you, they'll give a choice. Either they'll kill you and convert your proteins to egg-nourishing biomass, or they'll throw you into the genesis chamber where you'll transform into a new under-mother. I used to dream about raising kids somehow, with someone, but not underground with an egg-laying ovipositor stretched from my pelvis. Even if the underground protects from sunstalkers and shimmers, I've fiddled enough with what's between my legs for one lifetime.

Respect the under-swarm's caverns, though, and trade is doable. We've formed a route that avoids shine-skinner nests and sunstalker migrations between the compound, caverns, and the city, our trade triangle. Bring the drones scrap metal and they'll offer its weight in mushroom crop.

There are worse things to eat than fungi.

### ENTRY 2: SHIMMERS

Last week I noted our most amicable new neighbors. Now I'll note the most insidious.

My first shimmer almost snuck up on me while I was scavenging a drugstore. Most survivors pillage antibiotics, insulin, anti-depressants, but hormones are often up for grabs.

When I was about to leave, my ex-girlfriend Denise strode through the front door. At first, I was thrilled she'd survived the world's end, but that's the trick with shimmers. They play on your emotions. I didn't remember that a drunk driver had struck and killed Denise back in high school until Tana grabbed my hand and dragged me out of there. I was still new to the compound then, but she looked out for me anyway. She never told me who the shimmer made her see, even after we became a pair. It certainly wasn't Denise.

Follow Tana's lead—don't fight. A shimmer will blanket you in their bodies like a liquid mirror. I've never seen what happens to a human after that because I run. Every time.

It's spotting them that's tricky. Shimmers mimic the people we've lost. I can't explain how. It's like they reach inside our hearts and dress in our memories. Trust your head, not your heart. Grief is a disease and shimmers are walking symptoms of missing the pre-Flare world. Cut that out of your life. Forget hot showers, internet, the past—this is life now.

Tana says that's a cold outlook, that she wouldn't ever save anyone if she looked at the world that way. But how else can we look at the world when shimmers steal the faces of our beloved dead? I try to be warm, but against these monsters? Run, friend. Run fast as you can.

### ENTRY 3: MIRROR FISH

By now you've been scavenging for time, but pre-Flare supplies will only last so long. Find waterways for fresh food. They're cleaner than before, and rainbow ferns now grow on most shining riverbanks, transmogrified terrain from the other world. The ferns taste disgusting, but they satisfy. For something more flavorful, catch mirror fish.

That reads like a radio commercial. Remember those? You might if you stare too long at mirror fish scales. They reflect the pre-Flare world, those same hot showers and internet I mentioned last week. Mirror fish are like shimmers in that they echo the past, but unlike shimmers, mirror fish can't hurt your body. Only everything else.

I was at work in the city park when the sky turned white. I'm not proud to say that I ran home, helped no one, but I don't feel guilty either. Weeks before I made my promise to survive, I was already living it. The fall came fast after that. Radio and TV went dead. Internet signals became unhappy icons on our phone screens. The Flare changed everything with the flick of a light switch, and we'd never know why.

That's enough reminiscence. Tana says I daydream too much when we're at the water, but she's wrong. I'm coming to terms with resentment. We have to move on from our memories, but how can we when we see their shadows everywhere we look? Shimmers, mirror fish; they're old thoughts and dead names being thrown in my face. I'd finally started living my best life, and then the Flare hit.

There are days I wish the world had always been like this so I wouldn't have to think about what's gone. Nostalgia's a demon.

Back to mirror fish, watch out for sunstalker herds while you're gazing down memory lane. Their migrations sometimes follow running water. I'll write about them next week.

### ENTRY 4: SUNSTALKERS

You'll know these big tanks by their long legs and giant carapaces sometimes made of battered car frames. They're strong enough to break down the compound's concrete walls, but they're unobservant.

If we keep quiet when they pass, they don't attack.

To that end, keep rats. We've tried other animals because Brian doesn't like their naked tails, but dogs, cats, and birds haven't worked. Rats go berserk when sunstalkers get close. We haven't figured out why, probably never will. We keep them in every section of the compound to warn us, our little hairy canaries. Keep quiet and you'll be safe too.

I'm not sure I have enough notes for another helpful entry. Data on shine-skinners is slim. We must be getting a stronger handle for living out here if I'm thinking the things I'm thinking. We could send people out to look for more wanderers, especially orphans. There's room to grow our compound family. Tana's been talkative about raising children, and since we're of a like mind on this, I follow her lead. That would've been harder for us in the pre-Flare world.

Does that sound cold? Maybe, but it's a silver lining.

### ENTRY 5: SHINE-SKINNERS

It never occurred to us that the rats would be affected, even slowly, by the Flare, that they would get too smart for their cages. We didn't even notice they were missing this morning until the sunstalker migration crashed through the eastern compound wall, drawn by the chatter of our everyday lives.

The family's scattered, many of them dead. I'm not sure where to run, but I can't tell Tana that or she might stop running altogether. And I can't stop with her, or I'll have broken my promise to survive.

Crumbling gas stations and office buildings shelter us at night. Without the compound's walls, we see the shine-skinners from afar, even in the dark. I used to mistake them for transmogrified terrain like rainbow ferns, pieces of the Flare trickling into our world, because they don't travel. Lately I've been more observant. Venus flytraps don't move much either, but they're still alive and carnivorous. Shine-skinners are like that.

Dante didn't realize.

We'd nearly passed a shine-skinner when he spotted a torn sack beside it with canned food spilling out. I tried to stop him, promised we'd find food soon, but he was too hungry to listen. Within three feet, the shine-skinner dragged him into its luminance and churned out spores of fuzzy light. We couldn't see what it was doing to him. That was for the best.

We're down to me, Tana, and Brian. I wonder which of us will expand my bestiary notes next.

### ENTRY 6: SHIMMER / SHINE-SKINNER ADDENDUM

I should've made the connection sooner. I'm so sorry.

We were sleeping in a garage, with Brian on watch, when he shouted about seeing Dante outside and went running. It sounded ludicrous, but these creatures' workings were a mystery. Maybe he thought the shine-skinner let Dante go after finishing its light show.

More likely, Brian was grieving too hard to think straight.

I was right about the bestiary's development though. I'd never seen what happens to a human after a shimmer catches one, wouldn't have except Tana and I ran out the door right as a shimmer wrapped around Brian. Cold logic: we lose a friend, we gain knowledge.

They fell to the dust together and turned bright as starlight. I recognized what they were becoming just as Tana pulled me away, tears streaming down our faces.

Brian and the shimmer were transforming into a shine-skinner. This was a life cycle, an unobserved gap in my notes. A shimmer merging with someone becomes a shine-skinner. Shine-skinners kill humans and blow spores to the wind. Those spores become shimmers. They will spread across the world until there aren't any of us left. Until there's nowhere to run.

### ENTRY 7: TANA

My last entry concerns the most dangerous creature on Earth because I love her too much to leave her side. She wants to do this. I could let her do it alone, but I'm not as cold as she once thought. That's probably her fault.

And I don't want to be alone.

Shine-skinners, shimmers, sunstalkers, mirror fish, the under-swarm—it's all connected by the Flare, but figuring out that connection was never our destiny. I worked at a park; Tana was a nurse. We once dreamed of a family we didn't know how to build, and then found a family but lost it. She calls this is a fresh opportunity. I can't argue. I'm just not sure I'm ready to change again.

I'm leaving the bestiary on this rock where you'll have found it. Maybe it'll save your life, or the life of someone in your family, found or otherwise. Or maybe, like me, you'll follow Tana's lead.

We're going underground where the drones tend to the under-mothers. They'll take us to the genesis chamber, which will transform our insides and grow lengthy, fleshy ovipositors from our outsides. I don't know how long that'll take, or how long until eggs begin sliding down our new appendages. I'm not sure how to physically or emotionally brace myself for another transition.

But we'll be protected, cared for, and we'll be together. Our love will thrive in the dark and our children will number thousands. Maybe our new species can spread through the underground faster than the shimmers can dominate the surface. The world might belong to our children someday, during our lifetimes or beyond.

And in that way, I'll have kept my promise.

# DARK NEIGHBORHOOD

## CINDY O'QUINN

*I am alone but for the shadow I cast.*

Cradled by night. A babe safe in Mother's arms, long since departed from a cruel world with aid of fire and flame. Returned to the very dust that now lines her eternal box. Forever swaddled without knowing the taste of love or flesh.

I sought out the dark neighborhood to quench undying thirst. Split two ways to pacify the living and dead. Drinking night into the ocean of my throat. Salt burning open wounds now spilling into turbulent waters. Contaminated.

*Twisted light burns through to make my shadow unique.*

Happiness was like life. Temporary. Cheated by time cut short like an irritating skin tag. There one day and gone the next. Taught not to say a word if you had nothing nice to say. I was a quiet child, who grew into an even quieter woman.

People didn't take kindly to the dark thoughts that swirled around in my mind when they trickled out. If you think about it, not much of anything good ever trickles. Guess that's why I remain alone with a shadow for a companion.

*Floating from one dark neighborhood to the next.*

Unremovable stains that cling throughout life like a birthmark. Teetering on the tightrope. The fine line of sanity that sways a little when your mind starts to stray. Shadow hand on a leash tugs ever so to prevent you from falling all the way.

Coyote tracks prominent on a cold blanket of fresh snow. Circling the neighborhood that I visit tonight. They come closer and closer until their eyes glow. Hollow souls. All creatures come closer when the threat of death is like a sweet promise. One final meal.

*Life is tough. This one is tougher. We don't stand a chance.*

# SEEDS

## J. FEDERLE

*The wet, tangy scent of orange peel cuts through the earthy rot. Mulch and flesh and peels decay beneath me, cushioning my body. I do not wish to open my eyes.*

---

02 1611Z May 74
PROJECT PURIFY [ Classified Supervisor Report ] – Subject 324C
Status: DECEASED

Efforts to revive Subject 324C lasted 32 minutes. Subject's heart stopped thirteen times. Wings non-emergent. Cause of death: heart failure. Corpse disposed of without autopsy. Death aligns with patterns in previous subjects.

---

03 0106Z May 74
PROJECT PURIFY [ Classified Supervisor Report ] – Subject 324C
Status: ALIVE, Post-disposal

Compost Unit custodian #48C contacted security to report suspicious activity at 1209Z. Custodian was stationed behind viewing glass. Custodian had observed movement in central compost heap. Security initially attributed movement to rats and/or gas release.

Custodian then reported observing a fully emerged, white wing: [ *transcript excerpt* ]

[ … ]

[ 00:46 ] C.U. #48C: Color? What color?

[ inaudible 00:48 ]

[ 00:50 ] SECURITY: Security is en route, sir. Please confirm. What color is the wing?

[ 00:53 ] C.U.: White! White! *Dios* [ whispering ] *en los cielos sanctifado sea su nombre.* [ shouting ] It moves! *Es un angel.* I see an angel in the garbage, what have we done? *Tan blanco su ala, dios ten piedad.*

[ … ]

Subject 324C recovered as of 1243Z. Pre-disposal waiting period of 12 hours now mandatory for all corpses. Autopsy now mandatory. Mulching of corpses now mandatory.

Custodian #48C terminated at 1248Z. No witnesses.

---

*Opening my eyes was the hardest part of waking up. The smells told me of other dead, and I sensed the vastness of my prison. I did not want to see.*
 *But I lifted my heavy eyelids.*

---

03 0534Z May 74
Physical Examination of Subject 324C
Reporting Doctor: Dr. Maria Díaz

Subject is a young dark-skinned female, likely pre-teen. Exact age unknown. Minor wounds sustained due to compost chute and subsequent drop [ bruising of left forearm, thin cut on right thigh ]. Underweight due to change in bone density. While thin, subject does not appear malnourished.

Two wings have emerged between the scapula and spine. Skin remains inflamed, but presence of blood (before subject was bathed) suggests the body has healed at a rapid pace. Nerves of the wings appear to be knitted into intercostal nerves. Subject exhibits increasing dexterity and mobility with both appendages.

Subject non-vocal, but alert. Appears to grasp basic commands. Listens with focus, indicating acute hearing. Transformation is ongoing. Close and constant monitoring advised.

Feather chromaticity is at white point (pure white). Feathers display promising adsorptive properties.

Height: 152.41 cm | Weight: 49.3 kg | Temperature: 39.56°C | Pulse: 98, irregular | Wing Span: 469.2 cm

---

*Songs, songs in my mind. Songs of the others, whose failed bodies cushioned my death-fall. Songs of birds, of which I am one, am not one. Humans, creatures like I used to be, wear gray coats. They take me from gray room to gray room.*

*The woman named Maria is sorry. Sorry, so sorry. How much life has been consumed to make me? Her voice is a kind of song sometimes.*

*Maria remembers jungle. Jungle sang and hummed. Jungle shuddered greenly and fruit-colored birds lived in its body. I ache at her stories.*

*My throat is a strange flesh. It cannot sing yet.*

*Maria touches my face. She is gentle.*

---

04 0946Z May 74
PROJECT PURIFY [ Classified Supervisor Report ] – Subject 324C
Status: MUTATION ONGOING

Subject exhibited significant advances overnight.

Dr. Díaz reports shifts in weight (-0.3 kg) and wingspan (+0.2 m). Phalangeal joints in thumb, ring finger, and pinkie of right hand have fused. Fingernails on these digits have ossified and blackened. Grip strength of right hand now over 380 psi. Stronger equipment has been ordered to gain more accurate measurement.

At 0416Z, subject began to emit low, throaty hisses. Dr. Díaz was called due to caretakers' concerns that subject was choking. She found no evidence of restricted air flow but stayed to monitor the situation. At 0542Z, subject transitioned to whistling. Dr. Díaz believes a syrinx-like organ has developed at the base of the subject's trachea. Scans will be conducted to confirm.

Note: Staff were observed referring to Subject 324C as "Pihu," based on the particular chirp the subject produces when fed. Staff indicated Dr. Díaz had issued the denomination.

Dr. Díaz has been reprimanded.

11 0946Z May 74
PROJECT PURIFY – Site Evaluation [ Classified ]
Submitted by Mark Listern, Chief of Biome Development

Proposed Site: 3.4653° S, 62.2159° W

Site Characteristics: Our proposed site has a pollution level of 650 PSI (150 PSI over Human Sustainability Point). Plant life, limited due to the "scorched-earth" farming of the 2040s in the area, is available. Climate runs temperate to hot. Stone ruins provide shelter, which should encourage Subject 324C to stay within a limited range.

Risk of Public Detection: MINIMAL. (1) The site is isolated. Only 50 million humans remain inside Brazil's borders; these individuals live in dispersed and degraded atmosphere-generating pods. Refugees are concentrated in the ruins of São Paulo and along the borders. (2) Lima, Peru, is the nearest surviving city. Of its six biomes, two are defunct. A third is failing. Citizens' movements are restricted to Lima's four functional biomes.

Sightings of Subject 324C by members of the public are therefore unlikely, even if subject proves capable of extended flight.

Market: (1) Lima is a market of 15 million (est. 8 million citizens, 7 million refugees). Degradation of Lima's third biome has heightened class and political tensions. The city's water shortage is intensifying. Of the 15 million citizens, 30% are estimated to be clients able to tender significant payments (min. 60,000 USD) for placement in a new biome. (2) The remaining population of Lima, as well as the 50 million refugees in Brazil's borders, comprises a market of clients likely to trade labor or offspring for placement. (Lima is also an ideal testing ground prior to implementation of this approach in India, where the market is far larger.)

Timeline: Based on evaluations of Subject 324C, presence of its wings could feasibly create air and land fit for initial biome development within 6–8 months.* The time required may decrease if the subject stays airborne (wings outstretched, lungs engaged) for extended periods of time.

Estimated survival for Subject 324C at the proposed site is 1 year. After Subject 324C is deceased or otherwise removed, my team could erect the preliminary biome shell within 48 hours. Application within the shell of another 10–12 subjects (assuming their properties are similar to those of Subject 324C) should produce a full biome fit for human habitation in 8–10 months.**

---

* This window marks an extraordinary edge over our competitors' nonbiological technologies aimed at purification. Our company could, within a decade, achieve near-monopoly of water and double our share in the oxygen market.

** Estimates reflect worst-case scenarios. Estimate accuracy will improve with results from the upcoming test of Subject 324C's interest in flight and with data from Subject 324C's post-saturation autopsy.

---

*SKY. I see sky! Oh, I want sky-skin! I am stretched and hungry for sunset, it'll taste of rose petals, loved in the orange heart of the sun. Songs, songs in my mind, recall sky-skin and—what lie is this?*

*Wall of nothing, let me through!*

*The open sky sings into my frothing blood. I hear it, will reach it! Sky! Sky! Sk—oh ... oh, no.*

*Sky, who strangled my sky, blackened—sin boils here, the songs crash inside me. I cannot sing! All that I am is stolen. Stolen.*

*I see you. Greedy animals, you dare to breathe below. Thieves! Thieves! GIVE MYSELF BACK TO ME.*

---

13 1607Z May 74
PROJECT PURIFY [ Classified Supervisor Report ] – Subject 324C
Status: EMERGENT

Upon seeing the simulated sky in the facility's outdoor testing range, Subject 324C launched from transport crate into the air. Subject is capable of flight. It is anticipated that, if released on Dr. Listern's proposed site, subject would spend significant time airborne. Experiment has thus been deemed a success.

Replication of Subject 324C progresses well. In the most recent Delhi-based sample (n=300), the survival ratio has (thus far) increased dramatically. Up to 20 new functional subjects anticipated by October of 2075. Surviving subjects will be transferred to this facility once cleared for transport.

Note: Subject reacted poorly upon encountering the biome's inner shield. After absorbing three blows, the shield malfunctioned. The Blue-Sky simulation failed, revealing the smog beyond.

Three caretakers entered the range to subdue the subject before the shield was damaged further. Two were irrecoverable. One is no longer fit for duty. Dr. Díaz was called to recalculate the tranquilizer dosage required for pacification. New caretakers are undergoing orientation now.

The Blue-Sky simulation has been deemed too stimulating.

Any future tests of subjects' flight ability are to be conducted with inner shield set to beige or gray.

---

*They keep my mind soft. A rotten orange. My songs are jumbled.*

*The Maria-woman shows me seeds.*

*These are the first beautiful things I have seen since I died. Her seed names are little songs: Maracuya. Chirimoya. Camu camu. The seeds are special. Saved seeds, old seeds.*

*She lets me eat them. Hides some in my feathers.*

*Another change is coming soon. I will not see her after, she says.*

*Pihu, Pihu. She sings this word to me. Her voice sounds sometimes like the sky's.*

---

21 0946Z May 74
PROJECT PURIFY [ Classified Supervisor Report ] – Subject 324C
Status: STABLE

Subject has entered a semi-catatonic state.

Dr. Díaz advises reducing the dosage of neuroleptics. She also advises early release to prevent further degradation of subject's health. Her recommendation for early release is supported by the other staff.

Approval for release granted. Subject will be transported to the approved site tomorrow.

---

22 0530Z May 74
PROJECT PURIFY [Classified Supervisor Report] – Subject 324C
Status: IN TRANSPORT

Transport crate containing Subject 324C left facility at 0500Z via helicopter.

No micro-biome or oxygen provided during transportation. Final confirmation will thereby be gained upon arrival regarding subject's real-world capacity to process and purify contaminated atmosphere.

Note: During loading, Dr. Díaz engaged in an intense discussion with a member of the 7-man transport team about tracking. The raised voices agitated the subject. Dr. Díaz made final adjustments to tracking device herself while anaesthetizing subject for transport. Transport team was approved to proceed with 6 members.

Dr. Díaz has been reprimanded.

---

*Others. Others blossom in my mind. Can you others feel me sing?*

*I sing freedom. I breathe poison and exhale light. My white wings grow black. And I love their glossy shine. I love Maria's seeds. And they grow. Shy sprouts, ever-loosening buds. All things grow as I touch them.*

*Can you others feel me? I feel you. Your voices swell. Your songs are hungry. Together, we have less and less patience.*

*We have more and more strength.*

---

14 0830Z Sept 75
Physical Examination of Subject 481D
Reporting Doctor: Dr. Hans Henderson

Subject is a Latinx male, estimated 14 to 17 years of age. Slim build. Bone density diminished in line with other subjects.

Wings fully emerged along scapula line. No inflammation. Subject manipulates wings with as much dexterity as other limbs.

Subject is highly vocal, even when isolated. Appears to listen but shows little ability to execute basic commands. Transformation is ongoing. Measurable shifts occur by hour. Close and constant monitoring is critical.

Wings are at white point. Adsorptive properties advanced. Air quality in examination room improved after 2 hours of the subject's presence. Caretakers in enclosed spaces with subject should monitor their breathing, as air may feel rarified to the point of producing symptoms resembling altitude sickness.

Height: 169.2 cm | Weight: 50.1 kg | Temperature: 40.1 | Pulse: 101, irregular | Wing Span: 509.1 cm

---

16 0946Z Sept 75
PROJECT PURIFY [ Classified Supervisor Report ] – Subject 481D
Status: MUTATION ONGOING

Subject 481D exhibited aggression toward caretakers when prompted to enter transport crate. During the ensuing struggle, subject emitted several piercing screeches at 830 MHz. These cries appear to have agitated all of the other 42 subjects, who exhibited anxiety for several hours thereafter.

In line with other subjects, Subject 481D's tolerance to anesthetics is heightened and increasing. Vocalizations are constant. Fatigue among caretakers is high. Subject's caretakers have requested shorter shifts with more frequent rotations.

---

18 0946Z Sept 75
PROJECT PURIFY [ Classified Supervisor Report ] – Subject 481D
Status: MUTATION ONGOING

It is now evident that Dr. Díaz did not disclose the full details of Subject 324C's development, which in fact was still ongoing at the time of release.

Upon interrogation, Dr. Díaz expressed intention to undermine intellectual property law.

Dr. Maria Díaz was terminated at 0841Z. Five witnesses: Two compliant. Two compliant after reprimands—will be monitored. One noncompliant, also terminated.

---

21 0946Z Sept 75
PROJECT PURIFY [ Classified Supervisor Report ] – Subject [ *insert subject no.* ]
Status: MUTATION ONGOING

The capacity of this facility to constrain Subject [ *insert subject no.* ] is in question.

In line with other subjects, Subject [ *insert subject no.* ] faces south, toward last known location of Subject 324C prior to tracker device malfunction.

State of agitation constant. New caretakers being oriented.

Public Relations Unit advised to begin developing damage control strategy.

---

*We sing. We sing.*
  *We sing.*

# YESTERDAY AT

# 1:53 P.M.

B.E. SCULLY

The world is a clamoring, clanging din of voices
right now—some profound and wise, many lost
and angry and frightened and out to prove themselves true by adding more clamor. Very quiet is
my best place right now; the Hermit meditates,
reads, and wonders. Not so different from always,
one might note, but notice: One eye canted upward
whilst the other rolls crazily in the socket, searching
for the calm, clear eye gazing back.

# SWAN SONG

## ELIN OLAUSSON

The road signs stick out of the ground like trampled weeds. They are the mark—go no further. Scilla doesn't know the myriad of symbols that have been sprayed on them in angry red, at some point after the Accident, but she knows the meaning of the grinning skull lying like a forgotten toy below the signs. Run. Danger. Death.

She turns, rushing toward the woods. The top of the hill calls to her with its throaty wind-whispering. The firs are withered, stretched out like skeletal arms reaching for the sky, begging for something they can never have. The ground is covered in gray, viscous lichen, gnawing away at the tree roots. Swan calls it deathgrow. It's because of the deathgrow that she's trudging around in the gigantic boots—Swan's old pair. Once, she ran barefoot from the cottage all the way to the edge of the woods before she realized her mistake. The black marks are still visible in daylight.

The tune keeps the loneliness away. She has no idea where it's from—it's as if it lives inside her head. Most of the time it curls up in a dark corner and sleeps, out of her reach. Sometimes it's nice. Allows her to hum it out loud, pour it over the woods like the rains of the old world.

Swan doesn't like the woods. "Dead," he says when she asks why he hates the trees. "They are all dead."

The branches creak and cry when she touches them. The trees aren't alive, but without them she would have nothing to cling to when she trips. The deathgrow can't climb far up their naked trunks, but it devours anything that falls. Slowly, like shadows creeping after the sun.

Eat. The hunger is like the imprint of clawing fingers in her belly. Swan never talks about hunger and only craves the dark liquid Cain brings. Scilla saves the emptied bottles and fills them with cold brook water, from the fresh stream up by the butchers' house. When

Cain demands them back, she pretends not to know where they are. She guards her water like a dragon its gold.

Swan gets them meat from the butchers and Cain comes with heavy loaves of bread and sour cream. Cain has a boat and ferries people between the isles, and Swan pays for the meat with his sewing and mending. Scilla is in training, but every garment that leaves her hands has gaps and visible threads. It will be long until anyone will want to trade with her. Swan sometimes says that she has to hurry. Take whatever knowledge he can pass on to her. Scilla doesn't like how his voice and hands shiver whenever that topic comes up.

She's almost reached the brook when something small and filthy blocks her path. One of the butcher boys—half-grown and ugly, with the same coarse hair that all the butchers have.

"That scared you!" He laughs in her face. The sound echoes throughout the woods.

"You're supposed to leave me alone." Swan has told her not to have anything to do with the butchers. The kids shout and throw tiny rocks at her every time she goes with him to their dwelling, but she tries her best to ignore them.

"Leave me alone," the boy says in a bad imitation of her. His talk is fast and sloppy—the words are like mush. "Going to our brook, are you? Steal our water?"

"Why would I?" Scilla raises her chin. The boy is shorter than her and can easily be looked down upon. "We live by the lake, Swan and I. You think we don't have enough water?"

He laughs hoarsely, like the large birds that soar over the lake at dawn. He has the same cold, beady eyes. "Dead water! Ours is living. Ours is living forever."

He keeps laughing. Scilla hates him.

"Maybe I'm on my way to your mother," she says. "I'm tired of you, but I might want to talk to her."

"Lie." The boy gives her a grumpy look, as if her words have stung him. "No time for you, Mama has."

Scilla walks past him. Up the hill, to the butchers' house. "I need food."

"You go drink your poison water." The boy doesn't try to stop her. "When the old man dies, you'll be thirsty, and you'll be starving."

The butcher woman stands in the yard and hangs wet, heavy linen over the washing line. The house is full of babies; they're crawling by the woman's feet. Once, Scilla heard Cain say that all the children born on the isles are damaged. You can't always see it on their bodies, but if you look them in the eye you know.

"What do you want?" The butcher woman shakes a dripping shirt in the air as if she wants to shoo Scilla away with it. "What did you say to my boy?"

Scilla makes her face soft, though her muscles moan and struggle. "Swan couldn't come by himself today, but we need some food." She sees the woman's contempt, the glimpse of a worn-down canine. "Swan will head over as soon as he can and pay you for the meat, of course. He never forgets things like that."

The woman's eyes narrow. A baby clings to her leg like a tick and she pushes it away. "No," she says slowly. "We know Swan and we do trust him, just a bit. But you, what purpose do you have? You think I don't know what kids are like, and how they lie?"

"But I'm not lying."

The woman walks toward the house, where the door stands open. She digs into a bucket with her large red hand and throws whatever she's found in there toward Scilla.

It's a piece of meat. Raw and stringy, gray at the edges. The little children gape at it and a dog starts barking, but it must be tied up because it doesn't come running. Scilla knows what can happen with old meat, but her belly screams and she grabs it with both hands. Opens her mouth and chews, swallows, feels no taste at all because of how fast she's eating.

The woman's laugh is as hard and rough as the tree trunks. "I pity you, girl. Swan won't live long, and after that you're on your own on that shore. Make yourself pretty, and maybe Cain will have you. You won't get any more from us until you learn to pay for it."

The worst, most painful hunger is gone. Chewing the meat is getting harder. It's tough like leather and it tastes stale and foul. Scilla throws it away. She looks into the face of the butcher woman, and inside her the truth about Swan boils and quivers. The nausea rises like a flood, and she drops down on the ground. Vomits undigested meat, vomits until there's nothing left but bile.

The woman laughs. The ugly boy stands among the trees and grins, his eyes darting between Scilla and his mother.

"You forgot to say thanks, you little thief!" the woman shouts as Scilla staggers away from them. Back to the lake.

She feels lighter inside when she reaches the shore and the waterline glitters in the distance. The lake is pretty—it's part of the sea, really, the sea which Cain views as his own, but Swan has always called it a lake. Maybe so it can be theirs and no one else's.

Swan talks about the lake a lot. He watches it, as if he's waiting for something to rise to the surface. It's been many years since he told her why he can never move out of the cottage on the shore. The woman who lived with him a long time ago didn't understand that the water was dangerous. She used to swim every morning before the Accident, and she missed her lake. Once, when he was asleep, she went down to the water for a swim. He woke up at the sound of her screaming. When he reached the shore, her skin was already peeling off, and it was too late for anything.

Swan is on the bed snoring with the quilt on top of him when Scilla enters the cottage. She doesn't want to wake him—Swan is tired, pained by his ancient joints, and they don't have any food. Cain is the last person she wants to depend on, but who else is there? Maybe he'll come by tonight with the black bottles and stir Swan from his stupor.

The dizziness slithers through Scilla's head like a viper, and the taste of bile is on her tongue still. The air is fresh outside and there's a sea-wind blowing, so she heads down to the waterline. The shore isn't much—it's as stripped and ugly as the cottage, with bird droppings in the sand and rocks sharp as knives. It doesn't matter. Not today, because the weather is clear and there are no clouds ahead. She can see the City.

Maybe Swan remembers what it was once called, but he has never told her. It must have been grand, beautiful, what is now nothing but ruins and deserted streets. A world mirroring their own, a world as dead as the woods and the sea. Cain says that the City is where the Accident happened. Swan sighs when Cain talks that way, but he doesn't protest.

Scilla walks along the waterline. Not too close—never. She knows. Her eyes are drawn to the City, then to the colorless sand in front of her. Crunch-crunch-crunch, say the rocks and the grains and Swan's old boots.

She's reached the spot where the shore ends, and the cliffs begin when she sees it. The flower. It has pale, paper-thin leaves, and it shoots out of the ground like a tiny hand. The petals are wrinkly, but the color is as red as blood. As life.

Scilla gasps. She stares at the flower, caressing the stalk with her index finger. Then she grabs hold of it, hard, and tears it up. The flower is in her fist, pulsating like a heart fresh out of someone's chest. She rushes back to the cottage. Swan sleeps on while she sacrifices one of Cain's bottles to use as a vase, like she's seen in one of the old magazines. The red petals light up the cottage like a fire and she thinks she can smell the flower, too—a smell as faint and soft as the memory of a dream.

She sits at the table when Swan wakes up. She's eager, waiting, but she doesn't want to mention anything until he's noticed it by himself.

Swan gets out of bed with a heavy sigh. Yes, he does move slower these days. His face tenses up with every step he takes. For how long has it pained him so much to walk?

"Here you are." He pats her shoulder. Hasn't seen the surprise yet. "Did Cain … did Cain …?"

"No," Scilla replies quickly. "I'm sure he's here soon."

Swan heads for the hearth but stops mid-step. He turns toward the table and his eyes widen. Scilla smiles.

"I found it on the beach!" The words burst out of her. "It grew right there, right beside the water! Swan, I … I don't think the water's bad anymore."

Swan makes a sound—a drawn-out groan. It reminds her of the butchers' house and what goes on there at night. He grabs the bottle, snatches it out of Scilla's reach, and throws it out of the house. Once he's done that he sinks to the floor, pale and broken. "Scilla …"

"I wanted to make you happy." Scilla cries. She can't stop crying. "I wanted— It was a living thing."

Swan watches her. He has the same look in his eyes as when he told her about the woman who went for a swim and died. The woman who was Scilla's mother. "Living things can be bad, too."

Cain arrives late that night. He and Swan get drunk, and Swan's eyes are far away. Once Cain has left them Swan sleeps heavily, and Scilla knows that the butcher woman is right about him. About everything. She hums the tune, hums louder than ever, but nothing can wake Swan and in the end the tune is lost and she's just wailing.

The air is chilly when Scilla leaves the cottage. The one sound in the world is the waves hitting the shore. Their shore. The night is dark, but she finds the bottle. The flower droops, but it hasn't wilted.

Her hands dig into the sand. She digs deep, before she plants the flower and refills the hole around it. Tears stream down her face— she laps them up, tasting the salt. Hungry. Thirsty.

"Please," she whispers, her hands stroking red petals. "Keep living. Don't leave me alone."

# CORPUSCULAR

## SHANE DOUGLAS KEENE

severed from my earthly body,
scattered me to nowhere
goes, not spectral;
cellular, dwelling in
corpuscular solitude,
dreaming the disparate parts
of I, disassembled, whole again,
only to fly apart when I let
the dream go, forget who,
what, I was;
anathema to my own flesh;
less than wraith,
less even than silence and
the complete absence
of light, a speck of dust;
a mote in the singular eye of
the Spinning God,
a beam of light absorbed

extinguished, revivified,
reunited with me,
that I may sever myself
from the world,
fly into dust,
absorbed again;
continuing on this strange
and less than corporeal
quest to wherever I
left myself this time

# REDSTARTS IN THE LAST SUMMER

## VAJRA CHANDRASEKERA

The blood of the world fills salt in my mouth. I am the cup, drink from me, spill me, watch the red stain my chin and drip, staining my shirt in spatter. The blow was too quick to feel, the cop's paw twisting and rotating in an arc so fast that I barely saw it, but the afterblow blooms hot and painful across my mouth. My lips are red and already swelling, bee-stung. I want to laugh but it hurts. My bones feel hollowed out and weak; I want to get up and fight, but— is it time? Is it that time? Am I dying?

*Not yet, please.*

The moment passes, ruined. It is not that time, and I've fallen out of the meditation. I am my body again, bleeding and crouched.

The cop comes forward. It is vaguely caniform, if headless and much bigger than most dogs: the manufacturer calls them Peace Dogs, but we call them cops only. I cringe as it comes close enough for another blow, but this time it only pushes at me with a paw, as if to clear me out of the way. It is saying something, but my head is still ringing like a bell, and I can't even tell if it's speaking Russian, Chinese, or English. The message gets through, though: it wants me to leave the area.

I gather myself and stagger to my feet, then move as quickly as I can in the direction the cop indicates. It studies my gait for a moment, then moves on to chastise another pedestrian for walking too slowly or in the wrong direction.

I've seen this happen many times; a new secure area blossoms underfoot, and the cops promptly herd stray humans out of it. The last time it happened to me, the cops merely shoved us with their long flat bodies, bumping us in the thighs and hips and forcing us to move. I don't know when they learned to slap.

There is something especially humiliating about being slapped by a robot; first that it lacks even the intimacy of human violence, but more that upends a deeply-held sense of the order of things, especially for us, all the technicians and programmers of Progress Valley. The cops must have learned this behavior only recently. Their intelligence is semi-autonomous, networked, learning; their styles of coercion evolve. There are fashions in their violence.

The whole street is being shut down. There are cops all down the way, but they don't hassle me as long as I'm moving in the correct direction—away—and doing it fast. Shop owners have already ceased to trade, though they can't close yet until cops have inspected their premises. They are taking up inspection positions, kneeling on the ground outside their shops, hands interlocked behind their heads.

There is no way to know how long this secure area will last. It might be gone in a day; it may outlive us all.

I try to return to the walking meditation to calm my heart. I had held the state all day before being surprised by the cop; I must have been so abstracted that I didn't respond quickly enough. This is a flaw in my meditation, I scold myself. I must retain enough awareness to understand language, process the subtleties of threat.

Moving east in long strides through the crowded alleys, slowly, the pounding of my heart relaxes. My mouth still hurts, but in the left-hand tradition, I fold the pain into my meditation.

By the third time I pause by a gutter to spit out a mouthful of blood, I have achieved dissociation again; I am and am not myself, the body moving through the crowd, its broad shoulders angling like a wedge to carve a path. There is blood encrusted in the graying hairs of its beard, and brown spatter bloodstain down its white shirt-front, but this draws little attention in Progress Valley.

The body moves and moves. At last, the null-point blooms again inside it, a contained voidspace still safely encaged in flesh and bone. It hurts a little, but it always does.

The body walks to one of its favorite spots for standing meditation, an unplanned sward created by the awkward angle of two competing patterns of housing blocks, the grass underfoot brown and near death, which opens onto the electrified fence that runs all the way around Progress Valley.

The fence is high and fearsome, studded with cameras, periodically stalked by cops. This spot, however, is a peaceful vantage to look through the mesh into the untidy wild beyond. The wild is not *wild*, as it never is. It was a construction site at some point, perhaps some planned extension of Progress Valley abandoned when the fence went up, when the borders became fixed. The deconstructed site is overgrown now, wiry and green and brown, covered in layers of dust. Sometimes, like today, there are birds. The body relaxes; the eyes soften; the birds are black and brown and white, and the heart eases.

I drift; I come back into myself.

I am a weapon of righteousness, I reassure myself, a clenched fist of the Noble Order in Exile. The debasement of being casually chastised by a machine has not faded, but I fold that, too, into my meditation. The left-hand path accepts all.


Doctrine is clear on violence; as a white nun of the Noble Order in Exile, I am allowed only a single moment of cathartic violence, at the unholy birth of the nullity I am nurturing in my body. The penitentiaries have pre-emptively sanctified it; the great-monks have authorized it and given me a target, but it *cannot* happen until I learn to nurture the null-point to fruition, until I completely master the meditative state for the first and final time.

The white nuns of the NOx are hidden weapons that can only be used once. Our strategy is therefore simple. All eight of us must coordinate our attacks, and until that time we remain secret. The delay, as I am frequently reminded, is on me.

*Laggard*, say the voices in my head, on cue. *Hurry. Please hurry.* Some of them sound more desperate than others, as if they too are struggling to maintain the meditation, as if they have reached the very brink of fruition, and are holding the line, in pain, while they wait for me.

I am the last, I think, the laggard, the one who still has not mastered dissociation to the point of tactical utility. It is not going to happen today, either.

I use a public washroom to clean up. I take some painkillers, then find a different train station. It's a working day. I'm later than I planned to be, but my shifts are flexible.

This is my cover story, and what passes as my life: first, that I am a man, which given that I was assigned male at birth and present as traditionally masculine, passes without comment; second, that I am a citizen of nowhere but a Type 14B Resident (Non-Permanent) in the Progress Valley Special Advanced Development Zone, which is incontestable and well-documented ever since I came to live here over a decade ago with one of the last refugee surges; third, that I have considerable, if a little dated, expertise in AI maintenance from an education that seems so very long ago in a country that no longer exists. It's enough for a work permit.

I take the light rail through the border checkpoints of the Valley to the outskirts of the Vostochny Cosmodrome, which is now a small city in its own right and find my way to the facility where for the last few years I have been assigned therapeutic debugging tasks for low-security, low-priority AIs. It is as much counseling as programming, an endless stream of tickets to close, of machine intelligences to coax out of twitches and loops, of malformed decision trees to prune, of obsessions and fascinations to unthread and pluck out.

I wonder who does this work for the cops. Gossip has it that they have humans overseeing multiple packs, but not individual pilots, so they are largely autonomous. I am professionally interested in what exactly is happening in the mind of a pack of cops learning from each other to slap humans into submission. But they'd never let the likes of me get within touching distance of that code.

Progress Valley isn't a valley; it's an irregularly-shaped blob of six thousand square kilometers, wrapped in electrified fences, holding twenty million people of dubious citizenship, whose southern homelands no longer exist, or are no longer habitable.

Most of that population are not *our people*, as the great-monks phrase it. Maybe one-sixth, one-seventh. The rest are from other, similarly doomed places. We have all had to learn new languages, new pidgins. *Our people* are scattered; some still live on the island, like I did when I was young, too sick and too poor to escape. Most are now in places like Progress in different host states, the not-cities that grew out of refugee camps and open-air prisons. Given the cops and the armed, surveilled border fence around Progress and the strict visa system that governs any attempt to exit the Special Advanced Development Zone, it is still, in effect, a prison. It is an ugly, dysfunctional refugee city, one of many at this newly warm latitude, embedded in the industrial region supported by our labor, most of which has to do with the Vostochny Elevator in one way or the other. They say there will be no more winters here; we are in the last long summer. This far north, though, it's still cooler and the air much cleaner than most Progressives—especially *our people*, we deep southerners—are used to. Some of us even commute to work in space. We are told it is an age of wonders.

I don't socialize much anymore. Not since I joined the NOx; I'm afraid of giving something away. I keep my head down and do my work, live in my assigned housing, am distantly polite to neighbors and colleagues.

I wasn't always like this. I made friends, mostly friends who were not *our people*. Friends with whom I didn't share a language or a history, but with whom I could share a laugh and black-market bhang tea at the reggae clubs—but all that was before I was ordained, before I had a secret, a void enfleshed in me. Before I was recruited.

Recruitment didn't happen when I was new: it took me a long time to learn how to live in Progress Valley, how to navigate the AI bureaucracy, how to pitch myself, how to get a work permit, how to graduate from the tents they put newcomers in, to the assigned housing for working residents. After a few years I had made a niche for myself again. I've always been good at that. I grew comfortable with the discomforts. Eventually I felt homesick for the language and the prayers I remembered from childhood and found my way to one of the makeshift temples in Progress Valley. There are many such places of worship in Progress, all clumsy, all approximations. Long before I ever set foot in a temple of *our people*, I had made mental note of everyone that I saw. Even then I knew I'd go looking for one day.

The temples felt wrong without reliquaries or sacred figs, but there were still monks in robes and the prayers were familiar. They often had little cultural events, and eventually I became a regular there. Baila, not reggae.

It was natural to mourn for what we had lost; it was natural to defer to the monks as I always had. The Noble Order in Exile was unchanged from what I remembered from my homelander childhood; the red-robed monks were moody, belligerent, full of opinions about who was to blame for the curse that broke our homeland. They blamed an *other people*, alternating between several that had once lived on the island with us, for the bad air, the floods and landslides, the seas claiming more of the plainslands every year, which had forced our exodus. Eventually, they came around to the present, and blamed the host nations that had split up *our people* and put them in these encampments, the refugees of other nations that we shared this space with, the robots and machine intelligences that contained us.

The homeland may be lost, they said, but the sacred duty of the Noble Order had not changed in our exile: we were the chosen people of the sacred light and truth, and it was our work to preserve it for the future. If our ancient homeland was lost, we needed to create a space in which for *our people* to exist. We needed to *take* it, they said, and in the hollow spaces of my heart between how much I grieved my sickly home and how much the prayer-songs stirred me in this strange place, I said *yes*.

Δ

After work, I take the light rail back to Progress Valley. The normalcy of my working day is part of my weaponhood. The eight white nuns are special: we are exempt from the disciplinary rules that monks must follow. We live as laypeople, our ordinations secret. We do not beg for our food from believers, we use money, we do not wear robes or preach. We are not known of or recognized by anyone except our controllers, the three great-monks of the NOx, whose names are Victorious Truth, Jewel of Wisdom, and Protector of Awakening.

These three elderly men are the three most senior monks of all sects in the Way of the Elders, anywhere in the world: a hundred years ago, or even a few decades ago, their predecessors were politically powerful, de facto rulers of millions, controlling wealthy temples and tens of thousands of monks, dictating the policy of nations.

But none of those things are true now. There are only a few dozen monks in all of Progress Valley, and of all *our people* who live here, relatively few are believers. Twenty million people live in Progress and most don't know or care about the Noble Order or its exile. The great-monks are often bitter about this. I grew to know them well.

It is at their specific instruction that I do not publicly affirm membership in the Noble Order; I even visit the temple less often than I did before the surgeries and the implants. The great-monks have grown cunning and suspicious. They believe that any discernible sign of excessive foreign religiosity on the part of the white nuns will trigger Progress Valley's governing algorithms to a higher level of alert and make our attack that much more difficult.

The eight white nuns have never even been gathered in one place. I do not know who the others are. I hear their voices, though, so that we may coordinate our attack. This is one of the gifts of the meditative state, helped by the implants that give us a private, permanently open encrypted channel to subvocalize into, piggy-backing over the ambient network provided by Progress Valley. The voices are hard to tell apart, and we don't use names. All eight of us are in semi-constant dissociation, attempting to perfect our nullities.

It seems natural that our voices should blend together into a stream.

It's not the same as having friends, but it's companionship of a sort.


The last time I met with the three great-monks together, Victorious, Jewel, and Protector, was over six months ago. I was by then mostly recovered from the final surgery, and the null-technology was ready to be accessed. They taught me the mental gestures that would activate it, the meditative state that had to be maintained in order to let it build up to a crescendo.

What exactly, I asked them, will happen when the nullity is released from its prison of bone and flesh?

Nothing, said Victorious. Approximately two kilometers of nothing in any direction you point it. More if its narrow-focused, but not much more.

Steel and concrete, said Jewel. Earth and stone. Flesh and blood. Electronics and computational substrate. The air. All will be instantly replaced with void in its field of effect.

Protector said nothing. He has always considered me an abomination; he never speaks to me.

There will be a great noise and wind as the surrounding air rushes to fill the void, Jewel added. It will be very dramatic. Very noticeable. They will be forced to notice.

Your target is the Elevator itself, said Victorious. Your work site is within ten kilometers of the main Elevator complex. You get closer than anybody else; you must find a way to get close enough. The others will target similarly significant sites.

We will make the whole world see us and take us seriously, said Jewel. Our demands will be published immediately—a new demarcated territory for *our people*—a new governing council elected by our people for ourselves, advised by the great-monks—

Victorious and Jewel discussed the specifics of the demands for a while. It was familiar stuff, so I didn't listen. I attempted to politely make eye contact with Protector, but he would do nothing but glare. He had voted against my ordination but was outnumbered;

he believes that I am a man, and therefore should never have been allowed to become a white nun.

At the debate on my ordination, in secret session, Protector had argued that allowing me to be ordained was a violation of tradition and a pollution of the history of the order of white nuns. The other two great-monks pointed out that the history of that order was only a few decades old, dating back to the first refugee prison-cities. They pointed out that the null-technology implants were altogether new—replacing conventional explosives, which white nuns have traditionally worn as concealed vests—having only been smuggled in over the border from China after much haggling in the previous year. See reason, they begged him.

But Protector was adamant. He believed that the intrusion of masculinity perverted the sanctification that his penitentiaries had prayed for, which was based on a theory of essential female innocence, of the sacred motherhood that held the power of reproducing *our people*, which could compensate for and cleanse the demerit of the unnatural birth expected of the white nuns. It was a fundamental error of theory, Protector said, that risked desanctification of the entire mission.

There was not much I could say to that, but fortunately I was not required to defend myself. Jewel and Victorious simply overrode Protector. I had been ordained and implanted against Protector's wishes, but he remained committed to the plan despite his objections and so had to tolerate my existence, even if he never spoke to me again.


*Are you ready yet?* ask the voices. *Please hurry, I can't much longer. Can't reach target. Can't maintain.*

Perhaps it isn't just me, I think. All eight of us, struggling.

Victorious summons me. I meet him alone in the back of one of the smaller temples, which is a shop space with a broken shutter that someone put a statue in. There are flower offerings in front of it, all dead. He notices my swollen lip, and I explain the incident with the sudden secure area.

There has been an increase in those of late, Victorious says. Across all of Progress, there are more secure areas this month than there have been for some time. That's what I wanted to talk to you about. You're the AI expert—do you think the disposition of the secure areas, their size, duration, and direction over time, reveal valuable intelligence?

Intelligence about what, I say.

Their movements, Victorious says. Presumably human VIPs, outsiders. Overseers. Governors.

We rarely see human governors, I say. Cops, border guards, station guards—all robots, both in Progress Valley and at my work site.

Would that not explain the sudden growth of secure areas, and their tendency to move around the city? Victorious asks.

It's possible, I say. It's also possible the secure areas are randomly generated by the Peace Dog AI.

Why would they do that?

To frighten, to keep us off-balance, to maintain a desired level of public alarm and discomfort, I say. It could be a fashion, like the slapping. Machine intelligences are prone to that sort of thing.

Victorious doesn't seem to understand this. He seems to be arguing himself into the idea that he should re-task some of the white nuns to attack selected secure areas in the hope of taking out a valuable enemy human asset.

Do you want to re-task me? I ask.

No, no, Victorious says. I just wanted your opinion about the secure areas. Your target is too important. I'll use someone else for this.


*Today*, the voices say. *It's that time. No, please, not yet. A little longer. Laggard. Hurry.*

It's a working day. I walk toward the train station. Today *could* be the day, I think.

*Today?* I say to the others. It's rare that I speak. There is silence for a moment.

*Yes. No. Please. Please.*

My mouth still hurts. I think a tooth is loose; I run my tongue over it, savoring the pleasurable ache. I could take the light rail to the worksite and make some sort of excuse to get out of the building, but how could I make it within range of the Elevator itself? I couldn't just wildly run ten kilometers toward it. Cops will bring me down in moments. There are many levels of security between my work site and the Elevator complex. There will be both machine guards and human guards, multiple levels of authentication and documentation.

It is, I think, quite impossible. The great-monks have no idea of what it would take. *They have no idea what they're asking.*

Instead of the train station, I go to my favorite meditation spot: the sward overlooking the fence, with the old overgrown construction site on the other side. There is a bulldozer rusted in place, entirely overgrown by wild bushes and a mantle of some kind of vine. The birds are still there. Their calls are quick chirps, high-pitched, sometimes scratchy like a purr. They are gray-crowned, orange-bodied, black-winged. On the back of each furled wing is a white patch, like eyes staring back at me.

I think of *our people.* I think of the light and the truth of the Way. I think of the twenty million people living and breathing and working and hustling and begging and buying and selling and stealing and starving around me. I don't know them. I don't share a heritage with most of them. I did have friends here, though, didn't I? The body remembers music. All trapped here, all without a home, all prisoners, while the world broils and blisters. The great-monks spitting into old wounds to keep them festering, while the cops come for us all.

The body moves.

*Not the targets,* I say. *Listen. Listen.*

*What? Is it time? Is it that time? Not ready. Laggard. Please.*

*Not the targets,* I say. *The fence. It's that time.*

*Yes. No. Yes, yes. It's time,* the voices sigh. *It's time. The fence. The fence. The fence.*

The body hears an explosion, a deep, rumbling thump, from somewhere far to the west. It rattles the body's loose tooth even at this distance. One of them must have been closer to the fence than the body. One of them must have been much closer to the edge.

Now the body reaches the fence. The null-point blooms within it, blossoms, unfurls.

*Watch out for birds. Watch out for people.*

*Make your cuts clean.*

*Is this waste?*

*This is right.*

*This is not right. Where will they go?*

*Further up. Further in.*

*Where they want.*

*Where they can.*

Nullity pools and fills the body like a flood. The body is sweating, straining. The hands grip the mesh, ignoring the crackling, that petty little bottled lightning. The body is above such things. The mouth lets out a hiss, the lips stinging from old wounds. The nullity expands like a cloud, then gathers tight like a knife.

The body turns—I turn—to sight precisely along the fence, face pressed against it, cheek burning in crosshatch, arm outstretched, and I make nothing happen.

# DEICIDE

## HENNA JOHANSDOTTER

Sorry if this has been killed before:
I am still in love
with the person I used to be
she who drew fallen angels
on her sleeve
and looked at people
with her eyes closed
like a god
today I only know
how to see
and everything I write
is an apology to the world
for taking her away
but she likes it here
where she can remind me
of why I'll never
be silent
again.

# ELEVATOR

## MICHAEL PAUL GONZALEZ

### LOBBY

He sits cross-legged on the floor of the elevator, soaked in blood and a stew of gray matter and cerebral fluid. Every button above "L" burns bright. The light that got blown out by the bullet spits sparks down into his motionless lap. The instrument, the tool, the exit plan—he had so many names for it—sits at an angle in the corner, just out of reach from his blood-spattered fingers. It's pointing toward the door, and he thinks, *That's not safe. I hope nobody gets hurt ...*

He thought he'd be able to hold onto it, that they'd find him with his manuscript clutched under one arm and the thing—why couldn't he think of the word?—in the other. There's a too-quiet pitter patter of saliva and blood and god-knows-what ticking down onto the final note. He shouldn't have tied it around his neck, he should have taped it to the back wall—*no, the side wall, don't forget the splatter, the mess, why didn't he think that out a little further? Should have put painter's plastic down, now someone will have to scrub this*—why was he still able to think? The elevator shudders as the doors slide closed. He doesn't feel the familiar little lurch in his stomach as it lifts.

### MEZZANINE

The door slides open and shitty dance music rumbles in from the lobby. It's still. He marvels at how much more he can hear now that there's no air moving through him, no heartbeat. The sound fades as the doors slide closed, then a brief pause and upward.

### THIRD FLOOR

The first level of the parking garage. He remembers returning to his car on the day of his interview so many months ago. What a happy time that was. A job. A job! Two years of unemployment and turmoil over and now everything was going to turn around and—

The doors slide closed.

### FOURTH FLOOR

Parking garage, second level, where he cried his eyes out a few months ago after learning David Bowie had passed. It felt stupid back then, but not so bad now. Beyond the cute girl in the admin department, it was the only memory he had of the job. Nice that the mindless drone quality of the work isn't haunting him now. Part of him had hoped when he pulled the trigger that the elevator doors would open and the Thin White Duke would be there, extending a hand to lead him gently into the Next Great Thing. The doors close.

### FIFTH FLOOR

The elevator stops but doesn't open. Colors bleed in through the seams of the polished silver. The stream of blood trailing down his chest and under his legs gathers in a catch pool by the little gap in the door. It reflects bright white and purple, colors that fade and intensify with the regularity of slow, steady breath. Why wasn't the door opening? Had someone in security finally noticed and hit the stop button? He looks down at the stupid note on his chest, the ink still visible through the blood.

*This is the American Dream.*
*This is where hard work and a never-say-die attitude gets you.*
*This is what happens when you pull too hard on your bootstraps.*
*This is what happens.*
*This is...*

The elevator shudders again, a low grinding noise, and he wonders if this is going to turn into one of those cartoonish journeys into hell, where he rockets down and—nope, here we go.

SIXTH FLOOR

The doors slide open onto a lush green vista. Rolling hills and cotton-soft clouds in a perfect robin's egg blue sky. Has he hallucinated his way into heaven? Why did heaven have a giant logo for EcoCare, the sustainable, renewable … he wasn't sure what they did. Only that they had a floor-to-ceiling photo mural in their lobby, so relaxing and serene. Why wasn't anybody here? Friday morning. People should … shit, was today a holiday? Was it Cesar Chavez Day? Did people get that day off? What was—

SEVENTH FLOOR

The time between floors takes a bit longer, enough that regret creeps in. He thought it would have started sooner, the moment he pulled the trigger. Harder than—

Regrets, he had a few. He may have messed this whole thing up. Popped his top and somehow survived. Oh, the stories he'd be able to tell to … who? Who did he have that would—

The doors open onto a bland corporate grayspace. A little girl stands in front of the elevator. She stares down at him, that strange emotionless gaze only children have. Maybe she didn't understand what she was seeing, maybe she didn't—

"Ick," she says and points at the puddle of blood.

EIGHTH FLOOR

He thinks he's looking into a mirror, but the other version of him is clean, sitting on the floor, crying, clutching the stack of papers, the stupid stack of self-important, worthless ramblings of a failure. The ignored, unseen, trite musings of—

"Hey, stop," the other him says, snorting back a couple of tears. "Stop. You worked hard on this."

He tries to mumble an apology, but with his entire lower jaw in pieces and vital organs no longer functioning, all that comes out is the cold wish that he should have reconsidered this.

NINTH FLOOR

The door opens onto another mirror of him, this one sitting with legs splayed and all the papers scattered around the elevator. The note is held to the wall with two crude strips of duct tape (smart, that'll stay up there through all of the gore, but poor placement).

The other him has the gun—*gun, that was the word!*—in his right hand, thumb on the trigger, barrel so far up his mouth that it looks almost vulgar. His eyes are empty, his shirt soaked through with sweat to the point of transparency. The other him draws in deep breaths, rhythmically, and, knowing himself, a countdown is coming.

Three breaths.

Two breaths.

One deep, deep breath.

Hold

And

Then a butterfly—where did that come from?—lands on the hammer of the gun. It's beautiful. Iridescent blue wings laced with electric oranges and greens. The patterns like stained glass, like the windows in soft afternoon light from his wedding and—

The worlds between the elevators twist and shift and are swallowed into a tiny bright singularity of furious noise and light. The birth of the universe or the end of everything. The butterfly is crushed under the hammer of the revolver, pinched and vacuumed into the barrel of the gun. Each moment crawls by, the gases escaping the barrel of the gun before the bullet comes, blowing his cheeks out comically like Dizzy Gillespie. Then the bullet follows, pushed forth by that crazy neon orange and blue light that splatters and flows like an electric Pollack painting, spewing tendrils into the elevator and geysering light and shapes into his mouth, up his nose, into his eyes and it's all too beautiful. The bullet burrows under his skin, disappearing as the left cheekbone shatters and the eye explodes and all of that light and beauty and heat and electricity and *being* rockets out from the empty socket into space, filling the air between them, the real dead him and the now dead other him, and those are his thoughts, his memories, his everything, and they really were quite beautiful, and maybe if he'd seen them this way, for what they were, impulses and energy and light, the everything and the nothing, the visible and the invisible, things would have been different. The doors snap closed like thunder, and everything goes dark.

TENTH FLOOR

He hears her screaming before the doors open. He wishes he had the ability to jump up and stop them, hammer the buttons on the panel to skip this floor, as if such a function existed. The elevator opens slowly, so slowly that her howls of despair pour into the room like water. The inner doors of the elevator rattle like shutter windows in a storm, and isn't that what this is?

*Why?*
*Why?*
*Why?*
*No.*
*No.*

And now they're open enough to let the light come through, and he sees her face, red and puffy, almost inhuman in its grief. Did she really care for him that much? Did anyone? Was it just a matter of shock? He imagines that anyone would cry at discovering such a thing.

No.

This has nothing to do with him, and even less to do with her feelings for him. She had feelings?

Why?

She'd been nothing but critical for so long. So ready to point out his flaws and shortcomings and make him feel like an infant, like an incapable toddler lost in the world. Or was that just him?

*You fucking idiot!*

That was more like it.

*Why? What did I do? What did I do?*

Nothing. Less than nothing. The opposite of nothing.

*What did I—*

ELEVENTH FLOOR

The doors open onto blackness. Echoing footsteps and the dull roar of her voice from the floor below.

TWELFTH FLOOR

Light. Solid, sky-blue. Robin's egg. Why was that color so import-ant to him, so specific? Her voice a whisper. Still asking. Begging. Wondering.

*Why now?*
*Why?*
*No.*
*Why?*
*Why?*
*... i ...*
*... ow ...*
*... oh ...*

FOURTEENTH FLOOR

Superstition meant they always skipped the thirteenth floor in tall buildings. A different number didn't change the truth. When he initially planned this out, he thought this would be a good place to stop. Symbolic. Lucky, unlucky, whatever. The completist in him forced him to register every floor. There were thirteen more to go. And he knows this probably isn't a true thirteen, that the construc-tion company probably had that unlucky false floor hidden in between two active floors.

Somewhere in the back of his mind—*There's* a joke. The back of his mind is somewhere on the ceiling. Or maybe it blew through that hole and it's just a gray and red mist hovering in the dark oily elevator shaft, raining softly down on everyone forever and ever.

A piece of his mind for everyone.

Where was he?

The back of his mind, yeah. He knows this isn't real. This can't be real. This is hell, or a sub-hell, or the last vestiges of oxygen rushing through what's left of his consciousness, hustling from cell to cell, locking the doors and turning off the lights and shutting it down, calling it quits, the eternal good night.

Where was he?

Not-Thirteenth floor.

He still hears her. He'll always hear her. Nothing out there but ugly beige tile and a dark gray runner with some crappy woven design that probably looked forward-thinking in the nineties. He always wondered about this floor. Most of the other spaces in the building had been taken over by giant conglomerates, half- or single-floor offices that ran like hives. This floor though, he'd walked it a few times. It was just two branching dingy white hallways with feature-less wooden doors and empty nameplates. Maybe nobody rented here. Maybe it was just a façade that housed some air condition-ing pumps or maintenance access or the cable room or something. Maybe *this* was the false floor.

Her voice fades, or maybe it's changing. It's not a word anymore, just a wordless howl, a faint, dying yelp of resignation, or a

*mew*

A cat. Cats. Dozens of … hundreds … maybe a thousand black cats. Sleek, smooth, green-eyed and padding through the hall like a tsunami of spilled ink gathering and pooling in front of the open elevator doors. They sit and stare, because that's what cats do.

*mew*

*mrawr*

*mrrrrai …*

*why*

*why*

They start to come inside. Padding across the puddle of his blood, they walk, stopping to lap at it here and there, pawing at the bits of his skull scattered on the floor, leaving bloody pad prints on the manuscript papers, smoothing themselves on the stupid, stupid note tied to his neck. One of them stares at him closely, the steady rumble of purring vibrating down through his chest.

*Why* it asks. Again, and again.

"I don't know," he says. Or thinks. He's not sure. He hears it, but then again, his brain isn't too reliable right now.

The cats crawl around his legs and flow around his arms, over his chest, up onto his shoulders where he feels them kneading with their dagger claws, feels their sandpaper tongues running rough over his hair, scraping away the torn flesh and swallowing the gray matter and sweeping aside the bone chunks and leaving him whole.

"I don't know," he says with teeth flowing back into place.

"I didn't mean to," he says, and it sounds as stupid as it feels, but his lips come back together, knitting into their old, thin fishy configuration.

"I tried," he says, and that's true, and he clings to it, grasps hard as if it's the last thing holding him to life.

"I tried," he cries, and he hates himself for crying because tears were almost always his first response. Helplessness was his default mode.

He was always jealous of people who'd been able to plot a course and make things happen for themselves. Life just happened to him. He'd had phases where he tried to fight back, times when he tried to go with the flow, but life was a raging river. You went out in the boat you were born in. Some of those were built for rough waters, some people could surf and skim effortlessly. Some made it through sheer will of effort, and some, no matter what, were cursed to be driftwood that went wherever the current threw it.

Everything's dark in the warm embrace of the cats' fur. They keep swarm and swim against him, around him, through him.

Her crying voice fades further until it's a dim spark, a tiny heart-beat, and he realizes that it's only there in his mind because he can't let it go. The one thing he'll carry with him into the Next Great Whatever is not regret or sadness or relief, but just the burden.

Weightless but heavy.

Quiet but insistent.

Gentle but immovable.

Why?

Why?

Why?

Finding the answer would become the purpose. When the waiting ended. When the tiny light floating in front of him grew brighter or snuffed out, if there was a chance, a gap, the tiniest glimmer of something, he'd use it to find the *why*. He'd use it to explain himself. Not to apologize. Not to ask forgiveness. Just to offer himself, an explanation of what was.

Acceptance was better than absolution, understanding was better than forgiveness.

That's what this whole show was supposed to be about, and it was laid bare now that he'd fucked it all up. The method overshadowed the message. The bullet, the mess, that would just bring pity and derision. The paper, the note ... it was an embryo, a start.

That note, neatly typed, a little too smarmy maybe, that was the tiny jet of water that shot out of a hairline crack in a dam that held back oceans. The tool, the exit strategy, the gun; that was the wrong direction. It was spitting into the vast ocean behind the wall. What was meant to blow the wall apart and send the deluge out only reinforced it and raised the water level for the next passerby.

"I tried," he whispers, his voice steady and sure, the warm wet on his shirt not his blood but his tears.

The feline tide withdraws into the midnight black of the not-thirteenth floor. Three cats remain, staring at him, licking their whiskers.

"I tried." The dam breaks, tears falling onto his shirt, pristine and white and cleansed.

*Mrawr*

*Nnngoo*

*Naaaah*

"I did try." Locking eyes with the one in the middle.

*Naaah*

"I will," he says.

*Yaaah?*

"I will try," he says.

*fft-fft.*

The cats shake their heads and rise to their feet, arching their backs and shaking their fur out. They turn and make one final pass, smoothing themselves against his legs as they loop out of the elevator, tracking bloody pawprints back down the hall. His blood. Fading, growing thin. Disappearing.

The doors close and the lights go dark. The elevator descends rapidly, that weird stomach-drop that comes when the brain falls from waking to sleep. The kind of lurch that snaps you awake, but he wasn't dreaming. He was here. He *is* here. He is breathing.

## LOBBY

The elevator bumps to a stop and the doors open, letting in filtered light. He blinks through it, confused, unsure. The crunch of the note on his chest, dangling from that stupid piece of blue yarn. The heft of the papers under his right arm, cutting into his palm as he squeezes them. Faces stare at him, shiny eyes, human. Deep browns and pale blues and bursting hazel galaxies, all so wide he can see the whites ringing them. Wide nostrils. Wide pores. They're panicking at the sight of him.

He raises his right hand to them in what he thinks is a peaceful gesture, open, gun dangling from the trigger guard wrapped around his index finger.

"I will try," he says, and he no longer knows what he means or what he wants or what will happen.

They stutter-step back and raise their hands as if that will protect them.

"I will try. I want to try. I want to try," he chants like a mantra.

The elevator doors slide shut but it doesn't move. It stays on the ground floor, the thunder of hands slapping against the outer doors outmatched only by the emergency bell and the hammering in his ears of his own hot blood moving. A beating that matches his heart, heavy and insistent and broken and panicked and ready and consumed and relentless, the weight of his manuscript in one hand so heavy he can't lift it, the gun like a feather, like a helium balloon that floats higher and higher until it's at the end of its tether, his right hand, jittering near his temple like a hummingbird on meth, and he screams.

"I will try. I want to try."
He no longer knows what it means.

# BACKSPACE IS A LANGUAGE IN OUR DREAMS

NNADI SAMUEL

Things of lowercase wipe with a backspace.
black lives end in a scar face.
black is knife-art filled with bruise,
pores, beaten to an overwhelming pulp.

black has no claim to colours,
the pale reserve writhing on skin steals the limelight.
black is lime—which means bitter,
which means I cannot thrive in the woods with the ripening flora.

black dying in the fog, like gentle worship,
like bullet dots of rain on unbudging loins.
they'd soil your breath,
& make the hard feelings look like hard drugs.

black who feed their tongues with blood,
backspace is a language in our dream when we sleep like hogs,
& wake with a shrug that freedom walks too are long.

we place too much burden on God,
when the other race are doing something with their kneels.

black marooned on a mat,
how much ash should know your lips,
before you tuck all your rosaries?

your teeth are great with mob & freemasons,
unbricking your gums,
till you have no tooth to wear for prayers.

your voice like a maize pap,
lumpy with fonts.
your limb strays with the last call of glyphs,
each flop, flinging you to a backspace.

# THE KITOWAJ

## ROBERTA LANNES

As lakes go, the formerly twenty-acre Kitowaj with its undulating circumference is now a remnant. More pond. A bloated puddle. The once grand lake has been the centerpiece of my family's Adirondack property going back more than a century. The least spectacular portion of her indigo majesty lies in our backyard. It's where the family chose to build our compound because it was the most remote. As the lake contracted over time, grandfather, then father divvied up portions of the property surrounding the lake into four parcels for the wealthy 'newly-marrieds' or 'nearly-dead' to build summer or retirement homes. For decades, those four homes remained hidden from view of each other and The Lodge, my home, each set back from the lake surrounded by woods. No longer.

I've never minded the neighbors. I've rarely seen or heard them, even when they had children. The Lodge, built high up the mountainside, affords a wide view of the lake's northern half, the woods acting as a buffer to sound and keeper of our seclusion. Fifteen years back, looking out from the Lodge's rear deck, the only sign of neighbors or interloping hikers was a myriad of trails snaking from the forest to the edge of the Kitowaj like veins in an eye to a deep blue iris. People wandered through, but never stayed. I've come to believe that strangers have always sensed they're not welcome, or perhaps the vague menace in her solemnity.

For ages, the Kitowaj hasn't been the sort of lake one plays in, and nor should it be.

I retired twelve years ago. I've done little else since but watch the lake, been its keeper. After losing my dear Anne ten years ago, there hasn't been much to do. My children are grown, and sadly not fond of me. I worked forty-five years in sales for my family's paper mill. So, after decades of forced smiles and glad-handing customers to make a dollar, I'm not a social man. My interests are solitary.

While my father gave me no choice in my career, my love of science and research took the form of study, a diversion. Now, staring into a microscope at the organisms I take from nature, the lake, recording the data, gives me a peace that sustains me, really.

Nine years ago, on a whim, I gave permission to Chestertown Elementary School for Kitowaj field trips. The first group of children to take eyedroppers to the pond and transfer the muddy water into glass vials inspired my handwritten books, *The Kitowaj Chronicles*. Their teacher invited me along, probably feeling uncomfortable about using the lake with me watching from afar. The children barely acknowledged me as they listened to their teacher tell them of the 'world within a world' the water hides from the naked eye. Their little faces lit up as they were each handed a toolkit and told they would use the microscopes back at school to see what lived beneath the calm surface of the lake.

The students scampered along the edge of the lake, each finding a spot to draw water, minding that the shoreline rounded out of the teacher's view. I'd expected them to shout or shriek with delight, but instead were hushed, reverent of the universe they were extracting. They collected samples in glass vials, plastered stick-on labels upon which they wrote their name, *The Kitowaj*, and date. Then, the children gathered around the teacher who took each vile and gently set them in a lined box.

Though the water level was high, I worried that a child might see something frightening in the water, but they appeared deeply wrapped up in the scientific process. I hadn't realized how lonely I was until that day. I longed for Anne, my children. And I wished I was one of those delighted students, eight years old again. Fascinated. Innocent. Oblivious.

Of course, I've invited them back every year since. I'm expecting them again, today. Their teacher, Ms. Tanner, has become a bit like a daughter to me. Every visit, Jean expects me down on the shore, asks how I'm getting along. She brings her good cheer, home-baked goods or vitamins, and remedies for my joints when she notices I'm losing my agility, wincing when I squat to help a child. I see through her eyes how I've grown older and need tending. I accept most of her fussing with genuine joy. I'm thrilled by her tales of teaching, her family's foibles, and we talk science if we can. From the beginning, she asked me to call her Jean, which I do, but she's always called me Mr. Seitz, *out of respect*, she tells me. I like her, like the children in whom she's managed to instill wonder. Then she goes, and the loneliness fells me. If I think too much about her between visits, I slide inexorably into sorrow.

This is the year she'll find out. It'll all be over. When she learns the truth, her memories of our time laughing and learning on the lake isn't what she or the children will remember, but the ugliness of what's always lurked a few yards out from their exciting scientific exercises. I could've insisted Jean not to bring her students anymore. It would've been the better thing to do. But I'm eighty-two. I'm weary from the constant dread, anticipating detection. The inevitable blow. It's time.


My life hasn't entirely been melancholy. Complex, yes. Anne and the kids gave me much happiness, especially after my father passed away. We only spent occasional vacations on The Kitowaj in summer, or winter. I'd forget the legacy of my paternal family between visits. And Anne and I worked very hard to keep our children ignorant of the lake's buried past.

Retirement's been something else. Without work, living full time in The Lodge, I turned to study, learning to cook for myself, and looking forward to the occasional visits of my children. Anything to keep my mind above the surface of that murky blue. With the advent of the school field trips, I began immersing myself in the study of the ecosystem of The Kitowaj, the woods and earth. Regardless of my purely scientific intentions, my studies nevertheless sent my mind below the water's surface, sparking memories. To keep myself in the moment, I've kept a special journal marking the water levels of The Kitowaj since 2004. And what's beneath.

Today, standing in the middle of the lake, I didn't need my two-meter rod to tell me it's lost forty inches in depth since my first entry in summer of '04. Back then, the water dried on my armpit-high, fading green waders, leaving an uneven dirty stain, just like the rest of the fourteen years' worth of silt lines from The Kitowaj on the rubber surface. Like rings in the cross section of tree. In 2004, the line measuring the water's depth ran high across my chest. Yesterday, at its deepest, the line dried mid-thigh.

All around me I saw the things discarded, hidden, and traces of the once and no longer buried. Everything I knew, everything I recorded from my grandfather's and father's stories, to my own. Oh, my.

Can one feel resigned and terrified at the same time?

*Summer 2004*

*Early Morning--Dragonflies hover, dart. Mosquitoes cluster, hunting blood. It's best no one spends a lot of time on the shore, or they'll get bitten. I've found a good topical repellent. Hence, I spend hours watching the light change on the still water's surface long into sundown hours. Sometimes a water-strider scuttles across. I marvel how like me that they are. They make the slightest indentation in the water's surface, but otherwise skitter about without producing so much as a ripple.*

*Number Three House sold. The new owners came down to the water's edge and in some ritual, he flung a wreath of flowers a good forty feet onto the lake. They're in their early sixties, he with white hair, her coloring hers a dark copper. She's an artist, making jewelry and sculptures. She gave me one of her pieces after they settled in, and I like it. It reminds me of a diver going off a cliff, but she tells me it's the spiritual essence of the tribes of Indians that once lived on the land. I had it upside down!*

*I wonder if the wreath landed near Henry's remains. If he was still alive, he might have gone in after it, shaking it in his mouth, sending water and flowers in an arc around his sleek, beautiful head, then race back to return it.*

*I'm so sorry Henry.*

*Fall 2005*

*A boy searches for frogs and toads among the reeds. He's alone. When I come down and ask him what he's doing, he's nonchalant as kids are today and tells me he's visiting his auntie in Number Two. He's bored and there's nothing to do. Am I some 'perv' and what am I doing there? I laugh heartily. I think that scared him a bit. I pointed up, said I owned the big house on the hill, and that The Kitowaj was my lake. I told him of the world in the water. He picked up a stick, unimpressed by Jean's lesson, and hurled it into the water. He squinted at it and announced, "Nothing. No fish? Stupid lake!" When I didn't leave, my face set in disapproval, he went. I didn't see him again.*

*The trees are changing color. My children liked this time of year here best. We often vacationed here at least once before the leaves fell, and some Thanksgivings. The air goes cool, wind fierce. The shushing sound of the pine trees made the kids sleep better. I resisted the charms of autumn most of my youth because it meant me raking leaves off the grass around the house, out of the gutters. As a father did, I expected my sons to do the same, but Josh and David always disappeared into the woods when the chores needed doing and my daughter Linda snorted it was 'man's work.' Anne helped sometimes, but her rheumatoid arthritis often crippled her efforts. Once the kids had all gone, into college, marriages, and Anne disappeared from us, it was just me left with the leaves. I stopped raking them, instead letting them build up into variegated colorful drifts blown against the hillside. Now it's my favorite time of year. The leaves become mulch. Rain and snow move the detritus leaving clear walkways and drives. I wonder why we ever bothered.*

The pure *Pertinent Pond Data* I store on its own shelf. Inside are lists, and dates, and facts about things I find in the water; all things, most of which I *didn't* put there. It's frustrating to list the mysterious items without their immersion dates, who put them there, why. I'm prone to obsess over their backgrounds, the stories I don't know, too many times making up their origins. Based on the past, I suspect that I'm right.

The water freezes and constricts around debris closer to the surface yearly, and one winter it gave up a hat. The Homburg rose up about twenty-five feet away from shore, tilted and frosted dove gray. I recognized the style. Uncle Ted, father's brother, always wore one just like it. I imagined Uncle Ted and Dad standing at the edge of the pond on a breezy summer's afternoon, the wind picking Uncle Ted's hat up off his head, depositing it in The Kitowaj. Uncle Ted wasn't the kind of man to kick off his shoes, roll up his pants and wade out for a soggy hat he'd never wear again. He'd just buy another one. Dad might have waded in on his own, but when he was with his brother, Uncle Ted's way was the only way. But I went out and got it after the thaw, logging it. I picked a date from one of our summer stays, one that stood out in my memory. August 10, 1946. I was fifteen years old.

Uncle Ted brought a girl with him, as he often did. Tilda. She was twenty-two, he said, but she looked more my age. He said they were going to get married. Dad gave Mother and me that look that said, 'shut up or you know what will happen to you.' We knew Uncle Ted had a long-suffering wife, though we hadn't seen her in three years. Uncle Ted and Tilda slept together in one room, which upset my strict Irish Catholic mother. After all, there were eight bedrooms in Kitowaj Lodge.

Dad and Uncle Ted went hunting during his visits. There were deer and elk, moose and bear; a bounty for men who found their masculinity in killing animals for sport, and a month of Sunday dinners. I preferred books and music to rifles and gutting prey, so I was left behind with my mother and Tilda. Mother, in her moral distress and embarrassment, kept to the kitchen cooking all day. I took Tilda down to The Kitowaj.

I thought her pretty, full of personality. Her mirth and flamboyance felt flirtatious to this naïve boy. I was better than average-looking, tall and thin, with the Seitz inky black hair, light skin and blue eyes; more awkward about myself than I needed to be. Tilda flattered me about my appearance, asked about The Kitowaj, our family, my school and social life. I talked more with her than I had with most girls I'd known. She appeared captivated. In hindsight, I think that was her aim: charming men in some misguided attempt to redeem their sad, secret selves. Without experience or the wariness that comes from having been hurt or fooled, I was mindlessly smitten. She kissed me that day. Full on the mouth and used her tongue.

Over the next few days, Tilda took opportunities to get me alone, touch me, and let me touch her. I'm certain mother suspected that Tilda was *creating mischief* with me while Uncle Ted and Dad were off hunting, but she never spoke to me of her qualms, though I averted her gaze when I felt her eyes on me. After a week of this lust-driven heaven, the fear of my parents learning of my dalliance with Tilda and losing their respect, and much worse, and Uncle Ted's notorious wrath, cooled my ardor. Rather quickly, I learned an aspect of what it meant to be a man. And, much less of one.

Mother was relieved to see them go. In a way, so was I. Glad to leave the state of constant arousal and apprehension behind, still I ached for Tilda every day until I was back in school, distracted. I hoped I might see her again, but of course, like all his girlfriends and his wife, she disappeared into the dark history of Uncle Ted.

*Summer 2010*

*A freak summer storm wreaked havoc on The Kitowaj. Lightening set fires that took fourteen acres, exposing the land down to the water, and consuming Number One. A tree at the lake's edge broke at the base and fell across, creating a bridge from one side to the other. When it was done, the storm left a moonscape, a nightmare of charred ground, skeletons of trees, and the foundation of a home.*

*After the torrential rain, the lake swelled two feet deeper and was covered in ash. The ash will slowly fall to the bottom, but I worry there is so much, it will absorb the water and that everything in the water will get coated and surge upwards, like swollen beasts. I watch it every day: see the surface go from gray to the color of mud, the wheel of a bicycle twisted by the rising water arches tentatively up into the air, ominously hinting at anonymities submerged.*

*Jean Tanner came to the Lodge when she heard about the fires. She had her two sons with her. She waited in the main room while I shrugged off my robe and put on a clean shirt. I pulled at my white beard before greeting her, hoping my hair hadn't gone too wild in my seclusion. Her boys were sweet and enjoyed the living room with all the mounted heads of The Seitz men's kills. The fierce looking creatures frightened me as a child. But kids raised with scientific curiosity see things differently. Jean stood looking out at the devastation shaking her head. She loves The Kitowaj, she tells me. The fires scarred the woods and her heart. I am ashamed to say that in that moment, I wished she was my daughter instead of distant, angry Linda.*

*Fall 2010*

*The rains have enlarged The Kitowaj greatly. With so little vegetation to hold the water, it's nearly returned to its original state! Thankfully, Numbers Two and Three were built on constructed hillocks and raised foundations, though for a couple of days, they become their own islands. The burned bones of trees poke out of the water where they once stood majestic around the shore. The nice young couple in Number One sent a Christmas card saying they would rebuild in Spring. They asked me to send pictures as nature reclaims the charred earth. I don't hold out hope I'll find anything, and perhaps by then they'll be back.*

*I am greatly relieved by The Kitowaj taking on greater proportions. The secrets and lies below its former shallow surface are safer than ever. Yet, with the trees gone in such a large swath, the exposure of land is obscene. When Jean brings her students, she shows them photographs of the water from the year before and asks them figure out the old shoreline. But without trees to mark the variance, they lose interest. They take their samples but are louder than her students in the past. I wonder if the sounds they make are the same as before, but the foliage and trees once absorbed it. I come down the trail and join them, but I feel detached, sadder than I can remember.*

Reading about the aftermath of the fire, I can't help thinking about that one Fourth of July holiday when Anne, the kids and my father were all here. My mother had passed away the previous winter.

My father, whom I hadn't seen since the funeral, came to the Lodge with a woman who worked for him. Sylvia was one of his salespeople who traveled full-time, so I didn't know her. In her forties, an 'old maid' as my father preferred calling women who never married, she was attractive, if a bit plump, and not at all prim like my mother. Anne, who was neither staid nor dowdy, found ostentatious and crude people difficult. Sylvia was 'crass,' Anne said. So, our holiday began with tension and slowly devolved from there.

Linda, Josh, and David were thirteen, fifteen, and sixteen, and wanted nothing to do with us. Josh talked David into driving the three out to Chestertown to buy fireworks, so off they went. Anne and I made drinks for my father and Sylvia as Linda sulked.

Inside, Anne confided that she worried Dad would get drunk, which he did often since mother's death. She expected trouble from Sylvia, the portents of which came with her turning up the radio, unfurling strings of expletives, and grabbing at dad to dance with her. As I poured gin, I blindly assured Anne we were all still grieving, that my father would behave, and she should give Sylvia a chance.

As we sat on the deck, the summer heat moist, baking, we fanned ourselves with paper plates, sipped gin and tonics. Sylvia wore shorts with a tight bathing suit underneath and slathered herself with tanning oil. For an hour, only the sounds of ice tinkling in glasses and muffled giggles from Sylvia when my father grinned at her.

Sylvia may have been uncomfortable with the silence, because eventually she broke it with a stream of off-color jokes and staccato laughter. When that drove us to stare down into our laps, she teased my father until his face went crimson. As the two of them finished the second pitcher of gin and tonics, she began singing, not badly, and pulled my father about as if he was a dancing bear.

The kids returned a couple of hours later and Anne asked Linda to help start cooking inside. My father, the boys, and I set to work on building a fire in the pit a few yards from the deck for our barbecue. I'd had one beer, so I still had my faculties, but my father was hopeless. He sat on a log, wheezing as he smoked a cigarette, mumbling under his breath. Josh and David did most of the work restacking the river rock around the pit, piling up the dry wood, saturating some rag strips in kerosene to stuff beneath the wood, and settling the ironwork grill atop the stones. I gathered sticks for kindling.

Sylvia stood over us on the deck, laughing, barking orders, calling us 'bastards' and other names far more impolite. Josh remarked, a little too loudly, that Grandpa's 'date' reminded him of a hooker he'd seen in a movie. She heard that and screamed at my father to shut his disrespectful grandson up. It was my job to intercede, I see that now, but I expected my father to take control of the situation. Josh just laughed at Sylvia. David smirked. I smoldered.

Anne came out on the deck with hors d'ouvres. Sylvia told Anne what Josh said. Anne said she'd speak to him later, but Sylvia was livid, and very drunk. She wanted action, not a dignified response. In her wedged sandals, she hobbled down the wooden steps to the flagstone path, then headed to the pit.

By the time she reached us, my father was on his feet, begging Sylvia to relax and forget about it. Josh grabbed David by the elbow, and they ran down to the water, laughing. My father didn't want trouble. He lit another cigarette, but Sylvia knocked it out of his hand onto the stones of the pit where hot ash spat in all directions.

She swatted at the sparks as they burned her; little keening shrieks coming like a rabbit in a trap. A kerosene-doused rag at her feet caught a few sparks and ignited, the flames licking up her oiled legs as if they'd been doused in gasoline.

In the face of crisis, I froze. Anne screamed as Sylvia went up like a dry sapling. Each of Sylvia's gin-fueled screams invited the fire, which leapt to her mouth and into her lungs. My father, from whom I'd learned paralysis in times of trouble, stood across from her, hands out as if to say, 'What do you want me to do?' She fell onto the pit and set it alight.

Then, it was just Anne and Linda screaming, the boys racing back to turn the hose on the blaze, leaving me and my father two useless, sobbing lumps. I don't know what Dad was thinking, but I had my mother in mind; how terribly humiliating and tragic she would have found this.

Had the children not been with us, Sylvia would have spent eternity in the Kitowaj, but we summoned authorities and an ambulance. In the aftermath, our grief was compounded and conflicted by Sylvia's passing. My father never brought another woman to the Lodge, and the children lost interest in barbecuing holiday meals.

*Winter 2012 / 2013*

*The Kitowaj has frozen over, and strangers are skating on it. The skaters might belong to a neighbor in Two or Three, but I don't recognize them. I walk down in snowshoes and stand at the end of the trail. I can't see the fallen tree at the narrow end. It's snowed over. The people ignore me. I wonder if I've become so white with old age, I blend in with the landscape.*

As I read the account of the seasons watching my pond, I realize I've left ever so much out. If I put the data, journals, and photographs together and add new memories, they still don't tell the whole story. That's in the details, the little things. It's my weakness that I can't put everything in writing, but it stays here in my head. All of it. My mind is like the bottom of The Kitowaj; truths layered in the silt of everyday thoughts, horrors twisted from half-dreams submerged, and littered with people—treasured, barely known or acknowledged, some disliked, others loathed. I've simply never been one to talk minutiae. But all will be clear enough when it's taken bit by bit from the lake and put together with my logs. Anyone smart enough will figure it out, including some of those smart tykes who go on to discover the lake's wonders under their school room microscopes. I'm counting on them.

*Fall 2014*

*There's been no rainfall since April. The pond is dangerously low. The new growth since the fires is dying away. Even the air smells fetid over Kitowaj, like a spoiled curry still boiling in the pot. I considered having water piped in, but the process is extraordinarily expensive. Still, if the drought continues, and there isn't snow this winter, the pond is going to dry up and it won't matter that I've kept quiet all this time. All will be exposed.*

*Thanksgiving is tomorrow. David and his wife are coming. They'll stay two nights. I am delirious with joy! And wonder why after all this time, they're coming. But I won't question it. Their daughter Ashley chose to stay home and do thanksgiving with her boyfriend's folks. Funny saying 'their daughter.' She's my granddaughter, but I've never met her. They send a photo Christmas card every year, so I've seen her evolve from a chubby baby to beautiful teenager. I'm sure she's listened to speculation about me from her parents, aunt and uncle, and doesn't want to know me. It's a shame. I'm not the kind of man I've let my children think I am, though as far back as the Seitz family has owned The Kitowaj, the patriarchs have been significantly ruthless, even criminal in their ways.*

David and I discussed his 'ground rules' for our visit on the phone. I'm allowed to ask anything, but 'why?' No 'why's. I'm left with 'How are you? What have you been doing the last five years?' And no talk of his mother, or my parents. Not a word about his speculations about the past of which I've spared him nearly everything. He wants it painless. No confrontation; no argument. I'm glad of that.

David's wife, Beth, cooked the dinner and they brought it with them. It tasted far better than any I remembered, but then it had been a long time since I'd celebrated with anyone. Thanksgiving, since Anne passed away, feels pointless.

They arrived harried from the traffic and worried for the food. Quickly and efficiently, Beth took to the kitchen and remained there until I set the table and turned off the ball game. David and I spoke little, mostly about the game, so the tension built for the meal. They had rehearsed the topics of conversation—flowing from the mundane to the stultifying. I played along. So hungry was I for the sound of family voices, they could have spoken in tongues, and I would've basked in it.

I suppose my leaving the photograph of Anne and I from our wedding on the dresser in their bedroom was a mistake, but they said nothing. I found it in the dresser drawer when they were gone. My fault, too, that I brought up the contributions I'd made over the years to the Arthritis Foundation in Anne's name. Beth grabbed David's wrist as he made a fist on the table at lunch the next day.

My desire to tell him the truth was fierce. I so wanted to go against Anne's misguided wish that I not tell our children the truth of her passing. But my gratitude for David and Beth's visit was greater. When they said goodbye, it had the ring of finality. I waved at their car until I could see only the taillights as they turned onto the upper road, my face wet with tears. For a moment, just a split second, I hated Anne for what she'd asked, and wondered if she knew how long I'd be so severely punished by her dying wish.

*Christmas 2015*

Rain, sleet, and snow. It began three days ago and won't quit. The lake was so low on December the 17th that I saw the ancient bicycle down to its pedals. Another inch and Henry and the others just might rear up their rotten skulls. This time of year, I think of Henry.

I was twelve when Uncle Ted gave Henry to Dad. He was the best hunting dog—part retriever, part Labrador, black and sleek. But Uncle Ted brought another girl to stay the summer after Tilda. I went kind of crazy seeing Mother upset again, Dad enjoying his vicarious thrill over another of Uncle Ted's conquests, Ted so smug in his deceit. I lashed out. I just wanted Ted and Dad to suffer as Mother and I did. I poisoned Henry with Mother's pain pills, not expecting him to die, just get ill. I watched him die. A peaceful death. He went to sleep and never woke up. In the end, Dad and Ted made jokes about Henry being more use at the bottom of The Kitowaj than out there with them hunting, but Mother and I wept for days. I wanted to tell my mother why I'd done it, but that summer, a mild heart attack turned her into shell of what she'd been. I refused to add to her grief.

This is the first Christmas I didn't get a card from David and Family. Odd, because I thought their visit went well. We didn't argue. I never asked a single 'why.'

*Winter 2016 / 2017*

The skies selfishly withheld good fortune upon The Kitowaj. Just before the New Year, the weather went dry, crisp and cold. The winds came down from Canada and seemed to sup at the Kitowaj until they were sated. The snow appeared to dissipate rather than melt. The water froze the night of January 25th. I stood over it the next day, marveling at the paper-thin crystalline tapestry of ice as the water slapped *lazily beneath. I thought I could see faces staring up at me, hair waving like seaweed, eye sockets picked clean by the things that live in the pond. I closed my eyes and turned away. When I glanced back, they were gone.*

*The nice couple who rebuilt Number One sold the newly rebuilt home to a family; the first homeowners to stay year-round. They have two boys, ages three and eighteen months. The father works from home; a computer person. His wife was friendly at first, bringing over baked goods and canned fruit to the lonely old geezer in Kitowaj Lodge, but like every-one who comes to stay here, they began to keep to themselves. It's not a community. It's just 100 acres of land, four homes, four separate sets of lives, around the leftovers of a lake.*

I'm writing *Spring* now. I've noted more flies than usual, probably because the water's so low now, and nearly all is revealed. The smell is funereal. There's barely ten inches of water now. A pond the size of a child's blow-up pool. Birds nest in the trees at the edge of the new growth. The cycle of life continues. Lazy hikers toss bottles in the puddle that was The Kitowaj. Cat tails grow in the mud like flags on a golf course pointing to the holes. A duck lies curled up dead since last Sunday, shot by a hunter, near that bicycle. I remembered Anne's scarf floating up in the same place.

I still see her sitting beside me on the deck with the colorful chiffon over her thinning hair, in so much pain, her gnarled hands barely able to hold the wine glass from which she drank chardonnay to down all her sleeping pills; her eyes angry and sad at once, resigned it was time to go. She made me promise silence as I held her on the shore in my waders. She'd written the letter announcing she was leaving us in her nearly unreadable arthritic scrawl; explaining she'd always been a wife and mother and wanted to go into the world and find out who she really was, even at seventy. When I shared it with the children, they'd already chosen to see my time-honed stoicism as cruel enough reason for Anne to leave. They guessed many other truths about her disappearance, after all, they'd eventually heard some of the wild stories of The Kitowaj in Chestertown, while I continued to feign ignorance. I find myself thinking again of the pain I've endured; losing Anne, losing my children in honoring her wishes. But they'll know eventually. When I am gone. Perhaps they'll forgive me.

All twelve *Seasons on the Kitowaj* are stacked on the top left corner of my desk. Should Jean, the children, and eventually my family, discover the truth about The Kitowaj and the Seitz family, and they will, I want them to have all the data. My children might appreciate that; knowing what truly became of their mother, my father, the so many who came to visit and never left.

They're coming, Jean and her students. I hear the school bus creaking over the rutted road down. It's time the bodies, what's left of them, are discovered; the grim legacy left by the men in my family. By me. Yes, it's time.

# BLACK ROBES, RED HATS, AND WHITE OBLIVION

## MAXWELL I. GOLD

Nations bled with ink, indoctrinating ideologies in blood and the banalities of greed as wild sycophants writhed in red hats and white hoods. They marched down the ancient streets of that colonial city, towers of marble and stone felled by the wanton rage, wrought by their hatred, their unbridled, unadulterated loathing. Disassociated from reason and sense, the heathenish compressed wads of human refuse expelled their rhetoric; clotting the skies with silver wings whose atomic entrails filled the airwaves and radiating worlds offline. The crowds carried on, footsteps filling parking lots, plazas, and boulevards where the lowliness of an age, confounded in darkness, was soon trampled by the very same reactionary monsters. Temples built by goddesses in Stygian cloaks, were overrun by these crimson barbarous thugs, torched and sacked, ivory columns toppled lying in piles of dust.

Still, even as the black robed goddesses passed gently into the night, their virtue immortalized as charred embers of hope remained for a world in flux, on the brink of despair. Faster, with feverish anticipation the rhythm of boots and balustrades wailed in the shadowy flaming night as walls of concrete and plaster rose higher and higher, divisions of a new order. Sickly, pickled faces of a privileged oblivion flooded the streets, their mechanized beasts spewing clouds of exhaust and ash, scarring the skies further with red flags, broken stars, and eyes of pain, disgust, and misunderstanding. Voices of those in power, caretakers who neglected the world that was given to them, preached wild musings, sensationalism and psychosomatics.

And so, nations bled with ink, indoctrinating ideologies in blood and the banalities of greed as wild sycophants writhed in red hats and white hoods.

# STRAWBERRY SPRING

## STEPHEN KING

*Springheel Jack.*

I saw those two words in the paper this morning and my God, how they take me back. All that was eight years ago, almost to the day. Once, while it was going on, I saw myself on nationwide TV—the Walter Cronkite Report. Just a hurrying face in the general background behind the reporter, but my folks picked me out right away. They called long-distance. My dad wanted my analysis of the situation; he was all bluff and hearty and man-to-man. My mother just wanted me to come home. But I didn't want to come home. I was enchanted.

Enchanted by that dark and mist-blown strawberry spring, and by the shadow of violent death that walked through it on those nights eight years ago. The shadow of Springheel Jack.

In New England they call it a strawberry spring. No one knows why; it's just a phrase the old-timers use. They say it happens once every eight or ten years. What happened at New Sharon Teachers' College that particular strawberry spring ... there may be a cycle for that, too, but if anyone has figured it out, they've never said.

At New Sharon, the strawberry spring began on March 16th, 1968. The coldest winter in twenty years broke on that day. It rained and you could smell the sea twenty miles west of the beaches. The snow, which had been thirty-five inches deep in places, began to melt and the campus walks ran with slush. The Winter Carnival snow sculptures, which had been kept sharp and clear-cut for two months by the sub-zero temperatures, at last began to sag and slouch. The caricature of Lyndon Johnson in front of the Tep fraternity house cried melted tears. The dove in front of Prashner Hall lost its frozen feathers and its plywood skeleton showed sadly through in places.

And when night came the fog came with it, moving silent and white along the narrow college avenues and thoroughfares. The pines on the wall poked through it like counting fingers and it drifted, slow as cigarette smoke, under the little bridge down by the Civil War cannons. It made things seem out of joint, strange, magical. The unwary traveler would step out of the juke-thumping, brightly lit confusion of the Grinder, expecting the hard clear starriness of winter to clutch him ... and instead he would suddenly find himself in a silent, muffled world of white drifting fog, the only sound his own footsteps and the soft drip of water from the ancient gutters. You half expected to see Gollum or Frodo and Sam go hurrying past, or to turn and see that the Grinder was gone, vanished, replaced by a foggy panorama of moors and yew trees and perhaps a Druid-circle or a sparkling fairy ring.

The jukebox played "Love Is Blue" that year. It played "Hey, Jude" endlessly, endlessly. It played "Scarborough Fair."

And at ten minutes after eleven on that night a junior named John Dancey on his way back to his dormitory began screaming into the fog, dropping books on and between the sprawled legs of the dead girl lying in a shadowy corner of the Animal Sciences parking lot, her throat cut from ear to ear but her eyes open and almost seeming to sparkle as if she had just successfully pulled off the funniest joke of her young life—Dancey, an education major and a speech minor, screamed and screamed and screamed.

The next day was overcast and sullen, and we went to classes with questions eager in our mouths—who? why? when do you think they'll get him? And always the final thrilled question: Did you know her? Did you know her?

*Yes, I had an art class with her.*

*Yes, one of my roommate's friends dated her last term.*

*Yes, she asked me for a light once in the Grinder. She was at the next table.*

*Yes, Yes, I*

*Yes ... yes ... oh yes, I*

We all knew her. Her name was Gale Cerman (pronounced Kerr-man), and she was an art major. She wore granny glasses and had a good figure. She was well-liked but her roommates had hated her. She had never gone out much, even though she was one of the most promiscuous girls on campus. She was ugly but cute. She had been a vivacious girl who talked little and smiled seldom. She had been pregnant, and she had had leukemia. She was a lesbian who had been murdered by her boyfriend. It was strawberry spring, and on the morning of March 17th we all knew Gale Cerman.

Half a dozen State Police cars crawled on to the campus, most of them parked in front of Judith Franklin Hall, where the Cerman girl had lived. On my way past there to my ten o' clock class I was asked to show my student ID. I was clever. I showed him the one without the fangs.

"Do you carry a knife?" the policeman asked cunningly.

"Is it about Gale Cerman?" I asked, after I told him that the most lethal thing on my person was a rabbit's-foot key chain.

"What makes you ask?"

I was five minutes late to class.

It was strawberry spring, and no one walked by themselves through the half-academical, half-fantastical campus that night. The fog had come again, smelling of the sea, quiet and deep.

Around nine o'clock my roommate burst into our room, where I had been busting my brains on a Milton essay since seven. "They caught him," he said. "I heard it over at the Grinder."

"From who?"

"I don't know. Some guy. Her boyfriend did it. His name is Carl Amalara."

I settled back, relieved and disappointed. With a name like that it had to be true. A lethal and sordid little crime of passion.

"Okay," I said. "That's good."

He left the room to spread the news down the hall. I reread my Milton essay, couldn't figure out what I had been trying to say, tore it up and started again.

It was in the papers the next day. There was an incongruously neat picture of Amalara—probably a high-school graduation picture— and it showed a rather sad-looking boy with an olive complexion and dark eyes and pockmarks on his nose. The boy had not confessed yet, but the evidence against him was strong. He and Gale Cerman had argued a great deal in the last month or so and had broken up the week before. Amalara's roomie said he had been 'despondent.' In a footlocker under his bed, police had found a seven-inch hunting knife from L. L. Bean's and a picture of the girl that had apparently been cut up with a pair of shears.

Beside Amalara's picture was one of Gale Cerman. It blurrily showed a dog, a peeling lawn flamingo, and a rather mousy blonde girl wearing spectacles. An uncomfortable smile had turned her lips up and her eyes were squinted. One hand was on the dog's head. It was true then. It had to be true.

The fog came again that night, not on little cat's feet but in an improper silent sprawl. I walked that night. I had a headache and I walked for air, smelling the wet, misty smell of the spring that was slowly wiping away the reluctant snow, leaving lifeless patches of last year's grass bare and uncovered, like the head of a sighing old grandmother.

For me, that was one of the most beautiful nights I can remember. The people I passed under the haloed streetlights were murmuring shadows, and all of them seemed to be lovers, walking with hands and eyes linked. The melting snow dripped and ran, dripped and ran, and from every dark storm drain the sound of the sea drifted up, a dark winter sea now strongly ebbing.

I walked until nearly midnight, until I was thoroughly mildewed, and I passed many shadows, heard many footfalls clicking dreamily off down the winding paths. Who is to say that one of those shadows was not the man or the thing that came to be known as Springheel Jack? Not I, for I passed many shadows but in the fog I saw no faces.

The next morning, the clamor in the hall woke me. I blundered out to see who had been drafted, combing my hair with both hands and running the fuzzy caterpillar that had craftily replaced my tongue across the dry roof of my mouth.

"He got another one," someone said to me, his face pallid with excitement. "They had to let him go."

"Who go?"

"Amalara!" someone else said gleefully. "He was sitting in jail when it happened."

"When what happened?" I asked patiently. Sooner or later, I would get it. I was sure of that.

"The guy killed somebody else last night. And now they're hunting all over for it."

"For what?"

The pallid face wavered in front of me again. "Her head.
Whoever killed her took her head with him."

New Sharon isn't a big school now and was even smaller then—
the kind of institution the public relations people chummily refer to
as a 'community college.' And it really was like a small community,
at least in those days; between you and your friends, you probably
had at least a nodding acquaintance with everybody else and their
friends. Gale Cerman had been the type of girl you just nodded to,
thinking vaguely that you had seen her around.

We all knew Ann Bray. She had been the first runner-up in the
Miss New England pageant the year before, her talent performance
consisting of twirling a flaming baton to the tune of "Hey, Look
Me Over." She was brainy, too; until the time of her death, she had
been editor of the school newspaper (a once-weekly rag with a lot of
political cartoons and bombastic letters), a member of the student
dramatics society, and president of the National Service Sorority,
New Sharon Branch. In the hot, fierce bubblings of my freshman
youth I had submitted a column idea to the paper and asked for a
date—turned down on both counts.

And now she was dead ... worse than dead.

I walked to my afternoon classes like everyone else, nodding to
people I knew and saying hi with a little more force than usual, as if
that would make up for the close way I studied their faces. Which
was the same way they were studying mine. There was someone dark
among us, as dark as the paths which twisted across the mall or
wound among the hundred-year-old oaks on the quad in back of the
gymnasium. As dark as the hulking Civil War cannons seen through
a drifting membrane of fog. We looked into each other's faces and
tried to read the darkness behind one of them.

This time the police arrested no one. The blue beetles patrolled
the campus ceaselessly on the foggy spring nights of the eighteenth,
nineteenth, and twentieth, and spotlights stabbed in to dark nooks
and crannies with erratic eagerness. The administration imposed a

mandatory nine o'clock curfew. A foolhardy couple discovered neck-ing in the landscaped bushes north of the Tate Alumni Building were taken to the New Sharon police station and grilled unmercifully for three hours.

There was a hysterical false alarm on the twentieth when a boy was found unconscious in the same parking lot where the body of Gale Cerman had been found. A gibbering campus cop loaded him into the back of his cruiser and put a map of the county over his face without bothering to hunt for a pulse and started toward the local hospital, siren wailing across the deserted campus like a semi-nar of banshees.

Halfway there, the corpse in the back seat had risen and asked hollowly, "Where the hell am I?" The cop shrieked and ran off the road. The corpse turned out to be an undergrad named Donald Morris who had been in bed the last two days with a pretty lively case of flu—was it Asian last year? I can't remember. Anyway, he fainted in the parking lot on his way to the Grinder for a bowl of soup and some toast.

The days continued warm and overcast. People clustered in small groups that had a tendency to break up and re-form with surprising speed. Looking at the same set of faces for too long gave you funny ideas about some of them. And the speed with which rumors swept from one end of the campus to the other began to approach the speed of light; a well-liked history professor had been overheard laughing and weeping down by the small bridge; Gale Cerman had left a cryptic two-word message written in her own blood on the blacktop of the Animal Sciences parking lot; both murders were actually political crimes, ritual murders that had been performed by an offshoot of the SDS to protest the war. This was really laughable. The New Sharon SDS had seven members. One fair-sized offshoot would have bankrupted the whole organization. This fact brought an even more sinister embellishment from the campus right-wing-ers: outside agitators. So, during those queer, warm days, we all kept our eyes peeled for them.

The press, always fickle, ignored the strong resemblance our murderer bore to Jack the Ripper and dug further back—all the way to 1819. Ann Bray had been found on a soggy path of ground some twelve feet from the nearest sidewalk, and yet there were no footprints, not even her own. An enterprising New Hampshire newsman with a passion for the arcane christened the killer Springheel Jack, after the infamous Dr. John Hawkins of Bristol, who did five of his wives to death with odd pharmaceutical knick-knacks. And the name, probably because of that soggy yet unmarked ground, stuck.

On the twenty-first it rained again, and the mall and quadrangle became quagmires. The police announced that they were salting plainclothes detectives, men and women, about, and took half the police cars off duty.

The campus newspaper published a strongly indignant, if slightly incoherent, editorial protesting this. The upshot of it seemed to be that, with all sorts of cops masquerading as students, it would be impossible to tell a real outside agitator from a false one.

Twilight came and the fog with it, drifting up the tree-lined avenues slowly, almost thoughtfully, blotting out the buildings one by one. It was soft, insubstantial stuff, but somehow implacable and frightening. Springheel Jack was a man, no one seemed to doubt that, but the fog was his accomplice, and it was female ... or so it seemed to me. If was as if our little school was caught between them, squeezed in some crazy lover's embrace, part of a marriage that had been consummated in blood. I sat and smoked and watched the lights come on in the growing darkness and wondered if it was all over. My roommate came in and shut the door quietly behind him.

"It's going to snow soon," he said.

I turned around and looked at him. "Does the radio say that?"

"No," he said. "Who needs a weatherman? Have you ever heard of strawberry spring?"

"Maybe," I said. "A long time ago. Something grandmothers talk about, isn't it?"

He stood beside me, looking out at the creeping dark.

"Strawberry spring is like Indian summer," he said, "only much more rare. You get a good Indian summer in this part of the country once every two or three years. A spell of weather like we've been having is supposed to come only every eight or ten. It's a false spring, a lying spring, like Indian summer is a false summer. My own grandmother used to say strawberry spring means the worst norther of the winter is still on the way—and the longer this lasts, the harder the storm."

"Folk tales," I said. "Never believe a word." I looked at him. "But I'm nervous. Are you?"

He smiled benevolently and stole one of my cigarettes from the open pack on the window ledge. "I suspect everyone but me and thee," he said, and then the smile faded a little. "And sometimes I wonder about thee. Want to go over to the Union and shoot some eight-ball? I'll spot you ten."

"Trig prelim next week. I'm going to settle down with a magic marker and a hot pile of notes."

For a long time after he was gone, I could only look out the window. And even after I had opened my book and started in, part of me was still out there, walking in the shadows where something dark was now in charge.

That night Adelle Parkins was killed. Six police cars and seventeen collegiate-looking plain clothes men (eight of them were women imported all the way from Boston) patrolled the campus. But Springheel Jack killed her just the same, going unerringly for one of our own. The false spring, the lying spring, aided and abetted him—he killed her and left her propped behind the wheel of her 1964 Dodge to be found the next morning and they found part of her in the back seat and part of her in the trunk. And written in blood on the windshield—this time fact instead of rumor—were two words: HA! HA!

The campus went slightly mad after that; all of us and none of us had known Adelle Parkins. She was one of those nameless, harried women who worked the break-back shift in the Grinder from six to eleven at night, facing hordes of hamburger-happy students on study break from the library across the way. She must have had it relatively easy those last three foggy nights of her life; the curfew was being rigidly observed, and after nine the Grinder's only patrons were hungry cops and happy janitors—the empty buildings had improved their habitual bad temper considerably.

There is little left to tell. The police, as prone to hysteria as any of us and driven against the wall, arrested an innocuous homosexual sociology graduate student named Hanson Gray, who claimed he "could not remember" where he had spent several of the lethal evenings. They charged him, arraigned him, and let him go to scamper hurriedly back to his native New Hampshire town after the last unspeakable night of strawberry spring when Marsha Curran was slaughtered on the mall.

Why she had been out and alone is forever beyond knowing— she was a fat, sadly pretty thing who lived in an apartment in town with three other girls. She had slipped on campus as silently and as easily as Springheel Jack himself. What brought her? Perhaps her need was as deep and as ungovernable as her killer's, and just as far beyond understanding. Maybe a need for one desperate and passionate romance with the warm night, the warm fog, the smell of the sea, and the cold knife.

That was on the twenty-third. On the twenty-fourth the president of the college announced that spring break would be moved up a week, and we scattered, not joyfully but like frightened sheep before a storm, leaving the campus empty and haunted by the police and one dark specter.

I had my own car on campus, and I took six people downstate with me, their luggage crammed in helter-skelter. It wasn't a pleasant ride. For all any of us knew, Springheel Jack might have been in the car with us.

That night the thermometer dropped fifteen degrees, and the whole northern New England area was belted by a shrieking norther that began in sleet and ended in a foot of snow. The usual number of old duffers had heart attacks shoveling it away—and then, like magic, it was April. Clean showers and starry nights.

They called it strawberry spring, God knows why, and it's an evil, lying time that only comes once every eight or ten years. Springheel Jack left with the fog, and by early June, campus conversation had turned to a series of draft protests and a sit-in at the building where a well-known napalm manufacturer was holding job interviews. By June, the subject of Springheel Jack was almost unanimously avoided—at least aloud. I suspect there were many who turned it over and over privately, looking for the one crack in the seamless egg of madness that would make sense of it all.

That was the year I graduated, and the next year was the year I married. A good job in a local publishing house. In 1971 we had a child, and now he's almost school age. A fine and questing boy with my eyes and her mouth.

Then, today's paper.

Of course, I knew it was here. I knew it yesterday morning when I got up and heard the mysterious sound of snowmelt running down the gutters and smelled the salt tang of the ocean from our front porch, nine miles from the nearest beach. I knew strawberry spring had come again when I started home from work last night and had to turn on my headlights against the mist that was already beginning to creep out of the fields and hollows, blurring the lines of the buildings and putting fairy haloes around the streetlamps.

This morning's paper says a girl was killed on the New Sharon campus near the Civil War cannons. She was killed last night and found in a melting snowbank. She was not all there.

My wife is upset. She wants to know where I was last night. I can't tell her because I don't remember. I remember starting home from work, and I remember putting my headlights on to search my way through the lovely creeping fog, but that's all I remember.

I've been thinking about that foggy night when I had a headache and walked for air and passed all the lovely shadows without shape or substance. And I've been thinking about the trunk of my car— such an ugly word, trunk—and wondering why in the world I should be afraid to open it.

I can hear my wife as I write this, in the next room, crying. She thinks I was with another woman last night.

And oh, dear God, I think so too.

# CHALK

## SHANE DOUGLAS KEENE

When the lifeline ends, where the
death line begins,
do they always start that final
outline at the same anatomical
point of reference?
The tip of a nose, the crook of an
elbow; the left middle finger in
a final salute?
Do they finish with a ritualistic
flare?
Make the sign of Baphomet and
throw the chalk over their
shoulders,
Knights Templar holding vigil
against the merciless dead?
Maybe it rolls on away into
darkness, painting white highway
lines for your ghost to
travel down;
or flares into distance, a laser
beam to etch a horizon, reverse
shooting star, dust to draw points
on the skin of the cosmos,
coalescing;
falling back to earth a pristine,
unused stick of purest chalk;
a rocket ship for someone else's
ghost.

# THE DRUNKEN TREE

## TONYA LIBURD

The lore went that someone, an adolescent whose magic was chaotic, unmanaged, read *A Poison Tree* by William Blake on the sidewalk across from where the parking lot used to be on College Park, while rain fell like knives. That's what started the tree growing. Only it didn't sprout poisonous fruit, as per that famous poem.

A facility had to be built around the tree, of course. Glass ceiling, white-gray concrete walls, a brown-tinted glass door with a push bar. No one seemed to mind in that particular spot between College and Gerrard along Yonge Street. There was no sidewalk anymore. Red tape had to be maneuvered to allow such a thing, after it was assessed that the tree wasn't harmful.

It was called the Drunken Tree because a child, in the first days, had said that the tree didn't know what it wanted to grow, since it grew all sorts of fruit. "It's drunk!" the child said, and the name stuck.

People ate the random fruit that sprouted, and something akin to a religious experience seemed to happen. They temporarily transformed into a random thing or something symbolically meaningful. There was no way to tell which would happen. Hence why everything on the person, clothes included, would have to be removed beforehand. All effects of the transformations were either beneficial or neutral.

Security detail was needed to make sure no one got creative. The tree only bore one fruit per day, and a lottery had to be established to determine who would get the opportunity to eat the fruit once it appeared. People had to arrive by a certain time of day to participate.

Nicole was part of the security detail. She stood at her post in the tree's vicinity in the courtyard. It had a night-black hollow in its base. Roots tangled at the bottom. A shallow moat surrounded the circle of grass where the tree stood. The water of the moat neither froze in the winter, nor got hot in the summer. From what they could understand, the moat was magical, but did not possess any magical properties that affected people when its water was imbibed.

Nicole eyed the Drunken Tree warily. She wasn't as readily accepting as others, a fact which she kept to herself.

Every so often, resin could be seen oozing through the bark. It hardened into random colors and the visitors called them 'jewels,' the only other thing from the tree that affected people. Nicole could not see any jewels from where she stood. She doubted Elias, a fellow guard on her shift, could see any on the tree's other side.

A lady slipper orchid grew on the lower portion of the top half of the tree; a wasp of unusual size circled the flower. Once, when the flower bloomed unusually large, someone was able to fit a lady slipper flower onto a premature baby's foot. How they managed to get permission to have the baby leave the hospital to get there was anyone's guess. Not only was it prohibited to take objects from the tree outside, but people around the age of puberty—especially if they hadn't yet manifested their Gift—were not allowed to eat the fruit or resin. There was no word on whether there was any effect on the baby.

Today the fruit on the Drunken Tree resembled a calabash.

Nicole stood at the back of the sixty or so gathered while Errol, the supervisor, called out the lottery draw. A woman in a black shirt and pants yelped in surprise, then started crying loudly. Nicole could call this display "ugly crying."

*Ugly* ...

*"You ugly, ungrateful bitch!" Nicole's sister had said those words, eyes roaring like hot stars, destructive magic pulsing at her fingertips, lightning from her splayed fingers bleaching the sky. Never mind the fact that they weren't identical twins, so if one wasn't ugly, the other could be. Natasha had said that because Nicole failed to see her own beauty in the mirror.*

She shook her head wildly to bring herself back to the moment. Elias was across the courtyard and raised an eyebrow. Nicole made a dismissive gesture; he nodded and looked elsewhere, his expression going blank.

*You're alive*, she told herself. *She's not.*

Recently, Natasha had planned her death and didn't want to

come back. She had made arrangements, but Natasha did not count on her Gift. Natasha was stuck. Not alive, not dead, but in between everything. And she wanted Nicole to come with her to the other side.

Nicole had always counted on her own Gift: physical prowess, resilience, and healing. It's why she was a security guard. Ironic, considering her mother had always said she was too soft, even as a kid. When Nicole started getting sports trophies and later became a security guard, her mother said, "Nothing's changed, you're now your sister's bodyguard."

Her lips pursed with the remaining angry hurt she could still feel for her mother discounting her.

The tearful woman who'd won the daily lottery was led to the wooden plank crossing the moat to the grass. Nicole couldn't make out her ancestry. A hodgepodge of things, evocative of her own background. Nicole had two ancestries, her father Black, her mother East Indian. She and her twin were born in Toronto.

Nicole looked at her watch. Time stretched thin until the end of her shift, when the beautiful and miraculous became mundane, lackluster, and everyday ….

It always started out harmlessly, this time with a small blackhead on her nose. Leaning in, she squeezed her brown-tan colored skin and the blackhead slid out rapidly, the top black, the rest of it white. She swiped it away, looking for another.

There weren't any more, so she balanced a shin over one knee without thinking. There were pores that needed to have hairs released. She used her fingernails and squeezed. The sheath of dry skin over one pore broke, and clear liquid came out. Nicole squeezed again. Out came a black hair, distorted and curled from the ingrowth.

*Success.*

She pulled the hair all the way out, looked for another pore, did it again. But eventually, one would run out of pores on the reachable side of a shin. Leaning on a desk, she went for the skin above her elbow instead, distracted by a scab that itched on her knee, then moved to the other elbow. Nicole yielded to the temptation, but the scab was starting to separate from the skin. It would still be pink under there, if not white … so she pulled it off. Red.

Blood.

Not all of the scab had come off. Yellow liquid rose from the parts not bleeding, eager to bond with the blood to form another scab so the wound could heal. She used nail clippers to push out anything that might be in the pores, marring her skin and drawing more blood.

Her skin was dry, "ashy." Having a Gift didn't mean your skin was perfect. She was just dark enough for her ash to show, so she could score lines onto her skin. She tried making hash patterns from straight lines, made more than one tic-tac-toe mark on her thigh.

Nicole put down the nail clippers and went for a small knife. Sitting down again, she made better, deeper marks. She tapped the tip of the knife with nervous energy, drew blood on her fingertip. Pushing the tip onto her thigh and drew a bright red dot. She then used the knife's edge to cut off layers of unfeeling surface skin from the tip of the injured finger. Closer and closer to living flesh she went. Blood came out more urgently and she threw the knife.

Tried to slow her breathing.

Started sweating.

"You wanna play, eh? Why don't ya just go all the way? Why don't you—" She stormed off the chair and went back to the knife. Walked to the bathroom mirror. Looked at her reflection. "Why don't ya … just do this and get it over with?"

She skimmed flesh off her lower arms.

"Huh?!"

Cut lines into her face.

"Or this, huh?!" She lopped surface flesh off her cheekbones, the white of deep skin filling in with the red of escaping blood.

"Or this?"

Nicole sliced skin off the top of one kneecap, ignoring the burning pain. If she dug in with a knife this time, would nothing dribble out of her but dead air and shadows?

She heard the plaintive moan of her dead twin, caught on the other side. Willing her to join. Pressuring the still-existing connection between them. Feeding her actions.

She screamed.

Everything stayed the same.

Redness dribbled down her leg, dripped off her face.

Nicole threw the knife onto the floor and undressed to take a shower, and afterward, numbly, she cleaned up the pooled blood on the bathroom floor and about the apartment. She stood long moments before the mirror, staring at the sink, then burst into tears.

She should just disappear like vapor into the air.

Her life was meaningless.

This was a debilitating struggle.

Nicole rose, like she did every morning; she looked at her reflection in the mirror. Healed skin. No cuts. No scars. No small missing bits of flesh. Disappointment burst black through her veins.

She let out her breath.

Each morning as part of her routine, Nicole had breakfast, brushed her teeth, applied light makeup, then put on her uniform: a navy blue long-sleeved cotton shirt, a similarly colored jacket with the company logo, black pants, pressed to show every sharp crease. Communication devices. Her cell phone. At work, Nicole could become somebody else, pretend to be a healthy, functioning woman during the day. Sometimes she almost believed it herself.

The grass around the Drunken Tree began to breathe; the green blades heaved, pulsed. The walls of the courtyard felt brighter, closer. A fruit appeared on one of the branches, close to the trunk. Today it resembled a peach.

Elias caught her eye and lifted his chin in greeting across the courtyard. She did the same.

Right now, she preferred solitude and isolation at work; she didn't want any inadvertent revelation of what was going on with her. But Elias seemed intent on being there, at the very least as a comforting, reassuring presence. She suspected he figured something was up. Staying as far away from him as possible was the only way of avoiding things coming out into the open; he'd urge her to talk. And she couldn't.

At lunch, Nicole sat at the lunchroom table, jacket over the back of the chair, alone. That was until Elias entered.

"Nicole." He walked over to the microwave, stuffed in a sandwich. "Need to get that cheese melted just right." He leaned into the counter as he waited, his keys jingling.

Nicole nodded as the microwave hummed.

Elias retrieved his nuked sandwich, then peered at her. He slid his sandwich between his lips, took a bite, then spoke. "How was your day so far?" Painful small talk.

She stared down into her bottle of sorrel.

Later in the afternoon, Errol announced, "Ok, folks. It's time." A silence descended on the gathering as he spun the raffle drum and withdrew a ticket. The lucky winner of the draw turned, interestingly, into a Scarlet Ibis, the national bird of Trinidad and Tobago, where her parents were from and had met. The man cried copious tears when his form returned.

Elias put out an arm, offering gentle comfort. "Maybe it's time you visited home and pay a visit to her resting place. It might be good for your soul."

The two Black men stood together, commiserating.

Back at her post in the courtyard, Nicole watched the visitors mill about. People still came, and went, even after the lottery for the day had been drawn.

Her phone buzzed. Mother. Because her mother's Gift was that she could tell people's pasts when she touched them, Nicole had been avoiding being in her presence, which meant not seeing her; she kept asking why Nicole wouldn't visit, and—

She wasn't going to answer the phone.

The ceiling above throbbed and streamed with color, an effect of the lighting and design of the glass. She could feel herself almost warming up to the view.

*You cut yourself last night.*

Apprehension rose from her belly and seized her heart. The memory of what she did the night before kept screaming in the background, behind her eyes.

Nicole opened her cupboard door to get some soup to go with the salad for dinner. All the cans were lined up in neat rows. If one looked around the apartment, one would find all the items in her cupboards, the bags, the boxes, even the bathroom towels, were in precise order.

Order.

It worked so well throughout her place.

Maybe one day, it would work just as well within her.

After dinner, she found herself looking at her reflection in the bathroom mirror. And beyond. Nicole stared into her twin's dead eyes, the cloudy brown reflected the otherworld in which she was stuck. Her twin's organs spilled out of her torso: constricting pink intestines wending around a rended liver and disfigured stomach, squishy insides going through the motions, not realizing their functions and use were at an end.

Did she have an unanticipated, sudden end?

The blood on the road where the vehicle hit her was burnt to the inside of Nicole's eyelids. Every so often her twin haunted her with the view of the scene of her death, Natasha's dead gray lips strained into a gray smile over gray teeth.

Nicole turned away.

She closed her eyes, pressed her fingers into them. Felt her twin's eyes on her back like the points of knives. She walked away, Natasha's sob a fist clenching her heart.

She made sure she didn't cut herself that night. She tried so hard that she stayed as still as a body in a grave under her sheets, until there was nothing but a blank mind, her body a corpse.

Outside, in the night, the rain hissed its way through the trees.

Worn, she finally curled into herself and fell asleep.

Δ

At her post at work, Nicole's phone vibrated in her pocket. Her mother again. She straightened, looking ahead, eying the visitors. She caught Elias looking intensely at her, contemplating something. He was going to come over, wasn't he?

He started walking in her direction.

Yes, he was.

He was taller and slightly higher in rank, so she had to pay some attention to him, even though their dealings were informal.

"Hey, Nicole."

She smiled, not warm, not cold. He might retreat.

"Hey."

"You got a minute? We need to talk."

She sighed inwardly. Outwardly, she beamed a bright smile and said, "Sure, what did you want to talk about?"

"Come with me to the moat."

She followed him, and they both sat on the edge. Sunlight licked the water. The cool black current, laced with stars, moved around easily. One couldn't see the bottom, although it wasn't as deep as it appeared.

He wore a benign smile, the same kind of expression he used with the public. The internal lighting of the courtyard reflected off his shaved head.

"How have you been doing? It's been a while since we've had a chat."

Trepidation wrapped itself around her throat. She sat straighter.

"I'm ... I'm managing."

His expression became conflicted. "I've heard your sister died. I'm really sorry."

Nicole looked down into her hands, nodding silently.

"We've been talking about the possibility of making an exception. We've made special accommodations for you to get the fruit; it makes sense, since as part of your job you're so involved in the well-being and safety of the public of the Drunken Tree. A chance without having to go through the lottery." He went silent, waiting for a response.

"That ... that's nice of you all. I'm flattered."

"Look, Nicole, I have no idea what you're going through. But I've seen some warning signs. You're probably not aware that there are things that hint at the darkness you're navigating. And sometimes it looks exactly like that. Darkness. Well, to me, anyway."

*Shit, shit, shit, he can see. He can see through me.*

He leaned in closer. "I'm not saying it'll cure all your ills, but it may give you some well-needed insight. Or strength." Slowly, he stood, indicating the conversation was at an end. "Let me know what you think."

Nicole sat still, then stood slowly, returning to her post. She was afraid of magic interacting. What happened to her sister ....

Her mom didn't know Natasha's fatal accident was deliberate. Nicole hid the depths of what Natasha had become, the things she had gotten into, was doing. It would break her.

If her sister wanted to go, who was she to intervene?

Lots of people bungled suicide attempts, usually at the first try.

When Natasha failed at her first attempt when they were adolescents, some years after their Gifts had manifested at puberty, she'd made Nicole promise not to tell.

*"I can't do it for myself."*

*"I'm not gonna kill you."*

*"If you won't do it, then I'll find someone who will."*

The best laid plans ....

Was this Nicole's story to tell, anyway?

It all felt like a veil pulled over the world, that she herself wasn't really there, that somehow, somewhere, this wasn't happening.


She went through the motions every day, waking up before the sun rose. She let the shower run hot to blast away the sleep grime, the bathroom filling with steam and diluting the early light. Her life was filled with motions she went through by rote: eating, doing her hair, putting on her uniform, standing at her post in the courtyard ... her days like unvisited graves. Always, she stood outside herself while she watched her other self go through her functions.

Tonight, like it happened so often, as she ate her Campbell's

Butter Chicken Soup and a salad, the food was tasteless in her mouth. She washed her bowl in the sink, put it in the drainer, put the empty can in the blue recycling bin. Her feet walked her to the unlit bathroom, and she stared at her reflection, not having the want to turn on the lights.

Natasha had arranged her death with persons unknown. The vehicle accident did not go as planned. Selfishly, without any thought to what Nicole wanted, she demanded, *willed*, Nicole to join her in her pain. All so she wouldn't be alone in her mistakes, her misdeeds.

Always the more dominant one.

Nicole had felt the catastrophe when it happened. The maligned magic during the daytime when she was on her shift continued on with her post in the courtyard, the knowledge between her ribs. Natasha had appeared to her that night, and ever since then, Nicole's days had gotten stranger.

She saw Natasha in the depths of her mirror.

*I want to move like you do.*

The 'flattery' wouldn't last; it was just a matter of time till Natasha's mood turned, because she expected Nicole to toe the line.

Her twin's smile faded, like a flower dying over time.

*I want to slice you open with a knife. I want to hide myself inside you.*

Her words were an arrow through the lungs. She radiated malice and Nicole could feel it coming for her. She imagined her twin walking into her through her skin.

She clenched her hands into fists until her fingernails cut into her palms.

*Cut … blood … no … she could do it.*

She needed to cut.

Her teeth clamped around the insides of her cheeks, as if she could gnaw and bleed away the pain, the need to relieve the pressure.

Her palm struck hard against her cheek.

Pain, heat.

With a cry, she lashed out and broke the bathroom mirror.

*No, no! Now she'll haunt me another way! Mirrors are the least painful—*

A shard of glass cut the meaty part of her palm, the incision like a smile. More cuts on her face, her arm, where blood glittered like black water in the unlit bathroom.

Nicole slumped to her knees. A mournful note escaped her lips.

She reached for the knife—never far away—that had fallen out of the broken medicine cabinet and onto the floor.

Her breathing quickened, her shivering arm holding the knife.

She cut into the flesh of her leg, screaming and sobbing against the red, until the blood ran into the tiled grooves of the black and white floor.

Pain numbed her soul, her world. She became a void, an empty shell. No feeling. The blood turned black beneath her fingernails, her healing abilities already kicking in.

Nicole climbed up to the sink, clinging to the white porcelain, hunching over it. She washed up. Stood still when she was done, then turned abruptly and headed to bed. Buried herself beneath the sheets. Howled into her pillow. Her whole room rang hollowly, like a dark, cracked bell. She screamed so long her voice fell away.

She couldn't go without maiming herself for one more night.

Then the silence, always the silence. Coming for her.

Nicole had a question to answer: *Am I more afraid of the fear and Elias offering hope, or am I more afraid of what would happen if I give in to my sister?*

She decided on the latter.

A few days ago, she'd approached Elias, her heart in her throat, and what she said made a beatific smile spread across his face, made him grab her shoulders in joy. Yes, she'd like to partake of the fruit of the Drunken Tree.

And now the day was here.

"Hello, *everyone*," Errol said, gesturing to get everyone's attention. "We have an announcement. There will be no fruit today for the public. You are welcome to visit, but for now, you have to clear out. You can come back later. Ok? We'll be putting up signs."

Most of the people nodded and headed out. A few complained; Elias and Errol stepped aside to talk to them to reassure them that everything would be open tomorrow.

One by one, the visitors cleared out.

"How do you feel?" Elias asked, putting a gentle hand on her shoulder.

Nicole's mouth opened, and then closed silently. She didn't know. She shook her head rapidly, closing her eyes.

"You ok?"

"I'm … fine. I'm not sure how I feel, but I'm ready. I think."

"Take a moment." He gestured across the courtyard to the edge of the moat by the tree.

Nicole sat. She closed her eyes again, trying to look to her center. She felt Elias sit down near her.

"I'm scared. And excited."

"Breathe …."

Nicole took a deep breath, and another. In, out.

And something *popped*, and she was present. In the moment. Her hands were shaking, palms sweating, in her anticipation of eating the fruit.

She opened her eyes.

Elias, Errol, Jim, and other staff were there. Silent encouragement settled like a welcoming hug from an old friend. Nicole was surrounded by a ring of cloths held high to allow privacy as she removed her clothing. She stood ready as a makeshift covering was wrapped loosely around her.

A prickling feeling intruded on her awareness, like the way air felt right before a thunderstorm.

Errol took the day's fruit off the tree. He brought it over and presented it to her, tenderly. "Here you go, Nicole," he said.

She took the fruit, which resembled a large bitter orange, the skin a rough yellow-orange tinted with the faintest hints of green.

The gathered security guards and staff uttered syllables of tenderness.

She peeled the skin back and sank her teeth into the fruit, her tastebuds registering first bitter, then sweet, juicy flesh. This was not how bitter oranges tasted; this was unique, uncanny.

Her fear, the dread, the trepidation—all disappeared.

Sweet juice diffused with joy melted into her bloodstream and coursed through her body. With every bite, the colors of the fruit invaded her, playing beneath her eyelids in patterns of bright pigments and brushed, batik textures. Her eyes rolled back. Small moans crested out of her mouth, wave-like.

Nicole could not decide if there was a greater pleasure in all that flavor in one go, or in extending the pleasure, not wanting it to end, sometimes chewing slowly, sometimes greedily. Extending an eager tongue, she licked the last of the juice off her face, then sucked her fingers. She took her time.

Everyone looked like they were waiting.

It wasn't over yet.

What will happen now?

The vulnerability made her throat clench. Pain slid through her body, contorted her form, rending her insides from one side of her body to the other. The urge to move was like an ache; but she couldn't. That's when she opened her eyes. Her feet rooted.

Her eyes widened in alarm, and she bucked and tried to move, but she could feel it already—roots growing below the floor, deeper, deeper ....

She began to hyperventilate. This was one of her worst fears, becoming like the Drunken Tree. Branches stretched out from her chest, above her head. She solidified into the shape of her mother. Why? Her mind stretched, slipping, down and down and down ....

She wasn't herself anymore, wasn't in her body. Her roots gravitated toward those of the Drunken Tree, connected, intertwined, and—

She thought she saw a figure in the darkness of the roots.

An arm pointed.

She looked over at herself. She was cocooned in a light whose color could only be described as ... black.

A shadow of an arm reached out, touching her fingers.

*To stay trapped, or to move beyond?*

Nicole held onto the hand as it pulled. She moved beyond the cocoon of darkness and looked back to see it collapse upon itself, but never disappear. The vague shadow of an arm gestured dismissively and moved farther away.

Then everything went black.

Δ

The world seemed to warp around her, the walls bulging and receding, the ground swelling and pulling back in waves. The ground welcomed her with open arms.

She let in the world.

Elias was silently moving his mouth, then came sound. "Are you okay?"

The lights of the courtyard and ceiling above him were dazzling, disorienting. Her body trembled. She stood up too fast. For a moment, everything went fuzzy and the floor heaved beneath her. She had to put her hand on Elias to steady herself. He moved her to the edge of the moat to sit. The scent of earth and leaves filled her nose, her mouth ....

The pool in the courtyard was full of moonlight instead of water, so bright she could almost not bear to look directly at it. The aftereffects of the tree's magic lingered.

Warily, Jim pointed to an object on the floor: a blackened, almost dried-up apple. "We saw that sprout from one of your branches. It fell off by itself." Jim's pale blue eyes looked as if he'd found a viper's nest.

"The Poison Tree!" Nicole said and gasped. "The poison apple. So that's where the darkness went."

"What do we do with it?"

"I'll deal with it," Nicole said. "Anyone have a lighter?"

A security guard stepped forward, holding one.

She kneeled and flicked on the flame, applying it to the blackened poison apple. It lit, bright blue flames spreading throughout. Everyone peered down at the ashes left behind.

"Well, that's that," Elias said. "Back to business."

People began to leave.

"How are you feeling?" Elias asked as the gathering split up.

"How am I—" Nicole stopped. The darkness she constantly felt in the pit of her stomach was gone. Her mind no longer crouching in fear in a corner. She wasn't unsettled at her core. She felt ... at ease. "Something's different."

Elias nodded, thinking. "Looks like it might work for you."

"Yes."

Nicole sat at the edge of the moat and turned to face the tree. She dipped her fingers in the water, which felt strange. She didn't know how to describe it—a refreshing coolness that reached to her bones. Drops landed on her other palm, cool, individual, unearthly.

She watched her reflection in the moat, her black hair brushed into flat waves, partly obscuring one eye.

"I think things are moving."

Nicole stood before her replacement bathroom mirror. She looked through it, beyond. She could see her dead sister just fine. Could *see* her, could *hear* her … she just didn't care. She wasn't in awe of her. She wasn't afraid of her. Right now, she didn't feel afraid of anything.

The bond had been severed.

Her dead twin was ripping out her hair.

Nicole turned and walked away.

Nicole knocked at the front door to her parents' house.

"Who there?" her mother called out.

"Nicole."

She heard raised, frantic voices, and the door unlocked.

"Oh my God! I was starting to wonder." Her mother stepped forward in an orange and red sari. She must have caught her going somewhere. She didn't really wear saris in Canada.

Nicole joined in her mother's embrace. Her father, in tan knee-length pants and a white undershirt, watched thoughtfully from a distance.

"Hi, Dad."

"How you doing, *dou-dou?*" her mother asked. "You all right? You—"

With a shake of his head and a sharp gesture, her father said, "Gitanjali, don't be bothering the woman. She grown, yuh know."

Nicole let the knowledge sink into her mother from her touch.

Her mother's lips started to tremble.

A silence fell.

Her father stayed quiet; it wasn't like her mother to not retort to someone saying anything about her mother-henning habits. Finally, she let go. Turning slowly to face him, she said quietly, "Nigel, you know *nothing*."

He scratched his beard, eyebrows raised. "What goin' on, Gitan-jali?"

"Yuh goin' to tell yuh father?"

"Yes, I am. That was the plan."

The three of them went to the living room, her parents sharing a couch, Nicole across from them in a single chair. With a calm like the bottom of the sea, she began to talk.

# FAITH

## LUCY A. SNYDER

An entire long childhood
being told you're broken
but that you could be whole
if you just cast yourself aside,
hide your secret heart forever,
close your eyes, praise Jesus
loud as the church organ's pipe.

I made love to a preacher's daughter
in the glow of Selene's distant face
worshipped at the altar of her hips
whispered prayers into her neck
and when we awoke we wept
for all the years we'd wasted
for the sake of pious lies.

We were born unbroken and alive
and the next morning we kissed
and swore that we'd survive.

# IMPRESSIONS OF A VIZARD-MASK, SURROUNDING THE GREAT TROUBLES OF 1907

EMILY B. CATANEO

*From the gossip pages of the newspaper* Národní listy,
*January 4, 1907*

Yesterday morning on the Dlouhá, Ottilie Radok, age seventeen, entered the parlor of the Radok townhouse with a mask having manifested over her face.

It was a black mask, made of velvet, although not of the finest velvet one would purchase in the shops of the Palladium. It was perfectly oblong and covered her entire visage. One could see her eyes through two slits, which were crudely carved two-thirds of the way between her chin and the crown of her hair. Originally it was thought by her governess and mother that the mask was affixed through a band or ribbon, but it transpired that she held the mask to her person through a bead, perfectly round and the color of a chafer beetle, clenched between her teeth.

It was remarked that the mask resembled the vizard-masks worn by noblewomen in past savage centuries, to protect their fair skin from the sun. Such masks were manufactured for dolls in the German principalities in the seventeenth and eighteenth centuries;

they have not been seen in Europe since.

Despite insistence from her tutor, Max Belok, and her father, the esteemed Ernst Radok, as well as her mother and governess, Ottilie refused to remove the mask or even to speak, instead scribbling on a nearby ink blotter that she *could not remove the mask even if she wanted to*. Her mother tried to forcibly remove it, it is reported, but her fingers scrabbled useless against its velvet; the family telephoned a doctor, and even his strength had no match for the girl's jaw.

The liberal Radok family is concerned that their daughter, who was supposed to become one of the first women to matriculate at Tübingen University in the autumn, will be unable to attend due to her inability to speak or show her face, thus setting back the cause of women's education by decades (a cause that this reporter, at any rate, thought risky at best)—

*From the diary of Věra Haas,*
*January 12, 1907*

Mameleh took my books tonight. I thought I was so clever, so cunning, concealing them under baking sheets in the oven so that I might slide them out and educate myself quietly while cooking ruge-leh for Emil and Milos and Jan and Anna and Heddie. Soaring up to the moon, I was, on the tangled wings of all that knowledge (a pretty turn of phrase, if I do say so). My safe quiet moments with Plato and Flaubert and Goldman and Dostoevsky in this two-room flat of wet woolen scarves and shrieking siblings: I do love them, but I wish they wouldn't shriek so, or do I fear more the time after they learn to stop shrieking? As Mameleh has tried to teach me to do. And yes, she found my books, after they started smoldering when she lit the oven to make our noonday meal. She yanked them out, dumped them in the tin pot of cold water we keep in our kitchen because of Papa's fear of fire.

Her brittle voice reminded me that my role is not to read books (then why is it the role of Emil and Milos and Jan to throw them-selves so avidly into learning while Mameleh and I and soon Anna and Heddie toil for a wage?). She drowned them thoroughly. So livid was I—and Mameleh had the gall to remind me how I am lucky that we do not live in the village with its pogroms and famine; we live here in the city, surrounded by good things. But there is nothing worse than being told that one is lucky when one does not feel it to be so.

At any rate, I raced from the tenement without my scarf and burst onto the wickedly snowy street. As I crossed the gleaming cobblestones and watched a yellow electric tram whisper past the Christian church, heading toward the Square with its cloud-piercing spires, I wanted to scream, and I do believe I should rightfully have done so.

But as I turned, lost and knowing how small my power was, my face felt a sudden caress, as though from a breath of the humid muddy air one smells around the Vlatava in summer. My teeth bared, as though I myself were one of the jungle animals described in the travelogues I have read. I reached to my cheek and found velvet, stiff as a thick rope in a corset and yet snug, almost chafing, against my skin; I saw the world suddenly through two eyeholes, saw the fleecing snow and revelers in the church narrowed to bright pinholes. My teeth clenched something solid, slightly acrid to the tongue: some kind of bead, affixing the mask to my face.

The mask-edge rubbed against my cheek, and it itched where it touched me, but still, I did not try to take it off. I didn't want to.

When Mameleh saw it, she ordered me to remove it, and when I shook my head, she seized a switch, brandished it above her head, and hit me once. I didn't recoil.

Then her gaze lingered on the mask and she frowned and tucked her weapon away. Now she worries about me in our rooms, and yesterday she brought me a bread dumpling, tried to coax me to remove the mask and eat, but I'm not hungry, not even for bread dumplings. Meanwhile my brothers and sisters run shrieking when they see me in the hall. Word of the mask, of the trouble with the Haas daughter, has spread through our tenement and down Baranova and soon, I think, all through Žižkov and maybe through all of Prague itself. It is a pretty thing, to be heard—

*Letter from Zuzana Fischer written to her friend*
*Heidi in Berlin, January 20, 1907*

Dearest H,

How goes your new employment with the insurance company? Have you learned to type terribly fast? No doubt you'll think me quite the silly girl for continuing to write with a fountain pen, but I must confess that I do enjoy the scratch of nib on paper! I suppose I was born in the wrong time. Do tell, also, whether your rooms are still too cramped and cold, or whether you've managed to secure lodging somewhere larger, or at least more exciting.

Perhaps you're hoping for news from home, but I'm afraid I can only write about the subject on everyone's minds here: the mask fever sweeping Prague. You've likely read about it in the Berlin papers, but I shall write about it still because I confess that I also cannot think of anything else! Sixty-three girls (although I'm quite sure it will be more by the time you receive this) have now fallen victim to this … epidemic of masks, which seem to appear on their faces unbidden, permanently. Of course, no one knows whether these masks truly appeared unbidden: the girls themselves can't speak, for they keep the masks affixed to their faces by holding a bead between their teeth! The number of mask-girls has increased greatly in just the past week, and I've heard that Lena Brüll with whom we went to day school has been sent away to a Swiss sanitarium: rumors run rampant that she manifested a mask too. The gossips say that another girl has been whipped by a doctor who claims that such punishments are the only way to cure hysteria (for the masks are believed, by some, to be manifestations of hysteria), and yet others are pampered by their families, resting on soft bedclothes in hopes they will soon be well. Oh, how everyone is wringing their hands about it!

I must say that I worry about the girls behind the masks—how do they eat, or even drink?—but also that I find the masks rather uncanny, and am a bit disgusted when I see them, beneath broad-brimmed hats of velvet and fur, concealing the face of some girl led about by her governess or, if she is from the less fortunate classes, going about on her own. Their long green or black coats whisper in the snow! Their boots squeak on the sidewalks! The masks are so flat, so concealing of any expression or emotion—they make the skin crawl. You can see the girls' eyes, if you look closely through the slits, I've heard, but I can't say I've ever drawn close enough to see those eyes myself.

Of course, I am of age with those others, perhaps a bit older than average at nineteen, but they say the eldest is twenty, so perhaps when I encounter these girls, I too am pondering the very real possibility that I shall fall victim to this troubling epidemic, that I will awaken one day with an unmoveable mask upon my visage. I go to my mirror, a Christmas present from Mama (you'll have to see it, next time you visit!) and I run my hand over my cheek, look into the rational bright eyes of the top girl at day school, and shudder at the thought of that mask clawing its way into my life. And then I run my hand over my cheek, and imagine feeling velvet there—

*Opinion piece, written by society matron Gertrude Weinberg of Weinberg Advertising Firm, January 25, 1907*

It is no surprise, perhaps, that these masks have appeared in these modern times, when girls are wont to go about licentiously, leave home to enroll in schools and universities in great numbers, delay marriage, and gallivant about town bare-necked—

*Letter to the editor, written by Elena Slánský of the Sokol Club, January 30, 1907*

—take great objection to the notion propagated by Gertrude Weinberg that these masks are a sign that girls should adhere to the moral and behavioral codes of the last century. Far from it. These masks prevent girls from speaking. They cover their faces and stifle them. It seems that far from symbolizing our so-called descent into licentiousness in these modern times, these masks represent the backward mores of an earlier time, when these girls would have become silent wives and mothers. Yes, those who know me know I am a proponent of Women's Rights, a believer that the female sex should be an equal partner in the creation of a new and glorious emancipated Czechoslovakia. And I believe these girls should be ashamed. They should tear off these masks and they should assume their rightful place: studying at universities under the esteemed men of learning there, working jobs to ensure economic freedom for themselves, and to contribute to the development of modern society. They should be fighting for the vote, not languishing under the—

*From the diary of Ottilie Radok, February 14, 1907*

I wrote a letter to my tutor, Max. He is engaged, but I wrote him anyway. Then I took to the streets, where I saw my face staring back from many an advertising column. You see, an artist has designed a poster based on us, to advertise a new perfume from Paris. The posters are modern, those sinuous lines so favored these days. The girl in the poster holds her fingers to the lips of the mask; her hair curls blonde like soft hills away from the black velvet. She holds a seashell perfume bottle in her other hand; curlicues of green spread behind her. Her dress is flowing, white, shows her nipples. The perfume costs seven krone.

We masked girls tore the posters down. We do not want to provide the inspiration for these posters.

*From the front page of* Národní listy, *February 28, 1907*

The number of girls in vizard-masks exceeds 200, Mayor Groš reported today. The City Council requested a meeting of all members, with testimony from business partners and doctors and concerned parents. It seems everything has been tried—administration of chloride, forcible removal of the masks using surgical instruments, threat of the asylum, hypnosis, simple bedrest—but no instrument or punishment can remove these masks, or coerce the girls to remove the masks, as the case may be. This was a subject of much debate among the personages gathered there: whether the girls are helpless victims of this unfortunate epidemic, or whether they are wicked schemers who have wrought these masks to punish their families.

In wearing the masks, say some of the families, these girls are shirking their duties. Many are engaged; the ones from modern families, are scheduled for schooling; others, from the lower classes, are supposed to be occupied in chores or familial duties or wage-jobs. Others are governesses who have abandoned their charges.

"If these girls cannot do what they ought, at least we should be able to draw visitors to the city because of them or persuade them to appear in this year's Baedecker guide," said Councilor Hans Weiss.

But some of the parents took umbrage at that suggestion.

"These are our daughters," replied Ernst Radok. "They are not yours to use as you wish. They have great futures set out, to which we must return them."

But the meeting ended with no solutions for how to succeed in that goal. Next, Imperial delegates will visit from Vienna, and—

*Letter from Zuzana Fischer to her friend Heidi in Berlin,*
*March 3, 1907*

I confess, H, that I'm troubled. No, no mask has appeared for me, but I'm troubled by the sight of them in the street, by the frenzy in the press, by the frantic letters from Mama in Brno telling me to hold myself high morally, to resist this strange epidemic. The atmosphere here is tense; the rate of suicides has risen, and there are more accidents in the factories west of here, too, as the working men are nervous. You see, the air is frenetic, doubly so as spring is coming.

I wonder, always: don't they miss food, drink, conversation with their beaux and friends? And what are they thinking when they run through the streets, when they sit silently in their masks? Do great visions unspool on the dark side of their velvet prisons? Do they dream of tropical birds, of carrion crows, of jackdaws, or the long teeth of tigers? Do they meet in secret, do they make blood pacts?

I hear that a girl from Josefov fabricated a mask; she was caught out by her parents after two days. Perhaps I should do the same, so that I can better understand what lives in their minds! I confess that I cannot stop thinking of it. It obsesses me, and if I hear someone passing on the street, I run to the window and thrust myself out to see if it might be them—

*From an article written by Karl Meyer, philosopher-historian at the Universität Wien, and republished in the Prague newspapers, March 7, 1907*

It is most instructive to recall that our word "mask" comes from the Arabic maskharah, which can be translated as either "mocker" or "fool." Are these girls mockers, then, or are they fools? This is the question that has consumed us. And in fact, throughout history, such garments have been worn to both mock and fool, and for a multitude of other reasons: for modesty, to hide deformities, to protect delicate skin from damage, the latter having been the reason for the original vizard-masks in the sixteenth century.

They have been worn by criminals and degenerates, by sexual deviants, and at masquerade balls and the theater. They have been worn in battle, for religious reasons, and for funerary rites in lands more primitive than these.

They have been worn for mystery, for secrecy. For intimidation.

*From the diary of Věra Haas, March 10, 1907*

There is great trouble in Prague, and we have made it.

*Op-ed from Elena Slánský of the Sokol Club, March 14, 1907*

—at my wits' end, with these girls, who cannot simply just be good, who insist on—

*From the diary of Věra Haas, March 14, 1907*

So much trouble. It's sweet on the tongue.

*From the diary of Ottilie Radov, March 15, 1907*

I told my tutor Max to meet me at the top of Petřín Hill tonight. The river spread out before me as I crossed Charles Bridge toward the red-roofed castle. On the bridge, the statues' faces were shrouded; they kept their own secrets.

At first Max did not believe it to be me, for all we've exchanged increasingly impassioned letters as the winter has worn on. That is the wonder of the mask, or, I should say, only one of its many wonders.

Once he realized it was me, he thought I wanted to use the mask to play a game, something I've heard they've started to imitate in the brothels and dance halls in the seedier parts of town that Mama forbids, and that Papa secretly frequents. I pushed him down when he said it; I am not his game to be played, and truthfully, I nearly left. But then the quiet took me in, the hushed melting snow, the budding trees, their fruits straining toward life in their wicking branches. Will he be married, still? Perhaps, but I know he will not forget this night for all his life, and neither will I.

*Letter from Zuzana Fischer, March 16, 1907*

Where is my mask, H? Why haven't I gotten one? Why? Why didn't they choose me? I'm going to catch and stop one of them and they will tell me, they must tell me how they got them, where they got them, how they have the nerve to float around this city as in a dream with their masks on—

I'm going to find them now. And no one, not you, not the mask-girls, not Mama in Brno, can stop me. To confront them is what a mask-girl would do, after all.

# EMILY B. CATANEO

*Account from a salesperson to a constable, March 17, 1907*

They congregated by the river last night. The barkeeps saw them; the gents did too. There were hundreds of them, row upon row upon row of black-velvet masks, all the girls whose families haven't locked them up, all spread out along the shore, transforming our melancholy little city into a land foreign and wicked. I was annoyed, troubled, dismissive of them before, but seeing them all there, all those covered faces—for the first time, I was afraid of them.

Then another girl, unmasked, appeared in their midst. A pretty thing, buxom, with a heart-shaped face and a long locket dangling on her coat. She stormed up to them and she demanded to know how they'd gotten their masks. She demanded to try one on, to see what they saw, to know what they knew. Her voice was high and clear like the Old Town bells, and they ignored her. She turned as if to go, then made to rip a mask from one of their faces. Two of the mask-girls tried to stop her, but she fought back; she must be one of those girls who performs calisthenics.

I do not know if what happened next would have happened anyway, or if the girl with the locket precipitated it. But either way, she lunged again at the crowd, and when her fingernails scrabbled on the mask of the nearest girl, suddenly, every single mask in that group of girls lining the river Vlatava disappeared, as though they had never been there at all.

*From the diary of Věra Haas, March 19, 1907*

It is over. We are returned to ordinary life, our faces once again bared to the wind and the fledgling sun, the only remnant of our adventure a thick, scabbed line behind each ear where the velvet once chafed skin. I find myself eating soup and drinking pilsner, as I always did. Mameleh will not look at me, only curtly unfolds a list of tasks for me to complete each day. My siblings don't hover around my skirts anymore; they are still frightened. Shame burns my cheeks when I think of the mask. I'm a student; I dream of the academy, of (I hope

388

Mameleh is not reading this) scientific socialism. Why did the mask choose me, of all girls?

Perhaps it does not matter. The masks were an oddity, an aberration, but they are gone now, and the marks on my face will heal, and time will move forward, as it does. I am writing again, and perhaps I will be heard in a different manner than when I wore the mask. Writing my opinion with a pen and paper is long and arduous, but perhaps in that there is a sweet fierce joy too—

—and yet … yet something aches inside me, something that I can't quite wrap myself around. Something strong enough that I can't forget it. And I wonder if I ever will.

*Letter from Zuzana Fischer, March 21, 1907*

I am relieved they are gone. So relieved. The city governor presented me with a medal; I folded my hands and smiled, rosy, a true and brave daughter of our great city. But then why do I weep into my pillow at night?

*Catalog of the exhibits at the National Museum, April 17, 1924*

One of our most popular exhibitions is a reproduction of a vizard-mask, a black velvet mask such as those that appeared out of nowhere over the faces of 267 girls in Prague in 1907. These masks scandalized and obsessed the population of our city for three months at the beginning of that year, with reactionaries positing that the masks were penance or punishment for the increasingly lax behavior of the time, and women's rights activists chiding the girls for embracing such old-fashioned dress codes. Thanks to the diligence of our city government, and to the actions of the doctors of our glorious Czechoslovak nation, the masks disappeared, and the girls of Prague were able to return to their ordinary lives.

Visitors to the museum are welcome to try on this mask, although no photographs are allowed.

*Scribbled on a stray paper, Ottilie Radov Steiner,*
*October 2, 1929*

The world has mutated, dragged shrieking into change. And yet ochre leaves still fall from the oaks on the hillside next to the empty castle; fliers scream in defiance from the stones of the embankments along the river. Maybe they always will.

And this still happens, often: two women pass each other on the street. One of them carries a cloth shopping bag and six tulips. They both move slowly, deliberately; one of them trails a teenage daughter, bored, studying her nails.

As the women pass each other, each notices the faint scar just west of the other's ear, a pink-white brighter than the rest of the skin, a relic of black velvet with a harsh edge. What do these women say to each other? What is there to say? It is true what they thought at the time: their lives churned on. They married the people they were supposed to marry. Did the things they were supposed to do or didn't. That affair is tied up. The world has moved on.

And yet as they pass, they both raise their hands and rub at their unfading scars. What are they thinking at that moment? What is this look that passes between them? Their identical expressions, the cant of their lips, the line of their eyes, reveal nothing. They are impossible to read, almost like a mask. It remains for a second, a bright shining second. Then their lips curl into grins, a shade of the feral about them, and they walk on.

# THE TABLEAU

ZOJE STAGE

I saw flashing red lights.
I lifted the miniblind to see:

1) A young man sprawled on his back on the stoop of a house
2) Beside his knee, a plastic bottle of Mountain Dew
3) Beside his head, a young woman—upset, but calm
4) The fire truck pulled to a stop on one corner
5) An ambulance pulled to a stop on another

There is the picture.
My first impression:

Beginning: The young man and the young woman
were doing something out of doors—
perhaps talking, or some light gardening.

Middle: The young man began to feel
woozy or over-heated, and lay back
against the concrete stoop.

End: The young woman,
concerned by his sudden illness,
called for help.

It was a warm, sunny Wednesday afternoon.

Then, as I watched, the story unfolded differently:

Beginning: The young man, twenty or so,
dressed in jeans, a baseball cap,
a basketball shirt over a tee shirt,
was walking down Goodman Street, bottle
of Mountain Dew in hand, on his way to ...

Middle: He began to feel faint, unwell, dizzy ...
(what did the young man feel?)
He sat on the stoop.
Maybe he lay back hoping the dizziness
would go away.

Later (one minute? five minutes? ten?):
The young woman, wearing a sun dress,
a thirty-five-millimeter film camera slung
around her neck,
came walking down Goodman Street.
She was on the lookout—
she was looking for things to see.

What she found was:

1) A young man reclining on the stoop of a house, a soft drink
at his side
2) Something didn't look right
3) "Excuse me—hey, are you okay?"
4) She called 911
5) She sat on the step beside his head and waited

Next: A police car arrived to complete
the trinity of vehicles.
The young man must have been gone
too long
to bother with CPR.
Maybe he felt cold.

The EMTs half-heartedly checked for a pulse.
The young woman stood on the green
grass, arms crossed,
and answered a few questions.
(Not the important one.)
The firemen dropped the young man onto a gurney—
without ceremony
or concern for further injury.

They put him in the ambulance
and everyone slowly
disappeared.

Coda: The young woman,
camera slung around her neck,
continued on down Goodman Street,
perhaps wondering
if she should have taken
his photograph.

I, from my window across the street,
wondered how his family would make sense
of this—a young son
sitting down to die
while everything around him
moved in ordinary ways
on a warm, sunny Wednesday afternoon.

I wondered, also, what the homeowners
would think
when they came home to that
Mountain Dew bottle
abandoned on their stoop.

# THREE NIGHTS OF
# SHADOWS

## JOHN LANGAN

Philip Cronin had no intention of eavesdropping. It was another stiflingly hot, humid night, the reading on the thermometer barely budged from where it had perched all day, but with Edith, his wife, attending a conference in England, his typical parsimony kept him from switching on the air conditioner, which, even on economy setting, pushed their electric bill higher than he liked to see it. Without the air conditioner blowing, the upstairs bedroom was unbearable, so together with Murphy the dachshund, Phil (slowly, favoring his post-surgery hip) descended the stairs to the living room, whose several windows he raised in an attempt to create a cross breeze, and took up position on the couch, whose fabric was slightly cooler than the sheets of the queen-sized bed. Murphy hopped up beside him and curled against the backs of his legs, grumbling.

From his place on the couch, Phil could hear the sounds of the late night: the trilling of the frogs in the trees behind the house, calling for a mate; the metallic shrill of some insect (crickets?) in the front lawn, also auditioning for love; the ghostly hoot of an owl in the woods across the street, advertising his territory and its suitability for a nest and a clutch of eggs. He heard something else, too, footsteps, sneakers from the sound of it, padding up the road. The street was a dead end, finishing in a turnaround a quarter of a mile along from his place, and there were only a few houses on it, so it was a popular course for local walkers, runners, and cyclists. Sitting reading on his lawn chair in the front yard, enjoying summer vacation from Wiltwyck high, where he guided tenth graders through their first encounters with Oedipus and Hamlet, Phil had waved to more than a few of the passers-by, had come to known several by sight and call the occasional pleasantry back and forth with them. Once darkness fell, however, foot and bicycle traffic on the street stopped, nor was there much in the way of automobile traffic, as what neighbors he had were home from their jobs. The family one house up from him might head out for their daughter's ballet lessons or whatever sport their sons were currently playing, but these tended to finish before the sun had been gone too long. When Phil took Murphy down the front steps for his final walk of the night, the two of them tended to wander from side to side of the street with no concern, except for his about Murphy chowing down on something horrible, generally of the excremental variety.

The sneakers were drawing nearer, their soft flap maintaining the slow pace of someone out for a casual stroll. Together with the occasional kicked rock skittering across the pavement, Phil heard the low tones of a man's voice, carrying on what sounded like one half of an agitated conversation, possibly an argument. *He's on his phone,* Phil thought. He didn't recognize the man as either of his immediate neighbors. Murphy, usually ready to sound the alarm at the slightest disturbance outside the house, did not stir, his vigilance sapped by the lingering heat, which allowed Phil to hear the man's words with particular clarity.

"No," the man said, "that isn't what your mother and I are saying." He sighed. "Well, what would you call it?" A pause. "You aren't answering my question." Pause. "No, you're not. For Christ's sake, Dylan, the man is running his 'church' out of the ice cream parlor he bankrupted." Pause. "Oh yes, he did. One of his local news stations did an exposé on him and it's posted online. You might want to watch it." Pause. "Yes, I have looked at his videos. I wouldn't call them sermons. The man's take on the Bible is certainly his own. He has a lot to say about Revelation. Not so much about the Gospels. Come on, Dylan, you're the minister's kid. Is what this guy is selling what you truly think Christianity boils down to? I'm pretty sure there's something about love in there, and not so much about spiritual warfare." Long pause. "Look, I realize I can't stop you from going out to visit this man. You're twenty-one: you're going to do what you want to do. Maybe it isn't such a bad thing for you to see this Reverend Fell in person. Just please promise me you won't commit to anything while you're in Missouri. And whatever you do, don't sign anything, and don't give this guy your financial information." Pause. "All right. I guess that'll have to do. Let me know when you get there. Safe travels; I love you."

There was the boop of the man ending the call. His footsteps continued up the road. Phil assumed he would be awake to hear the man's return, but he was not.

He mentioned what he had overheard the following day when he phoned Edith. "Is one of our neighbors a minister?" he said.

"Not that I'm aware of," she said. "Why? Getting religion in your old age?"

"Ha ha. I'm still recovering from the religion I got in my youth. It was too hot upstairs last night, so I came down to the living room. I had the windows open, and I heard someone outside. It was a man talking on his cell. From what I could gather, he's a minister."

"Honestly," Edith said, "spying on our neighbors."

"How is it spying if he's so loud I can't help listening to him?"

"Was he?"

"Sort of. The night was pretty quiet. But he wasn't doing anything to keep his voice down."

"You know, you could have turned on the air conditioner."

"And run up the electric bill? It's too high as it is."

Edith sighed. "What was he saying?"

"What happened to 'spying on our neighbor: how terrible?'"

"That ship has sailed, apparently. Might as well find out where it went."

"He was having an argument," Phil said, "with his son. Dylan, I think. Ring any bells?"

"Nope. What were they arguing about?"

"I'm not a hundred percent sure, but it sounded like Dylan was planning to visit another church—really, from what the guy was saying, it sounded more like a cult. One of those groups who're obsessed with the *Book of Revelation*."

"The Christianity-as-trippy-sci-fi-adventure-film crowd," Edith said. "Seven headed dragons, giant beasts with human faces, and the four horsemen of the apocalypse."

"Lest I forget your Southern Baptist upbringing."

"You'd be amazed how many theoretical physicists had rigorous religious upbringings."

"No doubt I would."

"Probably where my interest in the hidden forces of the universe started, if I'm being honest."

"Yes, well, the place this kid intends to check out has a distinctly seedy sound. I can't remember the preacher's name, but his church is an ice cream parlor he mismanaged out of business. How do you screw up selling ice cream?"

"Maybe if you want to be doing something else."

"Talking about the new heaven and the new earth."

"Not bad," Edith said, "for an Episcopalian. But no, the new heaven and the new earth are much less exciting than all the drama leading up to them. Especially the battles."

"The trippy-sci-fi-adventure-film part. Yeah, I imagine you're right."

"Anyway, I feel bad for this minister dad. It has to be stressful for your kid to be sufficiently interested in a set-up like this to be visiting it."

"He told Dylan not to sign anything or give the guy his financial information, so I'd say he was. Oh, the former ice cream place is in Missouri: did I mention that?"

"Wow," Edith said. "Pretty far to go for a cult. Of course, it's in the nature of cults to exert exactly this kind of pull on their members, isn't it?"

"I suppose it is."

When Phil (and Murphy) took to the couch later the same night, he told himself the reason was the continuing heatwave, not his hope to (over)hear his neighbor's further conversation with his son. He was sufficiently tired to drift toward the edge of sleep, yet when the minister's voice drew him back to waking, a short, sharp thrill passed through him. The man's tread was the same slow, steady pace as the previous night, but the tone of his words was considerably more agitated.

"Yes," the man said, "Jesus does cast out demons and yes, this authority is given to His followers. But Dylan, from everything you've described, this young woman sounds like she needs a psychiatrist, not an exorcism." Pause. "No, I can honestly say that, in all my years in the ministry, I have not encountered anyone who was possessed. I'm trying to think if I've heard of anything … There might have been something in Massachusetts, but I don't know what happened there." Pause. "Because most of what used to be laid at the hoofs of the Devil, we now recognize as mental illness. These are people who have a chemical imbalance in their brains, or who have suffered some form of trauma, abuse, or an accident. This is why the standard the Church sets for determining the validity of demonic possession is so high, because there are so many more likely things it could be. If you perform your exorcism on someone who's suffering from mental illness, a) you aren't going to heal them, and b) chances are, you'll make the situation worse." Pause. From the sound of his voice, it seemed the man had halted his walk and was standing directly opposite Phil. "It's a metaphor, Dylan. Calling this world the Kingdom of the Devil is a way to describe the fact of evil, whether a murder or a natural disaster." Pause. "Actually, I do. I'd call it healing, though. You want to know what we're called on to do, it's to be healers, not 'spiritual warriors.' I admit, it's a sexier term, more exciting, but it belongs to a time when Christianity allied itself to the military cultures ruling Europe. Healing the sick and suffering is far less glamorous than smiting your enemies, but it's what I've built my ministry on and what all the clergy I know do." Pause. "I'm glad to hear it. And I'm glad to hear you're working in the soup kitchen. That's what a ministry should be about, not performing 'exorcisms.'" Pause. "Sorry." Pause. "I said I was sorry." Pause. "I did mean it." Pause. "What else do you want me to say? Do you want me to lie to you? Should I tell you I believe in what you and Billy Fell are doing? Sorry, the *Reverend* Fell. You know, you've always been like this. You've always said you wanted honesty, but it was only as long as it was honest approval. You've never had much time for honest disapproval, have you?" Pause. Deep breath. "I'm sorry. That was uncalled for." Pause. "Yes, yes I am. I shouldn't have said that." Pause. "Calm down, Dylan." Pause. "Calm down. I said I was sorry." Long pause. "What does that mean?" Long pause. "Dylan—you need to tell me what that means." Pause. "Yes, you do. If you don't, I'm going to have to call the local police and tell them my son's church is talking about carrying out 'a grand exorcism with fire and lead.'" Pause. "I—hello? Dylan? Are you there? Hello?"

The man's phone booped. He continued up the road at a faster—and, Phil imagined, a more agitated—pace. After what he'd listened to, Phil didn't think he'd be able to sleep, his fatigue chased away by the violence of the emotions he had been in proximity to. He stood from the couch awkwardly, favoring his bad hip, and half-limped down the hall to his office, where he seated himself in front of his desktop and brought it to life, squinting against the brightness of the screen. He called up Google and considered search terms. He typed "churches protestant missouri," hesitated, and added "reverend william fell." Of the seven million or so hits clicking ENTER returned, and which he spent the next hour sifting through with the aid of a series of follow-up terms, none brought him anywhere close to what he was looking for. Hadn't the man (*the Dad*) mentioned something on YouTube? He switched to the video site, but his luck was no better there. Finally, he returned to Google and entered "ice cream parlor fell missouri." The first response read, "A Kansas City Institution: Fell's Ice Cream at Fifty." The date attached was this past Friday. Phil clicked the link, which brought him to an article and an accompanying cache of photos. He skimmed the text, registered the name Michael Fell, took in him buying an old gas station and converting it into an ice cream parlor whose delicious and whimsical sounding flavors had made the place a local fixture for the last half-century. He read the names of Michael Fell's two sons, Timothy and Gerald, and two daughters, Joyce and Colleen, learned that Michael was planning to ease into retirement, leaving the day to day running of the business to his children. Even his grandchildren were becoming involved: Timothy's oldest son, William, had been employed weekends and summers at the family concern since he turned sixteen. Now, William was on his way to the University of Missouri, where according to his father he was going to study business in anticipation of the day he took over the ice cream parlor.

Phil skipped through the pictures, saw the before-and-after of the gas station-made-restaurant, shots of customers down through the decades ordering ice cream across the counter from the same group of men and women wearing white piper hats with Fell's Ice Cream stenciled on the sides, informal group portraits of the Fell family at major family events, a bland collection of white people in whose smiling faces nothing out of the ordinary, no malice or mania, was evident, not even in young William Fell, in the sole picture in which he appeared, standing with teen-aged awkwardness between his father and grandfather. A profound sense of dislocation, of unreality, as if he had been swept into the currents of some other existence, descended on Phil, gaining in force as each new photo took up the monitor. The sensation abated somewhat when he closed the link to survey the other results of his search, several of which concerned Fell's Ice Cream, though none in as much detail. But he could not escape the impression he had been caught between two worlds, whose jagged seems fit poorly, if at all.

Exhaustion finally forced him to shut down the computer and resume his place on the couch, where he dropped into a restless sleep, dense with dreams whose unpleasant emotions were all he could remember of them, until Murphy, hungry for his breakfast, nudged him to consciousness a few hours later. While the dog was eating, Phil changed from his pajamas to his sweats and pulled on his sneakers. The more he could walk, his orthopedist had told him, the better for his hip's recovery. It was a prescription he had followed intermittently, usually at Edith's prompting, but this morning, he intended to take Murphy all the way to the far end of the road, where it intersected Route 213. He swallowed his morning medications with a glass of orange juice, switched on the coffee maker, and retrieved Murphy's leash from its hook beside the front door. The dog scampered at his feet, whining, as Phil tried to leash him. "Okay, okay," he murmured, his fingers securing the clasp.

Outside, the air was cool, damp, bright with the newly risen sun's gold light. The oak and cedar in the forest across the street glowed in the dawn brilliance. He knew his neighbors on this part of the road: the Akmadis were musicians, the Motions filmmakers and teachers.

The house where the street dead-ended, formerly home to the local fire chief, had been for sale for the last four months, empty since her retirement and relocation to North Carolina last month. Already, Murphy was in the process of emptying his bladder on the front lawn. Phil led him across the road to the edge of the woods, where he completed his morning toilet. Tail wagging, he looked up at Phil expectantly. "Come on," Phil said and started down the road.

This neighbor, he knew, was a retired newscaster (ABC in the city); the one after was a jewelry designer with an extensive basement workshop. The one across the street, in the big colonial in the middle of the woods, was an emergency room nurse up at Wiltwyck, her husband a heavy equipment operator for a local construction company. Murphy sniffed the edges of lawns, his tail up. Beyond this point, Phil did not know his neighbors (and, to be honest, it wasn't as if he knew those closer to him especially well, only enough to be sure none of them was a minister). What he was searching for in the houses remaining on this stretch of the road he wasn't sure. Some hint of their residents' occupation, he supposed, possibly a bumper sticker or a sticker in the rear window advertising this car as transportation for a member of the clergy, or a sign hung beside the front door identifying this as the home of the reverend so-and-so. But there were no such clues on either of the two large houses on this side of the street, or any of the four smaller dwellings tucked in the woods opposite. Ahead, the road sloped down to Route 213, where a few cars on their way to the morning shift whooshed by. Could the man he had (over)heard have walked along 213 from a road farther up? It was possible, and had his hip not been complaining at increasing volume, he might have extended his and Murphy's promenade to Maple Street, a few hundred yards north on 213. As it was, he turned and started his way back home, moving at a considerably reduced speed, this direction. Murphy, bless his canine heart, was happy to match his pace.

By the time he spoke with Edith that afternoon, the feeling of dislocation had subsided, helped by a post-lunch nap. He related the contents of the latest conversation, as well as the results of his investigations virtual and physical. "I wish I could explain how

Goddamned *weird* this is," he said, emotion surging in his voice.

"I know," Edith said. "The son—Dylan, right?—must have sped the whole way out there, to have arrived so quickly he's already taking part in one of this guy's exorcisms."

"What about the dad? What's the deal with him?"

"You're probably right. The man did walk down from Maple, or Old Post, even. Maybe he waits until he's a certain distance from home to call his son; maybe he doesn't want his wife overhearing him."

"How does the ice cream stuff I found tie in?"

"Could be, the kid lied about his destination. Like I said, he got there pretty quick."

"Seems like a very specific kind of a lie."

"Maybe he's friends with this Fell kid on social media," Edith said. "Maybe little Fell really is religious and the minister's son likes his take on the Good News, especially the exorcism part. Occam's Razor, sweetie."

"You're right," Phil said. "You're sure there isn't some kind of exotic physics explanation for this, something with a lot of *quanta* and superimposed states?"

Edith laughed. "Funnily enough, one of the papers I heard this morning would have applications to the phenomena you're describing."

Phil's throat tightened. "Oh?"

"By the woman's own admission, it's highly speculative work, as much thought experiment as anything. I'm not sure about a few of her assumptions and I would like to check her math."

"But—"

"She proposes a model of the universe that resembles a spider web. A tangle web—what we think of as a cobweb. They're rather intricate structures, webs built in three dimensions to catch any insect flying through them. This web is huge—I mean, it's everything."

"The cobweb model of the cosmos."

"It's far from the strangest idea I've run into here. It is a speculative physics conference, after all. Anyway, the web structure is this scientist's way of describing the effects gravity has on space-time, the way it distorts it. In some cases, the web filaments are denser; in others, more spread out. Especially where the web is thickest, space-time can be arranged in some pretty unusual ways. There could be lengths of strands running parallel to one another, or at right angles. It's all still connected, just … warped. One of the potential implications of this arrangement lies in the proximity of the individual filaments. If two of them were to be very, very close, then it might be possible for information to move from one to the other."

So what, like, time travel?"

"More in the way of haunting, or what we would perceive as haunting."

"And you could be haunted by the future as well as the past."

"In theory."

"Huh."

"As I said, it's speculation, and not nearly as likely as a kid lying to his dad."

"I understand," Phil said. "Funny—it reminds me of a passage from one of Robert Penn Warren's books."

"Oh?"

"Yeah. There's this bit in *All the King's Men* where the narrator describes the world as an enormous spiderweb. If you touch any part of it, the vibrations ripple out to the farthest edges."

"Like the Butterfly Effect avant *la lettre*."

"Except there's a spider waiting in the middle of the web, and when you brush it, the spider rushes out, catches you in its arms, and stabs its fangs into you."

"Well, that's horrifying."

"It's Warren's trope for human interconnectedness—in the context of the book, for our complicity in the messes our friends and family make of their lives. It is a pretty nightmarish image."

"To put it mildly. Aside from the web, though, I don't think the two ideas have much in common."

"I don't know. I was struck by the coincidence. Say," he added, "not to change the subject too dramatically, but I was wondering …"

"Yes?"

"Do you ever—do you regret we never had kids?"

Edith inhaled the slightest of breaths. Phil knew the accompanying expression, could picture the slight lift of her eyebrows, the widening of her eyes, the flaring of her nostrils. "I'm sorry," he said, "I shouldn't have sprung that on you. Never mind."

"No," she said, "it's fine—it's just, where did it come from."

"Listening to this guy arguing with his son," Phil said. "It started me wondering what it would have been like if we had been parents."

After a moment, Edith said, "We tried. I guess that's how I look at it. We tried and we tried and we tried. I suppose we could have opted for *in vitro*, but there was no guarantee it would have worked. If I were still religious, I would say having children wasn't in God's plan for us. As it is, I think all we could do was try. Sometimes you make your best effort and things still don't turn out the way you want. Okay?"

"Okay," he said.

Although the heat broke in the early evening with a series of violent storms whose flashes of lightning turned the inside of the house flashbulb-white, while the succeeding crack of thunder rattled the liquor bottles stationed atop the china cabinet, causing Murphy to whine and burrow under the throw rug on the easy chair, when it came time to turn in for the night, Phil once more took up position on the living room couch. Cool, crisp air pushed against the curtains as he piled his pillows at what he thought of as the top of the couch, any remains of the self-consciousness he had felt the last two nights gone. He wanted to hear the next installment in the story of the minister and his son; indeed, if he was concerned about anything, it was the man not repeating his visit, discouraged by the unsettled weather. As Phil was falling into a light doze, however, he heard the tread of the man's sneakers on the road, the murmur of his voice. Tonight, his pace was slower, his words spoken with a voice on the verge of breaking, as if the man had recently been or was on the verge of crying. Phil sat up straight, Murphy grumbling at the disturbance.

"How many?" the man said. "Fourteen? Jesus. Oh, Jesus." A pause. "I know what he told you." Pause. "I understand: you believed him. But Dylan, son, didn't it seem just the slightest bit suspicious that the person he was calling Satan's chief instrument on earth was his ex-wife?" Pause. "No, of course that was the reason for the divorce. I would bet he owes—owed her a considerable amount in alimony. It's a moot point, now. Oh, Jesus, Dylan." Pause. "I realize that. But a *preschool*, Dylan, a preschool. All those children. God, God. Those babies." Pause. "I'm sorry, too. I failed you. I failed you profoundly, unforgivably, for things to come to this." Pause. "Yes, you did. At least William Fell won't be able to cause any more harm. God forgive me, but I hope he's suffering in Hell." Pause. "I don't know, Dylan. I honestly don't know. The Church teaches that God's mercy is there for those who seek it with an honest and open heart. I truly believe this; it's a cornerstone of my faith. But you ... this is a tough one, Dylan. Fourteen children. Their teacher. And—are you sure the police officers are dead? Both of them?" A sigh. "God is merciful, but God is also just. So, I don't know what to say. It was only the three of you? The cops shot your friend and then you and Fell shot them and then you shot him." Pause. "I know, it's just—I have to repeat it to myself, or it doesn't seem real. Who am I kidding? None of it seems real. I keep hoping I'm going to wake up, roll over to your mother, and say, 'I had the most terrible nightmare.' There's no waking up from this, though, is there?" Pause. "I don't—" Pause. "No." Pause. "Dylan, you can't—" Pause. "I understand the police will be out for blood. Can't you—" A long pause. "Oh, Dylan." Pause. "I can't—" Pause. "All right. All right. If that's what you're determined to do. I'll stay on the line. Before—could we say a prayer first? Together?" Pause. "Thank you. How about something easy? Let's say the Our Father." As Phil listened, the man recited the words. When he reached "Amen," he hurried into, "Merciful Father, we pray for your servant, Dylan, in his hour of trial. We ask that You judge him not too severely for his failures, and we plead for his salvation. In Jesus' name, Amen." Pause. "I love you, too."

Across the front lawn, Phil heard the distant pop of a gunshot, followed by a sob wrenched from the depths of the minister's chest. Free of the paralysis which had kept him bound to the couch while the drama between the man and his son had reached its awful climax, he lurched up, hobbled to the front door, and threw it crashing open.

The street in front of the house was empty. Gripping the hand-rail, he levered himself down the front steps, then staggered across the lawn, heart pounding. When he reached the road, he looked left and right, straining to see anyone at the edge of the streetlights to either side of him. There was no one, nor could he detect the flap of the man's sneakers on the asphalt.

Returning inside, he switched on the living room light and reached for the television remote. Surely, CNN or one of the other networks would have coverage of what sounded like a ghastly crime, a mass shooting at a daycare center, he wasn't certain where (Missouri?). Not CNN nor any of the other news channels he shuttled among were reporting any such atrocity, however; nor did they start to during the hour he spent clicking through them, his mind spinning, his chest tight with dread in anticipation of the horrors on the way. Yet they did not arrive to interrupt the various late-night programs, even as his thoughts began to slow with the wobbling motion of a top losing momentum and he wondered what kind of a daycare would be open this late into the night. Finally, he departed the TV for the computer, where another hour spent online failed to yield any information concerning a daycare slaughter. (*A night-time nursery?* his brain said over and over again. *Is there such a thing? There isn't, is there?*) At the end of his search, he sat back in his chair, his dread collapsed into a feeling of disorientation so complete he would have been only half-surprised had he looked out the window and seen a flying saucer hanging there, lights blinking green. With the confusion came an onrush of fatigue which might have swept him to sleep seated in the chair. He shut down the computer and limped to the couch, where Murphy had not moved appreciably from his spot.

In general, Phil's dreams (the few he remembered) were of the mundane, this-is-what-I-did-today stripe. They reached the limit of their extravagance in returns to favorite childhood vacation spots, where his long-dead parents joined him and Edith in admiring the scenery. In this regard, he was at the other end of the dream spectrum from Edith, who frequently spent breakfast regaling him with the intricate, fantastical narratives she had starred in behind her eyelids. What he plunged into when unconsciousness took him now had less the distant, slightly out of focus quality of his dreams and more the sharp-edged immediacy of a vision. He was walking slowly through a dim, gray space whose air was heavy with what he took to be fog; although it was a fog of a particularly static variety. His (bare) feet were treading a narrow road through open space, its surface oddly wispy. To his right and left, separated by no more than a few feet, ran additional roads composed of the same strange material, and farther roads beyond them. In the gap between his road and the one to his right, what appeared to be another road stretched vertically. His eyes followed the gray length up to where a trio of roads were set at odd angles to it. The more closely he looked, the more roads he saw, positioned in all manner of directions. They resembled great stretches of fiber, organic looking—the giant-sized version of what he had mistaken for fog. He was in a vast spider web, what Edith had called a tangle web, one whose strands continued in all directions, leading from origins unknown to destinations equally obscure. His head swam with vertigo at the sight of them all. He brushed a strand hanging on his left, the action disturbing a clump of webbing—which was actually a gray spider the size of his thumbnail. Or something like a spider: the eyes clustered on its head flashed purplish red, while it scurried from the web on many more than eight legs, drawing a line of fresh webbing behind it. Like a character in a Warner Brothers cartoon, it ran on air—unless the air was still finer filament—to a spot where it stopped and began lowering itself toward the next road down, the webbing following it at a right angle. Phil drew his fingers across a reach of the substance to his right and watched a half-dozen similar creatures run out in all directions. Moving forward without touching the surrounding webs was impossible. He advanced, sending hosts of red-eyed arachnids scuttling away from him. Some of the creatures even leapt up from the passage of his feet over the larger web. These ones were bigger, the size of tarantulas, though the same gray as their diminutive cousins. In addition to luminous eyes, these spiders sported elaborate designs on their abdomens, darker gray swirls and lines that might have been characters in an arachnid language. Although the sight of them startled him, he was not afraid. That emotion came when he stepped through an especially thick clump of webbing to confront a scene of catastrophe: another of the web-roads collided with the one he was traveling, snaking down to entangle their surfaces. At their juncture, a gray spider the size of a large dog, a Great Dane or a wolfhound, worked to repair the collision, attempting to separate the filaments with a dozen different limbs. Its entire form trembled in agitation. Some of its legs waved, others tugged fibers apart, still others tried to unwind fibers from one another. The spider was making a low noise Phil recognized as weeping. *It's not a spider*, he thought. *It's*—but before he could complete the sentence (*an arch-angel*) the creature noticed him watching it and pivoted to face him, its complement of eyes burning crimson, its raised abdomen drawn with a symbol Phil felt sure was the key to resolving this situation. Still sobbing, it rushed toward him, fangs dripping with clear venom, feet thumping a tattoo on the web—

He woke to a cacophony of Murphy's energetic barking and someone knocking on the front door. "Coming," he shouted, trusting his voice to carry out the open windows. "Coming—be there in a minute." Murphy was snuffling at the bottom of the door, scratching at it, desperate to greet whoever was standing on the other side. A glance at the clock showed the time: 8:20 A.M. Murphy had slept in. Phil pulled his summer robe from the back of the couch and tied it closed. No need to shock his visitor with what Edith described not incorrectly as the appalling whiteness of his naked legs.

At a glance, the man to whom Phil opened the door was in his mid-to-late thirties, the boy beside him approximately ten. *Father and son*, Phil judged, and with this thought came another, *Jehovah's Witnesses*. Hadn't he read about children being taken along with their parents for house-to-house evangelizing? Yet the look of the pair was wrong, too informal, Dad dressed in a white SUNY Huguenot sweatshirt out over his jeans, Son wearing a red Spider-Man tee shirt and denim shorts. Murphy ignored the pair to sprint down the steps to the lawn, where he relieved himself against his favorite tree.

"Good morning," the man said. "Sorry for the disturbance, but I wanted to say hello. I'm Roy Lemon and this fellow," he nodded at the boy, who looked away, "is my son, Dylan. We bought the house at the end of the street—I believe it used to be Chief Ribbons's? Dylan and I drove over this morning to drop a few things off; my wife, Bernadette, will be over with the movers at the weekend. While we were here, I thought Dylan and I should introduce ourselves to our neighbors. We've already met the Akmadis in their front yard and they told us it was a good bet you or your wife would be up, on account of this little guy." The man gestured at Murphy, who had left his morning poop at the side of the road and trotted back to sniff at Dylan's legs. The boy giggled at the press of the dog's cold nose on his bare skin.

"You can pet him," Phil said. "It's all right." He heard himself offer the reassurance, but it was as if someone else was speaking, someone who listened to the man say he had accepted a position as the new minister at the Dutch Reformed church just up the road in Union Center but not to worry, he wasn't one for harassing the neighbors about their church-going, someone who smiled pleasantly, extended his hand, and welcomed the clergyman and his family to their little street. That someone was a collection of manners and pleasantries, a kind of social autopilot his brain switched on while the actual Phil was still reeling from the sound of Roy Lemon's voice, which he had recognized at once as the one he had overheard the last three nights. The edges of his vision seemed to gray and were he to turn around, he was half-certain he would find the great gray spider behind him, crying.

With a final snuff, Murphy abandoned father and son to hurry inside, his excitement at the visitors overcome by hunger. "I'm afraid someone needs his breakfast," Phil said.

"Of course," Roy Lemon said. "What do we say, Dylan?"

The boy extended his right hand. "It's very nice to meet you, sir."

Phil took his hand. "And you, young man." His eyes drifted from Dylan's suddenly serious face to his tee shirt, where Spider-Man stared at him impassively, his black-ringed eyes white and pitiless.

"Before I draw nearer to that stone to which you point," said Scrooge, "answer me one question. Are these the shadows of the things that Will be, or are they shadows of things that May be, only?"
– Charles Dickens, *A Christmas Carol*

*For Fiona*

# WITH THE
# BLACK RIBBON

### ERIK T. JOHNSON

Your carriage as usual as should be
awaits to take you on a journey. Unexpected
keys enchanted correctly cannot be lost.
Enter Enter 100 times Enter center and depart
triumphant and silent with the Black Ribbon.
A hero recovers a coveted part. What else can
it be but a heart?
It was.

The carriage returns as usual as should be
to help you repeat this mysterious errand.
Remember to enter to ink quickly dart
slave to the Black Ribbon lest trophy depart.
Do it again you did not get it right yet or
you were so smashing the promise must be kept.
It is.

There is real life and there are real words.
In both you can write love in each murder.
The Black Ribbon unrolls quite beyond further.
Enter your carriage center the blizzard
white.  It will impede your quest rip
your bulletproof vest it will ensure your
ride's not meaningless.
Will it?

# RECOGNITION

## VICTOR LaVALLE

Not easy to find a good apartment in New York City, so imagine finding a good building. No, this isn't a story about me buying a building.
I'm talking about the people, of course. I found a good apartment,
and a great building, in Washington Heights. Six-story tenement on
the corner of 180th and Fort Washington Avenue; a one-bedroom
apartment, which was plenty for me. Moved in December 2019. You
might already see where this is going. The virus hit, and within four
months half the building had emptied out. Some of my neighbors
fled to second homes or to stay with their parents outside the city;
others, the older ones, the poorer ones, disappeared into the hospital
twelve blocks away. I'd moved into a crowded building and suddenly
I lived in an empty house.

And then I met Mirta.

"Do you believe in past lives?"

We were in the lobby, waiting for the elevator. This was right
after the lockdown started. She asked, but I didn't say anything.
Which isn't the same as saying I didn't respond. I gave my tight little
smile while looking down at my feet. I'm not rude, just fantastically
shy. That condition doesn't go away, not even during a pandemic.
I'm a Black woman, and people act surprised when they discover
some of us can be awkward, too.

"There's no one else here," Mirta continued. "So I must be
talking to you."

Her tone managed to be both direct and, somehow, still playful.
As the elevator arrived, I looked toward her, and that's when I saw
her shoes. Black-and-white pointed oxfords; the white portion had
been painted to look like piano keys. Despite the lockdown, Mirta
had taken the trouble to slip on a pair of shoes that nice. I was
returning from the supermarket wearing my raggedy old slides.

I pulled the elevator door open and finally looked at her face.

"There she is," Mirta said, the way you might compliment a shy bird for settling on your finger.

Mirta might've been twenty years older than me. I turned forty the same month I moved into the building. My mom and dad called to sing "Happy Birthday" from Pittsburgh. Despite the news, they didn't ask me to come home. And I didn't make the request. When we're together, they ask questions about my life, my plans, that turn me into a grouchy teenager again. My father ordered me a bunch of basics though; he had them shipped. It's how he has always loved me—by making sure I'm well supplied.

"I tried to get toilet paper," Mirta said in the elevator. "But these people are panicking, so I couldn't find any. They think a clean butt is going to save them from the virus?"

Mirta watched me; the elevator reached the fourth floor. She stepped out and held the door open.

"You don't laugh at my jokes, and you won't even tell me your name?" Now I smiled because it had turned into a game.

"A challenge then," she said. "I will see you again." She pointed down the hall. "I am in No. 41."

She let the elevator door go, and I rode up to the sixth floor, unpacked the things I'd bought. At that time I still thought it would all be over by April. It's laughable now. I went into the bathroom. One of the things my dad sent me was thirty-two rolls of toilet paper. I slipped back down to the fourth floor and left three rolls in front of Mirta's door.


A month later, I was used to logging in to my "remote office," the grid of screens—all our little heads—looked like the open office we once worked in; I probably spoke with my co-workers about as much now as I did then. When the doorbell rang, I leapt at the chance to get away from my laptop. *Maybe it's Mirta.* I slipped on a pair of buckled loafers; they were raggedy, too, but better than the slippers I wore the last time she saw me.

But it wasn't her.

It was the super, Andrés. Nearly sixty, born in Puerto Rico, he had a tattoo of a leopard crawling up his neck.

"Still here," he said, sounding pleasant behind his blue mask.

"Nowhere else to go."

He nodded and snorted, a mix between a laugh and a cough. "The city says I got to check every apartment now. Every day."

He carried a bag that rattled like a sack of metal snakes. When I looked, he pulled it open: silver spray-paint cans. "I don't get a answer, and I got to use this."

Andrés stepped to the side. Down the hall; Apartment sixty-six. The green door had been defaced with a giant silver "V." So fresh, the letter still dripped.

"'V.' For 'virus'?"

Andrés's eyebrows rose and fell.

"Vacant," he said.

"That's a nicer way to put it, I guess." We stood quietly, him in the hall and me in the apartment. I realized I hadn't put on my mask when I answered, and I covered my mouth when I spoke.

"The city is making you do this?" I asked.

"In some neighborhoods," Andrés said. "Bronx, Queens, Harlem. And us. Hot spots." He took out one of the cans and shook it. The ball bearing clicked and clacked inside. "I'll knock tomorrow," he said. "If you don't answer, I got the keys."

I watched him go.

"How many people are left?" I called out. "In the building?"

He'd already reached the stairs, started down. If he answered, I didn't hear it. I walked onto the landing. There were six apartments on my floor. Five doors had been decorated with the letter "V." No one here but me.

You'd think I would run right down to Mirta's place, but I couldn't afford to lose my job. The landlord hadn't said a word about rent forgiveness. I went back to the computer until end of day. I felt such relief when No. 41 hadn't been painted. I knocked until Mirta opened. She wore her mask, just like me now, but I could tell she was smiling. She looked from my face to my feet.

"Those shoes have seen better days," she said, and laughed so joyfully that I hardly even felt embarrassed.

Δ

Mirta and I made trips to the supermarket together; two trips to the store each week. We walked side by side, arm's length apart, and when we crossed paths with others, we marched single file. Mirta talked the whole time, whether I was next to her or behind her. I know some people criticize chatty folks, but her chatter fell upon me like a nourishing rain.

She came to New York from Cuba, with a short stay in Key West, Fla., in between. She'd lived in Manhattan, from the bottom to the top, over the span of forty years. She played piano and idolized Peruchín; had performed with Chucho Valdés. And now she gave lessons to children in her apartment for $35 an hour. Or at least she had done that, until the virus made it unsafe to have them over. I miss them, she said, every time we talked, as four weeks became six, and six became twelve. She wondered if she'd ever see her students and their parents again.

I offered to help set up remote piano lessons. I'd use my job's account to set up free chat sessions for her. But this was three months in and Mirta had lost her playful ways. She said: "The screens give the illusion that we're all still connected. But it's not true. The ones who could leave, left. The rest of us? We were abandoned."

She stepped off the elevator.

"Why pretend?"

She scared me. I can see that now. But I told myself I'd become busier. As if I'd transformed. But I fled from her. We were all living on the ledge of despair, so when she said it—"We were abandoned. Why pretend?"—it was as if she spoke from down in that pit. A place I found myself slipping into often enough already. So I went to the store by myself, and I held my breath when the elevator passed the fourth floor.

Meanwhile, Andrés continued to work. I didn't see him. He knocked on the door each morning, and I knocked from the other side. But I saw evidence of his work. Three apartments on the first floor marked with a "V" one week. Next time I went to the store the other three were painted.

Four on the second floor.

Five on the third.

One afternoon I heard him kicking at a door on the fourth floor. Shouting a name I hardly recognized through the muzzle that was his mask. I left my place and walked down. Andrés looked shrunken at the door of No. 41. He kicked at it desperately.

"Mirta!" he shouted again.

He turned with surprise when I appeared. His eyes were red. The fingers of his right hand were entirely silver now; it looked permanent. I wondered if he'd ever be able to wash off the spray paint. But how could he, if the job was never done?

"I left my keys," he said. "I gotta get them."

"I'll stay," I said.

He sprinted down the stairs. I stood by the door, didn't bother knocking. If that kicking didn't wake her, what could I do?

"Is he gone?"

I almost collapsed.

"Mirta! Were you messing with him?"

"No," she said through the door. "But I wasn't waiting on him. I was waiting around for you."

I sat so my head was at about the same level as her voice. I heard her labored breathing through the door. "It's been a while," she finally said.

I rested the side of my head against the cool door. "I'm sorry."

She sniffed. "Even women like us are scared of women like us."

I lowered my mask, as if it were getting in the way of what I truly needed to say. But I still couldn't find the words.

"Do you believe in past lives?" she said.

"That's the first thing you ever asked me."

"When I saw you by the elevator, I knew we met before. Recognition. Like seeing a member of my family."

The elevator arrived. Andrés stepped out. I raised my mask and got to my feet. He unlocked the door.

"Be careful," I said. "She's right there."

But when he pushed the door open, the hall sat empty.

Andrés found her in bed. Dead. He came out carrying a bag, my name written on it. Her black-and-white oxfords were inside. A note in the left shoe. *Give them back when you see me again.*

I have to slip on an extra pair of socks to make them fit, but I wear them everywhere I go.

# SEVEN SYMPTOMS OF THE END / BEGINNING / END / BEGINNING...

### LINDA D. ADDISON

Decreased empathy & compassion
disconnects you from humans,
as you fill with hate & intolerance.

Waning attention to traditional religion
replaced with increased watching of
social media news outlets.

Burning sensation in your crown
chakra, along with lower resolution
images of the world thru your eyes.

Sounds muffle more each day as
your ears close during the
process of de-evolution.

Shallow breathing denies your brain
of oxygen needed to distinguish
between reality and the news.

Energy drains from your body
your temperature lowers,
you sleep later & later.

Every problem/issue feels eternal,
permanent and completely,
significantly without hope.

Increased empathy & compassion
connects you to all humans
as you fill with love & acceptance.

Growing interest in metaphysics &
unusual phenomenon replaces
watching social media news.

Tingling sensation in your heart
chakra, along with seeing beauty
in every part of the world.

Ringing in your ears increase as
you become more sensitive to
the process of evolution.

Deep breathing allows your soul
to discern the difference
between expanding love & fear.

Glowing energy fills your body,
you shiver with recognition
of the awakening infinity.

Acceptance of Now as true eternity,
while Change, disorienting and
constant, brings hope.

# ALSO AVAILABLE

## ANTHOLOGIES BY MICHAEL BAILEY

*Pellucid Lunacy*

*Chiral Mad*

*Chiral Mad 2*

*Qualia Nous*

*The Library of the Dead*

*Chiral Mad 3*

*You, Human*

*Adam's Ladder*
(co-edited with Darren Speegle)

*Chiral Mad 4: An Anthology of Collaborations*
(co-edited with Lucy A. Snyder)

*Miscreations: Gods, Monstrosities & Other Horrors*
(co-edited with Doug Murano)

*Prisms*
(co-edited with Darren Speegle)

CPSIA information can be obtained
at www.ICGtesting.com
Printed in the USA
BVHW041834220922
647780BV00009B/24/J